The Murder
of a Queen Bee

Also by Meera Lester*

A Beeline to Murder (A Henny Penny Farmette Mystery)

*available from Kensington Publishing Corp.

The Murder of a Queen Bee

Meera Lester

KENSINGTON BOOKS
www.kensingtonbooks.com

KENSINGTON BOOKS are published by

Kensington Publishing Corp.
119 West 40th Street
New York, NY 10018

Library of Congress Card Catalogue Number: 2016945053

ISBN-13: 978-1-61773-913-2
ISBN-10: 1-61773-913-8
First Kensington Hardcover Edition: October 2016

eISBN-13: 978-1-61773-914-9
eISBN-10: 1-61773-914-6
Kensington Electronic Edition: October 2016

10 9 8 7 6 5 4 3 2 1

Printed in the United States of America

For my Scribe Tribe,
my readers,
and all the mystery writers—past and present—whose
books have inspired me.

Chapter 1

Speaking of flowers, behold the deadly beauties
that hide in plain sight.

—*Henny Penny Farmette Almanac*

Abigail Mackenzie reached across the lace cloth covering her patio table, lifted a corner of the bread from a bite-size tea sandwich, and grimaced. The bread had dried out, and the lettuce clinging to the mayonnaise had gone as limp as a rag in a wash bucket. If the egg salad filling had gone bad, it would be the final straw. Pretty much everything that could go wrong on this day had.

Heaving a sigh, Abby let go of the bread and sank back into the patio chair. She locked eyes with Katerina Petrovsky, her former partner with the Las Flores Police Department. When Abby left the force to buy and renovate the old farmette, they'd stayed best buddies, and when the situation warranted it, they still had each other's backs.

"Don't say it, Kat."

Ignoring the peeved expression on the face of her blond, blue-eyed friend, Abby stewed in silence. It was the hottest day in April, but for Abby, it had been raining cow patties from heaven. The intimate luncheon for Fiona Mary Ryan, who had wanted to talk to Abby as soon as possible without saying why, had seemed in jeopardy when Abby discovered dead bees at the base of her hives. Worker bees were a tidy bunch; they kept the hives clean and clear of bee corpses. Large numbers of dead bees at the hive entrances had meant Abby would have to open the hives and check them. Several neighbors in rural Las Flores kept bees. It wasn't unheard of for marauding bees to take over a hive, often fighting it out at the entrance. It was something Abby hadn't personally witnessed, but that didn't mean it hadn't happened.

Flinging open the door to the garden shed to retrieve her beekeeper basket containing her suit and smoker, Abby had recoiled at the stench of a dead rodent. Forgoing the rodent problem to assuage her concern about the honeybees, she had spent the next couple of hours smoking the bees and examining the ten frames in each hive. Relieved that there hadn't been a rogue bee invasion, Abby had searched for an increase in mites or anything else that might explain the die-off. Finally, it had dawned on her that farmers within a five-mile radius might have applied insecticide on their fields or chemicals harmful to bees on their garden plants. *And folks wonder why the honeybee population has been diminishing. When food prices hit sky high, maybe then everyone will take the issue more seriously and realize how much we need our pollinators.*

After disrobing from the beekeeper's suit and pulling off her jeans and T-shirt, Abby had showered the smoke scent from her body and hair. She negotiated a quick wardrobe change into sandals and a seventies-inspired peasant dress. Although she wasn't too crazy for the dress, with its embroidered detail on the bodice, she knew Fiona would love it. She wove her reddish-gold hair into a shoulder-length braid and secured the end with an elastic band. After sliding a chocolate sheet cake into the oven, Abby was setting about making the tea sandwiches when she heard Kat calling from the farmette driveway.

Finally, it seemed that the negative energy of the day had shifted into positive territory. Grateful for an extra pair of hands, Abby tossed a pinafore apron to Kat and put her to work dressing the table with a cloth of ivory lace and matching napkins. They laid out silver serving pieces and arranged the food—egg salad tea sandwiches, bowls of freshly picked strawberries, a rich chocolate sheet cake, and an antique sugar bowl filled with crispy gingersnaps. The tea in the vermeil pot smelled fragrant with leaves of spearmint and lemon balm, lavender buds, calendula flowers, and chamomile—Fiona's favorite. All that remained was for her to show.

Abby chitchatted with Kat—first about the flapper-girl haircut Kat now sported and then about the upcoming county fair and whether or not Abby should enter her honey and jams—and the time passed quickly. But all that talking made Abby thirsty, and she soon realized she'd forgotten to set out the water pitcher and glasses. After hustling back to the kitchen, she rinsed and cut a lemon into thin slices before dropping the slices into the clear glass pitcher and adding water. Glancing at the wall clock on the way back outside with the pitcher and glasses, Abby frowned, pursed her lips, and blew a puff of air. Fiona was over an hour late.

"What do you think's keeping her?" Kat asked.

"Darn if I know." Abby set the pitcher and glasses on the table. She dropped onto a patio chair, leaned back, and surveyed the surroundings.

The backyard ambiance of her farmette created the perfect setting for a tea party. Blossoms and birdsong in the apricot and cherry trees seemed to proliferate. The tall tea roses held aloft large peppermint-striped blooms. The verdant lawn appeared as green as a hay field in spring. Cream-colored flowers dotted the blood orange, tangerine, and lime trees, their scent permeating the backyard with sweet, citrusy fragrance. Quite possibly, her garden had reached its zenith on this very day. Abby secretly smiled at the notion that despite a shaky start, the day had turned so lovely. The garden seemed as pretty as a Monet painting, and the luncheon would be something that she and Fiona and Kat would talk about for a very long time—whenever Fiona managed to show up.

While Kat rambled on about the handsome new hire at the fire station, Abby strained to hear the sound of a car approaching on Farm Hill Road. As it sped past her farmette, Abby's thoughts ticked through plausible reasons for her friend's tardiness. If there had been an accident, surely someone would have called, since Kat routinely chatted up the police dispatcher ladies, and they always seemed to know how to reach her. And if Fiona had fallen ill, she would have answered when Abby phoned the cottage and the botanical shop Fiona owned. Abby quickly abandoned the idea that Fiona had suffered an accident while out searching for herbs, since she no longer hiked much in the mountains after being assaulted by a stranger. And if she did go out alone looking for wild herbs, she always took her cell phone. She hadn't answered that, either. So one glaring possibility remained—Fiona had bailed on their luncheon.

As her concern shifted to irritation, Abby grasped the stand of the patio umbrella and gave it an aggressive twist. With the shade now covering the food and Kat's side of the table, Abby moved over next to her former partner, leaving the spot in the sun for Fiona. Good thing Fiona loved the heat. Eyeing the herb garden from a new vantage point did little to assuage Abby's frustration. And her frustration level was rising by degrees, like the heat of the day. As if mirroring her mood, the drifts of lemon balm, elderflower, skullcap, sage, oregano, motherwort, and other herbs seemed to struggle to stay upright in the partial shade under the late April sun.

Kat finally spoke. "She might be helping somebody. You know what a sucker she is for every Tom, Dick, and Harriet with a sob story."

"True," Abby conceded. "She helped me a lot when I dawdled over whether or not to plant the herb garden—you know herbs can take over a place. I do appreciate how she spent hours with me discussing the culinary and medical uses of them. And it was her idea to put in a miniature medieval garden in raised beds, laid out with a Latin cross design. She was the one who found the illustration in an old gardening book." Abby waved her hand toward a cluster of raised beds on the east side of her property. "The garden was pretty this morning. Now it looks wilted."

"Oh well." Kat crossed her legs, repositioning the napkin over her lap.

Abby heaved a sigh. *Okay. Not interested. So luncheon tea parties are about delicious food, polite manners, and convivial conversation. Move on.* Abby changed the subject. "Fiona told me she'd recommended my honey and herbs to some of the local businesses," said Abby. "Already, Ananda Bhojana, that new vegetarian eatery, and Smooth Your Groove, the smoothie shop run by those commune people, have placed orders. And Fiona is stocking my honey in her Ancient Wisdom Botanicals store on Main. I mean, she gets a lot of traffic from Cineflicks, Twice Around Markdowns, and even the Black Witch."

"You don't say. The Black Witch, the only bar in town

and a biker bar, to boot. Bet they don't buy much honey. I mean, how many mixed drinks use honey as an ingredient?" Kat asked. She seemed unimpressed.

"Well, there's the Bee's Knees. It uses gin, lemon juice, and honey syrup." Abby struggled to think of others.

Kat rolled her eyes. "Seriously, Abby. Can you see a biker strutting up to the bar and ordering a Bee's Knees?"

"Point taken," said Abby.

In silence, the two sat staring up into the towering peppertree at the center back of Abby's property line. The tree's lacy green fronds and bracts of newly formed red berries hung in perfect stillness. Now and then a berry dropped into the chicken run.

"You ever grind those peppercorns?" Kat asked.

Abby nodded. "Once. Too much work. You have to clean, toast, and roast them first." Her stomach growled, long and loud.

"Sounds like you're as hungry as I am," said Kat.

Abby pushed a springy forelock of her reddish-gold hair away from her face and cupped a hand over her light eyes to gauge the position of the sun. "Where on God's earth can Fiona be? We could get sunburned out here without hats. Maybe we should move the food inside. Darn it all! Everything was perfect an hour ago."

Kat leaned forward. "My advice, girlfriend, call or text one more time, and if she doesn't answer, we will eat without her."

"If she didn't answer the six previous calls, what makes you think she'll pick up on the seventh?" Abby snapped, even as she tapped Fiona's number on her cell again and listened for one, two . . . five rings, with no answer.

"The tea is tepid," Kat said, touching the pot next to the perfusion of orange nasturtiums in a widemouthed jar.

"Dried bread, soggy sandwiches, and tea that probably should have been iced to begin with—"

"Oh, Kat, for goodness' sake, please stop grousing."

"Guess the heat and hunger are making a beast of me. I'm losing all sense of civility," said Kat.

"Well, you're not alone. My feathers couldn't be any more ruffled than if I were a hen with an egg stuck in her butt," said Abby.

Kat flicked at a small insect moving on the strap of her blue cotton sundress. The tiny creature spread its wings and flew away.

Abby blew air in exasperation. "It won't hurt you."

"How would I know?" Kat snapped. "There have been two cases of West Nile virus already reported in the county."

"Mosquitoes," scoffed Abby. "West Nile is carried by mosquitoes, not ladybugs."

"Whatever," said Kat. "I don't rehabilitate bugs, like some people." She rolled her eyes at Abby.

They sat in tense silence. Kat shooed the flies.

Abby fumed. After a couple of minutes, she reminded herself that there might be a good reason for Fiona being late. It served no good purpose for her to be locking horns with Kat.

"Sorry to be so testy, Kat," said Abby. "I'm worried and annoyed at the same time. I was in Fiona's shop yesterday and reminded her of our tea luncheon. I can't believe that in only twenty-four hours, she could forget. And . . . it's not like her to bail."

"I hear you, girlfriend." Kat used her napkin to wick away the moisture collecting on either side of her nose. "Okay, so here's an earthshaking idea—maybe she's in a funk. You did say she had hit the big four-o, right?"

"Yeah, but that was a week ago, and, anyhow, the forties are the best years of a woman's life."

"According to?"

Abby gave her a quizzical look. "Lidia."

"Vittorio?" Kat asked incredulously. "The old lady on Main, with the jewelry store?"

"The same."

"Yeah, well, Lidia should know. From the looks of her, she's hit the big four-o twice already. Maybe three times."

"Oh, please. Even if she is retirement age, she's still working. And Main Street hasn't exactly attracted a Ralph Lauren Home store, an upscale art gallery, or an artisan chocolate shop. Lidia and her handcrafted jewelry shop are our town's best hope for a bit of class now that the patisserie is gone."

"Suppose you're right about that."

Abby decided to wait five more minutes. Then she and Kat would devour the food and enjoy the rest of the day. Maybe they'd go antiquing. It would be Fiona's loss, and she'd have some explaining to do when they next saw each other.

"Fiona's store is nice in a hippie, Zen kind of way," said Kat. "But it bothers me that it occupies the same space as where the pastry shop used to be. I can't go in there without thinking about Chef Jean-Louis. Her herb-inspired, nutrient-dense, gluten-free, low-salt, low-taste bars made of who knows what can't compare to our late chef's exquisite madeleines." Kat reached for a tea sandwich. She parted the bread and tossed the lettuce onto her plate before taking a bite. Chewing, she said, "I think Fiona's a hippie, living in the wrong era."

Abby stared incredulously at her friend for throwing aside the lettuce. "Seriously, Kat?"

"What?" Kat asked. "Your chickens will eat this, won't they? Even if there's mayo on it?"

Abby shook her head. "Whatever." She reached for the pot and poured herself a cupful of tea. "Fiona sells good stuff. Almost everything is eco-friendly. And she isn't a hippie."

"Well, she dresses like one."

"In fairness, she wears those bohemian circular skirts, because that's the way the other women in the commune dress. You must have seen them. Some work here in town."

"Yeah, I know. I've been up to their compound, if you can call it that. We've had a lot of complaints. The families in those mountains do not like the drumming, chanting, and clapping. They complain of harmoniums droning on endlessly. And they don't like the weekly bonfires. They're afraid that one of these days a spark will ignite the mountain. It's a tinderbox up there, Abby. You know that."

"Maybe in summer . . . not right now," Abby said. "I was just up there last week with Fiona, checking on the progress of the commune gardens. From bio-intensive double digging to planting heirloom seeds, she's taught those devotees everything she knows. The gardens are lush and green and thriving. But don't take my word for it. You should go see them. The gate to their property is always open."

Kat stopped chewing long enough to say, "Nah." She wrapped a blond lock of hair behind her ear and pushed back her bangs, as if preparing to lean forward and do some serious damage to the pile of sandwiches. "And you couldn't pay me to live there. As far as I can tell, the place looks like a dumping ground of old buses, RVs, and shacks."

Abby corrected her. "The guru has a nice house."

"Well, he would, wouldn't he?" Kat said.

Abby shrugged. "The gardens produce an abundance of

organic vegetables. The commune residents have opened their facility to people who want to view and purchase the produce. They're also selling it along the roadside up there. Fiona told me the gardens are what she loves most about the place."

"If she loves them so much, why isn't she still living there?" Kat poured herself some tea and stirred in some milk.

"She moved into the cottage on Dr. Danbury's estate because she can't stand that guy in charge at the commune." Abby finished drinking her tea. She placed a silver tea strainer over her porcelain teacup, reached for the pot, and poured its lukewarm tea through the strainer into her cup.

"You mean Hayden Marks?" asked Kat.

"He's the one." Stirring a spoonful of rose-infused sugar into her tea, Abby said, "Got himself appointed the successor when the old guru left for India. But according to Fiona, Marks modified his predecessor's teaching to make it more understandable to Westerners, and then he changed how the commune worked, establishing a hierarchy of power, with himself as the supreme authority."

"Yeah, well, we know Mr. Marks," said Kat. "He's the charismatic son of an ex-con, who supposedly found solace in the Good Book and became a preacher."

"Really?" Abby arched a brow. "Fiona never said anything about that. Maybe she didn't know. But she sure couldn't abide that Marks insisted all the devotees call him Baba. It means 'wise old man' or 'father' or something like that. She found him to be the antithesis of a father figure, more like a dictator. For refusing to show proper reverence, she was asked to leave. Imagine that . . . for not calling him Baba."

"Baba-shmaba. A pig doesn't change its trotters." Kat's hand formed the shape of an *L*, for *loser*. She pushed back from the table and wiped her mouth with the napkin. "We've been watching that commune bunch for a while."

Abby swallowed another sip of tea and looked at Kat over her teacup. "I'm all ears."

"You hear the talk. Let me put it this way. Why would a peaceful sect of New Agers need firearms?" asked Kat.

"I don't know, but it's not illegal if they have permits."

"Yeah, well, according to the gossip along Main Street, they're stockpiling up there, and not only firearms. Do you want to know what Willard down at the hardware store says?"

"What?" Abby slid her cup back into its saucer and set both on the table.

"They've emptied his place of axes, freeze-dried food, and bottled water. He says he can't keep canning supplies or even basic tools like shovels in stock."

"Why?"

Kat devoured two sandwiches in quick succession and then wiped her fingers with the napkin. "Who knows? But you can't blame the locals for getting paranoid." She reached for the antique silver serving knife, slashed off a slice of the sheet cake, and dropped the slice onto a dessert plate, licking the excess buttercream frosting from her fingers.

Abby raised a brow. "You're like the sister I never had, Kat, so I hope you don't take this the wrong way. You're eating like a cop who doesn't care anymore whether or not she can make it over the training wall."

"Yeah, well, I missed breakfast, and I'm starving."

Abby brushed a crumb that had fallen from the silver serving knife. "I can see that. So eat, already. Getting back to the subject of the commune, I'm not taking sides, but we do live in the land of earthquakes, mudslides, and seasonal wildfires. Maybe Baba thinks a natural disaster is in the offing."

"Or the end is near, and they want to be ready, like that Heaven's Gate cult, who waited on a spacecraft following the Hale-Bopp comet," Kat said. "We can only hope the shovels aren't for burying the dead."

"Now, that's just too far-fetched," Abby chided.

Kat smiled and began nibbling the cake. She licked her lips. Holding the empty fork aloft, she looked at Abby. "Lord, have mercy, girlfriend! You nailed the cake." She took a bigger bite and writhed in pleasure. Swallowing, she reached for her cup of tea to wash it down and then did a little shoulder dance. "Um, um, um!"

"Glad it meets with your approval." Abby grinned. "I added last summer's raspberry jam to the buttercream."

Kat used the silver serving knife to coax a chunk of buttercream from the chocolate cake. After dropping the buttercream onto her plate, she scooped it into her mouth with her fork and licked her lips. "Don't know about it being an end-time cult, but it's a cult. Of that, I'm sure. But like I said, my peeps are watching. When Baba's gang breaks the law, we'll make the arrests."

Laying aside the fork, Kat poured herself a glass of water. "For the life of me, I can't imagine why anyone would join a commune or a cult. You have to give up your personal ambitions in life, sell your possessions, and donate all your money to the group. Fiona doesn't seem the type, although I can't say I know her that well." She pushed down the lemon slice and sipped some water from the glass.

Reaching again for the teapot to refill both empty cups, Abby felt as though Kat didn't understand Fiona's quirkiness. "She's just searching for deeper meaning, and perhaps joining that commune and dressing in that folk-boho style are an extension of that."

"Someone should buy her a watch and suggest she check the time once in a while," Kat said. "I'm not saying it to be mean-spirited, but it's thoughtless of her not to call and let you know she's been delayed."

Abby popped a piece of a sandwich into her mouth and nearly choked when the sound of gunfire rang out. After swallowing, she exclaimed, "Darn it, Kat! That ringtone is just plain annoying."

"Tells me it's Otto calling," Kat said, then licked her fingers and fished her cell from her pocket. After sliding a dry knuckle across the screen, Kat answered, "Hello, big daddy. What's up?"

Abby knew Sergeant Otto Nowicki wouldn't be calling Kat on her day off without good reason.

"Don't tell me. He's calling you in?" Abby whispered.

Kat nodded. "He's up at Kilbride Lake."

"What's going on?" Abby asked softly.

Kat shook her head and listened intently. She then whispered, "Canal patrol found a body in a burning car."

Abby stiffened. "A body?"

Kat listened, locked eyes with Abby. Her expression darkened. "It's Fiona's car."

Abby's stomach tightened. Her heart pounded. *Oh, good Lord.*

"So, it *is* a woman's body. Okay. See you in a few," Kat said. After thrusting the phone into her pocket, she grabbed a couple of sandwiches in a napkin and slipped them into her other pocket. "Could be a long night. I'm hoping it's not Fiona."

"Who else could it be?" Abby said, pushing away from the table. "I'm coming, too."

Tips for Making Rose-Scented Sugar

Rose-scented sugar is easy to make. All you need is a screw-top mason jar, granulated sugar, and scented roses that are fresh, fragrant, and pesticide-free.

1. Gather one to two cups of heavily scented rose petals that are free of blemishes and tiny insects.

2. Wash the petals, pat them dry with paper towels, and snip off the white part (which can have a bitter taste).

3. Alternate layers of sugar and rose petals in the jar until it is filled, leaving half an inch of space at the top.

4. Screw on the lid and set the jar in a cool, dark place for at least two weeks.

5. Sift out the petals before using the sugar.

Chapter 2

To repel moths in the garden, plant rosemary
and lavender; to keep them out of your closet,
hang the herbs in sachets.

—Henny Penny Farmette Almanac

Guiding her Jeep out of Las Flores and along the black-top roads that twisted through the foothills, Abby managed to keep Kat's vintage silver roadster in sight all the way to the summit. However, after the cutoff, which was only about eight minutes from downtown Las Flores, Abby lost sight of her former partner. After the cutoff, Abby negotiated the steep switchbacks of the narrow two-lane road until it dipped into a heavily forested area of pine, oaks, and redwood trees. Through the open Jeep windows, the mountain air smelled of sun-drenched earth and dried plant matter. Soon she turned off onto a link road leading to Kilbride Lake. The mountain lake supplied drinking water through a series of canals and reservoirs to Las Flores residents, as well as to the mountain people who lived on the western side of town.

Pulling off the road behind police cruisers and a fire truck, Abby guided the Jeep beneath a towering sequoia with a trunk nearly as wide as the fire truck Kat had parked behind. Abby jumped from the Jeep and slammed the door. The stench of burnt plastic, rubber, and human flesh turned her back. She opened the door and searched the vehicle for something to use as a mask. Behind the driver's seat, she found a package of work gloves. After ripping open the plastic bag, she removed a pair, then held them against her nose and mouth as she strode toward the coterie of first responders.

Firefighters from Cal Fire had already extinguished the blaze and were mopping up. Las Flores police chief Bob Allen and Sergeant Otto Nowicki assessed the scene. Kat, in her sundress, looked totally out of place as she stood next to a uniformed officer. Sheriff's deputies, a canal patrol agent, and the local forest ranger huddled together a few feet away, chatting, apparently awaiting the arrival of the coroner.

Abby's heart pounded as she spotted Fiona's car. She took in as many details of the scene as possible as she made her way over. A booming voice called out her name.

"What the devil are you doing here, Mackenzie?"

"Hello, Chief," Abby said. She lowered the gloves from her nose and stared at him. "I wanted to see for myself why my guest of honor didn't show up for our garden party today."

The police chief fixed one of his famous steely-eyed stares on her. "You know the vic?"

"I know Fiona Mary Ryan. Until I get a look at who is in that car, I won't be able to tell you if the woman is Fiona or not." Abby scrutinized the car. It had not been wrecked. There were no signs of any exterior damage beyond what the fire had done. So, there had been no roadway accident.

"Petrovsky says it's her," the chief said. "But another ID

couldn't hurt, since we found no purse or documents in the glove compartment. Get over here, Mackenzie."

Abby walked toward Otto, who was ogling Kat in her short sundress. Abby picked her way through the grass and weeds until Chief Bob Allen's voice boomed again.

"Watch out there!"

Abby halted. *You always could bark like a rabid dog, Chief,* she thought.

"Back up and go around," the chief snapped, as if addressing a rookie. "Can't you see the tire impression?"

Abby had indeed noticed the partial tire print and had sidestepped it by more than a foot.

"Get the crime-scene tape over there." Chief Bob Allen bellowed the order at the uniformed officer behind him.

Abby wanted to bark back, "Should have been taped long before now."

"If you'll recall from your academy training, Mackenzie," Chief Bob Allen continued, "that tire track could be a clue. It might belong to the killer's vehicle."

Whatever. Don't talk down to me. Abby knew only too well Chief Bob Allen's passive-aggressive personality after working for him for seven years. She took his barked comments in stride, because she felt pretty certain that the police chief had a deep-seated inferiority complex and felt his confidence elevated only when he was demeaning someone else. Abby returned the gloves to her nose. The stench of Fiona's body and the burnt car was overpowering. She peered inside the driver's side door.

Fiona's pale complexion was black and red in areas, but the bone structure was still intact. Her shoulder-length dark hair clung to her scalp in clumps, like tufts of wild weeds dotting an arid field. Abby looked at Fiona's neck. She took a sharp breath and peered more closely. Where was the necklace with the Celtic cross that Fiona always wore, believing as she did that it held a link between her and her pre-Irish ancestors, the Celts?

Abby fought back a wave of nausea. Oh, Fiona, what happened to you?

Fiona's attire suggested to Abby that she'd dressed especially nice for the luncheon—a gauzy white blouse, a chiffon gypsy skirt, lace leggings, and flats. The smoke and the agony of seeing her friend's body in such a senseless and sickening state caused her eyes to sting. But this was neither the time nor the place for an emotional display. Abby muffled a sob and wiped the gloves across her cheeks to erase any evidence of tears. Her throat tightened. *Do not cry. Not here. Not now.* She gulped hard and fought for composure. She would have only these moments to study the car and her friend's body. She sniffed hard, as if doing so might help her disassociate from her emotion and instead focus on the car interior.

The fire had claimed the front end and most of the dash. The driver's and the front passenger's windows were down, and the doors unlocked. The backseat was devoid of baskets and books, which seemed to accompany Fiona wherever she went. There were no signs of a struggle, no purse, no pills, or flammable liquids that might have started a fire. Nothing. *Weird.* Fiona seemed to have been sitting peacefully behind the steering wheel, waiting to burn up. Why hadn't she tried to escape?

Stepping back, Abby turned to face Chief Bob Allen. After sighing heavily and clearing her throat, Abby said. "It's her, Fiona Mary Ryan."

"What was your relationship with her?" Chief Bob Allen asked pointedly. He scrutinized Abby's face like he would that of a perp who might be hiding something. If he felt any sympathy for Abby's loss of her friend, he didn't show it.

THE MURDER OF A QUEEN BEE 19

"We shared a love of gardening." Abby swallowed hard against the lump that had formed in her throat. *Hold it together. Stand strong, straight-faced.* "Fiona owns the botanical shop on Main—Ancient Wisdom Botanicals. She was supposed to join us for lunch today but was a no-show." Abby swallowed hard. "Now we know why."

"What time was that lunch to be held?"

"Noon."

"Does she have family in Las Flores?" Chief Bob Allen asked.

"I don't think so. She lost her parents several years ago in a car crash. She has a brother. I've heard a lot about him, but I've never met him. Does a lot of international travel, I gather. When he's on the West Coast, he stays with her." Abby sniffed again and then waved the smoke away with her gloves.

"What about a husband, children?"

"Children, no. Husband, yes. She's married to Tom Davidson Dodge. Separated now. She goes by the name of Ryan. Divorce isn't final. He lives down the road, in that mountain commune, when he isn't staying with her, which he occasionally does. Or did. Their relationship was a little strange, but you had to know Fiona. There's a boyfriend, too, recently estranged. Laurent Duplessis."

"Duplessis. Unusual name," remarked the chief. He looked over at Otto, who was jotting down Abby's comments in a notebook, as if wanting to make sure Otto had duly noted that name.

"He's Haitian, I believe. I only met him once," said Abby. "Seems all right."

"Any idea where we can find this boyfriend?"

"Last I heard, he had rented a room over Twice Around Markdowns."

"All right, Mackenzie. Good information. Stick around. We're going to need your statement."

"Yeah, I know the drill, but thanks for reminding me."

"Coroner's van is here," said the chief, looking over the latest vehicle to arrive.

Millie Jamison stepped from the van, setting one black flat on the ground and then the other. A black dress with red piping showed her curves as she quickly slipped on a disposable gown, pulled booties over her shoes, and threaded her fingers into latex gloves.

"Oh, my, my," said Otto. "You'd never know she had a baby a few months ago. She's looking pretty hot."

Abby and Kat shared an eye roll.

"Really, Otto. Get over your bad self," said Kat.

Abby watched Millie make her way over to the body. "Glad she's here. She's good, no question. But when is the county going to hire a permanent chief medical examiner? Didn't the grand jury's report make that recommendation? Bringing a chief medical examiner on board makes more sense than having the two assistant medical examiners working cases with the coroner, don't you think?"

Kat shrugged. "It's all about funding. There isn't any. The system's working, so I guess the consensus is, if it isn't broken, don't try to fix it."

Otto strutted to the crime-scene tape and, lifting it, said, "We believe our vic is Fiona Mary Ryan."

"Noted. Thanks," said Millie, darting under the tape. She was clearly all business.

The local TV station van pulled in behind the coroner's vehicle, diverting Abby's attention from Millie to the crew. In a heartbeat, they were setting up for a live shot from the scene.

Abby shook her head and said to no one in particular,

"Boy, they got here fast." She knew the news reporters listened to the same scanners as the emergency responders, fire, and police. Fat chance of keeping the lid on the murder investigation, if that was what the chief wanted—and that was what he always wanted on any investigation. He hated bad publicity for the town and always tried to put a positive spin on negative news. But it was difficult to spin a murder, especially when the victim was a local businesswoman.

Abby watched Chief Bob Allen straighten his jacket, walk over to meet the news crew, and point them to a spot farther away from the body in the car. He probably offered to step in front of the camera, with the proviso that they wait for a shot of the car until the body was in the coroner's van.

"Well, here we are again, just like the old days," Otto said. "You still shucking corn and shelling peas, Abby?"

Abby smiled and nodded. She liked Otto. His wife, the West Coast regional director of an ambulance company, was gone a lot. Back in the day, when she was still on the force, Otto often offered to buy Abby and Kat dinner or drinks at the Black Witch, just to have a little company. But Otto could be annoyingly blunt.

"If you're asking if I'm still farming, the answer is yes," replied Abby. "Corn in the fall, peas in the spring." She smiled sweetly at Otto, then added, "Listen, guys, I've got a few of Fiona's things at my place."

"Oh, yeah?" replied Otto. "Like what?"

"Nothing special. A trowel, a scarf, and an armful of old books. She tended to write notes on scraps of paper and stuff them inside books. I doubt you'll find anything in them relevant to her death, but just the same . . ." Abby swallowed and took a deep breath. "I'll hand them over so you can give them to her next of kin."

Otto nodded. Kat stared expectantly at the coroner, who was approaching them.

It was the first time Abby had seen Millie in over a year, and Millie's countenance reflected a new mother's glow.

Stepping carefully, she ducked under the crime-scene tape to approach Abby, Kat, and Otto. Peeling off her gloves, Millie said, "Been a while since I've seen the three of you on scene together."

"Yeah, well, it looks like we pulled you away from something pretty special," said Otto.

"You look stunning," Abby chimed in.

"Hope it wasn't the christening," added Kat.

Millie smiled. "No. My hubby and I were at the symphony, on a rare date. I got the call in the middle of the 'Méditation' from *Thaïs*." Met with a blank stare from Otto and Kat, Millie looked at Abby. "You know that piece, don't you, Abby?"

"One of my favorites," Abby replied.

"Still pick up your violin once in a while?" Millie asked.

"Not really." Abby tried to sound indifferent, as if it didn't matter anymore. Millie sounded sympathetic, as if she knew that the thumb injury that had sidelined Abby's law enforcement career had also deprived her of one of her personal, secret pleasures, playing the violin. Her gun hand was also her bowing hand. It required a stable thumb. And hers wasn't. Safely locked in its case, the violin that Abby couldn't play but couldn't part with gathered dust on the top shelf of her closet.

Glancing at her watch, Millie asked, "So which one of you is in charge?"

Otto replied, "Technically, that would be me, although Chief Bob Allen is over there, doing the live interview, and you might want to talk with him, as well." Otto ran a hand over his crew cut and hitched his duty belt a little higher, as if doing so somehow elevated his stature.

"So, my best guess is the death occurred sometime between seven o'clock this morning and noon," Millie said.

"Ah, jeez, Doc. Could you be a little more specific?" asked Otto.

"Hard to say exactly. You know how this works. We might be able to get a little closer after the autopsy."

Otto nodded. "Cause and manner?"

"That, too, is hard to pinpoint in the absence of obvious signs of trauma, wounds, ligature, punctures, and cuts. We got severe thermal burns. Carbon monoxide poisoning is the most frequent cause of death in burn victims. But there's no cherry-pink and apple blossom–white skin mottling. That tells me she wasn't breathing during the fire. As I said, the autopsy will tell us more."

Millie's driver approached with a collapsible transport gurney, a body bag, and a form, which he handed to Millie. Otto presented a pen to Millie, and she filled out the form.

"So, here's the release number. I've put my contact info on there, as well," Millie said, handing back the paperwork.

Abby's thoughts raced. She had a zillion questions she wanted to ask, but this wasn't her investigation, and this wasn't the right time. Otto scanned the form and then looked over at the burned car. Kat's expression mirrored the solemnity of the moment. Abby felt her stomach tighten, knowing how they all had to compartmentalize emotions when dealing with cases like this one. Millie seemed to do it best. She respected the bodies and had deep empathy and compassion for their families. In that way, too, Millie and Abby shared a similarity.

Millie turned to leave, and Kat called out, "Before you go, Dr. Jamison, can you tell us with any certainty that Fiona did not just sit there and died of smoke inhalation? That's kind of hard to think that might have happened."

"Indeed," said Millie. "I'd think if she were still alive, she would have tried to escape, unless she was incapacitated, of course. But to answer your question, if she was in the car, breathing in smoke, we will undoubtedly see evidence of soot in her lungs during the autopsy." Millie flashed a sympathetic smile. "We'll get to the bottom of this. Unfortunately, we'll just have to wait and see what secrets her body gives up."

After Millie left, with Fiona's body bagged and tagged in the back of the coroner's van, Abby spotted Chief Bob Allen walking toward her, Otto, and Kat. Abby groaned. "Okay, guys. This is where I say, 'See you later.'" She knew that Kat and Otto would understand the strained relationship between their boss and her. The tension between them was old history.

"Understood. Go," Kat urged.

Otto nodded.

Abby gave them both quick hugs before hurrying back to her car. Otto and Kat were smart, diligent cops. Abby knew they would draw up a time line for the last twenty-four hours of Fiona's life. They would make a list of the people with whom she'd had contact and would make note of the reasons Fiona had associated with them. A person of interest would soon emerge. Abby knew that killers always had a relationship with their victims—however fleeting.

Passing through town, Abby stopped by the doggy spa to pick up Sugar.

"Zowie! Somebody looks better for an overnight stay at

the Diggity Do," she said, hugging Sugar, who seemed just as eager to see her. After taking the leash from the worker at the spa for pets, Abby walked an excited Sugar to the Jeep. She patted the car seat, and Sugar hopped in. Her tail wagged almost as hard as she panted.

Fifteen minutes later, back on the farmette, Abby poured herself a cup of cold tea from the pot she and Kat had abandoned. She strolled with Sugar from the patio to the backyard and sank onto the seat of the free-standing porch swing that she'd placed between two apricot trees. The cloying, sweet fragrance of citrus blooms permeated the air. A family of twenty crows that had taken up residence in the tall eucalyptus tree on the vacant wooded acre behind her property cawed in a raucous chorus. Abby rocked on the swing, hoping to push out the images stuck in her mind, images that sickened her as she thought about how Fiona might have died at the hands of her killer. What had been troubling Fiona? Why had she wanted advice from someone who had worked in law enforcement? Abby knew she might never get the answers to those questions, but she was sure going to try.

Dusk descended like a diaphanous veil over the farmette. Its hues of silvery violet and pale lavender reframed the landscape. A barn owl winged its way overhead, then disappeared into the dark canopy of trees. Abby struggled to fight back tears, which finally overtook her, hot and salty, spilling down her cheeks, wetting the fabric of the retro-hippie-chic peasant dress that Fiona would never see.

Abby rocked until the moon rose. Until her stomach was no longer knotted. Until her heart hammered no more. Her thoughts turned to the usual suspects: husband, boyfriend, known associates, and people harboring grudges.

Ancient Wisdom Botanicals had opened less than a year

ago—a year after Fiona and her husband, Tom Davidson Dodge, had separated. He lived most of the time at the commune, in an old VW bus that bore the rainbow colors and peace symbols of a bygone era and rested on railroad ties and concrete blocks. Tom had gotten a good deal on the van from a mountain mechanic who'd kept it over a dispute about payment for repairs the mechanic had done. But why, after separating, had Fiona and Tom occasionally still shared a bed at her cottage on Dr. Danbury's property? People in town knew that Fiona had wanted a child with Tom before her biological clock made it impossible. They also knew that even when she'd dated others during their separation, Tom remained her one true love.

Fiona's most recent boyfriend, Laurent Duplessis, could drum, sing, and attract more girlfriends than a Haitian masked booby could find fish in the sea. But his relationship with Fiona hadn't endured. She had liked that he seemed to know more about herbs than most people in town, particularly how to use them in Haitian food. His voodoo religion was, according to Fiona, mind-blowing, and they'd shared an interest in learning about various spiritual paths and practices. She had allowed herself to be comforted by him as her relationship with the commune people became increasingly strained. She'd let him work in her store for a while. But in a reversal of roles, she'd ended up as the caretaker of Laurent, who became increasingly irresponsible. When their relationship grew toxic, she had moved on. He hadn't. Abby recalled that Fiona had confided in her that she believed Laurent had been following her around. He had seemed to be stalking her. Just three days before the luncheon, she'd asked Abby for a meeting. Now Abby wondered if the purpose of the meeting was to find out about how to get a restraining order. Or was it something else?

She owed Fiona a debt of gratitude for all the help with the farmette herb garden. Abby vowed to repay the debt by finding out how Fiona had ended up alone and dead in a burning car, instead of dining on egg salad sandwiches in Abby's lovely garden, in the company of friends.

Egg Salad Tea Sandwiches

Ingredients:
6 hard-boiled eggs (chilled or at room temperature)
½ cup mayonnaise
¼ cup finely minced red onion
2 tablespoons minced sweet gherkin pickles
2 tablespoons coarse-ground mustard
1 teaspoon organic honey
½ teaspoon finely minced fresh dill
Kosher salt, to taste
Freshly cracked black pepper, to taste
12 slices white or whole-wheat bread
6 chilled, crisp lettuce leaves or 24 thin slices Armenian
    cucumber

Directions:
Peel and chop the hard-boiled eggs and place the chopped eggs in a medium bowl. Add the mayonnaise, onion, pickles, mustard, honey, dill, salt, and pepper to the eggs and mix thoroughly. Set the egg salad aside.

Stack 2 slices of bread on a cutting board so that they are completely aligned and cut off the crusts with a sharp knife. Repeat this process until all the slices of bread have been trimmed.

Spread a thin layer of the reserved egg salad on 6

bread slices. Top each with a lettuce leaf or 4 cucumber slices and then a plain bread slice to make 6 sandwiches.

Cut each sandwich into 4 squares or, if you prefer, 4 triangles with a sharp knife. Arrange the tea sandwiches on a large plate and serve at once.

Serves 4 to 6 (4 to 6 tea sandwiches per person)

Chapter 3

Don't get sidetracked by the hens' antics if the
rooster is in a foul mood.

—*Henny Penny Farmette Almanac*

Houdini, the rust-colored bantam rooster with weapon-
like spurs, eyed Abby, as if ready for attack. She
saw him.

"Did somebody get up on the wrong side of the roost?"
she asked.

She stepped up the tempo of her chores in the poultry
area, collecting eggs and hosing down the water dispenser
before refilling it. Keeping Houdini in her line of sight, she
plucked the aluminum feeder from its suspension hook and
added crumbles. Sooner or later, he was going to make his
move. Out of the corner of her eye, she saw Houdini begin
to pace. Hurriedly, she rehung the feeder. Sidestepping the
hens, Abby fetched the bag of wilted spinach and lettuce
leaves from the wheelbarrow next to the gate and dumped
the entire mound into the large cracked platter on the
ground. "Here you go, my darlings."

So Houdini had gotten his hackles up. Abby wondered
what had triggered his agitation this time. She was almost
finished with the chores when Houdini flew at her, screech-

ing a shrill warning and flapping his wings as though his tail feathers had caught fire.

"Oh, cool your spurs, big boy," Abby said, dodging the assault and grabbing the garden hoe. She held the hoe handle in a defensive position and eased out of the gate, stepping backward.

Like an opposing warlord, Abby locked eyes with Houdini. The rooster blinked first. Apparently satisfied that he had sufficiently established dominance over his domain, the rooster promptly herded Henrietta, Heloise, Tighty Whitey, Red, Orpy, and the wyandotte sisters with aggressive pecks. He stopped when finally they stood bunched together in a huddle under the henhouse. The bantam rooster began macho prancing. Abby had seen it before . . . and so had the hens. The girls watched in seeming boredom as Houdini executed the moves of his scratch dance, trying to entice them into exploring what his sharp toenails might have unearthed. On the off chance that he had uncovered a worm, two of the hens wandered over. No worms. Not so much as a grub or a speck of birdseed. They ambled off to a sunny spot for a dirt bath.

"Listen up, ladies, and you, too, Mr. Fancy Pants," said Abby. "Keep an eye peeled for hawks circling. I've spotted three already this morning. One is sitting sentry up there in that pine tree. I don't want to come home to a pile of plucked feathers and no chickens, and trust me, you don't want that, either."

After latching the gate, Abby picked up the basket of eggs, most in hues of brown, white, and tan, with a blue-green one from the Ameraucana. She walked to the water spigot in the middle of the yard. Sugar bounded over.

"You've been chasing my songbirds, haven't you?"

Abby leaned down and turned off the water to the hose. She would have filled the second water dispenser, as she usually did on hot days, but the rubber ring inside the screw-top lid on the older dispenser had snapped, making the dispenser unusable. Knowing that if a chicken went without water, it could stop laying eggs for up to three weeks, Abby made a mental note to keep a close watch on the water level in the sole dispenser. The temperature was expected to climb into the triple digits by late afternoon. On her way back to the kitchen, she plucked a stick from the grass and flung it into the air. Sugar bounded after it and trotted back, leaving the stick where it had landed under the white tea roses.

"Would it be asking too much to bring the stick back?" Abby knelt and massaged the dog's neck. "If you weren't such a cutie-pie, with a personality to match, I would have found you a new home long ago. But when the vet said your genes showed English pointer, beagle, and whippet, I got the idea that you might have a talent for tracking. That talent is useful in investigative work. Can you see where I'm going with this?"

Sugar pushed back and gave an impatient, high-pitched *yip*, *yip*. She might not be the world's greatest interpreter of dog speak yet, but Abby felt pretty sure that Sugar wanted a treat or a walk. But conversation . . . not so much.

"Okay, already. Let's find you a treat and get the leash."

In the kitchen, Abby searched for the bag of doggy treats. There were only three places in her unfinished kitchen where the bag could be hiding: on top of the double ovens, which had been installed without an upper cabinet; in the pantry of dry goods, next to the fridge; and in the drawer under the counter where she kept potatoes and onions.

"Shoot. Did you eat them all already?" Abby avoided eye contact with Sugar. Without looking, she knew that Sugar was gazing up at her with expectant eyes, making her guilt even harder to bear. How could she not remember having thrown out the empty treat bag? And, worse, why hadn't she ensured an adequate supply in the first place?

After grabbing her purse, the leash, and the car key, Abby slid open the screen door. "Come on, big girl. We'd better go get that gasket for the chicken water dispenser and more doggy . . ." She stopped short of saying the word. No point in getting the dog super excited all over again.

Twenty minutes later, Abby navigated the Jeep into the parking lot behind Crawford's Feed and Farm Supplies. She liked going in through the back door since there was always plenty of parking behind the building. Regular customers parked on the street out front. The store's employees parked at the rear, where truck deliveries were handled, where the bales of hay and straw were stacked, and where owner Lucas Crawford had a designated place for his pickup. Lucas had been widowed for almost two years now. His wife had died early in her pregnancy from virulent pneumonia. After the funeral for his wife and unborn child, Lucas had thrown himself into running the store, continuing to make deliveries around the county, and working on his cattle ranch near Abby's small farm. Up there, away from the town and the eager advances of women who wanted to console him, Lucas found solace in raising his grass-fed beef and riding his horses, keeping to himself.

When he had learned that Abby had bought the farmette downhill from his place, Lucas had made a special point of giving her permission to use his old truck if the need ever arose. He'd held on to his late wife's car, he'd told her, so there was no inconvenience. Abby smiled as she stared at his red truck. She'd borrowed it only twice—once to haul compost from the recycling plant to her gardens and another time to transport some lumber to repair the farmhouse kitchen. Each time she had washed the vehicle and had hung the extra key back on its nail on the wall inside the old gray barn where Lucas kept it.

The ringtone of her cell sounded, jarring her from her thoughts.

"Just a reminder. The estate sale is Saturday." Kat's voice practically trilled the words.

"What happened to hello?" asked Abby.

"You have caller ID, girlfriend. Just making sure you remember *not* to do the farmers' market. I thought we could take your car to the estate sale since your Jeep has more room than my roadster," said Kat.

"I've circled the date on my calendar, Kat. And yes, we'll take my Jeep. No problem."

Abby was more concerned about what the cops had discovered in their investigation of Fiona's death. With a killer on the loose in Las Flores, Abby could hardly think of bargain hunting. "What's new with the murder investigation?" she asked, tapping the speaker mode of her cell and setting the phone on the dashboard. She needed both hands to snap the leash onto Sugar's collar. The dog had already started barking her impatience.

"Lot of info, but few leads."

Sighing, Abby said, "So no one heard or saw anything?"

"More like no one is saying if they did. We're ruling out those closest to her and moving out from there. Checking alibis. Working the angles."

"Gotcha. So exactly where is the estate sale?" Abby asked, still struggling with the leash. Sugar wiggled worse than a bowl of gelatin on a picnic table during an earthquake. Abby had tried three times to connect the leash latch to the ring on her harness and finally gave up.

"Vineyard Lane . . . at the Richardson estate. Two doors down from where Fiona lives."

"Lived," Abby said, correcting her. Sugar whined. "Oh, hold on, Kat, while I deal with this dog."

"Where are you?"

"We're at the feed store, on a run for chow and treats. Parked around back."

"And I'm right around the corner. Be there in five. It'll give me a chance to check out Mr. Action Hero with the washboard abs. I can't for the life of me figure out why a man that good-looking hasn't remarried. He can't still be in mourning."

"If you mean Lucas Crawford, I'm watching him walk out the door right now. You better hurry, or you'll miss him," Abby said, instantly wishing she could call back her words. Kat was her dearest friend, but until Abby figured out why she felt those butterflies in her tummy whenever Lucas met up with her, she didn't want anyone—including Kat—complicating the situation. Not that there was a *situation*. And Abby could certainly understand why the single women in town might fantasize about the quiet rancher who lived a stone's throw up the hill from her farmette.

"Stay put, Abby. I'll be right there," Kat said and clicked off.

Abby laid the cell on the console. No point in taking Sugar inside until Kat had come and gone. Through the windshield, Abby watched Lucas check his phone before sliding it into his jeans pocket. Man, did he ever look good in slim-legged, boot-cut dungarees and a cotton flannel shirt. She hadn't seen him since those heavy winter rains, when he'd dressed in a knee-length slicker. Drought-stricken California always needed rain, but twenty-one straight days of it had worn heavily on the people who had to work in it, like farmers and ranchers. But her misery over the incessant rain and mud had had a bright spot when, at the end of that rainy period in March, Lucas had dropped by unannounced. He'd come to ask about the aged French drain around Abby's farmhouse. Was it still holding strong and redirecting the rising water?

He'd offered to bring her some sandbags if flooding seemed imminent. Abby smiled as she recalled how surprised she'd been to see him and also at the excuse he used to explain the visit. The French drain? Seriously?

She'd offered him coffee, a freshly baked cinnamon roll, and a towel to dry his face and his wet hair. His eyes, the color of creek water, gazed at her with such intensity that it seemed almost as if he could see into the depths of her heart. It was then that Abby felt the first flutter of attraction. That day in March, he stood facing her, dripping with rainwater like a drowned kitten, and gave her a rare smile. He took the towel she'd offered, shoved it through his curly, brown locks, and swallowed several sips of the steaming black brew. Under the intensity of his gaze, the butterflies in Abby's tummy took flight. She wondered then if he felt them, too. But she guessed not, since he suddenly said thanks, handed her the cup, gave Sugar a pat on the head, and left. That was the way of enigmatic Lucas, a man of few words, but full of surprises.

Now, as Abby watched Lucas climb onto the seat of his truck and slam the door behind him, she had to wonder why he hadn't been around of late. His red truck disappeared around the side of the feed store where an alley turned into the street. Most likely, he was taking off for a new delivery. Nobody provided that kind of customer service anymore. It endeared Lucas all the more to the people of Las Flores and his customers countywide. And today Abby was grateful that she'd parked under the dense walnut tree, next to a pallet of starter feed for laying hens, where she could secretly watch Lucas.

Kat eased her vintage roadster into a parking space just

as Abby slid out of the driver's side of the Jeep. She held Sugar on the leash as Kat exited her sports car and threw her arms around Abby in a demonstrative hug. Kat wore a navy pantsuit with a crisp white shirt, and a vintage brooch pinned to her lapel. Kat loved anything Victorian, from her cottage behind a large Victorian-style home in Las Flores to her collection of sterling silver thimbles and decorative combs, which she sometimes wore, although not today. Her blond tresses sported an expensive-looking cut and, with mousse, had been coaxed into an edgy style. Kat rarely wore makeup, although Abby could tell that today was one of those days when she did—mascara on her lashes and a sheer pink gloss on her lips.

"You get dressed up to come to the feed store? Impressive," Abby said, amused.

Kat grinned. "Don't be silly. I'm testifying in court today. But you, girlfriend, look like you're taking Fiona's death hard. You've got badger eyes."

Abby heaved a sigh. "It was a long night. Couldn't sleep thinking about the case. Anything you can share?"

"Not really. The people closest to her all have alibis, so we're going a little further out in her orbit, interviewing friends, customers, vendors, even the commune residents."

Before Abby could ask more questions about the investigation, she noticed Kat jerk her head toward the feed-store door.

"Did Prince Charming go back inside?"

"Nope. He hoisted some hay onto his truck and high-tailed it out of here."

Was Lucas the reason Kat had gotten so dressed up? She could have just worn her police uniform to court. Abby felt her stomach lurch.

"Your dance card is usually full, Kat. Are you saving a tango for Lucas?"

"Maybe."

Concealing her surprise, Abby asked, "What happened to the security guard?"

"Oh, that's so five minutes ago. But I recently had drinks again with the chef at Zazi's."

Abby brightened. "Oh really? So how did that go?"

"Oh, you know, he's nice enough. . . ."

"But?"

"I don't know. I prefer my tomatoes and onions on a plate, not tattooed on the forearms of the guy handing me the plate. Always . . . with the sleeves up. I've got nothing against ink, but I'm not feeling the sparks. Wishing I could find a nice Silicon Valley engineer type to hook up with. The trouble is, most around Las Flores moved here with a wife and kids."

"I'm not making the connection here between your chef, the engineer you want, and Lucas Crawford. Can you clue me in?"

"Well, Lucas, now, he's a looker. He's also eligible, available, and as you told me, he can cook."

Abby felt taken aback. Kat had remembered that detail. Momentarily caught off guard, Abby sputtered, "Yes, so I've heard. But he isn't really your type, is he?"

Kat's brow shot up. "And what type would that be?"

Abby fumbled for words, waved her hand, as if to dismiss the notion. "I . . ." She blew air between her lips. "I don't know. Polar opposite, maybe?" She wished now that she'd said something long ago to Kat about how she felt around Lucas.

"Polar opposite? Really?" Kat looked surprised. "Well, opposites attract, or so they say. Lest you forget, it was you, Abby, who suggested I be more choosy, set my sights higher. Lucas Crawford would be a great catch. Maybe I could get him off that ranch. He might enjoy dating a fun-loving cop."

Abby leaned against the Jeep, nodding her head. *He might indeed.* She'd said enough. She had trusted Kat with her life when they were partners on the force. Life had taught Abby a hard lesson about trust and betrayal. When Abby was in her midtwenties, her best friend, Josephine, had seduced Abby's then boyfriend behind her back. He had left Abby for Jo, then had ditched Jo to romance a female recruiter for the military and had soon joined up. Kat wasn't Jo. Abby knew that. If Kat only knew how a mere look from Lucas could stir Abby's emotions. But Kat didn't know. *And whose fault is that?*

Sugar wanted her treat. She clearly didn't like being tethered while Abby chitchatted with Kat. The medium-sized dog had lunged at a passerby and now had grown bored barking at a gray squirrel in the tree. Abby applied a reassuring pat on Sugar's head to calm her.

"Well, who knows?" Abby said to Kat with a smile. "Maybe Lucas will rock your world."

"The way I see it, Abby, Lucas needs a good woman in his life. The whole town felt bad when his wife passed away so young, being pregnant and all. I'd just like to be there for him."

Abby smiled. *You and every other single woman between twenty and sixty. But your heartfelt sentiment is sweet.* Kat was gorgeous, openly flirty, intensely funny, and had a heart of gold. If Kat wanted to start something with Lucas, Abby wouldn't stand in the way.

"Has he asked you out?" Abby asked, not sure she wanted to hear the answer.

"Not yet," Kat replied. "And I never seem to catch him here at the feed store."

Her spirits suddenly buoyed, Abby grinned. "So people

don't usually dress up to buy feed. What were you going to tell him you were shopping for?"

"Dunno. Don't have any pets. There's a mouse in my house. Maybe a trap?"

"Seriously?" Abby snorted. "Wouldn't that be just the thing? A trap?"

Kat chuckled. "I see what you mean." She glanced at her watch. "Listen. I have to go in a minute, but about the estate sale . . . I've heard there will be lots of antiques and dishes and farm tools."

"Great," said Abby, relieved the conversation had taken a new direction.

"I happen to know that old lady Richardson collected gobs of fine china. I'll be looking for porcelain and pottery marks while you hunt for garden stuff and old books."

"You know I like good china, too," Abby replied. "But back to Fiona for a moment. I saw a box or two of old gardening books in her shop that she planned to donate. What do you suppose will happen to those volumes?"

Kat's brow puckered. "I couldn't say. At some point, there'll have to be a funeral. Might be a good time to ask her brother, who has to settle her affairs."

"To hear Fiona tell it, he was the only stable person in her crazy quilt of a life. How's he taking her death?" Abby asked.

"Like a man who has lost a loved one to a murderer. He's grieving. Wants her killer brought to justice."

Abby nodded. "We all want that. What did Fiona's autopsy reveal?"

Kat glanced at her watch again. "Cardiac arrest due to asphyxia was the cause of death. No trauma to the body. The coroner's report is inconclusive. And, as you know, the toxicology report takes as long as it takes. For now, that's about all we have."

"Asphyxia?" Abby blinked with bafflement. "Drowning causes asphyxia. Inhaling a toxic gas causes asphyxia. Choking . . ."

"Before you ask me if she was choked," Kat said, "the answer is no. There were no marks on her neck or the rest of her body."

"Well, that's just weird," Abby said. She recalled Fiona's body in the car, with the front windows down. Fiona was seated behind the wheel and was leaning back in the seat. But her feet, as far as Abby could tell, didn't quite reach the brake or the gas pedal.

"You and I were a great team, Abby. We still are. But Chief Bob Allen told me not to involve you in this case, so what I tell you can go no further. Abigail, I'm dead serious about the need for secrecy. Otherwise, I could lose my job." Kat's expression reflected the sober reality of what she apparently felt.

"I would never do or say anything to jeopardize your job, Kat. I hope you know that." Abby suddenly lurched as Sugar pulled against the leash with a high-pitched *yip, yip, yip,* apparently after spotting a pair of squirrels scrambling along a limb of the tree.

Kat nodded. "Of course, but I need assurances that we're on the same page. So, here's a scoop. Fire investigators say an accelerant was used, but the coroner says no smoke or soot in her lungs, meaning—"

"Fiona was dead when someone torched the car," said Abby. She leaned against the Jeep door, shaking her head, feeling sorrowful all over again.

"Oh, but there were traces of emesis in her mouth," said Kat. "What do you make of that?"

"She threw up?" Abby asked, frowning. "You know, I've been with Fiona when she's plucked a leaf from a plant and chomped down on it. I often wondered how she always seemed to know whether or not it was poisonous." Abby scratched her head. "Maybe she knew from the bitterness or chalkiness or acidity. I don't know. Regardless, it's possible that this time she ate something toxic, something that caused her to vomit."

"No evidence of it in the car or anywhere we searched . . ." Kat's sentence trailed off.

"So if she was poisoned and threw up, the killer cleaned her up. Don't you have any idea where the killer took her life?" Abby asked, trying to make a linkage without enough facts.

"No, we don't. It's possible she was at her cottage, or someone took her someplace else. What's certain is that the murderer wanted the body and the car burned."

"To cover his tracks." Abby tried to wrap her mind around the puzzle. "Any sign of a struggle at her cottage? Or even the foul scent of someone being sick?"

Kat shook her head. "Nope. And there were no traces of botanical material on the car seats, floorboards, or in the trunk."

Abby scratched her head. "So here's a hypothesis. Fiona ingested or inhaled a lethal dose of something that caused her asphyxia. But it would have had to be quick acting, wouldn't it? She threw up before dying. Her killer cleaned her up and drove her to the site at Kilbride Lake. He staged her body behind the wheel, used an accelerant, and set the car afire to conceal his crime. Car torched, body burned, and the killer gets away." Abby waited for a response from Kat.

"It's plausible. The toxicology screen will tell us more," said Kat.

"But we both know forensic tests don't happen in the real world like they do on TV. A toxicology screen is going to take a while—two to three weeks or more. Right now, I think the murderer would have had someone to help with the move and the disposal, possibly a second person to drive a getaway car from Kilbride Lake."

"Makes perfect sense," Kat said. She glanced again at her watch. "Oh, my gosh, I've got to get to court."

Abby nodded. "Oh, before you leave . . . What about the tire print?"

"That piece of tire tread was awfully small. I don't think the lab will be able to use it," said Kat.

Abby nodded. "And Chief Bob Allen made such a big deal about it, as if I were a rookie whom he had just pinned. Whatever. I'll help the investigation any way I can, Kat, but for now I'd better hustle home before Sugar snaps this leash."

Kat was already climbing back into her roadster. "Let's get an early start Saturday, say seven thirty. Don't be late, or we'll lose out on all the good stuff."

"You just worry about getting the coffee ready. I'll bake lemon scones and bring fresh strawberries and crème anglaise," Abby said. She waved as Kat pulled away.

Abby dashed inside the feed store, with Sugar behaving like a dog who knew good behavior would get her a reward, and she and the clerk located a rawhide bone, a chew toy, and some dry doggy biscuits, along with a bag of dog food.

"Check back with us about that water dispenser gasket," the clerk said. "I'll let Lucas know we need more."

"Sounds good," said Abby. She left with her purchases in one hand and Sugar's leash in the other.

Watching Sugar devour her treat, Abby decided to take another look at where Fiona had lived and died. *We're already in town. That puts us halfway there.*

"What do you say to a drive into the mountains, Sugar Pie? Would you like that?" Abby fastened her seat belt, shifted the gear into reverse, and backed up the Jeep. Sugar cocked her head to one side. Looking over at her, Abby could almost swear Sugar was smiling back.

Abby stuck to the back roads through Las Flores, then drove through the mountains until she reached the red barn signifying the turnoff to Fiona's cottage. After navigating up the short gravel road, she parked at the mailbox and read the sign on the front porch: WELCOME LITTLE PEOPLE, FAIRY FOLK, AND BEINGS OF LIGHT. Abby smiled and wondered how Fiona had managed to persuade Dr. Danbury to let her put that up. But then again, who would read it, except maybe the mail carrier and the two of them? Of course, there was also the occasional transient Fiona brought home when rain or freezing temperatures threatened. A couple of weeks ago, Fiona had told her about picking up an Iraqi war vet who was hitching his way through the mountains to the valley of towns on the other side. He had slept on her couch for two nights. Abby sighed at the realization that for all her compassion, Fiona's rescuing personality might have been her undoing.

Turning off the engine, Abby looked for signs of life. Perhaps the doc would peek out the window. Dr. David Danbury had been a successful surgeon at the local hospital. He'd purchased the property right after marrying a pretty psychiatrist from Stanford University who was doing the rotation part of her residency program at his hospital. When their growing family outgrew the cottage, the doc built a larger house right next door and connected the two homes with a breezeway. Later, when the marriage failed and his wife moved back east, taking their daughters with her, the doc gave up his lucrative practice to make wine. He rented out the little cottage and eventually became an alcoholic recluse.

Fiona had confided to Abby that she and the doc had

initially got on just fine. But with booze on board, it was another story. The affable doctor turned into a pushy, mean drunk. He would talk about his life and insult each person as he remembered them. There was never a kind word for anyone. When Fiona didn't want to keep drinking with him, he insulted her, too, saying she was an emasculator, like his wife had been. After that, Fiona had to tread upon the proverbial razor's edge between being friendly with the doc and spurning his advances, which put her chances of staying in the cottage in jeopardy.

She loved her small home, positioned as it was in the middle of Dr. Danbury's ten-acre vineyard. At the back, there was a Christmas tree farm that bordered another forty acres of wilderness. The latter provided refuge for wildlife, a small stand of old-growth redwoods, and many indigenous plants. When Fiona decided to leave the commune for good, it had been a stroke of good fortune to find Dr. Danbury's cottage. She'd tried to stay in the doc's good graces by offering to plant him a garden that included heirloom vegetables and herbs. One day, he'd pointed to a swath of land near a large olive tree, which he said he'd planted years ago for the wife who left him. The doc had plowed a section under the tree and had told Fiona, "Plant there." That was the extent of his interest in gardens with anything that wasn't a grapevine or a Christmas tree.

Abby held Sugar's leash securely. She'd brought along the scarf Fiona had left at her house, Now, with Fiona's scarf in hand, she approached the mailbox and looked around. Maybe if she stood there long enough, someone would notice. She didn't want to look like a trespasser, a prowler, or, God forbid, an identity thief. She was, in fact, standing next to the mailbox. Mountain people didn't take kindly to strangers walking about, so Abby hung back and held Sugar in check by her side.

After a few minutes, when nobody had acknowledged her presence, Abby embarked upon the path through the grassless yard—a patchwork of poppies and plants growing in wild abandon near square-shaped raised beds of herbs. Chaotic and ordered, wild and cultivated, the garden seemed an accurate reflection of Fiona.

Raising the knocker over the carved brass female image on the front door of the cottage, Abby felt a twinge of sadness. She tried to push from her mind the image of Fiona's engorged, partially burned, black and red blistered face. She rapped the knocker three times. Waited. Rapped again. The dark green patina gave dimension to the brass face, accentuating the creases in the laurel wreath surrounding the woman's head. The banshee of Irish folklore, Fiona had told her, was a potent image—the harbinger of death. When Abby had asked Fiona why she would dare hang a banshee door knocker, Fiona had replied, "I felt inexplicably drawn to her. She's the woman of fairies and has power and magic. She foretells death through her wailing. The death is often violent—that much is true. But, look, there are lots of square knots in her cloak. They provide protection."

Humph! Some protection.

When no one answered the door, Abby put her hand on the knob and slowly turned it. The door flew open. Abby stumbled down two steps into a bright interior. Surprise registered on the face of the man who had opened the door from the inside. Sugar barked without letup.

"Who are you?" the man asked. He stood maybe five feet, ten inches. He had striking pale blue eyes and curly, brown hair with silver threads running through it. His face looked gaunt, and his puffy eyes were ringed in red, as though he had gone days without sleep.

"Abigail Mackenzie, formerly with the Las Flores Police

Department." Abby extended her hand. "Are you Jack Sullivan, Fiona's brother, the ethnobotanist she always talked so enthusiastically about?"

"You found me. What is it you want?"

Abby decided to be straight with him. He looked like he'd been through the ringer. "Sorry for your loss. To be honest, I'm looking for clues. Fiona and I were friends, and I made a promise to find the person who hurt her. I was hoping to take a quick look around, if that's okay with you."

If it was possible for his expression to harden, it did. "Excuse me," he said, "but the police have already been here. I've got funeral arrangements to make. I can't see any reason for them to send an ex-cop to poke around. So if you don't mind, please just leave. Take that dog with you."

Taken aback, Abby gave him a wide-eyed stare. "Your sister's passing has shaken me up, too. I didn't mean to be insensitive. Our whole community is worried that a killer is on the loose among us."

He glared at her.

Abby proffered the scarf. "It's Fiona's. She left it at my farmette the last time we were together. I meant to return it."

"Sure you did," he said, his tone conveying a biting sarcasm. "That scarf is your cover. You came up here to snoop," he said, warily eyeing her. "Did you think you'd unearth some salacious details about my sister's life? Juice up your copy? Hit on a provocative headline?" He tightened his hand around the doorknob, pulling the door open. "I'd really appreciate it if you would just go."

Abby's stomach clenched. "Look, Mr. Sullivan . . . you've made a mistake."

"I don't make mistakes about women like you. I can smell small-town reporter." His brows furrowed. "I've had to protect my sister from people like you in the past."

Her shock was met with a sobering stare.

"Ms. Mackenzie, do I have to ask you twice?"

"Of course not." Abby felt her throat closing up, her lips tightening. "My condolences." Tugging on Sugar's leash, she said softly, "Come on, sweetie."

Abby tramped from the foyer to the porch, then beyond the mailbox, and was at the end of the driveway, by the big red barn, before she realized she had walked clear past the Jeep. Turning around, Abby had one thought. What did he mean by having to defend his sister in the past? What did Fiona do?

Tips for Making Tea from Fresh Herbs

Homemade herb tea starts with fresh herbs picked at their peak around midmorning, after the dew has dried. If dust clings to the leaves, wash them and dry them with a paper towel. Drop two handfuls of the leaves into a one-gallon glass jar and fill the jar with water to within three inches of the rim. Add fresh organic orange slices or lemon slices or zest (wash the rinds before slicing) to the jar. Place in the refrigerator and let it stand for one to two hours. Strain the herb tea into tall glasses with ice. To sweeten the tea, add honey or rose-scented sugar. Some of the herbs that make delicious tea are the following:

- Mint—Choose from the estimated six hundred varieties of mint, including apple mint, chocolate mint, ginger mint, mojito mint, orange mint, peppermint, pineapple mint, and spearmint, to name a few.

- Lemon Balm—This is also known as balm mint, and it is a calming herb.

- Bee Balm—This herb is also known as wild bergamot. The red blooming variety, known as Oswego tea, was the tea of choice for the American colonists after the Boston Tea Party.

- Hyssop—This herb is used by herbalists to improve digestive issues. However, it contains a chemical that may affect the heart and lungs.

- Sage—This perennial mint has a long history as a medicinal and culinary herb. It was cultivated in medieval monastery gardens.

- Horsetail—Herbalists have noted that this herb's high silica content is beneficial for the hair, nails, and bones.

Note: Although humans have used herbs for thousands of years for culinary and medicinal purposes, it's always a good idea to check with your doctor before including herbs in your food and drink. Some herbs are more potent than others and may have unwanted side effects, and they can interact adversely with prescription drugs.

Chapter 4

An ant seeking a source of sweetness is as per-
sistent as an old boyfriend who is trying to get
back into your life.

—*Henny Penny Farmette Almanac*

The ants had found the honey buckets. Coagulating into
a black mass, thousands of them marched in lines like
an army on the move to cover the shelf above the washer
and dryer where Abby kept the honey buckets. She'd wiped
down one of the buckets after refilling the large jar for her
daily use—honey for tea, yogurt, waffles, and general good
health and well-being. She'd even gone so far as to swaddle
the bucket in plastic wrap, securing the wrap with duct
tape. But a single drop of honey left unwiped had been
enough to attract a full-blown invasion. Cleaning the mess
took most of the morning.

It was close to noon before Abby finished. She flipped
on the local farmers' network news, intending to eat a
quick snack before beginning the apricot jam–making
process, which would occupy her for the next two hours.
The cots were ripe, maybe too ripe to set up properly into
jam without having to cook out all the nutrients or add
pectin, and too much boiling or pectin would change the

texture. She considered whether or not it might be better to dry them instead. The hour she saved washing the jars and stirring the jam could then be used for another project. Maybe she would add manure to the three raised beds where she would then plant heirloom blue tomatoes, smoking hot Caribbean habaneros, and some sweet bell peppers. Suddenly, her thoughts filled with images of the myriad projects needing to be done around the farmette.

Swallowing a sip of sweet tea and nibbling on a peanut butter toasted sandwich, Abby focused her attention on the radio announcer reading the news. First up was a piece about the latest developments in the grass fire on the south side of Las Flores Boulevard, which was now "eighty percent contained." The announcer continued, "Partying high school students lobbed eggs against two vehicles parked on Cottonwood Lane last night. They also made off with boxes of produce outside Smooth Your Groove shake shop on Chestnut. A block away on Olive, vandals draped a tree in toilet paper and broke into a pickup truck belonging to a local man, stealing his rifle. And finally, the murder of a local woman is no closer to resolution today, as investigators have yet to identify a person of interest in the case. Services for Fiona Mary Ryan will be held at the Church of the Holy Names."

Abby winced. A sudden onset of sorrow soured her stomach. Tears burned at the backs of her eyes. Fiona's passing had been such a horrible shock, Abby had felt numb at first and later mercurial—normal one minute and tearing up the next. But what good were tears? They wouldn't bring Fiona back.

Dumping the remainder of the tea down the sink, Abby stared at the disappearing liquid and contemplated the case's complexities. After a few minutes, she washed and dried the cup and set it in the cupboard. Dabbing her eyes with a tea towel, she muttered, "I swear I'm going to find out who killed you, Fiona, if it's the last thing I do, though I doubt it will ease the guilt I feel. I should've demanded that you go to the police with whatever was bothering you. I didn't, and now . . . what a terrible outcome." For a fleeting moment, Kat's words of warning to stay out of the case intruded. But Kat needn't worry. Whatever information Abby might unearth from a few discreet inquiries, she would pass on to Kat and Otto. Studying the toast she no longer desired, Abby glanced up at the wall clock above the coffeemaker and noted the time—exactly twelve o'clock. Mountain traffic, she reasoned, would have thinned by now. She gave her last bite of toast to Sugar.

"Farmette work will wait for us, Sugar Pie. I'm going to help the good guys track down a bad guy who might still be in the mountains."

Sugar stretched her neck upward and let go a piteous howl, as if to protest being left behind while her owner tracked down a killer.

"Oh, don't worry," said Abby reassuringly. "You're coming with me."

The locals had superior knowledge. They knew what outsiders didn't about driving the mountain roads on the western side of Las Flores. They were familiar with the most treacherous stretches of the road, where it narrowed without shoulders or guardrails. A split second of inattention meant a car could drop a hundred feet. Hidden by dense brush and trees, a car and driver might never be found. The two most dangerous sections involved double S curves halfway between Fiona's cottage and Kilbride Lake. Previously, both had been the scene of traffic fatalities. Both accidents had involved people who didn't know the roads. Both had happened during bad weather. Today there wasn't a cloud in sight. Still, Abby wasn't about to tempt fate. She tapped the brakes as she entered the first of the curves.

Out of nowhere, a horn blared. A silver pickup screamed around the blind corner. It flew past Abby's Jeep, claiming the greater part of the twisting blacktop. Shoving the brake pedal to the floorboard, she felt the rear wheels slide. The Jeep fishtailed as she fought for control. Adrenaline raced through her body. Her heart slammed against her chest. Instinctively, she righted the wheel, and Sugar flew against her with a high-pitched yelp. The stench of locked brakes and burnt rubber permeated the Jeep. Coming out of the curve, Abby steered her car to the widest section of the shoulder and parked, set the hand brake, and cut off the engine.

Her hands shook. She leaned her head against the steering wheel and struggled for composure. Sugar pawed at the window, barking and whining without letup. Smelling pee, Abby lifted her head and realized the dog had peed on the seat. She ordered Sugar to stop barking, but she knew the dog was only feeling what she herself was experiencing—alarm and fear. Slowly and rhythmically, Abby began to stroke the dog's neck.

"There, there, girl," she cooed. "Scary, I know, but it's over." The dog yipped once, twice more, and then licked Abby's hand. "We're safe. That's what matters," Abby said. She hugged Sugar close.

Looking around for something to wick the urine—a napkin, a towel, or even an old shirt—and finding nothing, Abby remembered placing Fiona's scarf in the glove box before driving away from Fiona's cottage after her unsettling conversation with Jack Sullivan. This situation called for desperate measures. She pulled out the saffron-colored cotton scarf stamped in red with the symbol

Aum scripted in Sanskrit, the trident of Shiva, and the Kalachakra, the wheel of time. Abby thought that it was odd that Fiona, raised Catholic, had lived in a commune that embraced Eastern traditions. And it was strange, too, that she had gotten involved with a boyfriend who practiced voodoo Haitian style. But Fiona was a woman of many contradictions and interests. The search for spiritual meaning in life, a stint at commune living, and growing and selling herbs were all expressions of her free spirit. *Wherever you are, Fiona Mary Ryan, I hope you know I admired you, and I mean no disrespect by using your scarf this way.*

Abby compressed the scarf into a wad and dabbed it repeatedly against the wet spot. She thought about the maniac in the silver truck, a danger to anyone on the road. After dropping the scarf on the floorboard, Abby turned the Jeep around, maneuvered it back onto the road, and headed in the direction the silver truck had gone.

Only after she had passed the big red barn at Doc Danbury's driveway could she see down the other side of the mountain, where the road stretched out in long undulations. The silver pickup was tailgating a slow-moving winery truck loaded with oak barrels. Passing was impossible because of the line of cars streaming from the other direction. Abby accelerated. When she'd closed the gap between the Jeep and the silver pickup, she jotted down the license plate number using the pencil and pad she kept in the console.

After the last oncoming car had passed, the pickup shot around the winery truck. Just when Abby lost sight of the pickup, the winery truck pulled off, giving her an open view of the road ahead and the silver truck as it turned right onto a compacted dirt road. Abby continued to follow, undaunted by a message scrawled in white paint on an old fence board nailed to a tree—NO TRESPASSING. VIOLATORS WILL BE SHOT.

Eventually, she arrived at a stand of oaks at the top of a high hill. Pulling over in the shade, Abby watched the silver truck park near a rustic cabin. *Who would want to live in such isolation?* The answer came as easily as a bloom on a mustard stalk in springtime—woodsmen, potheads, drug dealers, survivalists, anarchists, and people desiring to disappear for a while. Abby wondered whether the truck driver belonged to one of those groups. Parked at such a high elevation, she could easily see the creek, the woods, and even the tall pole with the Christmas star on it that marked Doc Danbury's tree farm and his vineyard.

When the man climbed out of the truck and disappeared into the cabin's dark interior, Abby squinted against the sun. Difficult to tell, but she estimated his height to be six feet. Grungy clothes, a scraggly gray beard, and salt-and-pepper hair pulled back into a ponytail added up to a shabby appearance. Suddenly, it dawned on her who the man might be. He fit the description Fiona had given her of the man who'd assaulted her when she'd been out looking for herbs.

Abby tapped the number on her cell to speed-dial Kat. "I need a favor, Kat. Could you run the plates on a silver pickup? The man driving it is the same one, I believe, who accosted Fiona back in February. And he just ran me off the road."

"Are you all right?"

"Yes, I am."

"How can you be sure it's the same guy?"

"I can't. Not positively. My gut tells me it is."

"So this is where I ask you if you recall our chat outside

the feed store about how I could lose my job if Chief Bob Allen finds out I'm involving you in this investigation."

"I wouldn't ask, but that idiot drives like he's high on something. He's a danger on the road, and he frightened the daylights out of Fiona."

"Did she call the cops?"

"Well . . . no."

"So, you know as well as I do that scaring someone isn't illegal. If Fiona had feared for life and limb, she would have dialed nine-one-one. Any sane person would. But, as you've pointed out, she didn't. So what are you not telling me?"

Abby hesitated, swallowed hard. Fiona had asked Abby not to reveal anything about her encounter with the man, for fear of being arrested herself. But what did it matter now? Fiona was gone. "Here's the deal, Kat. I kept quiet about it because Fiona asked me to. She was trespassing on the man's property when he attacked her. When she wrestled free of him, she used his pickax, hitting him hard, I guess. Fearing for her life, she ran away. He might have been lying on the ground, unconscious and bleeding, but she couldn't know whether he would die or get up and give chase. And she never went back there again."

"And how do you know she was telling the truth?"

"I can sense when someone is lying. Fiona trembled when she explained to me what had happened. The way she was shaking, it was like the cells of her body remembered."

A beat passed before Kat said, "You'd better tell me the full story, and don't leave out anything."

Abby inhaled a deep breath and let it go. "February is mustard season. In late winter, you see how the mountain meadows and vineyards turn bright yellow."

"Yeah, yeah. Hot-air balloon rides and all that . . . Tell me something I don't know."

"So . . . in late February, Fiona went exploring on Doc Danbury's property, looking for wild mustard. There's also a forty-acre parcel that shares a boundary with the doc's land at the back, right?"

"Uh-huh."

"So, the doc told Fiona about the caretaker's cabin but assured her that no one lived back there anymore, so she felt safe searching alone for wild herbs. She'd gone pretty far when she wandered upon the creek and figured she'd also look for mushrooms and native herbs along its shady banks. She heard a twig snap. She said she spun around and was shocked to see a man watching her. He stood about six feet tall, had salt-and-pepper hair and a scruffy beard, and was dressed in a blue flannel shirt and stained jeans. She noticed one of his work boots had been wrapped in duct tape. He carried a pickax."

"Hold on," Kat said. "Was he working back there? Clearing the creek, building something?"

"Fiona didn't say, but she told me she wasn't afraid, at least not at first," said Abby. "They talked a bit, and then he became aggressive. He dropped the ax, lunged at her, and tried to drag her toward his cabin. She screamed and fought, and they fell. She threw dirt in his eyes and wrenched herself free." Abby caught her breath and swallowed hard, realizing how far-fetched the story sounded.

"Was that when she hit him with the pickax?" Kat said.

"Yes. After she had wrestled free, she grabbed the ax, took a wild swing, and hit his head. She said blood gushed out. The man staggered and fell. She said she ran all the way home and pounded on the doc's door."

"What did Dr. Danbury do?"

"Nothing. He didn't answer the knock. Fiona said he often drank a lot. Maybe he'd passed out."

Kat cleared her throat. "And then what did Fiona do?"

"Retreated inside her cottage," said Abby. "After that, she added a couple of new slider locks on the inside of her cottage door, but she still didn't feel safe . . . so she moved into her store for a while and slept on a fold-up cot in her office."

Abby waited for Kat's next question, but Kat remained silent. She had to be pondering the merits of Fiona's story.

After a moment, Abby said, "You know, she felt guilty for leaving the man bleeding like that and not knowing how badly he might be wounded. But, Kat, she feared for her life. I think that same man just sideswiped me less than an hour ago. Clearly, Fiona didn't kill him."

Kat cleared her throat. "I'm not convinced the two incidents are linked. And given that Fiona is gone, the story you've just relayed is hearsay, as you well know."

"I believed her," said Abby. "If you could have seen her . . . hands shaking, her lip trembling. It was like she was living through it all again. But, listen, I need you to run that plate. My situation at the moment is dicey."

"Oh, for heaven's sake, Abby. Don't tell me you followed him home."

Abby chewed her bottom lip. "He might be squatting in that caretaker's cabin."

Kat maintained a calm tone but exhaled a heavy sigh. "You see, this is what Chief Bob Allen was talking about, for crying out loud."

Abby recited the license plate number for Kat. "Sorry. I wouldn't ask, but . . ." Abby tried to think of some humble pie thing to say or offer to do for Kat.

"Oh, just hang on a sec," Kat muttered.

Abby waited in silence.

Momentarily, Kat spoke again. "The registered owner is Timothy Joseph Kramer. It'll take me a few more minutes to cross-reference to see if he has any prior contact history with law enforcement."

"I'll wait." It was a relief to know that Kat still had her back.

Abby stared at the cabin door. For a split second, she thought she detected movement. Yes, the screen door inched open. The man stepped out. He held a rifle. Abby's heart pounded in double time as she watched the man lift the gun to his shoulder and take aim at the 3:00 position. Then, to her horror, the man swung the barrel around and pointed it straight at her.

Abby dropped the phone. She thrust the Jeep gear into reverse and backed up. Cranking the steering wheel to the right, she floored the gas pedal. The crack of a gunshot rang out. She instinctively dodged. Ignoring the dips in the road, which thrust her body and Sugar's upward with such intensity that her head banged on the car's ceiling, Abby pressed on. One thought occupied her mind: *Get away from that nutcase as fast as you can.*

She drove to the main road and steered in the direction of Fiona's cottage. Approaching a turnout, Abby pulled off the road, taking comfort in the line of cars now passing her. Sugar panted hard. Who could blame her? Poor thing had experienced nothing but pandemonium this morning. Abby gave her a vigorous rub on her neck and back.

"Whew! That was close, baby girl. Remind me not to follow a rat into its hole when there is only one way out."

Kat came back on the line. "Abby? You there?"

Abby picked up the phone. "Yes."

"Sorry that took so long."

"Listen, Kat, he got a gun from inside that cabin."

"Gun? He's armed?"

"And dangerous. Took a shot at me."

"Abby, get out of there. Now. I'll send a couple of officers to pick him up. Says here Kramer has a warrant for assault and breaking and entering. I've already notified the county sheriff."

Abby breathed a sigh of relief. "Thank you. Listen, I can meet your officers if you like."

"Not necessary. What I want is for you to get off that mountain. There's no point in you staying in harm's way. We've got the doc's address, and one of the officers I'm sending grew up not far from there."

"Right. Listen . . . it's good to know you've still got my back," said Abby.

Now wouldn't be the time to tell Kat that Abby hadn't yet finished her business in the mountains. There was still the location of Fiona's car to check out. The police would have collected the car, of course, and taken it to the impound lot. But a visit to a crime scene could produce intangibles, such as a feeling, an intuitive insight, or a previously overlooked connection.

Sugar hunkered down on the seat; her large brown eyes focused on Abby. The dog whined.

"You put up with a lot today, sweetie pie. I promise I'm going to make it up to you."

After driving past the landmark red barn, Abby took the next cutoff to Kilbride Lake. She knew Fiona hadn't filed a report against Timothy Kramer, but she wondered if the assault on Fiona had been the only contact between the two. Might Timothy Kramer have had the motive to kill Fiona? Had he been stalking her? Was that why Fiona had wanted to talk to Abby and Kat? Had Fiona believed that she needed police protection from Kramer?

Abby put Sugar on the leash, and they took a long walk along the old Indian trail still used by the canal patrol officers and forest rangers. When Sugar seemed sufficiently exhausted and had slurped her fill of water, Abby secured the leash with an extension that allowed Sugar to rest in the dappled sunlight. Ambling away from Sugar and the Jeep toward where Fiona's car had been found, Abby walked slowly, eyes on the ground. She had not gone far when her cell went off. She didn't recognize the number. But after the call clicked off, she listened to the message. The volume of the man's voice rose only slightly above the din in his background. "Hope you got my postcard, Abby. It's been a while . . . way too long. Can't wait to see you. You know who this is, right?"

She stiffened. Her heart galloped. Oh, she knew who it was, all right. Hearing Clay Calhoun's husky voice took her instantly back to Valentine's Day the year before, when he'd left her in shock because he'd accepted a job on the East Coast. After planting a perfunctory kiss on Abby's cheek— as though he'd be home by dinner—Clay had driven off into his new life. Around the edges of her heart for months afterward, Abby had felt an inner wound that no herbal poultice could heal.

Her thoughts raced. *What postcard?* There had been nothing from him since he left. And what did he mean by "Can't wait to see you"?

Abby shook her head in dismay. Who knows what he meant by that? She congratulated herself for not taking the call. Talking with Clay would only confound her; it would be too confusing, and it was a conversation she didn't want to have. Right now, she had murder on her mind.

By late afternoon, Abby arrived at her mailbox on Farm Hill Road. After pulling down the hatch of the metal box with the chicken on top, she reached in and retrieved the contents, then flipped through the bills and the assorted junk mail. Then she saw it—the postcard. Her stomach knotted. Inhaling and letting go a long exhale, she flipped over the picture of Seattle's Space Needle to read the sprawling handwriting on the reverse. Large-size letters, big ego— that was Clay.

The memory of her heart breaking flooded her thoughts. The back of her eyes burned with tears, as if Clay's goodbye were happening all over again in the present moment. A little voice inside her head whispered, *You don't have to read it now.* She tossed the mail onto the seat and drove forward, wheels crunching on the gravel. After rolling to a stop, Abby got out and let Sugar race to gulp from her water bowl just inside the gate. She followed Sugar through the gate to the patio table facing the back of the property and the acre behind. Tossing the mail onto the patio table, she sank into a chair. Sugar barked and pawed at the door.

"No, sweetie. We're not going inside just yet. Get down now. Down. Let me rest here for a few minutes."

Sugar was relentless with the barking and pawing, so Abby walked to the aluminum garbage can at the corner of the patio, removed the lid and a rawhide bone, and tossed the bone across the yard. With Sugar chasing after it, Abby tried once more to relax, sinking into the chair.

The breeze stirred the hollow copper rods of a wind chime that had been harmonically tuned to play an ecclesiastical-sounding melody. Clasping her hands behind her head, she leaned back, closed her eyes, and drank in the sounds of the farmette's healing presences. Contented chickens clucked as they scratched in the dirt. A blue jay screeched as it flitted from the firethorn bush to the olive tree. Squirrels chattered their *kuk-kuk-kuk* as they scampered along the roof. Sugar whined, apparently wanting Abby to get up and play. After such a harrowing day, here, at last, was bliss.

Abby's thoughts drifted, but soon something she had seen moments ago began to trouble her. Then a realization took hold. The vertical blinds at the sliding glass door were closed. She had left them pushed back when she and Sugar had departed for the feed store. But she remembered locking the door. Suddenly, alarm bells sounded. Eyes flew open. Panic ensued. To close those blinds, someone had to have gone inside. Maybe was still in there.

Adrenaline pumping, she sucked in a deep breath and let it go. Abby rose slowly and crept to the fence, where she'd left a steel flat-headed tamper used to flatten the earth when patching the lawn. With the tamper raised in an assault position, she reached for the patio door handle, quietly pushed the door along the track, and stepped through the long blinds.

In the middle of the kitchen stood a hot pink six-drawer tool cabinet on locked wheels. A drill in a matching shade of pink and its charger rested on top of the open toolbox atop the cabinet. Frowning, Abby placed the flat-headed tamper on the floor next to the double ovens, took a step forward, and studied the toolbox. "What in the world? Who would . . . ?"

"Like it?" asked a familiar husky voice emerging from the bedroom hallway.

Abby looked up at her intruder, feeling her body shake against her will. "Darn it all, Clay! You're as crazy as ever. There's a law against breaking and entering. I could have killed you!" She knew deep down she would have let him in, had she been there, but it angered her that he was in her house without her permission.

She stared at him. Dressed in a white polo and jeans, he looked tan and fit, and taller somehow than his five feet, eleven inches, but he still exuded that rugged vitality and those good looks, which she'd always found irresistible.

The smile had evaporated off his face, but as he strode into the kitchen, those dark eyes still beamed with excitement at seeing her.

Sugar came bounding in through the open door. In an unusually vocal defense of Abby, she sounded a high-pitched alarm. Now Abby understood why the dog had made such a ruckus before. Sugar had known someone had come onto the property and had entered the house.

"I see you got a new protector," Clay said, crouching and holding out his open palm for Sugar to smell.

The dog backed up and barked nonstop.

"I'm a friend, not a foe," Clay said in a tone that clearly conveyed a calm self-confidence. But Sugar was having none of his small talk.

"It's okay, Sugar Pie," Abby said. She wheeled the tool cabinet aside, and Clay stood up. In one swift movement, he reached out and tenderly touched the hair at Abby's temple, letting a finger pull forth a reddish-gold curl.

Abby froze.

He clasped a hand beneath her chin and tilted her face upward. "I've missed you, woman." He leaned in for a kiss, but a quick maneuver enabled Abby to avert it. She turned toward the slider.

"We can't do this, Clay," Abby said, unable to face him. "Over a year of not hearing from you." Her voice cracked. She busied her shaking hands with opening the blinds.

Sugar sniffed Clay's loafers, his socks, and pant legs before retreating backward a few steps. She gave another fierce *yip, yip, yip*, as if to say, "You don't get a pass yet, mister." After running past Clay to the bedroom, the dog quickly returned, then gave a final *yip* as she trotted outside.

Abby left the slider ajar but slid the screen door shut. She watched Sugar chase a butterfly to the back fence, where the ten-foot Sally Holmes spilled over in a perfusion of blooms. A memory came flooding back to Abby of her planting the rose from canes Clay had gotten from a neighbor after she first bought the farmette. She shook off the memory and wondered how Clay had managed to get himself and the tool cabinet to her place. Maybe by taxi, since his truck wasn't on the property? But the question remained, but how did he get in? The realization came suddenly. He must have used his old key. Abby mentally chastised herself for not changing the locks, but what was the point now? The more pressing question was, why had he come back?

"I always told you one day I'd have to go, Abby. I never lied about that. But, Abby . . . Abby, turn around. Look at me."

He stood near enough for Abby to smell the soft notes of his Armani cologne. Like it or not, her body had longed for his presence. His hand stroked her hair, pulled the elastic band from the ponytail, letting her curls tumble loose, and then taking hold of her shoulder, he spun her around to face him. With both of his hands on her shoulders, she had nowhere to run.

Galvanized by the intensity of his gaze, Abby struggled to quiet her heart—make it still and unfeeling.

"If I could ever promise anyone a lifetime, Abby, it would be you. You are like a root of one of your plants, deep and strong and stable."

Abby felt her cheeks color under his gaze and waited for the *but* . . . and the excuse that would surely follow.

"But my spirit is restless. It's a curse," he said. He released his grip on her shoulders and leaned back against the kitchen counter. "Abby, you awake each day with the certain knowledge that you are exactly where you belong. But for me it's the opposite. Four walls are thresholds I have to break through. I wish I could settle. Why do you think I choose work that takes me all over God's creation? I keep thinking I'll find that one place where I belong. Put down roots. But I don't. I can't. I guess I'm flawed that way."

Despite her best efforts at control, Abby's heart hammered. "But what you did, it . . . was unthinkable. We never talked about your leaving. I thought you were happy here. And I thought you'd at least write or call or stay in touch. At least that."

Rubbing a palm over his cleanly shaven cheek, he spoke in a tone tinged with emotion. "I'm here now."

The ache in her chest moved to her throat. Abby swallowed against the lump that had formed. She pushed back. "It's not that simple, Clay. We can't just pick up and carry on like nothing happened. Why did you even come back?"

His face took on a tortured look. He swallowed. "The truth?"

"Of course, the truth," she said, her tone rising. "Always the truth."

"It's pretty simple. I tried living without you. It turned out to be harder than I ever imagined. I hoped that you'd forgiven me, that maybe you'd give me another chance."

Abby felt a shudder pass through her. "Just like that? You didn't think to check with me before just showing up? Before breaking into my house?"

"I didn't break in. I used to live here, remember? And I could never part with the key. Call it fate or whatever, but my inability to give it back maybe suggests that deep down I wanted us to have another chance."

"And how do you know I haven't moved on, Clay? Found someone else who makes me happy? You don't know, and yet you waltz in here like that could never happen."

His eyes registered hurt. "Is there someone else?"

Abby sighed. "That's not the point."

When he spoke next, his tone seemed tinged with regret

and longing. "I kept thinking about the way we used to dance through this old house before we got the flooring in—from the front door right out the back and into the field. We danced under the moon and danced even when there was no moon. I thought a lot about our dreams of building that wine cave, planting wine grapes, laying a massive stone courtyard, and filling it with pots of lime trees. You know, like those trees that shade the gardens of that place you always talked about wanting to visit in France."

"The Midi," she said. "Where they filmed *Chocolat*."

A hint of a grin flashed across his face. "So they're still showing films like that at Cineflicks, are they? That place is probably the only theater in small-town America that still serves homemade treats at the concession stand."

It was a point of civic pride for Abby, but she said nothing, knowing that it was possible he was baiting her.

Clay's expression darkened. "Believe me, Abby, when I say that no matter what I did or where I went, I felt an aching. Couldn't get rid of it. I know this is probably hard for you to accept. I had a longing that kept turning my thoughts to you and this place." His eyes conveyed unmistakable sadness.

Her resolve weakened. "Oh, Lord, Clay. Why couldn't you have just let things be?" Frustrated, she reached past him for the bottle of Napa Valley cabernet she kept on the counter, pulled open a kitchen drawer, and handed him the opener and the bottle. She collected two wineglasses from a shelf and gave one to him. Holding the other glass for herself, she waited while he poured the garnet-colored liquid.

"Shall we drink to our reunion?" he asked. His eyes crinkled, as if he was smiling with renewed hope.

Abby felt momentarily baffled that his mood could switch

so suddenly and now seem so buoyant under the circumstances. She considered her confused state. "How about we drink to clarity and trust? We'll need those for any salvage operation, if there's to be one."

She knew he understood that he might have ruined the relationship they had shared by his secrecy and the callous way he'd left. If they were to give love another go, it required a new paradigm.

Clay clinked his glass against hers. "Nice bouquet, lovely taste," he remarked. "Just like you."

Abby smiled in spite of herself and walked outside to check on Sugar. The dog bounded across the backyard, after a squirrel scampering on top of the fence, which Abby called the wildlife superhighway. The afternoon sun had disappeared behind the ancient towering pine. Its soft light, shining like a halo, splayed across the patch of green lawn, the raised beds of yellow and orange nasturtiums, and the bright green citrus trees interposed between the beds.

Sighing, Abby sat down in her grandmother's rocker and rhythmically rocked, staring at the fig, with its fruits beginning to swell. By late summer, they would become dark, aubergine globes, supersweet, ready for the picking. She wondered if he would be gone by then.

Clay sank into a patio chair opposite her, long legs stretched out, wineglass balanced on his thigh.

"At first I could only dream that you'd come back," Abby said, tearing her gaze from the figs to look directly at Clay. "Back then, I was in a terrible state. Days and weeks passed with no word from you. Hope faded that you'd ever return. I threw myself into the farm-work. Lord knows, there was plenty of that." She sucked in a deep breath and exhaled.

Clay didn't flinch or break eye contact with her. He listened, jaw tensing and relaxing.

"The first winter was the hardest. Not a lot to do with the bees and the garden during the rainy season. But now it's a new spring. I'm back in my skin, feeling like my old self. And my heart . . . Well, I guess it's grown stronger."

Clay nodded. "I'm sorry I put you through all that."

"Yeah, me too," said Abby. "What we had, Clay, that was special. I've thought about what I might feel when you returned. Joy, certainly, but also a sense of dread."

"Dread?" His brow shot up in surprise; his expression darkened. He sipped his wine, swallowed, and leaned forward to place his hand on her knee. "Why dread, Abby?"

Her heart raced. Her breath quickened. There was nothing to lose by holding her feelings inside. "Because, Clay, I know what's coming."

Honey-Drizzled Grilled Figs

Ingredients:
Extra-virgin olive oil, for preparing the grill
⅓ cup plain goat cheese (or try herbed goat cheese as a variation)
8 ripe fresh figs (Brown Turkey figs work best)
8 slices prosciutto
⅓ cup raw honey (Henny Penny organic honey preferred)

Directions:
Prepare the grill by brushing the grill grates with extra-virgin olive oil.

Fit a pastry bag with a medium round tip, and fill the bag with the goat cheese. Puncture the bottom of each fig to permit the insertion of the pastry bag tip.

Insert the pastry bag tip in a fig and gently squeeze the bag, pushing about 2 teaspoons goat cheese into the center of the fig. Do not overstuff, as this will cause the fig to split. Arrange the stuffed fig on a plate and repeat this process until all the figs are stuffed.

Heat the grill to medium-hot. While the grill is heating, wrap a slice of prosciutto around each stuffed fig.

Grill the figs for 2 to 3 minutes, flipping them once. Remove the figs from the grill to a clean plate, drizzle them with honey, and serve at once.

Serves 4 (2 figs per person)

Chapter 5

The rooster may raise a ruckus, but it's the hen
that rules the roost.

—*Henny Penny Farmette Almanac*

Clay had flustered her, but Abby was determined not to let that man confound her into losing the laser focus she needed to examine the place where canal patrol had found Fiona's body. Fiona Mary Ryan deserved better. Abby had asked Clay to stay in town until they'd sorted out their feelings. After much discussion, which hadn't ended until almost midnight, he'd agreed, but only if she promised to meet him for an early dinner the next day. He'd left her with the hot pink tool cabinet and a kiss before returning to Las Flores to book a room at the Lodge. Clay knew his way around town and her farmette. But she understood better than he that navigating the physical landscapes would prove far easier than the emotional terrain of her heart.

Abby pulled a hair clip from her blue-green work shirt pocket, and after flipping her head forward, she twisted her reddish-gold, shoulder-length mane out of her eyes. Bent over, hands on thighs clad in khaki-colored cargo shorts, she stared at the scorched earth littered with burnt wires and ash-covered shards of glass deposited by the towed car. Thank goodness she'd left Sugar at home, safely locked in the backyard, with plenty of water and food and access to the house. She hadn't planned to be long and wanted neither distractions nor the curious pooch pawing through the crime scene.

Fiona's body had been sitting upright behind the steering wheel, with her hands at her sides. Abby recalled that the seat hadn't appeared close enough to the pedals for Fiona's feet to touch them. Fiona was petite, about the same height as Abby's five feet, three inches. Someone taller must have driven Fiona's car to the site and erred by not returning the seat to the correct position for Fiona to drive. And if the killer had made that error, perhaps he or she had made others.

Abby stood and shielded her eyes to sweep the wilderness around her. Such a lovely, forlorn place—the type of place a hunter might enjoy, a bird-watcher would like, or lovers would meet for a private tryst. Her thoughts kept returning to the locals: they knew the terrain and the access roads. The killer might also be a woman in Fiona's orbit. Who stood taller than she had? Abby sighed in exasperation as she realized that almost everyone in town stood taller than Fiona had. Her thoughts went to the time line. Perhaps she would try persuading Kat to share the names of the people who saw Fiona in her last twenty-four hours.

As Abby thought about it, she realized she was one of them. She'd last seen Fiona alive on Saturday, when she'd driven into Las Flores to drop off the ribbon-tied sample jars of honey that Fiona sold in her botanical shop. Besides delivering honey, Abby had reminded Fiona about their luncheon the next day. When Fiona had excused herself to prepare a bank deposit, Abby had drifted around the shop for a few minutes, looking at the sale items. She recalled looking up when the ribbon of bells had jangled as Premalatha Baxter, the commune manager, and Dak, the new guru's bodyguard, stepped through the large glass door. Premalatha had asked Fiona about some herbal smoking compound that was out of stock. It had seemed an innocuous request at the time, but the exchange was puzzling. The commune didn't allow smoking.

Noon approached. Under the heat of the midday sun, Abby continued walking a grid pattern, searching. The tall grass led her thoughts to weed control and herbicides. Fiona would never use anything toxic on her plants, but Abby knew mountain families might. They could be a stubborn lot—liked doing things their way. They didn't like being told about the dangers of misusing fungicides, herbicides, or pesticides, regardless of what modern science had revealed about human health risks. They also didn't much like having a commune in their midst. They had made no secret about that, either. The doc and others knew Fiona's past included time spent in the commune. The locals didn't mingle with the commune residents. What if the killer was a local, knew the mountains, knew Fiona, and had tampered with her garden or herb patch by using an herbicide? Missing was a motive. Disliking someone because of where he or she used to live hardly qualified.

Meandering through stands of red-bark madrone, manzanita, and tan oak trees and finding little of interest, Abby was considering abandoning further searching when she noticed an old footpath overgrown with weeds that led up a slight incline. With dried leaves crunching under her hiking boots, she followed it. She soon realized that unless Fiona had been searching for trilliums, wild huckleberry, or poison oak, she wouldn't have found herbs here.

The more Abby looked around, the more convinced she became that this was a place chosen by the killer to hide his crime and not one that Fiona would have visited by choice.

Peering into a growth of poison oak and California broom, Abby spotted a paper smaller than a business card caught at the base of some weeds. Peering intently at it, Abby soon realized it was a medicinal patch, like one that could deliver a dose of nicotine. It looked like it had been recently dropped or discarded. Abby covered her mouth with her hand, and she considered whether or not it might be evidence. Deciding to mark that site so she could find it later, Abby propped a stick against a bush near the patch.

After hurrying back to the Jeep, she retrieved her cell phone from the console, found Kat's contact stored in the phone, called, and waited. "It's me again, Kat," she said. "I'm at the Kilbride Lake site. Who's running the investigation into Fiona's death? The county sheriff or Las Flores Police?"

"We are. Naturally, our investigation is cooperating with the sheriff's office. Why?"

"I wanted to notify the correct authority," Abby said. "I have a medicinal patch, like a smoker might wear."

"Really? Did you know Fiona to smoke?" Kat asked.

"No," Abby said. "But she told me once that Tom had tried to quit a few times."

"Did Fiona ever mention him using those patches?" Kat asked.

"No, but this patch might have relevance to the case. It's just a hunch."

"Yeah, well, let me get there and see for myself where you found it and what kind of shape it's in. Goes without saying . . . Don't touch it. Oh, and, Abby, be careful. We've issued a BOLO for Kramer. Our uniforms went to the area where the cabin is located, but he'd hightailed it out of there."

"I promise to keep looking over my shoulder until you get here," said Abby. "Let's hope your BOLO gets him found and into custody."

Abby knew that Kat would have to call county communications to get clearance to be dispatched to collect the evidence, and that this could take a minute or two. Time dragged. She took a picture of the evidence with her cell phone and waited some more. If Kat couldn't get away, Abby would send the photo by text or e-mail. But she didn't have to wait much longer. Eventually, Kat arrived. She wasn't alone in the cruiser. She'd brought with her Nettie Sherman, the Las Flores PD's only crime-scene technician. Abby had worked with Nettie, too, but hadn't seen her in a while. The last time was at police headquarters when Abby had been working a case, and Nettie had been hobbling around on crutches following knee surgery. Now Nettie hopped out of the cruiser like a new cadet.

Abby smiled and walked over to the women. Nettie looked svelte, having shed some pounds from her five-foot-seven frame now that she could run again. She could almost pass as one of Kat's relatives, with her jade-green eyes and hair the color of pine nuts. She wore her longish bangs teased off her face today and sprayed in place.

"Hi, ladies," Abby called out. "Good to see you, Nettie. Knee all healed?"

"Just about." Nettie held a large manila-colored evidence envelope, its bottom flap already secured with red sealing tape printed with EVIDENCE, CITY OF LAS FLORES PO-LICE DEPARTMENT.

"So, Chief Bob Allen has reassigned you back to CSI now." Abby grinned broadly. She knew how Nettie had hated that temporary desk job. But after her knee injury, she had had to be reassigned somewhere.

"Yep. Finally. That so-called light-duty desk job he gave me until my leg healed turned out to be the longest six weeks of my life. He had me hobbling to that damn coffeepot and the records room all day long. I hate to say it, but there were times when I found him more noxious than the scent of skunk on my mailbox post. And he had the gall to suggest that now that I was working at a desk, I could assume some other tasks, like repositioning the speed-trap trailer to slow traffic along Main and doing some DUI checkpoints. If you ask me, his micromanaging is off the hook."

Abby laughed. "Oh, Nettie, I feel for you. Can't say I miss working for the chief. So am I right that you are now the community service liaison, the CSI tech, and the property officer assisting Bernie down in the evidence room?"

Nettie shook her head, as if she couldn't believe it herself. "Complaining doesn't help," she said, adjusting the camera strap over her right shoulder. "Chief told me women multitask better than men. He said he meant it as a compliment, but we both know it was a lame excuse to give me more work."

"You just have to hang in there," Kat said with indifference. "He'll forget about you after a while, and it'll be someone else's turn to feel his wrath." Sniffing and gazing into the distant forest like a preservationist studying a stand of old-growth trees, Kat added, "It's what we all do."

Everyone fell silent. A beat passed.

Finally, Kat said to Abby, "Okay, eagle eyes. Let's get to it."

"This way." Abby walked toward her marking stick. Kat followed. Nettie brought up the rear.

After they'd covered a short distance, Kat said to Abby,

"Thanks for that tip on Kramer. I'm curious to see what a search of his cabin turns up."

After handing Kat the evidence envelope, Nettie took camera shots of the patch at various angles and then realized she stood in a growth of poison oak. "Oh, my gosh. Is this what I think it is?" Her eyes widened in a fearful expression. "I'm allergic. Good Lord, it's everywhere. I know this is my job, but if I go into that area, I'll be out on sick leave, suffering for who knows how long."

Kat tucked the evidence envelope under her arm and stuck out her free hand to pull Nettie from the growth. "Come on out. I'll get it."

"I'm sorry," Nettie said, trudging a yard or two away.

"If I didn't trust your sixth sense, Abby, I'd be leaving this trash right where it lies."

Abby nodded. "We can only hope it has a fingerprint, some sweat for a DNA test, a strand of hair or fiber, something with a linkage to Fiona."

"But it wouldn't be the first time that trash found at a crime scene was just trash," said Nettie. "On the other hand, sometimes you think a thing isn't important, and it ends up breaking open the case."

Noticing Kat's short sleeves, Abby removed her work shirt and handed it to Kat. "Slip it on. It might be a tad short, but no need to expose your bare skin to the poison oak. If you brush against it and get some of the oil on you, I've got vinegar in my Jeep you can use to remove it. It's an old Girl Scout trick. I'm not immune, but I don't seem to get those itchy, weeping blisters. Apparently, Nettie does. Just avoid touching it."

Kat slipped her arms into the sleeves of the work shirt and then slid her fingers into the nitrile gloves she kept in a holder on her duty belt. Gingerly reaching into the poison oak, she retrieved the white patch and dropped it into the evidence envelope.

"I can't imagine any woman in her right mind traipsing around up here alone," Nettie said as the trio walked back to the cruiser.

"Who says she was alone?" Kat chewed her lower lip, as she did when she was trying to puzzle through something. "She might have arranged to meet someone."

"All we know is that somebody killed her," Abby said. "We don't know where, how, or who."

Kat said, "She had lots of friends, some, admittedly, rather strange."

"Yeah," said Nettie, slapping at the small flies lighting on her as she walked. "Like her current squeeze, Laurent Duplessis."

"They broke up a while ago," Abby said, correcting her.

"Whatever," said Nettie. "Strange coupling, if you ask me, but there's no rhyme or reason to why some people are attracted to each other."

"True," said Kat. "But you have to marvel that in the midst of building a botanical business, she still managed to have a social life." Kat opened the cruiser door and placed the evidence envelope inside the vehicle. She slammed the door and walked to the shade. There she sipped water from a bottle she'd retrieved from the car. Nettie got a bottle for herself and handed one to Abby.

Abby chafed at Kat's comment. The implication was that if Fiona could have a social life, why couldn't Abby? Kat was a study in contradictions—being a cop who tended to keep a low profile about her police work, she could also be a social butterfly. Abby wondered if Kat would ever understand why the farmette work offered a solitude that nurtured her, even if the work seemed never to end. Kat would probably never appreciate why Abby stuck with it when it generated so little money, and why Abby had so little time or energy to build social relationships or find romance. Only another person who loved living close to the earth, like a farmer or a rancher, could appreciate Abby's lifestyle. Not everyone needed or wanted the world's constant distractions and drama.

As the trio sipped in the shade, Nettie said, "Duplessis sings, as well as plays the drums. I heard him once, back when Zazi's tested out local musicians during the restaurant's early-bird dinners. Some were chosen to perform during evening meals, as well. I expected jazz, not Caribbean, with all that drumming." She rubbed her arm, as if already sensing the start of a poison-oak rash. "Lot of nervous energy. Oh, and he's a smoker. Saw him light up with the other musicians outside afterward. Just saying."

Abby shook her head. "According to Fiona, he liked smoking herbs through a hookah. Less harsh on his vocal cords. Apparently, among the young Haitians in North Miami, where Laurent grew up, the herb of choice is *Cannabis sativa*. From what Fiona said, he was always careful never to overdo, as he had a thing about alertness. Relaxed was okay, but losing control was not. And he was a controller."

"So he used marijuana. Did he also sell it?" Nettie asked.

"Possession with intent to sell is a felony under health and safety code one-one-three-five-nine," said Kat.

"Now I know this isn't my imagination. I feel itchy all over," Nettie said, running a finger around the neck of her uniform shirt.

Kat might have been looking at Nettie, but her thoughts were clearly somewhere else. "So, Abby," Kat finally asked, "are you trying to make some linkage here between

Laurent's weed smoking, the nicotine patch, and Fiona's murder?"

"We're trained, are we not, to allow the evidence to lead us to a conclusion. Not sure yet," said Abby. "But if he smokes dope, you've got to wonder if he's got a criminal past. You know as well as I do that drugs and alcohol are often linked to violent crime."

"So true," Nettie said. "So maybe drugs played a role in her murder."

"And yet he's not the only person in Fiona's world who smokes." Abby dabbed the perspiration from the corners of her nose and her forehead with her shirttail.

"Yeah?" Kat's eyebrows shot up. "I'm listening."

"I heard Premalatha asking Fiona for a special blend of smoking herbs this past Saturday," Abby revealed.

"Oh." Kat's eyes grew wide. "And what time was that?"

"Two-ish."

"Did she walk in with anybody?"

"The guru's bodyguard Dakota, or Dak, as he calls himself, was with her," Abby said. "You know him. He's heavyset, with a stocky build. Tats all over. Never says anything, never smiles, and never looks you in the eye. But here's what's interesting. Why would Premalatha ask for smoking herbs when the commune doesn't permit smoking?"

Nettie stepped back and swatted at a cloud of gnats. "Maybe for the teacher, Baba. Unlimited power must be nice."

"So you think Baba sent his bodyguard and manager to buy herbs?" Kat asked.

"Maybe," replied Nettie. "And that's not a crime. But which herbs was Fiona blending for smokes?" asked Nettie, stepping back some more and waving away the gnats.

Abby said, "Skullcap, marshmallow, uva ursi . . . I think there might have been others. I never actually heard anyone ever asking for weed or cannabis. And I do not believe Fiona would get mixed up with anything like that. That would be so out of character."

Kat asked, "So Premalatha and Dak were asking Fiona for smoking herbs. Anything else you haven't shared?"

Abby thought for a moment. "Fiona said she was temporarily out of stock and offered to mix a version of the compound if they could wait a day. Premalatha didn't want to come back." Looking straight at Kat, Abby took a deep breath and asked, "What's Premalatha and Dak's alibi for the morning Fiona was murdered?"

Kat shot her a quick warning look but answered, "They vouched for each other."

Abby shook her head, inhaled deeply. "Well, that Premalatha is one cold fish, and I think there was no love lost between her and Fiona."

"Why do you say that?" Kat asked.

"On the way out of the store on Saturday, she paused at the door and asked Fiona, 'What did he ever see in you?'"

"He . . . ? Who was she referring to?" asked Nettie.

Abby shook her head. "Don't know."

Nettie mused, "But 'What did he ever see in you?' sounds like a jealous barb over a man."

Kat withdrew a notebook from her shirt pocket and flipped through the pages. "So, the men intersecting Fiona's life included Laurent, the ex-boyfriend, and Tom, the soon-to-be ex-husband. There's her brother, Jack, and her landlord, Dr. Danbury. The former teacher is out of the picture, but we still have Hayden Marks and Dak, the bodyguard."

Abby looked out over the deep blue lake. "So if a man was the reason Fiona was killed, you'll have to find a linkage between the two women and the men they both knew.

Just out of curiosity, what was Premalatha's alibi for the time Fiona died?" Abby asked.

"The guru vouches for Premalatha, and she alibis Dak," Kat replied.

Nettie chimed in. "They eat lunch together, but all the other stuff, like meditating, doing yoga, or reading, they do alone. But as commune manager, Premalatha always supervises the preparations of the guru's meals."

"They were all together in the dining hall at twelve thirty," Kat said, adding, "This business of meditating in your room leaves everyone essentially unaccounted for until those lunch preparations start. It's proving difficult to nail down the commune contingent, but we're working on it."

"And what about her husband, Tom Davidson Dodge?" Abby asked. "I'd be curious if he slept at Fiona's the night before her death."

"He did. He says he left her in bed at six forty-five Sunday morning for a job on the other side of the summit. The work involved renovation for a local winery. The thing is," Kat said, "that the winery has been closed for a few weeks. No one can vouch for him until around nine."

"So no other persons of interest, no promising leads?" Abby asked.

Kat sighed and shook her head. The chatter on Kat's radio had picked up. She frowned as she cocked her head toward the radio to zero in on dispatch's message. Looking intently at Abby, she said, "You must have spooked Timothy Kramer. He has evaded the BOLO, and now his cabin is on fire. Cal Fire's on the way, and Nettie and I have got to go."

Abby nodded, and her heart raced at the implications. Another fire perhaps deliberately set. Now, what exactly was Kramer trying to hide? Abby's thoughts ran rampant. There was no way to know for certain that he had set the fire. But if he had, why would he do that, unless he was attempting to cover up something? she mused as she watched Nettie and Kat get into the cruiser.

Kat started the engine and prepared to make a U-turn. She stopped for a moment, rolled down the window, called out, "No telling where Kramer is now, Abby. I can count on you, right? To go straight home?"

Smiling to reassure Kat, Abby replied, "That's a ten-four."

Twenty minutes later, Abby drove along Chestnut. She wheeled into the parking lot of Smooth Your Groove, where she bought a cup of green tea with blended mint and almond milk. Rather than nursing her tea in the smoothie shop, she opted to stroll four blocks down Chestnut to Main Street to take a look in the window of Fiona's shop. She had a lot to think about, and a walk would be just the thing to clear her head.

Passing Lidia Vittorio's jewelry store, Abby resisted the urge to check out the latest marcasite offerings. With no money to blow on earrings, she avoided looking at the window displays. Next, she strolled past Cineflicks and peeked at the latest consignment displays in the window of Twice Around Markdowns. Finally, standing in front of Ancient Wisdom Botanicals, she wondered how to gain access to Fiona's shop without breaking the law. But as she stood before the door with the CLOSED sign facing the street, she could see someone had turned on the interior lights.

After depositing her smoothie cup in the nearby trash receptacle and tightening her grip on the shoulder strap of her purse, Abby pushed against the door handle. To her surprise, the door creaked open. Tiny bells on a red ribbon announced her arrival. New Age instrumentals played softly in the background. Fiona had programmed the music to come on when she flipped on the shop lights.

Abby called out a greeting. "Hello. Anybody here?"

No answer.

Her senses went on high alert. She stepped across the welcome mat and ventured past a bamboo table display of soaps wrapped in paper and tied with twine. Well, this was odd. Who was in the store, and why weren't they answering her shout-out? Suddenly, Abby felt a little shiver. The soft lights and the soothing New Age music did little to calm her nerves. Inching forward, she eased past a large display of Ayate washcloths, loofahs, and aromatherapy massage oils. Instinctively, her right hand reached for a weapon on a duty belt she no longer wore. She heard a snap.

"Hello. Who's there?" Clearly, she was not alone. She quickly considered possible intruders. Fiona's husband, Tom, topped the list. Jack, Fiona's brother, surely had a key. What about Laurent? Fiona had said he'd come here whenever they fought. *Who else?*

She crept past a rounder of all-natural fabric clothing. She slipped past a bookcase tightly packed with new and used books on the culinary, medicinal, and apothecary uses of herbs. Rounding another glass display case, Abby saw bottles of essential oils, a selection of teas, and a basket of herbal smudge sticks tied with red cotton thread. She bumped the basket with her elbow and quickly righted the smudge sticks and the boxes of tea.

At the shop's rear on Lemon Lane, a dog sounded an alert, barking incessantly.

"Hello. Anybody back there?"

Abby stepped into the room at the rear of the shop that served as Fiona's office. File cabinet drawers stood open. Manila files and their contents lay strewn about on the black metal surface of the desk. Upon spotting the back door slightly ajar, Abby hurried over and yanked it wide open. She saw Laurent Duplessis dashing toward a green sedan with a dented front fender. He tossed a black briefcase across the driver's seat to the passenger side before jumping in and starting the engine. The car lurched forward, engine revving, tires squealing.

Abby raced into the cloud of exhaust. Wildly waving her hand in the air, she yelled, "Hey . . . stop. . . . Somebody stop him!"

She pulled up, breathless, retrieved the little spiral notebook she habitually kept in her shirt pocket, and jotted down the license plate number. Turning back, she quickly returned to Ancient Wisdom Botanicals. As she stood in the middle of Fiona's office, staring at the mess, her imagination conjured a visual of what had just happened. Laurent Duplessis had been searching the small office, but for what? Had he found it?

The way Abby saw it, Laurent looked out for Laurent. With Fiona, he had had a free and easy lifestyle. He could wake up whenever he wanted. He could smoke dope as he liked, and he could hang out at the beach. He could party and play drums half the night and then waltz back into Fiona's cottage when he got hungry or needed sleep. What a deal. Maybe the best one Laurent had ever had. Most women would have kicked him out long before Fiona had. When she finally ended Laurent's free ride and broke things off between them, she still helped him find a place to live—the apartment above Twice Around Markdowns.

Walking to the front of the store, Abby took out her cell phone and tapped the number for the Las Flores PD. "Abigail Mackenzie here. I want to report a crime," she said. "Ancient Wisdom Botanicals on Main Street has just been burglarized."

Tips for Cleansing or Consecrating a Space with an Herbal Smudge Stick

The burning of herbs to release scented smoke in order to cleanse a space of negative energy or a negative presence or spirit, or to consecrate a garden or a sacred space, is not a new practice. The ancient Greeks, the Egyptians, Romans, Babylonians, Hebrews, Tibetans, Chinese, and Native Americans all practiced smudging. You can easily make a smudge stick with herbs and flowers from your garden. You'll need the leaves of herbs and wildflowers (optional), scissors, and cotton thread or string.

- Pick a bouquet of sage leaves and wildflowers. Trim the stems of the wildflowers so that they are three to four inches long.

- Use the thread or string to tie the flowers around the sage leaves.

- Lace the thread or string up and down the bouquet, tying it tightly.

- Hang the smudge stick to dry for several weeks before using it in a well-ventilated area.

Chapter 6

Honeybees have five eyes—compound eyes
on either side of the head and three small
ocelli on top—enabling them to see
ultraviolet light and detect color.

—*Henny Penny Farmette Almanac*

Within minutes of Abby's call to the Las Flores PD,
two officers arrived on scene and secured Ancient
Wisdom Botanicals.

"You are positive the man you saw was Laurent Duplessis?" one uniformed officer asked.

"Yes," Abby answered.

"And he was definitely inside the shop?" the other asked.

"Well, I can't say positively. I believe so," she replied. "My friend Fiona never left drawers open and file folders strewn all over the place. When I spotted Duplessis, he was the only person I saw out back, and was running like his tail feathers were on fire."

Abby patiently answered every question put to her until they got another call from dispatch. Watching the cops get into their cruiser, she considered briefly chatting up Laurent's landlady but just as quickly dismissed the notion.

The cops would certainly do a knock and talk in their follow-up. If she preempted them, they'd surely see it as interference.

Standing in the sunshine on Main Street, Abby glanced up at the sign above the door of Ancient Wisdom Botanicals and wondered if someone new would buy the place. She couldn't imagine Fiona's brother hanging on to it. According to Fiona, he was more at home in rain forests and living amid primitive cultures than modern ones. Maybe that store space was jinxed. Previously, it was the site of the pastry chef's murder. With the chef's death, Las Flores had lost its innocence. Now, once again, a killer was on the loose in their lovely small town.

Abby felt hot. Her skin prickled. Was it the afternoon heat or a hormonal response to all the drama? *Whatever.* She slipped out of her long-sleeved shirt, exposing bare shoulders except for the straps of her turquoise tank top. She tied the shirt around the waistband of her jeans, pulled her thick hair into a more secure ponytail, and began walking back toward Lidia Vittorio's jewelry store, where Main intersected Chestnut. Maybe she'd get the Percy Sledge CD from the glove box and during the drive home listen to it to get into the mood for her date with Clay.

A smile slipped across her lips as she remembered how Clay had called her in the first weeks after she'd moved to the farmette. He'd dialed her on his way to buy lumber at the big-box DIY store. Wrist deep in the dirt where she had been harvesting garlic, Abby had shaken off the soil from her hands to take his call. He'd told her to tune in to the local radio station and then had hung up. Abandoning the bulbs on yellowed stalks, Abby had walked to the patio and turned on the radio in time to hear the refrain of "When a Man Loves a Woman." Even thinking about that moment brought a smile to her lips. It was the first time Clay had put words to his feelings for her, albeit through song lyrics belted out by another man. But that day her knees had gone weak as she listened.

As she approached the corner of Main and Chestnut, Abby felt a newfound sense of joy and hope bubbling through her being. How wonderful it would be if that old excitement she used to feel with him could be rekindled.

"Abby, wait up."

Turning, she saw Clay jaywalking across the street, dodging a car, to catch up with her. He wore a baby blue polo shirt, open at the neck, slim jeans, and loafers.

"Just thinking about you," she remarked with a smile. "What brings you to Main Street? Visiting old haunts? Renewing old friendships?"

Clay flashed a disarming smile. "And why not? I made a lot of friends here. I can't believe how many people missed me."

Her smile withered. *Does it always have to be about you?* "Look, I haven't forgotten our date tonight. You did say six o'clock, right?"

"Yeah, but seeing as how you are already here . . . got a minute? I've got something to show you."

Abby sighed. It was useless to protest once Clay set his mind on something. Best to just go along. She nodded. "I'm game."

He put his hand on her back at the waist and gently nudged her toward Lidia Vittorio's shop door. After pulling it open, he braced it with his foot while Abby walked through. In frosted diffusers with bamboo reeds on the countertops, the shop's signature scent of ginger and pear permeated the interior. Soft music and spotlighting that splayed off the highly polished surfaces created a welcoming ambiance for the handful of customers browsing the gem-studded offerings.

"My old eyes must be playing tricks on me," called out

Lidia. "Abby, dear, it's been such a long while." Lidia wore a classic tailored black dress with a black lace Peter Pan collar. At the center of the collar, she'd pinned her favorite cameo. She wrapped her thin arms around Abby and hugged her tightly.

"What's kept you away, my dear?" Lidia asked, pulling back from the hug and holding Abby at arm's length to look at her. "Oh, to be young again . . . I dare say you don't need jewelry to enhance your beauty, like some do." Scooping threads of silvery hair away from her face, Lidia pinched the strands together and tucked them back into her coiled braid, held in place at the nape of her neck by hairpins. "Sorry you missed our big sale on marcasite on Valentine's Day." She smoothed her coif with her hands, blue veined, with tissue-thin skin, and nodded an acknowledgment to Clay.

At the mention of Valentine's Day, Abby flinched. "You couldn't feel any worse than I do about that, Lidia. I was elbow deep in bare-root season, and then in March I was spraying organic oil all over the fruit trees before they leafed out. And now that the weather has already turned warm, I'm expecting my bees to swarm."

"Well, dear, it sounds like you are working awfully hard." Lidia turned her attention to Clay. She smiled broadly, revealing the stains of habitual tea drinking on her uneven lower teeth. "Perhaps your friend Calhoun here could help you out." She smiled, as if she was conspiring with him in some grand scheme.

Abby looked at Clay. His face instantly wreathed in a boyish grin; his dark eyes gleamed due to his apparent happiness that Lidia had remembered at least part of his name.

"Oh, I'm itching to help her," Clay said.

Abby's brow arched upward.

Clay thumped the glass display and spoke in a voice tinged with excitement. "I've got plenty of ideas for fixing up the place," he said. "Starting with ripping out that master bath. From the looks of it, that bath was an afterthought to the old bunkhouse. I wouldn't be surprised if the back of the shower stall was breeding mold."

His remark seemed unduly critical, but Abby believed he meant to emphasize his vision for making the place pretty and more functional. She sighed. "What do you expect of a two-room farmhouse built in the late nineteen forties?"

Clay said, addressing Lidia, "What Abby needs is a bathroom with a marble floor, a couple of big view windows, and a spa tub with jets."

As much as Abby liked that idea, she wished Clay would use a little more restraint in his conversations with townspeople with whom she would have relationships long after he had taken off again. Lidia didn't need to know how dilapidated the farmhouse was. It would only give her reason to worry about Abby. Locals took a strong interest in the welfare of their own. That was just the way small towns were.

What was clearly apparent to Abby now was that the drill and the tool cabinet Clay had brought to the farmette had been part of his plan all along to ingratiate himself back into her life. So be it. If he insisted on building a new master bath, she'd be an idiot not to let him. And while he was at it, he could finish her kitchen, too. Then, immediately, Abby felt guilty for having such thoughts. The less emotional, more rational side of her mind took over. *Give him a break. Accept him for who he is. Or end it. But stop punishing him.*

"I saved it for Calhoun," Lidia said, winking at Clay and leading them to a glass display case. Lidia's bony fin-

gers unlocked the case and pulled out a small box. She set it on the counter and opened it, exposing a pair of earrings. She picked up a hand mirror.

Abby's heart skipped. Her breath caught in her throat as she stared at the earrings. A chiming sounded as customers entered the shop, but nothing could draw Abby's attention from the gold earrings in the shape of honeybees before her. Each bee's eyes were small cabochons of aquamarine. Diamond chips formed the head. The thorax was embellished with citrines, while the embellishment for the wings and dark brown abdominal bands featured chocolate diamonds.

"Excuse me, will you?" Lidia said. "I'll just see what the other customer wants. Be right back, dear."

"Of course," said Abby, taking the hand mirror from Lidia. She held an earring against her left ear. "Oh, my gosh," Abby remarked. "These are exquisite."

"The eyes there," Clay said, pointing to the bees, "are roughly the same color as yours." He seemed quite pleased with himself for noticing.

"Ha. I wish," Abby said. She peered at the shade of blue green, but she secretly liked the red in the citrine and its smoky-brown undertones, because she could see them reflected in her hair where she stood under one of the counter spotlights. "These beauties do not go with my old shirt and faded jeans." Abby lingered a moment longer in front of the mirror, holding first one earring up to her ear and then the other one to her opposite ear. Finally, she sighed. "I've never seen such lovely earrings."

"Let me buy them for you," Clay said.

A beat passed. Abby thought for a millisecond. They were over-the-top beautiful, but with a thousand-dollar price tag, they were also expensive. And where would she ever wear them? He would spend his money, and the ear-

rings would sit in her jewelry box. "How sweet of you to offer, Clay. I don't know what to say, except, well, I really couldn't accept them. They're lovely but too pricey."

Abby placed the earrings back in the open box and then reached for his hand and wrapped her palm around it. Looking into his wide-set dark brown eyes, she said softly, "You don't have to buy me presents. People should be able to find their way back...." The words trailed off into a sigh. "How can I say it?"

I don't want to hurt you, but why rush us into beginning again? she thought.

"Time ... I just need time, Clay. That's all I ask." She squeezed his hand and found it eager, warm, and willing to hold hers. She searched his expression for signs he understood her confusion.

Although he nodded in acquiescence, his expression seemed to have darkened. He pulled his hand away and busied both hands with rearranging the earrings in the box. With resignation written all over his expression, Clay finally closed the lid.

Abby turned to see where Lidia had gone. And when had Tom Davidson Dodge entered the store? Abby watched Tom, thin-boned in a T-shirt and jeans, with a navy watch cap hiding a head of curls, take several items from his brightly striped Peruvian bag. He set them on the counter's glass surface. Lidia emerged from the back room with a vial of liquid and a scale in her hands. She faced Tom on the opposite side of the counter.

Tapping Clay on the arm, Abby placed a finger against her lips and cocked her head in Lidia and Tom's direction.

Tom held up a braided gold chain with a Celtic cross dangling from it.

Abby sucked in a deep breath. *Oh, my gosh. You can't be pawning Fiona's favorite necklace. If that isn't cold-hearted, what is?*

Tom placed the necklace on the counter and reached into the bag again. He plunked a wedding ring set next to the necklace. Then he reached into the bag again and pulled out a silver cuff bracelet embedded with semiprecious stones. Abby watched Tom look for a reaction from Lidia.

"They belonged to my late wife," Tom said in a soft tone. "Heirlooms they were, she told me. The rings have to be worth a small fortune. She said they once belonged to her great-grandmother from County Kerry."

"Well, yes, that would make them estate pieces, wouldn't it?" Lidia smiled politely. "The necklace has a solid resale value. However, gold is not worth what it was a while back. How much do you want for everything?"

"I was thinking ten grand," Tom replied.

"Oh, dear, that would not be possible. Even if they were worth that—and I don't believe they are—I'd have to pass." Lidia laid aside the loupe she'd picked up, and stared frankly at him. "You do understand that I have to resell these items for a profit."

"Yeah. So then what could you give me?" Tom asked.

"Well, let me see." Lidia stroked her lower lip with a forefinger. "Gold is going for slightly more than a thousand per ounce, but a lot depends on the purity and the weight of your pieces, of course." She reached under the counter and pulled forth a scale, then set the rings on it and noted the weight. Then she pulled a vial of liquid from under the counter and placed a drop on the rings. She repeated the process for the gold necklace before returning the scale and the small vial to the shelf beneath the counter. Lidia picked up the loupe and used it to study the

Celtic cross. "The craftsmanship is superb. Would you take six hundred for this?"

Tom seemed antsy, shifting his weight from side to side. "I guess so. What about the other stuff?"

Abby looked at Clay, shook her head slowly, and raised her hand, palm to the floor, to indicate that they should stand down and stay quiet.

Fiona had confided in Abby that the Celtic cross necklace was worth close to two grand. Lidia was driving a hard bargain. The fact that Tom would accept less than half of what the object was worth perplexed Abby. Did he not know the value, or was he just desperate for money? What alarmed Abby more was why Tom was hawking the jewelry in the first place. It was behavior that was unbecoming, to say the least, and highly suspicious, since those valuable pieces had belonged to his dead wife. That raised a whole bevy of questions about who would profit most from her death. Was he Fiona's designated heir? Who had her will?

Abby motioned for Clay to follow her. They left the bee earring box on the counter and quietly walked out of the jewelry shop into the sunlight. From down the street wafted the scent of red beans, rice, roasted jalapeños, and grilled sausages, reminding Abby that she had long ago digested the peanut butter toast she'd had for lunch. She disregarded her hunger and hastened toward the traffic light.

"Abby, hold up. Zazi's is open," said Clay, his voice tinged with hopefulness. "What say we grab a table and you tell me what's going on?"

"Later, later." Abby kept up her brisk walking pace. The traffic signal flashed the white pedestrian walk light and sounded the familiar *ding-dong, ding-dong, ding-dong*. Abby raced across the intersection. She gestured to Clay to

catch up. After dashing inside the Dillingham Dairy building, the first floor of which was taken up by police headquarters, she headed straight for the window where a male
police officer staffed a desk behind bulletproof glass.

"You might want to let the homicide team know that the
husband of Fiona Ryan is pawning her jewelry at Village
Rings & Things across the street!" Abby exclaimed, sucking
in a deep breath. "It's just a hunch, but he could walk out of
there with enough moola for a flight to Timbuktu. Just so
you know."

Tips for Inspecting a Honeybee Hive

Make routine hive inspections. Conduct inspections every ten days. Changes in the apiary can
happen quickly. When inspecting a hive,
approach it from the rear or the side and do the
following:

- Check for dead bees at the front of the hive. This
  is normally not a grave concern; however, a large
  pile of dead bees could indicate a recent pesticide
  poisoning.

- Look for spotting in the area at the front of the
  hive and also on the hive boxes. Spotting is an
  indication of illness in the colony.

- Ensure that the hive entrance is open to permit
  easy access for the bees during the honey flow,
  when pollen-laden bees fly fast toward the hive.

- Lift the hive up to assess its weight; a heavy hive
  indicates a hefty honey store.

- Check for overcrowding and, if necessary, add a second story to the hive to accommodate the increasing population, or the bees will swarm.

- Reduce the hive entrance to a small opening if you suspect that predators or bees from other hives are robbing the hive. This is often indicated by bees darting back and forth or fighting in front of the hive.

- Observe worker bees pushing out dead bees to clean the hive. This is normal.

Chapter 7

Thyme spices up vanilla cake. Lavender glorifies pudding. Basil intensifies butter, and rosemary elevates potato. But what herb knits a broken heart?

—*Henny Penny Farmette Almanac*

With Clay's hand on her elbow, Abby walked out of the Las Flores Police Department and reentered the late afternoon light filtered through the crepe myrtle trees along Main Street. Friday afternoon pedestrian and street traffic had gotten worse now that the days were growing longer and the weather had turned warm. Summer hadn't officially arrived yet and wouldn't for a few weeks, but people in the outlying valley towns had already begun their summer caravans through Las Flores and the mountains to the beach communities. Every weekend, the traffic would back up for miles.

"How do you know the jewelry that guy was pawning belonged to his dead wife? Did he kill her?" Clay asked, releasing Abby's elbow to take her hand. They strolled toward the crosswalk. "What say you bring me up to speed while we eat?" he said. "I'm starving."

Abby pulled Clay to an abrupt stop. "Could you give me forty-five minutes? I'd like to run home, shower, and change first." She cocked her head slightly to one side. "It's been one thing after another, and I've been out in the heat all day. I'd like to clean up, slip into something a little more feminine."

He leaned down and kissed her neck. "Not necessary." He was smiling, but Abby could tell he didn't want her to go. "You look fine, and we're already here." He glanced at her sideways and thumped the pedestrian walk button on its metal pole with the side of his hand. "And regardless, Zazi's has a restroom. Can't you freshen up there?"

Abby flinched. He'd missed the point. She wanted to hear their song on the drive home. She wanted to wash and primp and feel pretty again. She wanted a sentimental and sexy reunion. It had been so long.

"Jeez, Clay, we weren't even supposed to meet for another hour." Abby flashed her sweetest smile. Noticing his jaw tensing, as if he was holding back his growing frustration with her, Abby let her smile fade. She tried another approach. "I have an idea," she said. "While I pretty myself up, you grab a stool at the bar at the Black Witch and have a glass of that Kentucky bourbon you like so much. I'm sure the boys around the dartboard will want to hear all about your travels."

"Probably," Clay said. "But I thought you would."

Ouch. His remark stung, but Abby wasn't about to let him see her react.

After a moment of tense silence, he said, "If it's so important to look good while you eat, Abby, then, by all means, go on home. Don't worry about me. I can find some way to cool my heels." His eyes darkened. Abby recognized his shifting mood.

She stared at the concrete. The pedestrian walk light began flashing, accompanied by the *ding-dong* repeatedly sounding, but neither she nor Clay moved.

He let go a long, audible exhale. He stared at the tall building across the street. His lips tightened into a severe line, and then, after a beat, he said, "Go on home, Abby. I'll see if Zazi's can rustle up something to tide me over until you get back. I'm too eager, I guess. I just want to spend some time with you."

She knew this maneuver. He would tell her to do whatever she wanted, but if he didn't also want it, he would make her pay for her choice by closing down emotionally. She hated his silent treatment. It was the classic passive-aggressive ploy. Abby shifted her gaze toward the theater marquee. A little foreign film from Hong Kong, *In the Mood for Love*, was playing for another week. Maybe she would see it. Maybe they would see it together. Or not.

A struggle had begun between her heart and her mind. Clay had come back. He'd said he couldn't live without her. Maybe she was creating an unnecessary problem. Surely she could set aside her desire to be romanced and just muster more generosity of spirit. But then again, if she gave in, wouldn't they just revert to their old way of being together? Nothing would change. That wasn't what she wanted for her life. If they were going to have a real chance of starting over and building a relationship that would thrive, this moment might be pivotal. Her thoughts raced as she remembered something Fiona had said about how two people could believe they loved and needed each other, but that didn't necessarily mean that they should be together or that they would even find enduring happiness. Sometimes coming together was just to finish off karma. Fiona had pointed to her own failed relationship with her husband, Tom, as an example. An icy finger of fear suddenly twisted around Abby's heart.

"On second thought," said Abby, "just forget about me getting all gussied up. We'll just grab a seat at the picture window at Zazi's, have a glass of old-vine zinfandel, dine on the bistro special, and watch the sun set on the mountains. Just like back in the day." She'd gone an emotional distance with Clay. Her heart was stronger now. She could choose to appease him, but on her terms. She'd let him buy her dinner. But that was all.

Clay locked eyes with her. The tension in his face relaxed as a smile played at the corners of his mouth. "That's my girl. I don't like the idea of a killer on the loose and you out there on the edge of town by yourself. Guess I've come back just in time."

Oh, really? You have no idea how silly that sounds, do you? "My neighbors are great," Abby said, thinking of Lucas, who lived up the hill from her farmette. "And I've got Sugar and my gun."

"So you don't need me?" Clay said, as if she'd just rejected him.

"I didn't say that."

"You didn't have to."

Abby released his hand as they stepped into the crosswalk. She pulled the strap of her purse tighter against her shoulder as a sudden hot gust of wind kicked up. The trees planted along the sidewalk bent and swayed, strong yet pliant. *We need to be like those trees, Clay, able to withstand whatever comes at us and still grow. I'll have dinner with you, listen to your stories, and smile at your jokes. But when it's time to go home, I'm going home alone.*

Inside Zazi's, Abby settled into the four-poster chair Clay had pulled out for her. She gazed out the bistro's front window and decided to file their tension-filled exchange under "knee-jerk reactions" and let it go. The window afforded a view of Main Street and beyond to the south, where the blue-green mountains towered behind the red barrel-tiled roof of the centuries-old grain mill. The wealthiest Las Flores families chose the mountains' southern slopes to build their mansions, up high, where the view overlooked the downtown. They hid their estates—some with vineyards—behind tall stone walls with gates. But the downtown merchants had a daily reminder that the mountains hid the nouveau riche. During certain times of the day, the sun would strike the glass windows on those lofty ridges, transforming the mountainsides into a mosaic of shimmering light, just as it did now under Abby's pensive gaze.

Clay ordered a bottle of zinfandel, touted on the wine list as having been produced from locally grown grapes on vines planted around 1910. The dutiful, dark-haired, white-aproned waitress who had encouraged Clay's choice scurried away, then returned a moment later with the bottle and two glasses. She coupled the task of opening the bottle with a soliloquy on the importance of having the correct wineglass, because of how it directed the flow of the liquid so that it hit certain parts of the palate. In different ways, this enhanced an appreciation for the wine's aroma and flavor. But opening the bottle proved impossible when the corkscrew malfunctioned. Clay offered to have a look; it seemed as good a moment as any for Abby to freshen up. She excused herself and left for the powder room.

Abby splashed cool water on her cheeks and washed and dried her hands. After pulling a comb from her purse, she freed her reddish-gold locks from the elastic band and coaxed them into thick waves that graced her bare shoulders. She untied her pale green work shirt from around her waist, slipped her arms back into it, and fastened it, leaving the top button undone, so a sliver of her turquoise tank top peeked out. Clay would like that, although he surely would prefer that she left the shirt off. She tucked her shirt into her jeans; this showed off her figure, kept trim and muscular by all the farmette work. Even if it didn't matter to Clay, it mattered to her that she did not look as though she'd just finished cleaning the chicken house before taking a seat in Main Street's best restaurant. Just as Abby unfastened her belt buckle and unzipped her jeans to tuck in her shirttail, two ladies entered the powder room, in the middle of a conversation.

"Edna Mae should know. She's lived here all her life. If she says that the community up there has become a cult and the town would be better off without them, then there's got to be something dark going on up there. Edna Mae has never known a stranger. And there's not a bigoted bone in her body," said the woman with hazel eyes and short gray hair. The wrinkled lobes of her pierced ears supported shiny gold hoop earrings. She held open the powder room door for her companion, a tall, freckle-faced woman with glasses and wearing a cream-colored shirt over brown leggings.

"So why is there a commune up there?" the freckle-faced woman asked. She flashed a fleeting smile of acknowledgment at Abby before disappearing behind the toilet door adjacent to her friend's stall. "I thought it used to be a convent."

Abby had zipped her jeans and buckled her belt and was reaching for her purse to leave when she heard the woman with the hoop earrings, now in the first stall, answer, "The nuns sold it to a builder who defaulted. A real estate developer grabbed it, the one that Zora Richardson married, I think." The woman lowered her voice. "Rumor has it that he's in cahoots with the commune's new leader. That murdered Ryan woman and her husband, I heard, were mixed up somehow with that commune, too. That new leader has attracted the riffraff that are coming into town. Don't know much else about the dead woman except that she had a husband *and* a boyfriend."

Abby's antennae went on high alert. While straining to hear the rest of the conversation, she rummaged for makeup in her purse.

"So who killed her?" asked the freckle-faced woman.

"I heard the husband did it."

Abby stared in the mirror at the reflection of the woman's spiky gray hair as it appeared and disappeared at the door's upper edge, looking like a rat bobbing along the top.

After unlatching the door, the woman stepped out and continued her conversation with her friend. "You and I can fly back to Milwaukee, but Edna Mae will never leave Las Flores." The woman looked at Abby with a forced smile and proceeded to wash her hands. "I just hope for her sake they make an arrest soon."

Abby returned the woman's smile. "The murder of Fiona Ryan is just awful, isn't it?" said Abby, jumping into their conversation. "Our police are a good lot, though. They'll find the killer," she said with confidence. She searched for items in her purse until she located red-tinted lip gloss. Using the lip brush, she swept a wide stroke across her bottom lip. "I couldn't help overhearing you mention Edna Mae, the owner of the antique store. Are you related?"

"I'm her cousin twice removed on her mama's side," the freckle-faced woman replied.

"Nice lady, that Edna Mae," Abby replied. She pulled a paper towel from the dispenser and dabbed at the corners of her mouth.

"Spirit as pure as bleached linen, and she's got the low-down on those commune folks," Freckle Face said as she exited her stall and waited her turn at the sink. "Dark and unrighteous acts going on up there."

"That so?" Abby twisted the lid back on the gloss and dropped it into her purse. "Like what?" Abby tried to sound shocked.

Freckle Face heaved a long sigh. "What's that they say about idle hands doing the Devil's work? That dead girl romancing two men? Could be that they're all into polygamy."

Abby winced. Her friend Fiona had been free as a feather, but polygamy? *No way. Absolutely not.* But before Abby could utter a word in Fiona's defense, the gray-haired woman corrected her friend.

"Polygamists are people with multiple spouses. The dead girl had only one husband . . . and they were separated." The gray-haired woman stepped to one side and pulled a paper towel from the dispenser. Wiping water from her hands, she spoke in a matter-of-fact tone. "Is there anyone in town who doesn't believe those people live out on the fringe?"

"What do you mean?" Abby asked.

"A cult of Satan," the freckle-faced woman stated decidedly. "Arcane arts."

"Arcane arts?" Abby asked, wondering if the woman was referring to telling fortunes, scrying, or conducting séances. "What exactly do you mean?" Abby hoped to find out what the women thought they knew about the inner workings of the commune.

Freckle Face chimed in. "They do séances to contact dead spirits. I heard that leader up there reads the Good Book differently than other men of the cloth."

The gray-haired woman pushed her fingers through her locks and said, "You hear talk around town. He's got a thing about the number eight, justifies some of his actions with Old Testament verses about the eight wives of King David. Maybe he thinks he's king, too, and requires eight women to dote on him."

"Oh, my goodness!" exclaimed Abby. "How narcissistic!"

Apparently encouraged by Abby's interest, Freckle Face added in a hushed tone, "Eight women sleep on the floor of his room every night. They call it energy balancing. The chosen ones wear a necklace—a black knotted cord with a figure eight symbol."

Abby shook her head, as if in complete disbelief. "You don't think someone in that commune might have had a reason to hurt that woman who is dead now, do you?"

The two women looked at each other.

The freckle-faced woman flicked water from her hands and spoke up. "Well, you've got to wonder what happens when a woman like that falls out of favor with the so-called prophet."

"Or if she incurs the jealousy of the other women," the gray-haired lady remarked thoughtfully. She quickly reapplied her lipstick and looked at Abby. "Several of those commune people work down at Smooth Your Groove. I'd be careful about eating anything there. Who knows what they're putting in those smoothies."

"Thank you. I will," Abby said, lifting her curly hair with the front of her hand and flicking it from her bodice over her shoulder. She plucked the reddish-gold strand clinging to her shirt and let it drop to the floor.

"Yes," chimed in Freckle Face. "You can't be too careful."

The gray-haired woman adjusted her scarf, tucked her purse strap over her shoulder, and waited for her friend. "We're here for a mini reunion," she said. "Edna Mae and the two of us went to nursing school together, but that was aeons ago."

"Really?" said Abby. "That's so nice."

"Edna Mae's retired now. That antique store is her second career."

"Lovely how you've remained friends for such a long time," said Abby, rolling the cuffs up on her shirt. She glanced at her watch. "Ooh, and speaking of time and friends, I've got to get back to my date, or he'll come looking for me." Abby opened the powder-room door and glanced back at the two women preening in the mirror. Their conversation had shifted from murder and the commune to the Amish quilts Edna Mae now carried in her shop.

On the return trip to her table, Abby thought about the "cheap trinket on a cord" remark and the symbolism of the number eight. What might seem like the mindless prattle of outsiders could have relevance. She made a mental note to look into it.

Clay whistled softly. "You had me worried, woman. I was beginning to think you'd slipped out the back door and left me for good." His dark eyes danced. "I would have come after you. We've got plans."

Abby arched a brow. "Oh, do we?" She plucked the white napkin from under her fork, shook the fabric loose, and laid it across her lap. Clay poured the wine and intercepted Abby's hand as she reached for her glass. He drew her fingers to his lips, kissed each with tenderness, as though reacquainting himself with the feel of her flesh.

"To a fresh start with the only woman I have ever truly loved. The one who has claimed my heart and soul. To you, Abby, my main squeeze."

Shouldn't that be "my only squeeze"? Her thought remained unspoken as she lifted her glass and touched it to his. He probably hadn't even recognized his faux pas.

Clay took the lead in filling in the blanks of his life from their year apart. He had always enjoyed talking about himself, and this time was no exception. As Abby listened, she realized as perhaps never before how thickly Clay could lay on the Kentucky charm. He was as smooth as the old-vine zinfandel they were drinking. Eventually, he got around to a topic besides himself—the farmette—and inquired about her renovation projects for the summer.

Abby told him of her desire to rip out the aging shower-tub combo in the master bath. "There's mold growing behind that cheap vinyl enclosure. I just know it," she said. She sipped the red liquid, relaxing into the warm, contented mood it evoked.

"And I've got a plan to fix that," he said, with a grin that bared nearly all his pearly whites.

"Well, I like the plan you conjured up while we were inside Lidia Vittorio's jewelry store," Abby said. "I can't afford a marble floor or a fancy jetted tub, although I'd love them."

"We'll see," said Clay. "There are several architectural salvage yards in the county and at least three stone suppliers who fill their Dumpsters daily with castoffs from custom cuts. With permission, we might be able to find enough similar pieces of marble to lay a small floor."

Abby looked at him in surprise. "Do you know anything about cutting marble?" she asked. "It's stone. Thick stone. A slab of a mountain."

Clay smiled like a Cheshire cat. He devoured an appetizer-sized serving of bruschetta, mozzarella melted over chunks of heirloom tomatoes and fresh basil on a toasted crostini that had been generously brushed with olive oil. Wiping the corners of his mouth with his napkin, he leaned forward to gaze at her with smoldering intensity. In a tone of supreme confidence, Clay said, "All you need is the right tool for the job . . . and the knowledge of how to use that tool. And, thank the Lord, I've got both."

Abby's cheeks flamed at the double meaning. Her pulse quickened. "Oh, I'm sure you have. But if mold," she said, in a not too obvious shift in the conversation, "is in the drywall, that section will have to be removed." She guided her finger around the rim of her wineglass. *Sip the wine more slowly.* It wouldn't do to lose her objectivity, and he seemed intent on weakening all her defenses. "Is it so simple?"

"Oh, it is. Trust me," he replied.

Trust. Not so easy. Abby sank deeper into her chair, only faintly aware that she drew comfort from the solid support of the oak planks.

Leaning in, he put his hand over hers. "A tub for two is on my wish list."

"Flooring and kitchen shelves are on mine," Abby muttered hastily. "There is almost no storage space, and I'm tired of that plywood subfloor in the living area. It looks okay covered with an area rug, but how much nicer the space will be with warm hardwood floors. But that will be a big project." She didn't want to sound too depressing. But when everyone else talked renovation, they were dreaming of new doors, windows, crown molding, and countertops, but she wanted finished walls and floors.

"Everywhere you look, Clay, there's a project," Abby said. "Once upon a time, I was working from a master plan for the farmette. Now I tackle what needs fixing before the next rainy season sets in . . . and pray that the tap on the money trickle doesn't dry up. I've got honey, eggs, produce, and herbs to sell, but the real money comes from my part-time investigative work for the DA. And at present, there isn't any."

Clay leaned back in his chair, nodding, reassuring her

that things would change now that he was back. "I'm home now, Abby."

The wine had lowered her emotional barriers. She leaned toward Clay, as if to share a secret. "You know," she said after polishing off the last sip in her glass, "I dream of buying that acre of land at the back of my property. The heirs who own it are lovely people, and right now they don't want to sell. But maybe they'll have a change of heart someday if I come up with the right amount of cash. Who knows?" Abby leaned back in her chair. "With the additional acre, I could get goats, make cheese to sell, and still have enough room to increase my hives and the number of chickens—which means more honey and eggs. If I could fix up that old house back there, I could rent the farmette house for yet another income stream." Suddenly, Abby's face flushed with warmth. With a sheepish grin, she quickly added, "A pipe dream, I know."

Clay rubbed his chin. "How much do you think you'd need?"

"Well, that's just it. It's not on the market."

He pointed to his watch. "We could always auction off this baby."

She knew how difficult it would be for him to part with the designer watch. He'd set the watch as a reward for achieving his dream of making a six-figure income. And he'd done that on his last job.

"A down payment, maybe," Abby said with a sigh. "But you know as well as I do, California land is like gold. That acre behind the farmette won't come cheap." She lifted her glass and waited for Clay to refill it. After taking a sip, Abby held the wine on the back of her tongue and then swallowed. She felt warm and inexplicably happy, reveling in the anticipation of good things to come. Maybe this was Clay's greatest gift to her—inspiring ideas, imparting hope, sending her spirits soaring with the belief that anything she truly wanted was possible if her belief, desire, and will to manifest it were strong enough.

Clay gazed at her with an expression that Abby interpreted as both soulful and contented.

She studied his youthful, tanned face, the faint frown lines threading across his forehead and around his eyes. He certainly didn't look forty-two. He exuded vitality from his rock-hard body. Abby doubted that any woman could remain immune to Clay's charm and intensity. And until she sensed a wind of change blowing again toward their relationship, she would enjoy the buoyancy of spirit his presence brought her. At that moment, Abby realized she would give him a second chance.

They agreed upon a dessert course of fresh ewe's cheese and honey, along with an espresso with a lemon twist for Abby, while Clay enjoyed most of the second bottle of zin. Abby offered to drive him back to the Las Flores Lodge.

With his arm draped over her shoulder, she helped him as he stumbled to the door of his room. Clay leaned against the door frame and faced her. He pulled her close, as if with an awareness of cloth and skin separating their beating hearts, and he wanted more. He tugged on the elastic band holding Abby's hair and freed the mass of waves and curls, which came cascading down upon her shoulders.

"God, you're beautiful," he whispered. Leaning in, he grazed her mouth with his, caressed her lips in a series of tender, sweet kisses, murmuring how much he loved her between each. Then, in the next moment, he smothered her mouth with a commanding mastery. Finally pulling back, he smiled, as if with secret knowledge of the depths of her soul.

Even Abby felt surprised at her eager response to his sensual hunger. The emotion of the moment had rendered her pliant, even weak. She'd longed for that kiss, and yet now that it had come, it confused her. She didn't want to feel weak with Clay. Why did he still have the power to seduce her?

Suddenly, he reached for the doorknob. "Babe, the hallway is spinning," he said, slightly slurring his words.

"Uh-oh," said Abby, hesitant to point out the obvious. *You've had too much to drink.* She heaved a sigh. "Give me the key. Let's get you inside."

She waited while he fished inside his pants pocket and finally produced the key. After unlocking the door, she helped him to the bed, where he sprawled out. Abby tugged off his shoes and fetched him a glass of water. She'd heard somewhere that booze dehydrated the body and the brain. A glass of water for every glass of wine could help avert that morning-after headache. When she returned with the water, Clay lay quietly snoring. Abby kissed him on the forehead, set the glass of water and his key on the nightstand, and locked the door before pulling it shut behind her.

She decided to use the shortcut through town to the farmette. The road twisted back through a piece of the mountain and eventually dropped down onto Farm Hill Road. She'd be at her door long before midnight.

From Las Flores Boulevard, she turned onto Main Street and stopped at a red light. Enjoying the fresh night air wafting in through her open windows, Abby heard a familiar laugh and looked in the direction of the ice cream parlor. There she saw Kat giggling like a schoolgirl as she wiped drips off the bodice of her sundress and quickly licked a double-layer cone. Had the police made an arrest? Or did they have someone in their sights? Why else would Kat be out for ice cream when the cops were expected to work the case doggedly until it was solved? Abby had even thought that they might have to cancel their date for the upcoming estate sale. Then, seeing Lucas, Abby's heart lurched.

After strolling out of the ice cream parlor with a handful of napkins, Lucas Crawford smiled as he handed the napkins to Kat. Abby's stomach tightened. Lucas—that gorgeous man of few words, with soulful eyes the color of creek water—appeared to be sharing a sweet moment with her best friend. What was up with that?

Honey-Lavender Ice Cream

Ingredients:
2 cups whole milk
⅛ cup fresh lavender leaves
2 tablespoons honey, plus 2 teaspoons
¼ cup granulated sugar
2 large eggs
1 cup heavy cream

Directions:
Combine the milk, lavender, and honey in a medium saucepan and bring to a gentle boil over medium-low heat. Stir occasionally.

Remove the saucepan from the heat and let the milk mixture rest for 5 minutes. Next, strain out the lavender and return the milk mixture to the saucepan. Bring the milk mixture to a simmer over low heat and cook for 5 minutes. Stir often.

Beat the sugar and the eggs in a medium bowl with

an electric mixer set to medium speed until the mixture is pale yellow, thick, and well blended, about 3 to 5 minutes.

Add half the milk mixture to the egg-sugar mixture and whisk together. Pour the egg mixture into the remaining milk mixture in the saucepan and cook over low heat until the mixture coats the back of a wooden spoon.

Remove the mixture from the heat. Stir in the heavy cream. Freeze the mixture in an ice cream maker, following the instructions provided by the manufacturer.

Serves 6 to 8

Chapter 8

Drink a tea of rose petals and rosemary sprigs
to heal the heart's conflicts.

—Henny Penny Farmette Almanac

Abby eyed a tight space behind the long line of parked
cars at the Richardson estate sale. "Sheesh. Looks like
the whole dang town is here."

Kat groaned. "I might have guessed. Flyers have been
plastered all over downtown. We should have gotten an
earlier start."

"Well, we're here now," Abby said with optimism. She
maneuvered the Jeep behind a sleek black Hummer with
the license plate letters SVC-WHIZ. Convinced that a fling
between Kat and Lucas wouldn't last even if they did get
something going, Abby entertained the hope that Kat
would soon find a new Mr. Right. Maybe a nudge in that
direction couldn't hurt. She pointed to the plate and said,
"Looks like he's here!"

"Who?"

"That new boyfriend you wanted—the Silicon Valley
engineer type. But finding him in the throng . . . well, that
might take a little sleuthing."

"My luck," Kat replied, "he'll drive a beater, his wife will be the whiz, and that Hummer will be her wheels." She swung her long legs from the Jeep to the ground as the wind tousled her short, blond locks. She slammed the Jeep door shut and walked around to Abby's side.

Abby suppressed her eagerness to ask Kat about Lucas and the ice cream moment and decided she'd wait for the right time. From her perspective as Lucas's neighbor and a frequent shopper at his feed store, Abby had some insight into the man. He wasn't the kind of guy who would jump into any relationship without giving it prudent thought. She doubted he could be hurried. Perhaps his meeting Kat had been a chance encounter. End of story. But there was no denying Kat's dark mood today. Abby was pretty sure her friend would get her groove back during the estate sale. She just needed to find some special item at a bargain-basement price. And Abby was going to help her find it.

Clicking the Jeep's lock button on her key and starting the short hike down the road, Abby glanced briefly past the red barn that led up to Fiona's cottage and Doc Danbury's house. Both the cottage and the main house had their doors closed and their blinds down. With the houses set back from the road, the residents could easily spot visitors or intruders. As she walked, Abby thought about what Kat had said on their drive up the mountain. Tom Davidson Dodge looked the most promising as a suspect, but the case was weak. The evidence was circumstantial, but he didn't have a verifiable alibi. Cops knew the killer was the last person to have seen Fiona alive. It was Tom's bad luck that he'd slept at his wife's cottage the night before she was found dead.

The fog was lifting, and the birds were singing. Abby's tummy was full of Kat's strong coffee, herb omelets, and a miniature lemon scone with chilled crème anglaise and fresh strawberries from her farmette garden. All seemed right in Abby's world, except for the niggling doubt that Tom Dodge is the actual killer.

As they walked, Abby's thoughts shifted to Clay. How bold Clay had been to invite himself along on her outing with Kat after Abby had briefly mentioned it. She'd talked him out of it that morning in a phone text, placating him with a promise of a home-cooked meal . . . soon. If Clay were to move back to the farmette and continue to be generous with his money, it would take the edge off her financial situation, at least for now. Still, Abby chafed at the idea of needing Clay's help. She wondered whether or not to broach the subject with Kat and finally decided to go for it.

"You'll never guess who has walked back into my life . . . Clay Calhoun. Can you believe it?"

Kat turned and looked at her, wide-eyed. "Oh, no. I thought you'd never see that man again. So what's his story?"

"Not clear."

"Never is with him. Surely he's told you where he's been and what he's been doing?"

"Nope."

"What do you want to bet that he's jobless now? Or he's had a breakup with whatever new woman he found after leaving you high and dry."

"I don't know," said Abby. "I'm just trying to be present with it."

"Take my advice. Don't let him get under your skin, girlfriend, unless you want to get hurt again."

"Yeah, yeah . . . I'm picking up what you're putting down, Kat." Abby believed Kat had her best interests at heart. If she didn't welcome Kat's input, she should have avoided bringing up the subject of Clay in the first place. "Look," said Abby, pointing into the yard where the estate sale was being held. "I see a gorgeous armoire."

Vintage furniture made up the bulk of the sale. Antique armoires, carved wooden headboards and footboards, along with cabinets, a chest of drawers, two desks, and assorted chairs, stood in one area. Banker boxes of books were lined up in neat rows on a threadbare Oriental carpet—a bargain at a dollar apiece. Bakeware, pans, lids, and assorted serving pieces were scattered about on several old tables. Lamps and other household bric-a-brac covered utility tables like the one Abby carted to the farmers' market on the first and third Saturdays during summer.

Kat made a beeline to a table that held old silver-plated serving pieces and post–World War II/midcentury curios, along with small collectibles, china, and sundry pottery pieces. Abby followed and asked the question that had been at the back of her mind on the ride up the mountain.

"You said the BOLO your peeps put out on Laurent netted him at SFO. So where was he going?" She picked up a deeply tarnished but otherwise lovely old pie server with a claw curve, decorative engraving, and a filigree handle.

"Where else? Port-au-Prince," Kat replied with a frown as she attempted to decipher a pitcher's pottery mark.

"Going home to Haiti. Figures." Abby laid aside the pie server and picked up a nineteenth-century opal-glass rolling pin imprinted with a poem. "You see this?" she asked Kat, who loved all things Victorian.

"Yeah. I'll pass. It's an old sailor's souvenir—a collectible for someone, but not me," said Kat. She spied a Devon cottage creamer. "Now, this is sweet. . . . Johnson Brothers. You got to wonder how Zora's mother came by it." A beat passed. "But I'd want it only if the sugar bowl came with it, and I don't see one."

Abby followed her to another table and watched as Kat plucked a bone china gravy boat with an ornate floral pattern to study. "This is nice, too." She turned the boat over in her hands. "Ha. I guessed it. Another Johnson Brothers. There is a crack in the handle and a chip in one of the blue flowers," she bemoaned, returning the item to its matching plate.

"So about Laurent . . ." Abby handed Kat a demitasse cup and saucer in the 1930s flow blue style. "Why hightail it out in such a hurry?"

Kat inverted the cup, as she had every other piece. "He said his mother had taken ill and the voodoo healing spells have not helped. But, of course, we know that he wanted to escape prosecution on a burglary charge." Kat pointed to a hairline crack through the center bottom of the cup. She set it back on the table, apparently not deterred from searching on.

"I'm insanely curious about what you found in his briefcase," Abby said.

Kat brushed a lock of her blond hair behind an ear and hoisted the straps of her empty cloth bag a little higher on her shoulder. "He didn't have a briefcase."

"But . . . ," Abby stammered. "I saw him toss a black briefcase into a green sedan before he drove off."

"No green sedan, either. We caught up with him. He was locking the doors of his old beater pickup and getting ready to board a bus from the long-term airport parking."

Abby frowned, confused. "So what happened to that green sedan?"

"He told us it belongs to a mountain mechanic friend, who loans him the car whenever Laurent schedules work on his truck. Apparently, he went to Fiona's store to retrieve his black zippered portfolio containing publicity photos of him and local bands. Thought her shop more secure than his apartment."

"Really?" Abby sighed heavily. "I *didn't* make a mistake, Kat. I know what I saw. And I think I know a briefcase from a portfolio."

"Of course you do. But we couldn't find the briefcase, and he's not admitting to even owning one."

Now thoroughly perplexed, Abby pointed to a framed tapestry. "Did you let him go?"

Kat looked over at the tapestry and made a distasteful face. "We couldn't hold him on burglary. He had a key to Fiona's shop and free access, he says. But he began to sweat when I asked him about his immigration status. So we've got him cooling his heels in a cell until ICE can interview him." Kat reached across a table of mismatched plates to retrieve a lavender-glazed teapot with a silver lid. Beaming, she handed it to Abby. "Speak to you?" Kat asked. "Fraunfelter with an Ohio stamp on the underside."

"It does," replied Abby as she pulled the round ball on the silver dome and the lid lifted, revealing a chain that held a four-cup tea-leaf strainer inside. "So cute. You seldom find these with the strainer and the round rubber ball that releases steam," observed Abby. "I'm sure it belongs to the twenties flapper era."

"So buy it," Kat said, apparently happy that at least one of them had found something.

"Well, I think I will . . . but it depends on the price Zora wants for it," Abby said. "You keep looking."

"I'll be over there." Kat pointed to the side of the house where stacks of framed art rested against an old wheelbarrow.

Weaving through the crowd with the teapot in her arms, Abby finally spotted Zora. The tall, thin woman in her late thirties wore gray slacks with a pale pink oxford shirt and a gray, hip-length vest. Over her outfit, she had put on a frilly strawberry-patterned apron with oversize pockets embellished with pink rickrack. She was counting out change for a woman who had just purchased a large chamber pot. Abby smiled, imagining how lovely a mass of purple petunias would look in that pot on a wide gray porch with white trim. Suddenly, a burly, balding man with a chair pushed in line in front of Abby.

Excuse you. What is it about yard sales that bring out bad manners? Rather than listen to him haggle over the price, she moseyed over to a bench that wrapped in a semicircle around the trunk of an ancient oak. Seated in the shade, she could avoid the pressing in on her by others and quietly browse the contents of a box that someone had placed on the bench. After setting the teapot down beside her, Abby picked up a book from the top of the stack in the box. She recognized it as a dust-covered volume of Culpeper's *Complete Herbal*. Absorbed in thumbing through the pages, she didn't see Jack Sullivan stroll up.

"Mackenzie, isn't it?" His tone conveyed no hint of the causticity that had characterized their last conversation.

"It is," Abby replied while assessing the handsome man with curly, brown hair streaked with threads of silver. She squinted up to see intense pale blue eyes gazing back at her. He wore tan cargo shorts with side pockets near the knees, a navy stretch polo, and running shoes with white ankle socks.

"Fiona's books," he said, looking at her intently.

"Seriously? You're selling them?"

He nodded and pointed toward Zora. "She dropped by yesterday. Said I could bring down to the sale whatever I was clearing out of the cottage. I'm afraid it all has to go." He paused for a beat and looked at her intently.

His warm, friendly demeanor perplexed Abby. It was certainly a different vibe from that of their last encounter.

"Listen, I know I made a mistake with you," he said. "Any chance we could put that behind us?"

Caught off guard by his sudden admission, Abby tilted her head quizzically, as though she hadn't heard him right.

"I'm not usually so high-handed," Jack said. He gestured to the open space on the bench on the other side of the box. "May I?"

Abby nodded.

He sat down, chewed his lower lip, as if trying to figure out how to engage her. "My thoughts seem to be duller and more muddled than usual since I arrived in your charming hamlet," he said, looking over at her. "I'm obsessing and not sleeping."

"Try a spoonful of honey in chamomile tea." Abby had hardly spoken the words before she wished she could call them back. An ethnobotanist would know the herbs that could help with sleeplessness.

He nodded. "Tried it. Under normal circumstances, it works. But nothing is normal now, is it?"

Abby shook her head. She considered whether or not to ask if he knew anyone who'd want to harm his sister as she watched Zora listening politely as the bald man argued over a fair price for the tufted armchair. Zora shrugged, and the man stomped off, leaving the chair for Zora to put back. Instead, she sat down on it. With no one else in line, Abby realized it was now her chance to ask the price of her teapot. She laid aside the book to stand. Jack spoke.

"I treated you shabbily," he said in a voice tinged with humility.

Abby sat back down. "Oh, forget about that. Completely

understandable," said Abby, her gaze darting between him and Zora.

"Accept my apology?"

Abby managed a feeble smile and nodded.

Jack continued, "You said you were Fiona's friend. Did you see each other a lot . . . ?" His words trailed off.

"Quite a bit. She was great fun. Always saw the bright side of things."

"That she did. I'll wager she set your ears afire with her stories." He blew a breath out through pursed lips. "Got that from our mother's brother . . . Quite the storyteller, he was." He looked as if he was weighing what more he could say. A beat passed, and sadness took over his features.

"Give yourself time, Jack. You've had a shock, and grief can be crazy messy and confusing. Even when you have prepared for a passing, it still leaves a hole in your heart."

His light eyes locked onto Abby's. He looked away toward the line of trees and wire fencing that hemmed the property. "You know what's bloody awful?"

Abby shook her head.

"I can't get a straight answer about how she died. They're saying maybe poison." His jaw tensed.

Abby spoke softly. "It takes some time to process the pain. Grief is like that. It's a sneaker wave that creeps in to wash over you. It takes you under. Then it brings you up again to an unknown place. All the while, you're gasping in despair." Abby swallowed. "But with time, the pain lessens, and your heart heals."

His eyes blinked as he stared at the ground. Finally, he looked at her with curious, questioning eyes. "You lost someone, too, didn't you? Whom did you lose, Abigail Mackenzie?"

She tensed. His question had triggered the old, familiar

ache. Hoping to reclaim her equilibrium, she searched for light amid the negative spaces in the leafy oak canopy. The conversation was one she didn't want to have.

"Family member? Lover?" He continued to probe.

Abby's fingers tensed around the edge of the bench. She wasn't about to confess to a total stranger that the reason she'd entered law enforcement could be traced back to the death of her younger brother during her first year in junior college. He had been visiting her over the Christmas holiday and had asked her to run errands with him, including a trip to the bank. It had been a blustery, rainy day, and she'd been baking cookies and watching Jane Austen's *Pride and Prejudice* on cable. She couldn't miss the ending of her favorite movie, so she'd declined his offer. There had been a robbery at the bank just before closing. Her baby brother had been in the wrong place at the wrong time. Becoming a cop had been a way for Abby to deal with her anger.

She shrugged off Jack's question. "Cops see a lot of grief."

Jack's gaze seemed piercing now. "Fecking senseless loss. How do you come to terms with it?" His voice cracked.

"Counseling," said Abby. "It's a process. Acceptance is the last stage."

As the ensuing silence engulfed them, Abby pushed down her sadness. She felt terrible for him and for herself and for everyone who'd cared about Fiona. Her hands sought something to do, and she reached for the book again. She stared at its cover while spurning the tears stinging at the back of her eyes.

Jack sniffed. He reached over and pinched the book's cover between his forefinger and thumb and opened to the frontispiece. "Fiona was so excited when she found this at a yard sale back in Holyoke. Mid-teens, junior year in high school, I think, and before the auto crash that turned our lives upside down. With our folks gone, we had to finish our growing up in the care of relatives in Boston." He turned the page. "She pinched the corners, wrote in the margins. If the book weren't in such terrible condition, it might be worth something. It's a first edition, nineteen forty-seven."

"Yeah?"

"Far older editions are still in circulation." He released the book into Abby's hands and leaned back against the tree trunk.

Abby thumbed through the pages, noting Fiona's underlining and pencil notations. Some seemed pointless, as if she'd been doodling in the margins, thinking about something else. The most common mark was a figure eight. Sometimes a cross or a *T*, and in other places the Aum symbol. There were astrological signs next to names. Abby searched for the photograph of a monastery garden laid out as a Latin cross. Not finding it, she stretched up and then relaxed her shoulders. What did it matter? She had the real thing, the herb garden that Fiona had created just for the farmette.

"Nicholas Culpeper," Jack said, "the author, was a physician and a botanist and also an astrologer. He wrote the first version of his *Complete Herbal* in sixteen fifty-three."

"Really?" exclaimed Abby. "Now, that would be quite the first edition to own, wouldn't it?"

He let go a mirthful laugh. "Culpeper's observations about the characteristics of herbs were extraordinary, but linking herbs to astrological signs and planets defies modern explanation. Of course, in his time, it was undoubtedly considered rigorous, muscular thinking, I suppose. I mean, the man searched for symbolism and linkage."

"May I ask you a question about that?" Abby turned to lock eyes with him.

"Certainly." He flashed a quick, mercurial smile.

"Do you know of any special meaning associated with the number eight?"

"Symbolism, you mean?" He thought for a moment. "Well, in the great religious traditions of the world, there's the eightfold path in Buddhism. Then there's the Jewish ceremony of the circumcision of a male child eight days after his birth. An eight-pointed star symbolizes Lakshmi, the goddess of wealth in Hinduism. And, incidentally, it is also the symbol of the ancient Babylonian goddess Ishtar." He paused to think. "In the early centuries of the Christian church, baptismal fonts were generally eight-sided. There's ample evidence of them in the walls of ruined churches throughout Ireland." Rubbing his chin, he added, "In botany, the genus *Coreopsis*, I recall, produces flower bracts divided into two series of eight."

Abby's eyes widened. A smile played at the corners of her lips. "And let's not forget there were eight maids a-milking in 'The Twelve Days of Christmas,'" she said.

"That too." He grinned. "And the eighth month in our calendar year is August, the month of the astrological sign Leo. In tarot, the Strength card."

Abby looked at him with wonder. "Holy moly!" He'd seen her innocent question as a challenge, and clearly, he didn't want to fail in meeting it.

"And in mathematics, an eight on its side symbolizes infinity, while in the Chinese culture, eight symbolizes prosperity. Shall I go on?" he asked.

"That's quite sufficient. How did you come up with all that right off the top of your head?"

Jack's grin grew deeper. "It is a little association game I play to remember things. Now I have a question for you."

"Shoot."

"Why are you intrigued by that number?"

"I see Fiona has drawn figure eights throughout the book."

"Is that so?" he said. "I hadn't noticed. Can't imagine why she would. But what say you keep this book? I'm pretty sure my sister would have wanted you to have something with which to remember her."

"Why, thanks," Abby said, cuddling the book against her bosom.

Jack rose and motioned toward Zora. "I've got to talk with her about handling these books and a bunch of other stuff. When I've completed the cleaning out of Fiona's cottage, I'll have to deal with the botanical shop."

"So you're going to sell the business?"

"Sadly, yes. I know how much she loved it." He took a step away before spinning around to face Abby. "There's no chance that you . . . well . . . Would you be interested in helping me go through all her stuff?"

"Sure, if you want me to." Abby wasn't about to pass up the opportunity to scrutinize Fiona's possessions for possible clues to her murder.

"She was a voracious reader," Jack said. "And a writer, too. I counted twenty-five journals, if you can call them that. People who keep journals mostly just jot down their thoughts. Not my sister. She stuffed hers with scraps of paper, letters, notes, feathers, found objects, bits of glittery things, broken seashells, all kinds of stuff."

"Just another reflection of her free spirit, I suspect," Abby replied.

His rugged features lit up at her positive spin on his statement. "You clearly understood my sister as others haven't. So when would you like to start?"

"Well . . ." Abby thought about her farmette work, her farmers' market obligations, and the promises she'd made to Clay. How much longer could she reasonably expect him to wait before moving back in? And if Clay knew she was planning to spend time with another man—even if it was for a good cause—might it not provide him a reason to leave again? *Oh, but why am I even thinking about that now?* Abby felt her forehead creasing into a frown.

Jack's facial expression darkened. "Look, I don't want to make any demands on the rest of your weekend," he said, "but how about Monday morning, say, nine o'clock?"

His tone made it sound like an entreaty.

Mustering courage, Abby replied, "Okay. I'll bring breakfast." Had that sounded too eager or forward? she wondered. Breakfast meant conversation, and she had a lot of questions for him.

"You can bring your dog, if you don't think she'll get in the way. I like dogs. I do. Sugar. That's her name, isn't it?" His thick brows arched mischievously; his pale blues widened.

You like dogs. Could've fooled me. "Wow. That's quite a memory," Abby said.

The breeze tousled his curly, brown hair as he leaned over to grip the box in his large hands and hoist it high into his arms.

"It's selective," he said with a wink and walked away.

Tips for Growing Kitchen Herbs in a Container

Plant seedlings of your favorite culinary herbs
in a terra-cotta pot with a saucer, a wooden box

filled with potting soil, or even a large bag of soil that you have made a rectangular opening in on one side. Maintain a regular watering schedule. Choose from any of the following culinary herbs: basil, chervil, chives, cilantro, dill, English thyme, French tarragon, lavender, lemon balm, lemongrass, oregano, rosemary, savory, and sorrel.

Chapter 9

Sweetened by sugar or salted by brine, a pickle
strikes a nice balance . . . unless the pickle's a
jam and you're caught in the middle.

—Henny Penny Farmette Almanac

Leaving sleepy Las Flores for the mountains on Monday, Abby looked forward to spending the day in Fiona's cottage, helping her brother pack her belongings. Last night, she'd told Clay she needed another day or two to stow things away and make room for his stuff. Surprisingly, he had accommodated her without too much protest, but he hadn't spared her his sad-faced Eeyore expression.

As for Jack, she sincerely wanted to lend a helping hand. Apparently, he didn't know a soul in town other than his sister and her estranged husband. But as Abby thought about it, she realized that sometimes in the most innocuous of settings and situations, one learned things. One little detail, overlooked at first, could sometimes break a case wide open. Abby took her time negotiating the Jeep around ever-higher curves until the fog abruptly yielded to sunlight. In the forest clearings, she observed the low ceiling of clouds still hanging over the valley floor. But once she'd pierced the gray shroud of fog, the sunlight of the mountains dazzled through canopies of towering blue-green redwood trees. The morning air carried the humid scent of pine sap, wild thyme, and decayed plant material.

At Dr. Danbury's big red barn, Abby turned onto the weedy gravel driveway and drove up to Fiona's cottage. She cut the engine and sat for a moment, wondering if she should have dressed more conservatively. It was going to be a hot day, and she'd chosen loose, cool clothes—a lacy black camisole and a see-through white cotton shirt with three-quarter sleeves. The shirt hung several inches over black cropped pants with side and rear pockets, in case she needed to stash a note or two for safekeeping. The only thing not color coordinated was the chartreuse bandanna around her shoulder-length red-gold curls. *But why am I thinking about clothing now, as if changing anything at this point is even an option?*

She glanced at the shed that served as Dr. Danbury's garage. The door had been thrust wide open. Inside, a partially covered, mud-splattered all-terrain vehicle, or ATV, had been parked at the rear, behind the spot where the doc customarily parked his Volvo. The Volvo was gone. Abby couldn't help wondering where the doc had gotten off to so early today. The other weather-beaten shed—the one closest to Fiona's cottage and where she kept extra stuff for her store—had a sturdy lock hanging from its latch. Abby grabbed the cloth bags of breakfast fixings from the passenger seat. She scooted out of her Jeep and strolled to the cottage door.

Surprised that the banshee door knocker was missing, Abby knocked three times before the door swung open. Jack, fresh faced, with his brown and silver curls bouncing in every direction, greeted her in bare feet. Wearing blue jeans and an unbuttoned white shirt with the cuffs turned up a couple of rolls, he seemed happy to see her and made a sweeping gesture for her to enter into the step-down living room. Light flooded the interior through the bank of windows offering a sweeping vista of green mountain ridges running north and south, parallel to the Pacific Ocean. Stacks of boxes awaiting assembly, bags of packing peanuts, and rolls of tape had been piled in a corner by the fireplace for the work ahead. The fragrance of freshly brewed coffee and the soft strains of Celtic music playing in the background created an ambiance that Abby liked. A lot.

"I've got eggs, herbs, an onion, a bell pepper, cheese, whole-grain muffins, and some andouille sausages," Abby said, hoisting the bags into his arms. "All I need is a frying pan, a bowl, and a wire whisk. In two shakes of a lamb's tail, I'll cook up breakfast."

"Sounds wonderful," he said, leading her to the kitchen and placing the bags on the rustic barn-plank table, which, with its ladder-back chairs, took up most of the room.

He finished buttoning the shirt over his exposed muscular chest and tucked the shirttails into his trousers. "What can I do to help?"

Everything about him seemed different—gone was the anger of their first encounter and the forlornness of their second. Today he exuded a quiet self-assurance. Abby could only speculate that the shock of his recent loss had morphed into acceptance of its undeniable reality.

In a voice exuding sweetness and warmth, she replied, "Could you empty the bags?"

"That, I can do," he said in a tone tinged with relief. "Holding my breath, I was, out of fear you'd ask me to cook something. I've eaten all the canned fish and devoured the box of crackers. Any more of that diet, and I'll be growing me feline fangs." His eyes shone with impish mirth.

Abby smiled back. "Someone's in rare form today."

"I finally got some sleep . . . and a hangover . . . to thank for it."

Abby reached for a spatula from a glazed crock of utensils on the counter and pulled opened a cabinet door. "Where can I find a bowl to scramble the eggs?"

"There." Jack pointed to the adjacent cabinet.

"So," Abby said, taking down a bowl, "what happened to the door knocker?" She gave him a sidelong glance. Faint laugh lines on either side of his blue eyes crinkled while he seemed to be thinking through a response.

"Just . . . well . . . gone." He reached into the bag nearest him and pulled out a carton of eggs and the hunk of cheese wrapped in plastic. After peeling away the plastic, he removed a knife from the set on the table, sliced off a sliver of cheese, and popped the piece into his mouth.

"Yeah? Where?" she asked, probing.

"Back there," he said, waving the knife toward the back of the house. "Or there." He pointed the knife in the opposite direction.

Abby set the bowl on the counter and gave him a bewildered look. "Well, which is it?"

"I suppose the landlord disposed of it when he cleaned up the broken glass." Jack chewed his lip like a small boy confronted over having been caught red-handed in some questionable act.

"Wait. What glass? I'm confused. The cottage door has no glass."

"Oh, right you are. So, it was the glass window at the back of the house."

Abby detected a bit of beating around the bush. "This

sounds like a fishy story, which you need to start from the beginning, now that you've hooked me."

"Heaved it, I did," he admitted, feigning a thick Irish brogue, "toward the East Coast, and I might have uttered a curse as I sent it flying." His face bore a sheepish expression. "Aye, and nearly ripped my arm from its pit."

Abby sucked in a breath. "Ohhh, so you tossed that pretty little knocker away?"

"That I did. The winds were howling something fierce, and there was nothing to slow the wailing over the mountaintop. But the gusting was to my advantage, or so I thought. Once thrown, the object would be carried by the wind even farther from me. The problem, I soon discovered," he said before pausing to swallow, "was that the wind was blowing directly at me. But I, being a wee bit tipsy, hurled that banshee with all my might. I could have sworn it was gone for good."

"Was it?"

He exhaled heavily. "Nay. She landed a foot away. But the Irish have a saying. 'He who isn't strong must use cunning.' So, I summoned my strength and hurled it in the opposite direction."

Seriously? Not only did he look like a leprechaun with that wild hair, but now he sounded like he'd kissed the proverbial Blarney stone. She resisted the urge to laugh out loud.

"I suppose 'twas then I heard the window shatter."

"Oh, no . . . Don't tell me." Abby put her hand over her mouth to hold back the laughter. "That door knocker was an art object, Jack. Surely you didn't believe it had anything to do with Fiona's passing."

"No, of course not." He continued in his affected dialect. "But I had a deadly buzz on. Opened the door for a little night air, I did. Then I spied it hanging there. It ignited my anger something fierce. I ripped it off and sent it flying away from the cottage. And then I picked it up and turned to fling it again. That's when the glass shattered, and the landlord came staggering out to ask what the bleep I was doing."

"What did you tell him?"

"What could I say? Out chasing ghosts? I didn't mean to break his window."

Abby leaned over the bowl and howled with laughter. "Oh, Lord, have mercy," she said after regaining her composure.

His deadpan expression shifted to a sly smile. He did a shoulder roll before laying aside the knife to reach into the other bag. He pulled out the mushrooms. "Ah, fungi. These will add flavor without the hallucination that some find so annoying."

Her laughter erupted again.

"Ever been to a fungus fair or foray?" he asked. "I hear that in California, mushroom connoisseurs engage in those sorts of activities."

"Well, I don't." Abby took the button mushrooms from him. "My luck, I'd pluck a basket of deadly toadstools."

"Or a psychoactive *Psilocybe* species with hallucinogenic properties," he uttered in a flat monotone.

"That too." She had expected a somber mood from Jack, but she found the unexpected display of humor rather delightful. However, it did seem strangely juxtaposed against the deep sadness she'd witnessed in his eyes during their first encounter. Abby understood only too well how shock and mourning could take all kinds of expression. Just because someone felt grief deeply didn't necessarily mean he or she couldn't experience moments of lightness and humor.

Laughter could serve as a counterbalance to the burdensome, at times unbearable, weight of sorrow. She liked this side of him—it was so very much like Fiona.

Jack took the bowl back, washed the mushrooms, and laid them on a cutting board for slicing. "These will taste great in the eggs," he said, dropping the accent.

"Absolutely," Abby said. "Especially with chives, parsley, and a teensy bit of English thyme. Just a little of each." She focused on chopping the herbs, along with the onion and bell pepper. Next, she grated a half cup of cheese. Removing the casings from the sausage took a minute more. She cut them into slices under his watchful gaze. "I'd ask you to beat the eggs, Jack, but with your sore shoulder from all that heaving . . . well, I'm happy to do it," she teased.

"I'll be in your debt for that," he said.

When the eggs were frothy, Abby made the omelet. "So, tell me, did Fiona always share your interest in plants?"

Jack set plates and silverware on the table. "Not in an academic way. Fiona loved edible garden plants and herbs she could grow and eat. I, on the other hand, harbored an interest in all kinds of plants in cultures, and how indigenous people use their plants throughout their lives in foods, medicine, and spirituality practices. That is the very definition of *ethnobotany*—my field of study." He tore two paper towels from a roll to use as napkins. "Fiona got serious about herbs after she suffered a bad reaction from taking milk thistle for a liver cleansing along with the allergy drug a doctor had prescribed for hay fever."

"Here in California, milk thistle grows wild like a common weed. So Fiona used it as a liver tonic?"

"Yes. She would often fast and cleanse. But after that adverse reaction, she was much more diligent, reading voraciously about herbs and never using them as tonics or medicine unless she understood their drawbacks, as well as benefits."

Abby turned off the burner. She cut the omelet in half with the metal spatula and slid the halves onto the plates.

Jack pulled a chair out for her and sank into the other one. "In fact," he said, "tradition holds you can use milk thistle in emergency situations involving poisoning by *Amanita phalloides,* the death cap mushroom. That's because milk thistle seeds have silymarin—a chemical that protects liver cells from toxins."

Abby held the whole-grain muffin in her hand in midair. "So, if Fiona knew that she'd come in contact with some toxin or poison, she'd likely know the antidote to take, right?"

Between forkfuls of omelet, Jack said, "Oh, yes. I think so."

"Unless she couldn't," Abby said, speculating, before she pinched off a piece of the muffin and ate it.

"Wouldn't that beg the question of why she couldn't?" he asked.

Abby nodded. "When we know that, I think we'll have the key to solving her murder." Abby washed the bite down with a swig of coffee. "Tom spent the night with her and left here early in the morning on the day she died. Would she have gotten up and made breakfast for him?"

"Of course," said Jack. "For Fiona, making a meal was a means to demonstrate love." Jack leaned in, as though sensing Abby was about to make a point.

Abby set the muffin aside. "On the day the cops found Fiona's body, this kitchen—in fact, the whole house, according to my sources—looked like a cleaning crew had just serviced it. Two people for breakfast and showers meant a kitchen to clean, a bed to make, and bathroom laundry and towels to throw into a basket or the washer. Someone cleaned up."

"It had to be Fiona," Jack answered. "She kept a tidy house." He forked a sliver of green on the edge of his plate and stabbed a piece of omelet, then ate it with masculine gusto.

"Suppose that makes sense. Did you know she was coming to have lunch with me on my farmette?"

He shook his head. "If she told me, I didn't remember. So you see, my memory *is* selective."

"Talk to me about poisoning. What kinds of poisons might she have encountered around the environs up here?" Abby asked, using her fork to break apart the omelet. She took a small bite, savoring the taste as she chewed.

"Well, around the cottage, most likely, the doc keeps pesticides, herbicides, fungicides to deal with weeds and pest infestations. Could be that there are several species of spiders, insects, snakes, mold, mushrooms, and all manner of plants, perhaps even some that possess powerful neurotoxins. Certain plants can exert a paralytic action or adversely act upon the cardiopulmonary system, causing stoppage of the heart."

"For example?" Abby eyed him intently.

"The death cap, for starters. Some say it took the life of the Roman emperor Claudius, although it is possible that eating a mushroom painted with a poisonous toxin could have done him in. The death cap has taken more lives throughout history than any other mushroom, but it's not quick. After ingestion, it could take maybe fifteen to sixteen hours to kill."

"What might someone ingest that would have a shorter action time?"

"You mean fast-acting plants?" He pursed his lips and blew air through them. "You've got deadly nightshade, monkshood, and hemlock, which killed Socrates. Let's not forget *Digitalis purpurea*, also known as foxglove. For generations, it's been grown at the back of flower gardens, but every part of the plant is poisonous. Its leaves look like comfrey leaves, which also has toxic properties. People who are allergic to foxglove could experience fatal ana-phylaxis. But I believe there would be signs of an allergic reaction to foxglove contact or ingestion."

"Like what?"

"Hives."

"I didn't see any hives on Fiona," Abby said, deciding to spare him the details about Fiona being clothed and burned, which had limited her view of Fiona's exposed skin. "If Fiona had ingested a plant poison, I think it would have had to be fast acting or at least have taken her life within the few hours given as the time frame for her death."

"Well," said Jack, "depending on the poison, the coroner or medical examiner might find traces of it in her body or possibly the by-products. Plant alkaloid poisoning, such as you might see in monkshood, could happen as quickly as within half an hour of ingestion."

"But wouldn't the medical examiner or coroner need to be looking for those alkaloids?"

Jack turned his gaze on her. "I couldn't say. Do you think someone used a poisonous agent to kill her?"

"My sources in the police department tell me they are taking a hard look at Tom as a person of interest," Abby said matter-of-factly. "Do you think Tom capable of hurt-ing her?"

Jack trembled slightly and shook his head in an immedi-ate denial. "Not the Tom I know."

Abby took a slow sip of coffee, giving him time and hoping he might elaborate.

"Fiona loved him, you know. Right up to the last. She

believed their marriage would work if he could just break his ties with the cult. I guess she saw something in him that he couldn't see in himself."

"What was that?"

"Fatherhood. Fiona wanted to start a family. I'm not saying there weren't issues."

Abby brows shot up. "What kind of issues?"

"Fiona tried to wrest Tom free from the clutches of the commune, which she said of late had become a cult. She told me they blocked her at every turn. But she kept trying. She told me that she thought they had changed tactics and had someone keeping tabs on her."

"Like a stalker? Did she say who?"

He folded his arms across his chest and stared off into space. "I don't know. Maybe more than one person."

"Did she ever mention the name Laurent Duplessis?"

"To her," said Jack, sipping his coffee, "Duplessis was a dalliance, nothing more. But I gather, to him, she was everything good about America. He believed they had a future."

"I'm sure he did." Abby reached for the pot and refilled Jack's cup before pouring the last of the coffee into her own. "So why was it so hard for Tom to break free from the cult?"

"Brainwashing and rigid rules. You are required to relinquish all your possessions, money, and all links to the outside world, except if you are making money, which you must give to the compound. Fiona couldn't bring herself to return to such a tight structure and swore she'd never raise a child there. According to her, they were grooming Tom. They had convinced him that he had the potential to be the new leader when the time came for the current cult leader and the commune manager to start new branches throughout the world."

"Do you mean Hayden Marks and Premalatha Baxter?"

"Yes, those two." Jack finished the last bite on his plate, dabbed his mouth with the napkin, and nodded. "I can't imagine Tom hurting Fiona. Kill the goose who lays the golden egg? What would be his motive?"

"Yeah. My thought, too. But maybe it was someone else who had the motive and some way to stack the deck against Tom. In effect, forcing him to kill," said Abby.

Jack shook his head. "No. I can't see it."

Abby wondered if he knew about the jewelry incident. She took a deep breath and watched Jack's expression closely as she broached the subject. "Tom was caught pawning their wedding rings and jewelry."

The color blanched from Jack's face. His eyes locked onto hers.

"You didn't know?"

He shook his head in disbelief. "That makes me sick." He leaned forward, rested his elbows on the table, closed his eyes, and pinched the bridge of his nose.

Abby said, "Hard to believe, I know. But it's true. I was there." She rose and collected the dishes, placed them in the sink. "I wonder if you might show me Fiona's garden. I've seen what she grows in front of the house, but she has a patch on the north side, right?"

He ran his hands through his hair and looked up. "Yes. It's lovely." After pushing his chair back from the table, he rose and strolled from the kitchen to the back door. "Mind the hole there." He pointed to an opening in the floor large enough for a child to climb through to reach the crawl space beneath the house leading to the rear of the structure. It was partially covered with a rug.

Abby sidestepped the hole. "I've been up here to see Fiona a couple of times and never noticed that hole. Wonder why Dr. Danbury hasn't fixed it." Abby let the back door slam behind her.

"Because of Paws, Dr. Danbury's cat. The good doctor would forget to feed and water the cat when he was drunk. At least, that's what Fiona told me," he said, leading Abby to a large area uphill from the cottage, fenced to keep out the deer. "Paws liked hanging out with Fiona, and why wouldn't he? There was all the canned fish in the world in her cupboard." He chuckled, holding up a large tree branch for Abby to pass beneath.

"I've yet to see that cat," Abby said.

"The cat wasn't the only creature to enter through that hole, either." Jack leaned down to unwire the gate.

"As floor holes go, it's pretty large," Abby said.

Jack wrestled open the garden gate. "Finding a lizard in her shoe," he said, "freaked Fiona out. Another time, a chipmunk found its way in and raced around the house until Fiona got it to go back out through the hole."

Abby smiled. Leaning down near a row of parsley, she plucked a green leaf and chewed on it. "So Fiona took in strays of all kinds, not just humans?"

"That she did."

Fiona's garden had clearly reached it apogee, evidenced by the riotous color of both sun-drenched and shade-loving plants—the latter protected by two apple trees with thick, stubby trunks on the garden's southeastern axis. In the full sun, crimson climbing roses sprawled over the wire fencing, while sunflowers dazzled with their bright yellow blooms.

Pointing to a stand of colorful hollyhocks, Jack asked Abby, "Did you know that evidence of *Alcea rosea*, or the hollyhock, was found in the grave of an early human—a Neanderthal dating back some fifty thousand years?"

"No, I didn't know that." Abby enjoyed his ability to

pull out—seeming out of the blue—facts about common plants, as it enriched her experience of being in the garden with him.

"Foxglove blooming right on schedule . . . late May," she said, pointing to the purple and white blooms atop four-foot spires along one side of the fence. "And just look at those delphiniums," said Abby, "just beginning to show color. They're gorgeous."

"And deadly," Jack said. "Seeds and very young plants, if ingested by cattle or other farm animals, are highly toxic."

"And over there, feverfew!" exclaimed Abby. "I love its daisy-like flowers, always so cheerful. And chives, bee balm, and lots of herbs I don't recognize are growing along that row there."

"Just point to them, and I'll tell you what they are," offered Jack. He stood near a narrow footpath. With green shoots poking up everywhere, it looked like the others Fiona must have tried to weed without success. As Jack strode the narrow paths, he began to point out to Abby various plants, calling out their Latin names, as well as their common ones. "Fiona favored the old heirloom perennials and open-pollinated plants," he said. "She liked seed saving, because plant diversity all over the planet is shrinking with every generation, and she wanted to do her part to save some of these old favorites, which soon will be gone forever."

"Well, I believe she was right about species loss," said Abby. "It also happens to be my philosophy."

He stopped and turned to look at her. "I see why my sister liked you so much. Fiona may have been, as you say, a free spirit, but I detect an independent spirit in you, as well. I like women who know their minds, blaze their own trails. I'd love to see your garden."

His proclamation had taken her by surprise. Abby hoped

her expression revealed only her amusement and not her concern that it could be awkward for her if Clay was present. But despite her misgivings, she heard herself say, "Sure."

They returned to the house. Jack wrote out his cell phone number and, grinning, handed it to Abby.

Abby felt a subtle ripple of excitement. She plucked the paper from between his fingers and tucked it into her back pants pocket. "We'd better get to packing," she said.

The morning hours quickly passed, and by the time Abby glanced at the clock over the fireplace, her stomach was growling. It was nearly four o'clock. They hadn't eaten since breakfast, unless you counted the stale nuts, crackers, and cheese that had fortified them as they sorted, cleaned, wrapped, and packed each room in turn. Fiona's books had been carefully placed into boxes, and the boxes labeled with the word LIBRARY printed with a black felt-tip marking pen. These they had stacked behind the front door. She had counted out the items in Fiona's dish pattern and had noticed only one cup missing, while the remaining dishware and extra pots and pans had been wrapped and tucked into boxes for Jack to decide how to dispose of them. Fiona's clothing and shoes had gone into bags for the women's shelter and had been piled along the living-room window. Perishable food items and toiletries had gone into garbage bags. Jack would go through everything else when he had the time.

Abby stood and stretched as the CD of Portuguese fados finished. She had listened to the music of the world: country tunes, Peruvian pan flute, Urdu *ghazals*, folk music, Hindi devotional *bhajans*, movie scores, and Gregorian chants. Fiona's eclectic musical taste was nothing short of amazing. Who but such a free spirit could feel inspired by music spanning such diverse traditions and cultures? And Jack seemed to enjoy it, too. He had chosen to spend his life in a discipline that would take him to diverse cultures in the world as he studied plants and their uses. Had they both received some exotic gene in their makeup, or had they been influenced by someone in their formative years? Abby made a mental note to ask him.

Picking up a towel to fold, Abby gazed at Jack, who stood in the kitchen doorway with glasses of iced tea. She put down the towel and sank onto the couch. He handed her a glass and stretched out next to her to sip from his. After catching sight of a picture among family photos scattered about on the floor, he picked it up and stared at it. In a field, a boyish-looking man embraced a young, dark-haired woman who was attempting to tuck a dandelion flower in his hair. The sun seemed to be rising and casting its warmth and glow upon them.

"She met Tom," Jack said, his voice cracking, "at the Wash and Dry in Boulder Bluff. It's where she landed when she first came to California. She was in a group of women who shared a vision of living a more spiritual life apart from religious dogma. They learned to be midwives and herbalists and earth mothers in every way. It was her journey, and try as I might to dissuade her and point her toward a real education, she stayed with that group."

"Marching to her own drumbeat," Abby said after swallowing a sip of the tea. "You have to admire her for that."

"By their expressions, you can tell they are in love, can't you?" Jack asked.

Abby stared at the image and nodded. "Yes, seems so."

A moment of silence ensued. Jack swallowed several sips of tea and then announced, "I want to see Tom. Is he in jail or at the commune?"

"Easy enough to find out," Abby replied.

"I have to ask him," Jack said. "I have to know." His tone sounded resolute. He impaled her eyes with a soulful gaze. His expression appeared full of strength and determination.

She nodded in agreement.

"You take her journals. See if you can learn anything. Before we put Fiona in her eternal resting place, let's you and I face him. I will know if he's lying."

Abby looked up to meet his gaze. "I do hope so, Jack."

Tips for Creating Drama in a Garden of Flowers

- Color: Plant drifts of plants with blooms in the same color for maximum impact.

- Paths: Create paths from pea gravel, stones, packed earth, or another material that meander into secret sitting/viewing areas. Or use the paths as linear elements in formal gardens.

- Statuary and Garden Art: Choose garden art or statuary that finds resonance with the type of garden you are creating. For instance, use whimsical pieces in cottage gardens and regal pieces in parterres or other formal garden designs.

- Surprise: Tuck a tea table, a whimsical element, a stunning mosaic birdbath, or a fountain in a hidden place, to be discovered by visitors to the garden.

- Theme: Consider a theme-oriented garden. For example, include plants with red and orange blooms to symbolize seduction, plants with white blossoms to represent purity and peace, or plants with flowers in primary and secondary colors to symbolize impressionism.

- Tiers: Use the three-tier approach to plant height: place the tallest plants in a bed to the rear, those of medium height in the middle, and the smaller bedding plants at the front.

Chapter 10

Don't be tempted to put eggs in your pocket if
you're passing by the henhouse in your
bathrobe. Forgetting about those eggs could
add an hour of cleanup to your workday.

—*Henny Penny Farmette Almanac*

Woman, get a move on!

Abby read Clay's text message twice. A sense of indignation and fury brought a flush to her cheeks. Clearly, Clay felt pissed. She should have expected it. Their plan had been for her to take him from the Lodge to the farmette at some point in the late afternoon. She hadn't known that the work of packing up Fiona's cottage would take so long. When Abby had realized how tardy she would be, she had done the decent thing and had sent Clay a text with an apology and a new ETA of 6:30 or 7:00 p.m. at the latest. And that home-cooked meal might have to be a midnight supper, but what did it matter? He could just cool his jets. Her day, however, would be exhausting and long. Why was she welcoming Clay back into her life when he was already making demands on her? What was up with that?

After a deep breath, Abby put the phone down and tried

to breathe away the tension she felt. Her being late was becoming a pattern when it involved Clay. Was it a message from her subconscious to face her fears about starting up again with him? She did love him, but they shared a painful history, and a lover once wounded was forever changed. He had scarred her heart. The way she saw it, his emotional interior remained impenetrable, in spite of what he'd said about being unable to live without her. Now he would be in one of his dark moods again.

As her damp palms clenched the steering wheel and adrenaline pumped through her body, a twinge of anger drove her foot against the gas pedal. She felt the Jeep respond as she navigated into the passing lane along the straight section of the road back to town. She wasn't speeding, but she'd been driving faster than usual after turning from the mountainous spur road onto the highway. She hoped that a deputy sheriff or one of Las Flores's finest wasn't hiding in the thick blooming acacia along the roadway. From writing tickets back in the day, she knew all the places where the cops could radar while remaining half hidden; accordingly, she braked before passing each one. The sunset was still a couple of hours off, but what did it matter now? Clay would still be hungry. And she would still be late.

Sorting through Fiona's personal items had proven to be a daunting task, more so than either she or Jack had anticipated. They'd lost track of time while organizing and packing up the cottage. When she had realized she'd be more than an hour late meeting Clay, Abby had sent the text. His terse reply had seemed irascibly impatient. But as she thought about the day she'd just spent with Jack Sullivan, the anger and frustration fell away. She couldn't recall the last time she had laughed as hard as she did, in fits and spurts, at his unstoppable witticisms and funny stories. Perhaps her company and his use of humor had somehow helped him get through the otherwise somber task of sorting through his dead sister's possessions.

The hours had passed quickly, and they'd tarried far too long as they examined the small treasures Fiona had collected: clipped articles, pictures, strange found objects, and religious paraphernalia. Abby glanced over at the box of journals now resting in the passenger seat. Jack didn't have time to go through them, but he thought someone should, instead of relegating them to a bonfire, lest they contain information helpful to the murder investigation. And Abby had been only too happy to take them.

She slowed the Jeep to the posted twenty-five miles per hour after taking the Main Street exit. From there, she drove straight to the shelter. Someone had hung the CLOSED sign on the front door, so Abby continued around back. After spotting a large empty bin, she came to a stop, climbed out, dumped the black plastic contractor bags of Fiona's clothing and household items, returned to the car, and headed straight to the Las Flores Lodge.

Eight minutes later, she pulled into the driveway and spotted Clay pacing the wide stone veranda. His computer bag rested near the front steps. He trudged past a potted fuchsia on leaden feet, his hands thrust deep into his jeans pockets, a scowl creasing his forehead. When his expression brightened upon seeing her, Abby felt her tension evaporate.

"Hi, handsome," Abby called as he dashed toward the Jeep.

After hopping in, Clay tucked the computer bag behind the seat, buckled up, and heaved a long exhale. "Finally! I've got the appetite of a grizzly for that home-cooked meal you promised."

"I'll get right on that," Abby said, thrusting the gear into reverse and turning around the Jeep. "Just as soon as

I feed the dog, check on my bees, and lock the chickens in for the night."

"I see how it is!" he exclaimed. "In order of importance, I'm dead last."

Abby shook her head. "Seriously? You didn't just say that."

"Well, I'm growing weary of no wheels, those four walls where I'm staying, and the air conditioner humming twenty-four/seven. If I turn it off, all I hear is traffic and the sounds of the town. I'm a country boy at heart, Abby. I'll be the first to tell you, I'm looking forward to shutting off the alarm and waking up beside you to the call of that rooster of yours. What's its name?"

"Houdini." Abby merged into the traffic on Las Flores Boulevard, heading northeast toward Farm Hill Road.

"So named because?"

"He was herding my hens through a hole in the fence, trying to make a run for the border."

Clay chuckled. "I see. Taking his women with him. Smart guy." He adjusted the seat to accommodate his long legs and leaned back. When Abby braked for the red light at the intersection of Main, he unlatched his seat belt, leaned over, and planted a sloppy kiss off-kilter on her lips.

"Hey, that'll get you arrested, mister. I'm trying to drive here," she said.

"It's still there, woman. I can feel it," he declared in a jubilant voice while reattaching his seat belt.

"What's still there? What are you talking about?"

"Love. You still love me."

"Oh, *really?*" *You can't possibly know how I feel when I'm not even sure myself.* Although Abby wanted to call him on his tendency to jump to conclusions, she also realized this wasn't the time or place. She wrinkled her nose at him instead.

"I'll wager you've been thinking about me all day, haven't you?"

Abby recalled her day with Jack. *If only you knew! How is it I never noticed just how maddeningly full of yourself you can be, Clay Calhoun?*

He continued, "Because I've thought of nothing but you today. Ever since I woke up and remembered. Still can't figure out why you didn't stay awhile after that smooch."

She looked over at him momentarily, arching her brow with interest. "It was a good night kiss, Clay. You knew I had to get back. And besides, you didn't feel well." Admittedly, he looked kind of cute and sexy today. He'd gotten his dark brown locks shorn, probably that morning, while she'd been up at the cottage, helping Jack. With the cowlick and sideburns gone, Clay's equally dark brown eyes, lashes, and brows dominated his features.

He flashed a dimpled grin. Before she could say anything more, he added, "All I can say is that you're a good kisser, you little seductress."

"Yeah?" Abby tried not to show her surprise. She hadn't seduced him. He, however, seemed to be the one on a relentless pursuit. But it was nice he'd remembered their kiss even after drinking the better part of two bottles of wine. Had he also recalled how much of a struggle it had been to climb the front steps of the Lodge? Or to get through the lobby and to his room with her five-foot-three-inch frame as his only support? That hadn't been sexy. But in a moment of weakness at his door, she'd yielded to passion. To say she hadn't enjoyed it would be lying. But clearly, he'd read a lot into it.

After a pause, he said sheepishly, "You need me, Abby.

Haven't I been punished enough? I want to leave the dog-house."

Abby chortled. "I wouldn't characterize the Las Flores Lodge that way. The facility has lovely rooms and all the amenities anyone could want."

"But it doesn't have you."

"True," Abby said. "I've just been busy, and I wasn't expecting you to visit. I have all the bed linens to wash and groceries to buy. That reminds me. I ought to make a stop at the feed store to get more crumbles and scratch grains for the chickens. Not only that, but also some ground corncob for the henhouse floor, which I first have to clean, and then there's—"

"Now you're just being silly." His tone grew soft and serious. "We have done this before, Abby. I can lighten that load you're carrying all alone. I want to help. I want to be with you."

And how long would that be exactly? Abby thought about that line used by Bernie, who worked in the evidence room at the police station. *I'm here for a good time, not a long time.* Her stomach tightened. She hated having doubts about Clay. But always at the back of her mind, the same old question drummed on: how to fall back in love and trust again after a betrayal.

"I see I'm going to have to woo you again," he said. He leaned back and closed his eyes. "Well, that's okay, Miss Abby Mac."

A smile toyed at the corners of her lips. He'd used his pet name for her. In the early days of their love affair, he would come into the farmhouse at night from whatever project he had been working on and call out, "Miss Abby Mac, I'm home." Then he'd act like he'd been working at some forklift plant all day and missing her. He would take her into his arms, snuggle his face against her neck, and tell her how much he had missed her. Remembering those moments felt like a balm on an old wound. It put to rest, if only momentarily, Abby's self-torturing doubt.

She focused on driving the last stretch of Farm Hill Road, deep in thought about clearing space on her calendar to accompany Jack to a jailhouse interview with Tom. She was about to mention her busy schedule to Clay when he broke the silence with a declaration of his own.

"I've made arrangements to have my truck shipped from the East Coast. It arrives at the farmette next weekend."

Abby didn't try to hide the shock her expression surely must have registered. "You did what? Aren't you getting a little ahead of yourself?"

"Why put off the inevitable? I'm ready. You're ready."

"I haven't said that."

"You didn't have to. Your kiss last night said it all."

After they'd arrived at the farmette, Abby declined Clay's offer of help with the chickens. Still peeved, she pointed him to one of two lidded garbage cans on the patio, where he'd find Sugar's dry food. Her water and food bowls would need filling. Then he could help himself to some tea from the pitcher in the fridge and amuse himself while she dealt with the hens. Following that, she'd make dinner. And he'd just have to wait until she was good and ready!

As she walked toward the henhouse and the chicken run, a racket overhead impelled Abby to look up. Large black crows flew in an erratic back-and-forth, straight-line pattern, as if trying to drive away some threat hidden in the towering pine tree. She strained to see what had gotten the crows so riled. Then she spotted it—a hawk with a wingspan of maybe four feet and a seven- or eight-inch reddish tail lifted off a tree limb. It swooped straight across the farmhouse, rose up high above the chicken run, and alighted in the aged, gnarled oak that rose majestically on the vacant wooded property behind Abby's.

"Whew. That was close, ladies," Abby said, approaching the gate of the chicken run. "And thank you, Houdini, for rounding up the girls and bunching together like little frozen statues. I don't believe that a hawk can penetrate the hole in the poultry-wire ceiling of the run, but all the same, I'll put Clay to work on it tomorrow."

Suddenly, she didn't feel so miffed at Clay. If she played nice, he might prove useful in banging out some of the projects, like the chicken run and the bee house, which she longed to complete but never seemed to have enough time to do. She poured a helping of scratch grains from the twenty-five-pound bag into a large pottery saucer on the ground and checked the hanging canister of food. Still half full. After dumping the stale liquid from the water dispenser, she listened momentarily for its refilling with fresh water.

Clay met her as she crossed the lawn to the patio, where the strains of sultry jazz floated across the evening air. "We always had music playing, regardless of what we were doing. You remember, Abby?" He reached out to her and pulled her close, kissed her hair. "We are good together."

Abby's guard went up, although she wasn't entirely sure why. This was what she'd wanted, wasn't it?

Sugar left her bowl of nuggets and bounded across the yard, then jumped on Abby with a happy *yip, yip, yip.* Abby pulled back from the embrace and knelt to hug the dog. When she stood up, Clay had walked to the fence and was staring into the deserted wooded acre behind Abby's farmette. Although food preparation was the last thing on her mind, she walked to the kitchen and grabbed a pot from under the counter and started water boiling for pasta. After setting out the olive oil, pine nuts, and parmesan cheese, she inserted the blade in the food processor. She dashed outside to the patio herb pot to pluck a handful of fresh basil to add to the other ingredients. With the pesto made and the pasta still bubbling away, she washed some organic tomatoes and then sliced the tomatoes and fresh provolone for a Caprese salad. From the cupboard above the counter, she pulled half a loaf of sourdough bread, which would pair well with cultured butter flavored with fresh basil and garlic and made less than a week ago. It was simple fare, but just the kind of home-cooked meal Clay would enjoy.

Clay plugged in the twinkle lights that Abby had strung around the partially framed patio. Her dream was to one day turn it into a screened-in room that allowed light and air in, while keeping out flies, bees, and mosquitoes. But until then, it afforded a place away from the hot kitchen in the cool night air without having to flip on the outdoor lights mounted on the wall.

"I have a confession, Abby," Clay said in a serious tone. He twirled the pasta on his plate around his fork.

"Another one?" Abby asked, leaning back against the patio chair cushion. "So, go on. . . . I'm all ears."

"I've ordered lumber. The local DIY guys will drive it out in the morning."

"Here?"

He snorted, "Where else?"

"Lumber? For what?"

"The master bath."

"How could you know what to order when you haven't taken measurements?"

"Who says I haven't? That first day, when I brought the tools out here and waited for you in the house, I borrowed your new measuring tape."

"Oh . . . Will these surprises of yours never end?"

"It's part of my master plan," Clay said with a broad grin. "Get ready for this place to transform."

Transform, huh? Your master plan? What about mine? Abby mustered a polite grin and pushed back her plate. Leaning back against the chair cushion, she listened intently to the chorus of peepers and crickets. Perhaps their sound could drown out the voice inside her head that complained about him moving too fast. She searched the deepening violet sky for the early evening star as Clay began to spin a spell, talking through his ideas for the bath but never once asking for feedback or her opinion. She knew any plan he conceived would be an improvement on that nasty, cheap shower enclosure around the chipped tub, but why hadn't he asked her what *she* wanted?

Empowerment could take many paths, and maybe this was hers. Although it had been a long time coming, she was beginning to understand that passion could carry them only so far. Before their romantic love could become an enduring bond that could last a lifetime, there had been an abrupt rupture. And the great irony was that during Clay's absence, she had found stability from learning to trust the surest voice around her . . . and it had emerged from deep within her being. Now that selfsame voice sounded a niggling doubt that she could ever be a dutiful wife waiting for her man to come home after another of his far-flung trips.

When he got up and pulled her to a standing position to kiss her, Abby mustered a generosity of spirit, rationalizing that if she could allow herself to relax into his embrace, her misgivings might evaporate. The sweet moment ended almost as it began when Clay began swatting at the mosquitoes puncturing his bare forearms.

"Our cue to go inside, I guess," said Abby.

"You want help rinsing the dishes?" Clay picked up her plate and put it on top of his and then loaded the silverware and glasses.

"Nah. I'll do the dishes. You relax."

"Couch or bed?"

"Suit yourself."

By the time Abby had finished the dishes, made a cup of green tea with roasted brown rice, and locked the sliding glass door to the patio, Clay had fallen asleep on top of the coverlet. Clothed only in his underwear, he had stretched his tan body across the middle of the bed and was tangled in the sheet. Abby retrieved the laptop at his side and briefly noted the screen display of bathtubs. After turning off the laptop and placing it on the floor, she paused to look at how Clay's body curved against her bed pillows and sheets. Just like in the old days. All she could think about over the past year was his coming back to her. Here he was. But her desire to crawl in next to him was weaker than her desire to read Fiona's journals. She padded barefoot away from the bedroom, with Sugar trotting right behind her.

Abby sank onto the oversize leather couch with her cup of tea. She reached for the journals, an eclectic mishmash of styles, colors, and shapes. From the dates inside the journals, Abby soon figured out the chronological sequencing and put them in order. Some of the journals were plain composition books with lined pages, like those used by high school students. Other journal covers sported elaborate designs, perhaps appealing to Fiona's imagination. Scanning the first of them, Abby realized that the disparate artwork on the journal covers found resonance in Fiona's cursive ramblings. She had written some passages in a careful cursive, while scribbling others. In the earliest journals, Fiona had kept a record of her meditation practice. She wrote about how the teachings of different gurus jibed or conflicted with her Catholic upbringing. Through her inner spiritual experiences and analysis, Fiona had unwittingly charted the intellectual and spiritual contours of her mind.

> *I feel the surge of energy in my spine, at my heart. Then my throat. My body spins. Awareness expands. I'm on the ceiling, then turning, facing down to look upon my body. How strange that I am there, as a body, but also here, as the mind. Who is it that sees me?*

Abby swallowed the last of her tea and set aside the cup. She grappled with Fiona's ideas of duality, not sure why it mattered so much. A gentle breeze stirred the long copper tubes of her harmonically tuned wind chime. The notes sounded peaceful, like a spiritual hymn. The breeze grew stronger, entered the open screened door to caress Abby's arms and legs. By lamplight, she read on.

Abby realized that Fiona's yearning to be fully present in her life as a spiritual being—equally at home in the in-visible and the visible world—lay nakedly exposed across her handwritten pages. For a moment, she felt conflicted about continuing to read. Fiona would not have wanted her life dissected, as cops were obliged to do when working to solve a murder. And although exuberantly free-spirited, Fiona probably would have balked at having her sacrosanct journals combed for clues by others. Thinking about putting aside the journals, Abby reminded herself that the search had to be done by someone. That being the case, Fiona likely would have wanted the reader to be a friend.

Abby meticulously thumbed through the pages, then suddenly stopped. She ran a finger under sentences in a section about a seer who foretold a bright future for Fiona. Elsewhere, she read about Fiona's desire to make sense of her dreams. She read, too, about instances when Fiona's inner vision collided with physical reality.

I pray and meditate today, as usual, in the big blue paisley chair next to the window. I feel the bliss of the religious rainfall Samadhi. It feels strong. My resistance diminishes the bliss. It eventually subsides. Dr. Danbury's other cat, Clea, is pregnant. I've been feeding her, and now she climbs into my lap. She starts birthing her babies. I get up and put her on the towel in a box behind the couch. New life . . . a beautiful thing to witness.

Abby lost herself in Fiona's world as page after page of entries revealed the restless spirit of a woman who refused to live her life on the train tracks of habitual routine and mindlessness. During the last three months of her life, Fiona had written about relief at ending the dalliance with Laurent Duplessis; her deepening love for her husband, Tom; and her fear that someone wanted to harm her. The anxiety showed up in entries posted at all hours of the night, some of them about nightmares with dark imagery. Fiona had clearly tried to extract meaning from them. Tucked into those pages, Abby found a brown wool scapular bearing the face of Jesus. Making a mental note to give it to Jack, she thumbed through the next few pages and found papers that had been shredded. She realized after reassembling them that they were the divorce papers Fiona had never signed. On the last page of that journal, Fiona had written the date of the Friday before the weekend she

died. In the margin was the numeral eight and snake figures. *He's setting me up. I know what's going on now, and
I have proof.*

Abby turned the final page and found a key taped to the
inside back cover. She stared at it, speculating about what
it might open. Seeking answers, she'd found more questions. Now she was stumped. Her neck ached. Eyes were
tired. She laid aside the book and reached for the soft
blanket draped over the couch. Pulling it over her, she
turned off the table lamp.

Before her mind's eye, a bizarre gallery took form—images of Fiona's inner circle. The snake that Fiona had interpreted as a dream symbol of deceit and betrayal had
figured prominently in more than one dream. Abby wondered what could link the partial tire track, the smoker's
nicotine patch, Fiona's necklace, Laurent's missing briefcase, the journal notations of a snake, the number eight,
and that key. She stifled a yawn, knowing that she needed
to let her brain rest, if only for an hour. Perhaps things
would become clearer after the sun came up.

Tips on Cleaning Eggs to Sell

Don't dunk dirty eggs in water and wash them.
You'll remove the bloom, the natural coating
that prevents bacteria from entering the eggs.
Instead, do the following:

- Rub the shells with a dry cloth to remove poop
  and other debris.

- Use a pot scrubber, a loofah, or a sanding sponge
  to gently sand off dirt, debris, or poop.

- Or dip a clean cloth in warm water (20 degrees Fahrenheit warmer than the temperature of the eggs) and wipe the eggs clean.

- Avoid submerging the eggs in water or allowing them to stand in water. Instead, try briefly spraying the eggs with water and then wiping clean.

Note: Clean eggs that are commercially refrigerated at 45 degrees Fahrenheit and 70 percent humidity will keep for about three months. In a standard refrigerator with less humidity, the shelf life of an egg is about five weeks.

Chapter 11

Two roosters will not a harmonious henhouse
make.

—Henny Penny Farmette Almanac

The one-room post office adjacent to the police station smelled of paper dust and a lemon-scented disinfectant from a recent mopping of the green tile floor. Abby wrinkled her nose and walked straight to the wall of mailboxes to retrieve her business mail, hoping that the stench wouldn't hang on her white blouse and navy blue crop pants. When her key failed to release the box-locking mechanism, she soon realized why. She had taken Fiona's journal key from her daypack's zippered pocket instead of her mailbox key. Using the other key, she removed the mail—most of it junk—from the box before closing and locking it. Abby tossed the circular ads and discount cards in the large corner recycling bin but held on to the bee catalog she'd requested from a Sacramento-based company.

Leaving the post office, she noticed the attention-grabbing catalog cover. It featured a completely assembled painted hive with ten top bar frames, metal frame rests, an inner cover, and a lid—all for the unbelievable sale price of eighty dollars. A completely assembled and painted hive box for under a hundred bucks? No way. Something must be missing! She glanced up at the pedestrian walk light, which gave her the go-ahead. Abby stepped into the crosswalk and stole glances at the catalog cover as she made her way to the other side of the intersection.

A car horn blared. Tires screeched. Abby's hand flew out for balance and hit the hot hood of an approaching car. Adrenaline rushed through her. Her heart pounded. In a single movement, she clutched the catalog to her chest and gripped the shoulder strap of her daypack in order to race across the intersection.

Only after the champagne-colored BMW Alpina B7 started to roll forward through the intersection and turn onto Chestnut, where Abby stood at the corner, did she see the driver. Premalatha Baxter and her passenger, Dak Harmon, glared at her, as if the incident had been Abby's fault. Had they been carelessly speeding? Or had they tried to scare the wits out of her? Abby took a deep breath and shrugged off the incident. With murder on her mind, as it had been of late, she could be overreacting.

Except for her friendship with Fiona, Abby's dealings with the commune people had been minimal. She'd just as soon keep it that way. But she couldn't help wondering how anyone in that commune could afford a car that cost in the neighborhood of over a hundred grand.

The BMW rolled along Chestnut, toward the commune-owned Smooth Your Groove, with Abby watching and trying to shake off the tension her body still registered. After sliding the catalog into her daypack and zipping the daypack shut, Abby hitched her pack over her shoulder and set off again. Her cell phone vibrated in her pants pocket. It had to be either Jack or Kat replying to Abby's earlier texts. From Kat, she wanted to find out if Tom Dodge had been arrested, as reported, or simply detained for questioning. And from Jack, she wanted to know if he could help her figure out what lock Fiona's journal key might turn.

Glancing at her cell phone's screen message, Abby felt the dark energy from the near accident lift as she read Jack's short text: **See you in a few**. Abby kept a watchful eye on the parked BMW until she approached Lemon Lane, where she turned right. No harm in taking a look at the shops facing Main Street whose back doors opened onto Lemon Lane. That was where the delivery truck, vendor, and hired help activity took place. Fiona's shop, now shuttered and locked against the likes of Laurent and anyone else, held the most interest for Abby. She saw no one around Fiona's shop. But at the rear of the other shops, the activity was as brisk as that at the entrance to a beehive illuminated by the first rays of morning sun.

On the approach to Tilly's Café, the seductive scents of pancakes, maple syrup, bacon, and fragrant coffee drew her inside. She waved to Pedro, the short-order cook, who was slaving away over an egg scramble on his commercial grill. He lifted his spatula in acknowledgment as she claimed a counter stool and dropped her pack onto the adjacent seat for Jack. She didn't have to wait long for him to show. Within five minutes, the bell on the front door jangled. Abby looked up and felt a lurch of excitement as Jack strolled toward her.

He seemed in a cheerful mood, calling out with an affected Irish accent, "Well, look at you there. How are ya?"

Abby smiled. He seemed to enjoy speaking with an Irish brogue when in a good mood. Or whenever it suited him.

The twentysomething waitress grabbed menus, sauntered over, and plunked them down on the gray Formica countertop. She turned over the coffee cups. Pushing back a tuft of pink hair that had slipped over her ear, she asked Abby, "Know what you want?"

"Just orange juice for me," Abby said.

"I heard that," Pedro called out. "No harvest pancakes and scrambled eggs? I know you love them."

Abby laughed and called back, "Oh, yes, I do, but I cooked eggs before I left the farmette this morning."

Jack stared at the menu. Damp and loose curls in a halo of light brown clung to the sides of his face and his forehead. His whisker stubble further accentuated his angular cheeks and nose, making him look like a rugged sailor.

Definitely eye candy, Abby thought. She tried to gauge the waitress's reaction to him, but the girl was all business.

"Your order, sir," the waitress said.

Jack laser focused his baby blues on the face of the pink-haired waitress. "Something with a wee bit of elixir, if you'd be so kind. The stronger the kick, the better."

"Seriously," Abby said, shaking her head. "And what about breakfast?"

"Well, if you insist," he said with a sly grin. "A pint of plain will do. Rich in cereal, grain, yeast, and alcohol."

Abby arched a quizzical brow.

"What?" he asked with a broad grin. "It's got your four main food groups, plus some extra benefits!"

Tapping her notepad with a fake fingernail, the waitress seemed to lose patience. She raised a pencil-thin brow and said, "We don't serve alcohol here. You might try the Black Witch, a few doors down."

"He's teasing," said Abby.

Jack continued grinning. "Now, don't you be losing patience with me. I'll just be having what she's having," he said, with a nod to Abby.

"So . . . two glasses of orange juice?" A defiant brow arched as the waitress scribbled the order.

"Hang on." Jack winked at Abby. "Aye, and the breakfast special . . . a feller needs filling up after living on tins of salmon, sardines, and crackers for days." Winking at Abby again, he explained, "Getting sick of cat food."

The waitress cocked her head. "So you're changing your order from just juice to the special now?"

"Indeed." Jack seemed to enjoy annoying the young woman.

The waitress exhaled heavily and walked over to give Pedro the grill order.

Jack reached for Abby's pack with one hand and grasped her elbow with the other. A warm shiver from the touch of his hand on her arm sent Abby's thoughts spinning and her heart racing. *This is just silly. Stay focused, and get a grip.*

He guided her to the last table at the back of the room. "She'll find us," he said, cocking his head toward the waitress. "Here it's a little more private for us to talk," he said in a serious tone, devoid of the accent.

Abby laid aside her pack and took a seat.

When Jack pulled a chair out from the table, the chair legs screeched over the ceramic tile flooring, and Abby flinched. Her thoughts flashed back to the crosswalk incident. Her nerves jangled; her stomach churned.

"Can you believe those commune people nearly picked me off in the crosswalk?" Abby's face flushed with heat.

"What do you mean?" Jack's eyes expressed alarm as he dropped her pack on the floor next to her chair and took a seat. "When?"

"A few minutes ago. I had the green light to walk and was in the middle of the crosswalk. She had to see me."

"Hold on," said Jack. "You know the driver?"

"Yes. Premalatha Baxter, the commune manager. She was with that gorilla, Dak Harmon, the leader's bodyguard.

The commune business must be turning a nice profit for her to be driving a brand-new BMW."

Jack leaned in, his expression dead serious. "Why would you be on their radar?"

Abby blew a puff of air between her lips. "I'm guilty of being friends with Fiona and with you. You are Tom's brother-in-law, and he's one of them. So as far as I can tell, that's it. Well, unless being inquisitive is an affront to them. I do ask a lot of questions."

"My advice, if you want it," said Jack, "is to cut that Premalatha a wide berth."

Abby nodded.

"So your text said you had found a key," he said, leaning back into the chair.

Abby nodded and reached in her watch pocket, then placed Fiona's key on the table. "Taped to the inside cover of one of Fiona's journals. Any idea what it unlocks?"

Jack turned it over. He stared at her, seeming baffled. He shook his head.

"At first I thought it might go to a post office box." Abby fished out her mailbox key and dropped it next to the journal key. "See what I mean?"

"Yes. They're quite similar." Jack's gaze was riveted on her face and then moved beyond the keys on the table to the open collar of her white eyelet-trimmed blouse.

Her fingers flew to the blouse's undone top button. Abby's cheeks burned. "What about a safety-deposit box, like at a bank or a credit union?" Abby asked, hoping she might shift his attention.

"It's possible, I suppose." His expression registered faint amusement, but he stayed on topic. "But which bank and which box number?" Raking his hands through his curly locks, he said, "Maybe Tom would know."

"That's what I thought. Next point . . . who gets access

to a box in a financial institution? As Fiona's husband, Tom is her next of kin, barring a surviving parent, which doesn't apply, since your parents predeceased you both. And she bore no children, right?"

"Right."

Abby looked up as the waitress arrived with their glasses of orange juice. Before continuing, she waited until the young woman had departed for the area where Pedro plated the food. "Do you know if your sister made a will?"

"The police asked me about that," Jack said. His pale blue eyes locked onto hers, and for a millisecond, Abby felt a slight shiver of pleasure. "In her original will, Fiona left everything to that old teacher from India and his organization. But then, when the old man left and Hayden Marks took over, Fiona told me she was quitting the commune life. A year after starting her business, she told me she'd revised her will."

"Oh, I'll wager the homicide team would want to see that . . . find out who stands to gain financially from her death."

"They asked me for it."

"And . . . ?"

"I would have given it to them if I knew where to find it." His long, tapered fingers rubbed the stubble on his jaw. "We didn't find it in the cottage. We both know that. Was there no mention of it in her journals?"

"No." Abby leaned in, tilting her face slightly up toward his. "If we could locate the box this key fits . . ."

"Maybe we'd find the will." Jack's tone sounded conspiratorial.

"Except for one inherent problem." Abby sighed.

"What's that?"

"Let me lay it out. Let's say Fiona had a safety-deposit box where she banked. A bank employee could open the box and look for her will. That's good. The banker would try to determine whom she named as executor of her estate. That's good, too. If Fiona named you, you would get access to that box. But here's the bad news. If it's not your name, but someone else's, most likely, the bank would try to contact that person."

"What if they can't find that person or he's in jail?"

"You might need to consult an attorney. I'm not an expert, but I think the bank employee would most likely turn the contents of the box over to the county probate clerk."

"So, we need Tom's help?"

"Yes, I think we do." Despite her churning tummy, Abby finished her juice and leaned back in the wooden chair. "Jack, can you think of anything else about Fiona's life? During her last days, did she fall out with anyone, like an acquaintance or a business associate? Can you think of anything at all that might have bearing on the case?"

Jack chewed his lip in silence, apparently mentally parsing the details of his sister's last days and weeks of life. His pale blue eyes drilled into Abby, although he seemed unaware of it. Still, Abby felt energy, like a whisper, passing between them. Her grandmother Rose, who had had a rich and imaginative inner landscape, would have counseled Abby to notice it without naming it. Naming something would confine and narrow the scope of it. But even as Abby's thoughts whispered, *Fiona*, her hands grasped for the cool Formica tabletop. A beat passed. She reached for the keys.

Jack snapped out of his reverie, took the keys from her hands for a final comparison. Then, pressing both keys back into her palm and cradling her hand in his, he said, "You know, I talked with Tom by phone right after I learned of her passing." He choked up, hardly able to utter an intelligible word. "He asked if I could handle the burial if he chipped in some money. He said he just wasn't up to dealing with it. And one more thing . . . ," Jack said, with his eyes narrowing. "Tom told me he felt responsible, but wouldn't say why."

"Not exactly a confession," Abby said, only too aware that Jack was still holding her hand. She gently pulled away from his grasp and slipped the keys into her pants pocket.

He downed his juice and set the glass on the table. "I don't think Tom would hurt an ant, and certainly not Fiona. What I can't fathom is why he'd try to pawn her jewelry. Why can't the police eliminate him as a suspect? And why— if he knew anything at all about that key you found in her journal—did he not mention it to me during our phone call?"

Abby absentmindedly tapped a fingernail against the table surface. "Fiona pretty much penned the narrative of her life in those journals. Toward the end of the last journal, she wrote about her foreboding sense of doom, her nightmares, and moments of extreme anxiety. It appeared that she had panic attacks, without knowing why or seeking help. I suppose, put into perspective, all her observations could add up to a premonition of her death." Abby breathed in a shallow, quick breath to push away the raw emotion she felt.

Not a minute later, she remembered the scapular. "Oh, jeez, I almost forgot," she said. She unzipped her pack, fished out the religious item, and handed it to Jack. "I found it in the same journal as the key," Abby said, zipping the pack and dropping it onto the empty chair beside her.

After dabbing his mouth with his napkin and laying it aside, Jack took a close look at the scapular. He smoothed the strings connecting the two square pieces of brown wool and just stared at it.

Seeing his eyes fill with tears, Abby looked away. She watched as the pink-haired waitress across the room arranged plates of food on a tray, picked the tray up, and started walking toward their table. The young woman set before Jack a steaming plate of scrambled eggs, a bowl of fruit, a side of sausage, a platter of pancakes, and a serving of toast. Jack sniffed and cleared his throat. He slipped the scapular into his pocket.

"Enjoy your food," said the waitress, before sashaying away to grab the coffeepot and head to another table.

"I should have warned you that they serve large portions here." Abby chuckled.

He said, wiping his eyes with his napkin, "Good. All I need are some bangers and beans to make it a true Irish breakfast."

Watching him first devour the mixed fruit and then a slice of toast, Abby said, "You know, Fiona was never going to divorce Tom. I found the papers, which she'd torn up and tucked inside a journal. Do you suppose Tom knew?"

Jack nodded and helped himself to a forkful of sausage and egg. "Like I said, in the end, they may have chosen different paths for the life that each wanted to live, but they loved each other. Of that much, I'm sure."

The bell on the restaurant's front door jangled. Abby looked up to see Otto Nowicki, in his blue uniform and black boots, his shiny silver star on his chest, heading to the counter. After waving him over, Abby watched as he changed course, making a beeline to her.

"Gotta say, Abby . . . you must have a good reason to be hanging here at our café when you've got all that healthy food at your place," Otto remarked.

Abby smiled and presented an open palm toward Jack. "Otto, this is Jack Sullivan, Fiona's brother."

"I know," Otto replied. "Mr. Sullivan and I have already met." Otto extended a thick pale hand, which Jack shook vigorously.

"Of course you have," Abby said.

Pulling out a chair for Otto, Jack asked, "Have you arrested my brother-in-law, Tom Dodge?"

"*Detained* is the word. For questioning," Otto replied, eschewing the chair.

"But I heard on the radio that Tom has been arrested," said Abby.

"That's the local media for you. Rushing to a headline, they beat out the competition. We haven't charged anyone. Nor is an arrest imminent."

Abby looked at Jack, knowing how much he wanted his sister's killer to be found and locked up. The dejected look on Jack's face could have chilled the butter pats on the hot pancakes. Jack put down his fork and stared at Otto.

"What did he have to say," Abby asked, gently probing, "about pawning his dead wife's favorite necklace and jewelry? He had to know that would look suspicious."

"He did. And it was," Otto answered. "But not illegal. He said his wife had given them to him in case he ever needed money. He wanted money now for her funeral." Looking at Jack, Otto said, "I asked you, sir, if this was true. As I recall, you said it would not be unlike your sister to give him the jewelry. And you also said he'd told you he needed help with the funeral expenses."

"And both statements are still true," Jack said.

"So you detained Tom but didn't arrest him?" Abby asked.

Otto wrapped a thumb around his duty belt. "Yep. But we requested copies of those pawn receipts from the jewelry shop owner. As for Tom Davidson Dodge, we've cautioned him to stick around. I assume he's back home by now."

"You mean up at the commune?" Abby said in an attempt to clarify Otto's statement.

"Yes." Otto shifted his attention from Abby to Jack. "I want to let you know, Mr. Sullivan, that there'll be a couple of our guys in plainclothes keeping an eye on things at the funeral. Okay with you?"

Jack nodded.

Abby pushed back a lock of reddish-gold hair from her forehead and once again straightened the open collar and tugged down the eyelet-trimmed sleeves of her blouse. "A quick question before you go, Otto. I'm trying to reach Kat. Is she working today?"

"If you call patrolling the fairgrounds work."

Abby chuckled. "Of course. I forgot she was pulling that duty. I'll catch up with her there. It'll give me a chance to find out if any of my jams and honey did well in the competition."

"You do that, Abby." Otto turned away and ambled over to a table where he could sit facing the room.

"Doesn't he like our company?" Jack asked.

"He's not unsociable," said Abby. "If he eats here alone or with other cops, he'll get a free meal. The owner likes having cops around, and cops like to sit with their backs to the wall. Call it self-preservation. He's in uniform, a clear target for cop haters and killers on the loose, even in a small town."

Tips for Keeping Roosters and Hens Safe from Predators

- Bury the bottom of a poultry-wire fence around a chicken run about eight to twelve inches to deter foxes and raccoons.

- Weave a poultry-wire ceiling across the top of the chicken run to thwart attacks from above by hawks and eagles. A poultry-wire ceiling also keeps chickens from flying out of their protective zone.

- Running a double layer of poultry wire around the chicken-run fence can keep foxes and raccoons from tearing through the fence and attacking the chickens.

- Use a strong, heavy-duty poultry wire that is 2.0 to 2.5 mm thick for best results.

- Electric fencing works, too, as a deterrent to wild predators; however, it must be incorporated into the fence at the top and the bottom. This is not a good option if there are children and pets on the property.

- Always lock your chickens in the henhouse for the night.

Chapter 12

The sixteenth century had its own version of
smoothies: smoldering passions were cooled by
drinking water sweetened with honey, sprinkled
with florets from lavender buds, and spiced
with cinnamon, nutmeg, and cloves.

—*Henny Penny Farmette Almanac*

"Hold up there, daddy longlegs!" Abby exclaimed.
She and Jack were strolling along the sidewalk on
Lemon Lane, the short paved street that ran between the
fenced play yard of Holy Names parochial school and the
rear entries of the shops that faced Main Street. The key
she'd found in Fiona's journal had piqued her curiosity,
prompting Abby to suggest that she and Jack visit his dead
sister's shop. With his hemp-colored cargo shorts swinging
around muscular legs and his moss-colored T-shirt pro-
claiming his activism with the slogan MY LIFE DEPENDS ON
PLANTS, Jack, with his elongated strides, had Abby speed
walking to keep up.

"Do you think you could slow the pace a bit?"

Jack turned to look at her, as if not fully registering what
she'd just asked. Erasing the thoughtful, brooding expres-

sion that had claimed his unshaven face, a slight grin emerged at the corners of his mouth and widened into an impish smile.

"Where did you get those long legs?" asked Abby.

"Well . . . we can't all be little people," Jack jested in his affected Irish accent. "Blame it on my gene pool."

Abby smiled. "Was your father tall?"

"Ha! No taller than a rasher of pork-belly bacon stretched full out. But Uncle Seamus, my mother's brother, now he was the fir in our family of fruit trees. With uncut hair and his tweed cap on, he stood five feet, eight inches tall. And that was barefoot in his boots. He was fully an inch taller than the rest of our clan in Sneem."

"Sneem is a funny name. Is that near where you grew up?"

"No, but I have cousins there. A river splits the village into two parts, and relatives of mine live on both sides. One side sits nearest to the North Atlantic coast, and the other looks toward the Macgillicuddy's Reeks, Ireland's tallest mountains. Sneem is a pinprick of a place but, in my estimation, one of the loveliest in the world. We might come from what was once a village, but those of us in our tribe who are short—not me, of course, but the others here and afar—make up in attitude what we lack in height."

Sashaying sideways to avoid colliding with a wall planter, Abby lost her balance. Jack caught her and held her steady in an embrace until she pulled away. Her heart hammered erratically. *Thank you for blocking my fall. I'm not reading anything into it. Let's just keep moving.*

Even after they had resumed walking toward Fiona's shop, passing Cineflicks and Twice Around Markdowns, Abby still felt flustered. She pulled the shoulder strap of her daypack a little tighter and muttered, "Such a klutz. I can't believe I didn't see that. I could've smashed in my nose."

"And what a shame that would be," said Jack. "I rather like that nose, especially the freckled bridge, which looks as though the fairies have dusted it. And those eyes . . . the color of the sea along the Cliffs of Moher."

So, this silver-tongued devil is flirting with me. Best to ignore it. But Abby was beginning to think that his playful demeanor and overt flirtation could crumble the resolve of even the most stalwart woman intent on resisting him. His flattery made her nervous.

Abby mustered a feeble smile. There were a lot of things she wasn't sure about, but one thing she knew for certain: it would be a bad idea to flirt with Jack, even if he'd started it, because they soon would be alone inside the shop. One thing could lead to another, complicating and confusing the well-defined parameters of their current relationship. And she already had invited Clay back into her life. No, this was business, and they would keep to it. As they neared the shop's back door, she considered what she could say to tamp down any amorous intention he might harbor.

"You know, Jack, I mourn the loss of friendship with Fiona. Your sister was beautiful, smart, accomplished, and one of the funniest women I have ever met. She lifted self-deprecation to a high art, often remarking about how light-weight she was."

"Aye, lightweight and short, that Fiona. Served her right for refusing to hang with me from the backyard oak or drink water from the secret well in the woods."

And there's the accent again. Charming, to be sure. But do you not know I'm trying to be serious here? It occurred to Abby that Jack's remembering his and Fiona's youth helped him with his grief.

"And she refused to sample the ale Cousin Jimmy brewed in his basement." Jack's grin accentuated the deep dimple creasing the left side of his face.

Abby locked eyes with him. His look warmed her to her toes, weakened her knees. *Oh, good Lord. Seriously?* She reached out to the stucco wall, then ran her hands the six inches to the back door. Avoiding his gaze, Abby wondered if he felt it, too. She promptly changed the subject and injected a serious tone. "Speaking of secret places, I can think of only three things in Fiona's shop with keyed locks. Two of them are file cabinets, and the other is her desk drawer," Abby said. "I'm hopeful, though, that we might find something the key unlocks and, even more importantly, whatever she's hidden that Laurent Duplessis sought when he tossed the place."

Jack slipped the key into the back door keyhole and turned it until the mechanism released the lock. "You could just ask him."

"I'll get right on that," Abby replied. "Just as soon as we find him. Last I heard, he was being detained for a chat with immigration officers. They might have deported him, or if he managed to clear things up, he could be in Haiti or still around here. That said, I haven't seen him lately, but I'd sure like to know what he was looking for that he thought he could hide in that briefcase of his."

"I'll wager he was shoplifting while he was searching for whatever had gone missing."

Jack pulled open the door and motioned for Abby to pass. She flipped the light switch to the on position. The music started. Abby stared at the room's disarray. Files and papers littered the floor, the cabinets, and Fiona's desk. Jack swore under his breath. He picked up a book from the desk and returned it to an empty slot in the bookcase.

"I want to find that guy. All I need is about eight and a half minutes," he said.

"To do what?" asked Abby.

"Beat him into a brisket and whack his cabbage," said Jack.

"Seriously?" Abby tightly clamped her jaw and stared at him. If it weren't so funny, it would be sad. How could an otherwise intelligent man believe that a round of fisticuffs could fix anything?

Stepping from behind Fiona's Queen Anne desk, with its inlaid leather writing surface partially covered by files, Abby took note of the cut-glass bowl of peppermints wrapped in cellophane and the old-fashioned Rolodex. The latter seemed incongruous with the tech world of nearby Silicon Valley. She inserted the journal key partway into the lock of the desk drawer. When it didn't fit, she opened the drawer and searched it. Maybe there was a secret compartment, like the ones Kat would sometimes locate in period furniture whenever she and Abby went antiquing. After searching the drawer, Abby knelt and felt around underneath, but soon surmised that Fiona's desk had no such secret hiding place.

Jack walked around the small office, picking up folders from the floor and slapping them against the desktop. He fumed, "All heart, that Fiona. And just look at the jokers she attracted into her life—idiots, ne'er-do-wells, and Duplessis, who epitomized them all." He picked up another pile of folders from the floor and dropped it alongside the stack on the desk. Glancing at Abby, he quickly added, "But among her associates, you, Abby, were the exception."

"Duly noted," Abby said. Her attention flitted around the room, from pieces of furniture to a wall calendar hanging near a collection of nature photographs in cheap black frames. A dinner plate–size wall clock hung above a tall metal filing cabinet that stood between the wall and the doorway that opened into the showroom. She tried the file cabinet lock, but the key didn't fit in that lock, either.

Jack plucked a peppermint from the bowl on Fiona's desk, twisted and peeled off the wrapper. Popping the candy into his mouth, he pointed to a small credenza supporting a multifunction printer. "There's a keyhole we haven't tried." He held out an open palm, apparently indicating that he wanted Abby to give him the key, as though with a different hand, it might unlock something.

Abby walked away from the tall filing cabinet and handed him the key. After opening and closing each of the credenza drawers, Jack squinted at the lock and tried the key. It didn't fit. He then scanned the room for anything else with a lock.

"You've got to wonder why she had locking cabinets and drawers when she didn't lock any of them," said Abby, strolling to the credenza.

"Maybe she wasn't the only person with access." Jack passed the key back to her. He peeled away the cellophane from another mint.

After pocketing the key, Abby pulled open the credenza's top drawer and took note of its three separate compartments. She then thumbed through business payables, IRS documents, license renewals, liability insurance, employee records, tax returns, and a massive file of legal documents. Leafing through the legal material, Abby recalled a comment Jack had made to her when they first met. Maybe now was the right time to ask him about it. She glanced over at him. Apparently having decided to eat the whole bowl of mints, Jack had plopped down in Fiona's chair. He was hunched over the bowl.

"These candies are seriously addicting," he declared. His face remolded into a sheepish expression.

"Listen, Jack," said Abby. "I've been wondering about something. That day when Sugar and I showed up at Fiona's cottage, you accused me of being a reporter and said you'd had to protect your sister from small-town reporters in the past. Why? What had she done that required summoning her big brother from far-flung ports of call to protect her?"

His brows knit in a pained expression. "Accusations . . . mostly."

"Of what? Against whom?"

"A woman died," he said, crushing a mint between his teeth. "But it wasn't Fiona's fault. She was just . . . there."

Abby rolled her eyes. Clearly, she was going to have to wheedle the story out of him. "Jack, please."

He peeled away the wrapper from another mint as meticulously as if he was removing a floret from a lavender bud. Finally, he said, "Fiona was living in a community in the foothills of the Sierras, learning about herbs while serving as an apprentice to a local midwife. She worked there as a doula."

"A what?"

"Doula, a labor coach. No medical training, but in every other way assisting before, during, and after the delivery. She said the midwife used herbs in her practice to induce labor or ease the pain of labor, herbs that have been used and deemed safe for centuries."

"All very interesting," said Abby. It truly was, but how had the woman died? And what did that death have to do with Fiona? She glanced over at Jack just as he finished unwrapping yet another mint. He popped it into his mouth.

"So . . . what happened?"

"Well, that's about it."

"Well, a woman died, Jack, so there must be more to it," Abby said, no longer trying to hide her frustration. After stepping away from the credenza, she reached over to retrieve the bowl of mints.

Jack made a tsking sound. "The woman had the baby, but . . . then the trouble began."

"Tell me. I'm all ears."

Jack sighed. "It bothers me to talk about it."

"I can see that," Abby said, deciding to try a different approach. She flashed a disarming smile, leaned in toward him, and gave him back the bowl.

"I can't be seduced that easily," he said, with a wink.

Abby straightened her back, put her hands on her hips, and shook her head.

His pale blue eyes focused on her. "The labor was long. It was the woman's first pregnancy. Only pregnancy." Jack cleared his throat, picked up another mint, thought the better of it, and dropped it back into the bowl. "The baby had turned the wrong way in the womb. And it had grown too large to fit into the birth canal. The midwife was trying everything she knew, but the husband and the woman's mother called an ambulance after twenty-two hours. At the hospital, the doctors performed a C-section and saved the baby. The mother suffered a brain embolism. Fiona felt devastated. Of course, everyone did. A few weeks after the birth . . . well, and death, Fiona and her midwife friend were sued by the deceased woman's family, who claimed they should have sought medical intervention, instead of waiting for the frightened family to do it."

"Oh, my gosh. How terrible for everyone involved," Abby said. She walked back to the credenza and removed the drawer. Kneeling, she guided her fingers around the inside top lip, as she'd often seen Kat do.

Jack heaved a heavy sigh. "The deceased woman's family lost the suit. But that didn't stop them from trying Fiona in the court of public opinion. It was an act of God and nobody's fault, but they continued to contact the media and to make it open season on Fiona and the midwife."

"And that's why Fiona ended up here?" Abby tried to angle her arm up and inside the credenza to continue her search.

Jack nodded. "She had heard that Las Flores had a commune in the mountains above the town. She wanted a fresh start. And she needed new friends. So she took the Ryan name and continued working with herbs. She never looked back."

"Found something," said Abby as her fingers felt a ridge. Unable to make out the object, she reached for her daypack and removed a small flashlight. She turned it on, and the circle of light revealed a business envelope taped to the credenza's top underside. "Eureka!"

Jack jumped up and hurried to her side. "What is it?"

"Dunno yet." Abby's stomach felt the flutter of butterflies. She tugged at the tape securing the envelope and then pulled the envelope out before laying aside the flashlight.

"Open it," Jack said.

"No, you do it," said Abby. "Better that a family member does it."

Jack slid a thumbnail beneath the envelope's top flap and eased it up. He pulled out a folded piece of paper and another key, which looked to be identical to the one Abby had found in Fiona's journal.

He handed Abby the key and she stuck it in the same pocket that held the other key.

She read the note. Cocked her head to the side and frowned. "Well, this is strange."

Jack stared at her, waiting for her to explain.

"See here?" She pointed to a sequence of numbers. "One. Nine. Seven. Five."

Jack considered the numbers in silence for a moment. "Hold on . . . That is her birth year."

Abby continued, "And below those four numbers are letters. *E. L. O. H.*"

"It's not a word, is it? What are we to make of that?" asked Jack.

Abby studied the paper. "Perhaps it's a password with four letters and four numbers. Although, using your birthday as a password is never a good idea." Her brow furrowed. "It could also be a mnemonic. You know, like FCGDAEB. Fat Cats Go Down Alleys, Eating Bread."

Jack stared at her as if she'd lost her mind.

"Letters of code. In that particular mnemonic, each word stands for a note in the order of sharps in music. The word *Fat* stands for F sharp. *Cat*, for C sharp. And so on. There's a mnemonic for flats, too."

"So the fact that there is a sequence of numbers, code that must be deciphered, and an identical key can only mean what?" asked Jack. He stared at her, fingers across his mouth, as if to keep from diving into the bowl again.

"Beats me," said Abby. "But it suggests that Fiona might have hidden something and then devised the memory prompt so she'd know where she hid it. She cleverly concealed the prompt so no one would find it or the item's location. It's rather elaborate. Where would she get an idea to do such a thing?"

Jack ran his fingers through his hair, leaving it tufted near the crown. "We used to pretend as kids that we were spies. We made up secret words and codes."

"And that suggests something else," Abby said, pursing her lips. "Your sister apparently could trust no one. When she called me, she needed advice but didn't want to talk about it over the phone. But instead of telling her I would be right there or insisting that she go to the police, I waited and planned a luncheon. By then, it was too late."

Jack's expression grew tender. "She never made it. And you've been blaming yourself ever since." He advanced a step toward her. Anticipating a hug, Abby got busy returning the flashlight to her pack.

Jack tapped his watch face. "I'm supposed to meet the priest at Holy Names in about ten minutes. We're going over last-minute funeral details. Come with me, Abby."

Abby felt she should protest that she had other things to do, but Jack's pleading expression made her reconsider. "Well, I suppose so, if it won't take too long. I'm working through a long to-do list today."

"I'll help," Jack said with a broad grin. "I owe you. But just one more little thing."

"And that is?"

"I'd like to see Tom sooner rather than later. Could we do it together after I meet with the priest?"

Abby began figuring out how to rearrange her schedule to accommodate his request. Could she still squeeze in seeing the DA about some part-time work, make it to the feed store to buy some calcium for the chickens, and pick up the extra nails for Clay at the big-box DIY? She sighed, "I suppose." Somehow, it would all get done; if it didn't, there was always tomorrow.

Jack locked up Ancient Wisdom Botanicals. They crossed over to the other side of Lemon Lane and turned the corner.

In a matter of minutes, they approached the gate in front of the Church of the Holy Names. Just as Jack opened the gate and stepped into the churchyard, Abby felt her phone vibrate and heard the ring that told her Kat was calling.

"Good to hear from you, Kat."

"Sorry it wasn't sooner," Kat told her. "We had a fracas at the fair. Cowboy poets were going at each other. Can you believe it? Hurled cobs of roasted corn and discarded cones of cotton candy from a Dumpster. They weren't playacting. And little kids were watching. Took a while to sort it all out, but we did. Anyhow, I got called back to the station. Where are you? What's up?"

"Surprised to hear you are working the fair when the investigation into Fiona's death is in full swing. But hang on a sec." Abby pointed to her phone, whispered Kat's name, and pointed Jack toward the rectory adjacent to the church, where the priest lived and maintained an office. She sank onto the bench positioned directly in front of a life-size statue of the Virgin Mary.

"Thanks for waiting, Kat. So to answer your question, I'm roasting on a hot bench in front of Holy Names, waiting for Fiona's brother to finish his meeting with the priest. And then we're going to see Tom Davidson Dodge. I thought you could tell me Dodge's whereabouts."

Kat replied, "As far as I know, he's up at the commune. And I'm at the service station, gassing up the cruiser. I'll swing by if you can hang tight for five minutes."

"Of course." Abby tapped the END CALL button and left the sunbaked spot in front of the Virgin to stand by the gate until Kat arrived. She found herself wishing she'd brought along her wide-brimmed straw hat for protection against the sun's searing rays. Just then, an ambulance siren wailed from the direction of Las Flores Boulevard. It grew louder on the ambulance's approach up Main, in the direction of Chestnut. When a series of short beeps told Abby the ambulance had entered the intersection by the post office, she resisted the urge to check it out, in spite of her impulse to find out what the emergency might be. Five minutes passed. Then ten. Abby wiped the beads of perspiration gathering across her nose. What was taking Kat so long?

Presently, Kat pulled up to the curb and climbed out of the cruiser with a water bottle. Abby noted droplets clinging to the vehicle's windshield and bumper.

"You stopped to wash the car?"

"Yeah, well, you know Chief Bob Allen's controlling nature, constantly worrying about the department's image as if it were his own. Cars have to be cleaned and gassed up. Uniforms pressed. Boots shined. Tasers and shotguns returned and locked up. I'm surprised he hasn't whipped out that tiny measuring tape on his key chain to check the length of our hair and fingernails. Next thing you know, he'll have us waxing our nightsticks."

Abby chuckled. "I feel for you, Kat." She motioned Kat toward a stone bench under an ash tree that provided shade. As they walked to it, Abby said, "I heard an ambulance pass. It sounded like it was headed down Chestnut. What's going on?"

"It's the smoothie shop. Dispatch took the call about a middle-aged man complaining of chest pain, nausea, and fatigue. Probably overheated," Kat said. She took a swig from her water bottle before sitting down with Abby on the bench. "So Fiona's brother is with Father Joseph?"

Abby nodded. "Planning a funeral is such a personal thing. . . . I thought it best to hang around out here until he's finished. Then he wants me to come along while he talks with his brother-in-law. Wants to ask Tom face-to-face if Tom knows anything about the murder."

Kat locked her baby blues onto Abby. "You won't be shy about sharing information if you learn something we don't already know, now will you?"

"No problem. Just tell me what you know." Abby grinned.

Kat made a contorted face. She smoothed a wrinkle from her uniform shirt and stretched out her long legs. "Well, I can tell you that as far as we're concerned, Tom's in the clear."

Abby frowned. "Even though he was with Fiona the night before and the morning of her death, and he has no alibi for the time of death, and he pawned her jewelry? How did you rule him out?"

"He passed the poly. He offered to take the test right away to eliminate himself as a suspect."

"Wish we could catch a break in this case," murmured Abby.

"We just have to keep digging." Kat sniffed and gazed philosophically out over the churchyard.

"So why were you working the fair?" asked Abby.

Kat removed her hat and ran her fingers through her sweat-damp blond tresses. "Why else? Chief Bob Allen said somebody had to do it. And Otto was planning to meet with a couple of San Jose homicide detectives to help us in Fiona's case." Kat took another swig from her bottle. "I would have rather met with those detectives, but I swear, Abby, the chief has got me on speed dial for grunt work. But if I complain, I'll get the horse poop detail until the fair ends. Pardon the pun, but that's not fair."

Abby smiled. She leaned against the bench back and stared at a lady beetle crawling across Kat's boot. "Oh, I hear you."

"And pee-yu, does that horse dung stink when you are downwind of it. I don't know what they feed those horses, but there are piles of manure everywhere. There's a ready supply, if you could use some."

Abby looked up and made a face. "*No.* That stuff is too fresh. Like a fine wine, poop has to age."

Kat laughed. "You didn't just say that!"

"On that acre behind mine, where the stone house is, the heirs had some guy come out last fall and dump a load of horse dung, apparently to keep down the weeds. This year, wild oats sprouted everywhere. The oats have turned from green to paper dry now, and my chickens love them. I'm no expert, but I do know some things about manure."

"It's a dubious distinction," Kat said with a chuckle. She glanced at her watch and stood up.

Abby rose, too. "In farming, like in detective work, Kat," said Abby, "you can't help but notice when you're knee-deep in a pile of crap. Know what I mean?"

Kat nodded.

A moment passed in silence as the downtown clock-tower bell chimed twice to mark the hour.

"Before you take off, Kat, I've got a question. Do you know of any reason anyone might want to run me down in a crosswalk?"

"Were you jaywalking?"

"Of course not."

"Catch a glimpse of the driver or the license plate?"

"Not the plate, but the driver, yes. Premalatha Baxter. And she had that creepy Dak Harmon with her."

Kat screwed the cap down on her water bottle. "He's an ex-felon with a rap sheet for assault with a deadly weapon. Personally, I can't see why a preacher or a commune manager would need muscle like that. Also, I can't see why you'd be a threat, especially to them. You don't have business with those people, do you?"

Abby's expression clouded. "Not much directly, but the smoothie shop buys my herbs and honey."

"I've heard they don't like people bad-mouthing their peaceful community," said Kat. "But you would never openly criticize their policies, now would you?"

Abby shrugged.

"So why worry? People fly up that ramp from the highway into town without slowing, in spite of the speed being posted. They don't pay attention. That said, be vigilant." She smoothed her hair and put on her hat. "What you and I both need is a girls' day out. With Clay back in your life—"

"Yeah, well, it's not the same anymore. You haven't told anyone about us, have you?"

"Didn't have to. Ours is a small town, Abby. Five minutes after he registered at the Lodge, it was all the gossip at Maisey's."

"Oh, great." Abby rolled her eyes. "I should've known the gossip mill would start spitting out speculation as soon as somebody saw him."

After walking Kat back to the gate, Abby gave her a hug. "So where's the evidence pointing you now?"

"We got an anonymous tip to check out the commune's businesses, in particular their financials. So we're sniffing around."

"Personally, I think that bunch has been led astray by a rigid idealist with a belief in a Bible-based utopia," said Abby. "Those commune residents have always been a hardworking bunch. But under the cultish leadership of the new guy, they seem more like a slave labor force turning over their paychecks to the guru. I can't imagine one of them killed Fiona. What would be the motive?"

"Well, she was pretty outspoken about that new leader

and the changes he has been making. Perhaps she rubbed someone the wrong way. Three days before the murder, Fiona was seen in the smoothie shop, arguing with Premalatha Baxter, who had authorized changes to the smoothie recipes. Fiona claimed that people might get sick and that Premalatha didn't have enough knowledge to be mixing things up like she was doing."

"Fiona was outspoken, for sure," Abby said. "I hadn't heard about the confrontation over changing the ingredients. But the shop had a right to change recipes. Do you think Fiona's complaint led to her murdering Fiona?"

"Tick off the wrong person and crap can happen. Fiona might have been right about misusing herbs. Her tox screen showed high plant alkaloids and traces of fruit and berries in her stomach. Sounds like a smoothie to me."

"Holy chicken feathers! But who made it for her?" Abby's thoughts zeroed in on the obvious. "Premalatha?"

"Not if we're to believe what she told us," said Kat. "She called Fiona and briefly spoke with her around the time of the murder and, therefore, couldn't have been there. She told us in retrospect that she was shocked at how normal Fiona sounded. Cell phone records back up her story."

Wondering if she should tell Kat that the day before Fiona died, Abby had delivered farmette herbs to Smooth Your Groove, Abby decided to shift the focus of her questions. "So, Kat, no customers of the shop have become ill from consuming the new versions of the smoothies, have they?"

"Matter of fact, they have. Nettie cross-checked the logs of the ambulance company calls with the hospital," said Kat. "She found out that the EMTs have responded three times in the past two months to transport people with stomach pains. All three said they'd had smoothies within half an hour of feeling ill."

Abby thought about that for a moment. Her brow furrowed in concentration. "Except the morning she died, she hadn't gone to the Smooth Your Groove shop, right?"

"Right."

"But someone could have delivered a smoothie to her that morning."

"With Fiona's body having such high alkaloid levels of aconitine, you've got to wonder how she got that poison in her system. In that respect, ingesting a smoothie with the poison in it makes a lot of sense," said Kat.

Abby took a deep breath. Her thoughts free-associated at a dizzying speed as she considered the horrific death aconitine poisoning could cause. Suddenly, the warning Abby had received from the two women in the bathroom about not eating at Smooth Your Groove flashed through her mind. Abby turned and looked directly at Kat. "I overheard something in Zazi's powder room, I think you should know."

Banana–Chocolate Mint Smoothie

Ingredients:

2 ripe bananas, peeled and cut into 2-inch pieces, plus 1
    ripe banana, peeled, cut into 2-inch pieces, and frozen
½ cup almond milk
1 tablespoon unsweetened cocoa powder
1 scoop good-quality vanilla ice cream
1 tablespoon organic honey, optional
10 fresh chocolate mint leaves, washed and torn

Directions:

Place all the banana pieces into the glass jar of an electric blender. Warm the almond milk in a microwave oven or on the stove and then whisk in the cocoa until it has dissolved. Pour the chocolate almond milk into the blender. Add the ice cream, honey, and chocolate mint.

Pulse until the mixture is just blended. Turn the blender on high and let it run for about 2 minutes, or until the smoothie is well blended. Pour the smoothie into chilled glasses and serve at once.

Serves 2

Chapter 13

Noxious weeds are like unsavory people: even
in the most convivial company of flowers and
herbs, they emerge to sow seeds of ugliness.

—Henny Penny Farmette Almanac

"It was an old nudist camp back in the day," said Abby.
She pointed to the sign at the commune's entrance as
she steered the Jeep toward the wide metal gate and braked.

"Tarweed Lodge," Jack read aloud. "Nudist camp, you
say. Do we have to disrobe to go in?"

Abby wrinkled her nose. "Good heavens, no." She pointed
to a large chain and padlock and the wooden sign wired to
the gate. White painted letters provided visitor instructions:
BUZZ THREE TIMES FOR AN ATTENDANT.

Jack jumped out of the Jeep. "I've got this."

As she watched Jack tap the buzzer, Abby's thoughts
turned to the locked gate, and she searched her recent
memory for a time when the gate had ever been closed,
much less locked. Abby leaned out her driver's side window. The scent of pine and juniper permeated the hot
mountain air. She searched to see where the buzzer wires,
secured to a branch of a nearby juniper tree and looped to
a pole, led. It appeared that the wires had been strung to

other trees all the way up the gravel driveway, until they disappeared behind a roof strut of the first of several rustic cabins. Her gaze swept back to rest on Jack.

He stood with his backside to Abby. He had plunged his hands into his cargo shorts pockets and was shifting from one foot to the other while he waited. Someone had to let them in. When no one showed, Jack strolled back to the car and stood by Abby's car window. "You might as well cut the engine," he said. "I don't see Tom or, for that matter, anybody. We could be here awhile." He slipped off one of his tribal-colored sandals and shook out a small stone. "Definitely the wrong shoes to wear in the woods," he muttered.

Abby turned off the ignition and left the keys in place. After leaving the Jeep, she strolled into deep shade, curled a thumb into the hem of her white cotton shirt, and pulled it from where it stuck to her damp waist and back. "I'm wilting, even here in the shade. Tom said he would meet us at the gate, didn't he?"

Jack's brows knitted. "Yes. But maybe he had to get permission or something. I'm not exactly sure how commune protocol works."

"Well, it seems to have evolved into more of a cult than a commune, with a bunch of new rules and restrictions," said Abby. She wondered how much access to the place they would be given. When previously she had come here with Fiona, the gate had never locked, and the buzzer hadn't worked. "Listen, Jack, once we're inside, take your time talking with Tom. And don't mind me if I disappear for a few minutes."

Jack looked at her askance. "Why? Abby, what are you planning?" Before she could reply, he said, "Don't make me have to track you down. I'll be worried."

"See? That's what I mean. You needn't worry about me.

I'll be fine. I just need a little time to nose around. There's been a lot of speculation about what goes on up here."

A male voice called out to them, and Abby glanced over her shoulder toward the driveway. Down the packed dirt path strolled two men and Tom, dressed in a surfer shirt, jeans, and well-worn construction boots.

"You found me," said Tom. "Hello, Abby. Last time I saw you here was a couple of months back, with Fiona." He managed a weak smile, and Abby returned it. He appeared hollow-eyed and haggard as he waited behind the gate while his sandy-haired companion and the other man, who had a gray goatee, proceeded to open it.

"Two people to open a farm gate?" asked Jack.

"Rules," said Tom.

The man with the goatee pulled a rolled-up flyer from his back pocket and handed it to Abby, but Abby was watching Jack size up Tom. After a moment, Jack opened his arms and drew his bereaved brother-in-law into a bear hug.

Glancing at the flyer, Abby skimmed past the image of a basket of vegetables to the address of their local farmers' market and a booth number, where the commune sold its vegetables and herbs. It also listed Smooth Your Groove's address under the image of a cornucopia of berries and other fruits. The rest of the page featured quotes from satisfied customers. Abby smiled as she realized no surnames were used, and the given names listed appeared to be those of commune residents. It just seemed bizarre that some marketing genius at the commune had thought up the idea of flyers for visitors and potential customers, whom they now locked out.

Following Jack and Tom up the incline, Abby stayed out of their conversation and wondered how she was going to slip away for some serious snooping. After weighing a couple of options, she finally surmised that it would just be easiest to wait for an opportunity.

"You okay?" Jack asked Tom when the men were a few yards from the fork in the path. Abby knew the right side of the fork led to Tom's van. After a few more steps, she spotted it parked roughly sixty feet away, in the shade of a mixed grove of pine, redwood, and oak trees.

Tom shrugged. "I've seen better days."

Jack put his hand on his brother-in-law's shoulder and said softly, "Then why stay here? Fiona told me how much the commune had changed from the cooperative community it used to be. And even Abby here thinks it's become a cult."

Tom didn't reply. He thrust his hands into his jeans pockets and kept walking toward the fork.

When they reached the split and turned right, Tom's commune companions parted company with them, taking the left side of the fork. Abby stared at them as they marched in lockstep like mechanized soldiers toward a long barnlike structure, which she recognized as the commune's meeting hall. She wondered if they might even be former military.

Her worries that the staff might not respect Jack's right to talk privately with Tom were unfounded. Soon the trio arrived at Tom's rainbow-painted van. The giant driver's door sported a faded peace symbol that hearkened back to the hippie counterculture movement of an era long past. The vehicle had been positioned on a platform of railroad ties and concrete blocks. A thick layer of pine needles covered the van and the two folding chairs positioned next to a stump near the van's rear bumper. Abby surmised that during hot evenings, here in the dappled shade, Tom perhaps quietly enjoyed the cordial company of a friend. Or maybe not. She'd heard the group's leader expected everyone to work long hours. Upon being paid, residents turned over their wages to the commune manager. She used the funds for the support and welfare of their small community.

Jack offered her one of the chairs. Abby declined.

"No, thanks. I want to see the garden. I know the way," said Abby.

"You can't do that," Tom said.

"No worries." Abby played it off lightly. "I've been here before." She wasn't about to hang around and argue. She walked away as quickly as possible to the garden, which was surrounded by cyclone fencing to keep out the deer and other wild animals. She gauged the time to be roughly two thirty, so they were approaching the hottest hours of the day. She certainly felt it. Panting and perspiring, she glanced back at Jack and Tom. She could see their lips moving but couldn't hear a word. Elsewhere, the grounds remained eerily quiet. Even Tom's escorts had disappeared. Where was everyone?

Abby sprinted along the length of the garden fence to the weather-beaten garden shed and peered around the corner. About a dozen men and an equal number of women were filing into the long building into which the other two men had gone. Abby recalled Fiona had once described the meeting hall as a place where the community held biblical lectures, meditation sessions, and initiations. Abby judged the distance from where she stood at the shed to the nearest window in the rear wall of the meeting hall to be about ten feet. Dodging the sight lines of people wouldn't be all that difficult, because there were trees and bushes, but dogs were another matter. Still, she had neither heard barking since their arrival nor seen any tail waggers running around. Everyone had entered the hall now, except for one bull-sized, muscular man in a gray, sleeveless shirt.

She couldn't see his face. Abby took a deep breath. It was now or never. She sprinted through the stand of trees into a clearing.

Her heart raced. She crouched amid tall blue-blooming ceanothus and the yellow-flowering flannel bushes that grew up against the back of the building, hoping no one had seen her. She wished she'd worn a dark top with her navy crop pants. Hands against the wall, she rose from a squat to an upright position next to the window. Layers of dust had created a dense film on the glass. Blowing hard on the glass set off a cloud of dust, but the thick layer remained. The window probably hadn't been washed in years. The opacity might have suited the nudists who hung out here back in the day, but if cleanliness was truly next to godliness, why hadn't the windows been washed by these God-fearing, utopian-minded people?

Using the heel of her hand, Abby gently rubbed away the dirt from the bottom corner of the window and peered in. She spotted Hayden Marks approaching the dais at the front of the room. He wore a plain white kurta tunic with an ochre-colored clergy scarf and loose pajama-type pants over his tall, thin frame. He stopped short of the dais stairs, folded his hands in a prayerful *pranam* greeting before those gathered, and bowed slightly. He then strolled up the carpeted wooden stairs of the dais and assumed a seated position on a red-cushioned divan at the center. He looked out over the room and straight toward the back window. In a panic, Abby pushed back from the window. She dropped to a crouch. Could he see her? Did he see her? Had bright light streamed through the peek hole she'd made?

After a minute, she mustered enough courage to look in again. Hayden Marks's eyes were closed, while eight women in four pairs placed before him flowers, a platter of fruits, a wooden bowl of coconuts, and a black tray with a bolt of white fabric. They also laid before him a stack of currency tied in a red ribbon, prayer beads, colored stones, and crystals. There was a board with backing to make it stand. On the board's eight hooks hung silver figure-eight neck-laces. For his part, Hayden remained still as a statue, with his hands resting in his lap. Behind him were pedestals holding sacred images from the Bible. The pedestal nearest him held a canvas painted with the image of an Old Testa-ment king surrounded by eight women. *So that's how old Hayden convinces women to do his bidding . . . by making it a biblical tradition.* He would be the first cult leader to reinterpret Scripture to serve his purpose. She was pushing the heel of her hand against the window to enlarge the peek hole when she became aware of the scent of patchouli.

A female voice behind her hissed, "What are you doing?"

Abby spun around. Premalatha glared at her. Abby's stomach churned. She struggled to think of what to say. "I . . . uh . . . was just curious. What's that all about . . . ? Some kind of initiation?"

Premalatha, who was wearing a long-sleeve tunic and a mid-calf skirt, adjusted her scarf—similar to the one Hay-den Marks was wearing—and as she did, the patchouli scent intensified. She glared at Abby with a steely-eyed stare. "That's none of your business. You can't just waltz in here anymore like your friend the queen bee, who used to be the teacher's pet. Her teacher is gone, now she's gone, we've got a new teacher, and I'm his pet. So get out."

Abby pushed past the shrubbery. Standing in the open, she gestured toward the garden. "I've been here before with Fiona. Many times. I just wanted to see how all the herbs and veggies were coming along. What's with the new restrictions?"

"None of your business."

"I have every right to be here. I've driven Jack Sullivan here. Tom Dodge's brother-in-law."

"I know who Jack Sullivan is. He had the good sense to call. We gave him permission to be on the property. We haven't extended that permission to you. We've posted signs. You are not welcome."

"Well, that seems a little harsh for a peace-loving community. You commune folks used to welcome people to come see the garden and to learn about your way of life."

Her expression hardened. "Now we don't. We hand out flyers." She pointed back toward the gate.

Abby pushed back. "Are you all afraid the murderer might enter the grounds? That the killer might come for you, as he did for Fiona?"

Premalatha slid her hands into the pockets of her paisley-patterned skirt. "Why should I care? We voted Fiona out. I say good riddance to that troublemaker. Somebody just did us all a favor."

"It's bad luck to speak ill of the dead. I've heard the wheels of karma grind exceedingly fine."

"Our power comes from a visionary leader who receives messages from on high." Premalatha's expression seemed flat; her eyes empty.

"I see," said Abby. "You mean like establishing a bunch of rules, locking down your facility, and taking the hard-earned wages of every worker here?"

Premalatha stared at her. "What do you know?"

"That's just it. I don't know. But I see Hayden Marks is right there inside the hall." Abby jerked her thumb toward the meeting hall door. "I'd just as soon get answers to my questions from him."

"He's busy . . . and you're leaving."

Abby's lips tightened into a thin line. "Did you kill Fiona?"

Premalatha snorted. "You're not the police. Just some farm chick who sticks her nose where it doesn't belong. Just like Fiona, who isn't going to be missed."

"That's not true," Abby said hotly. "Her brother is grieving, and her husband looks like a broken man."

"Tom is lucky she's gone." One of Premalatha's skirt pockets took on a cylindrical shape, and it was pointed toward Abby.

Did she have a pistol? But even if it was just a harmless felt-tip pen being used to threaten her, Abby recognized intimidation when she saw it. In her peripheral vision, she detected an abrupt movement. Jerking her head to the side, she spotted Dak, who had slipped up like a rattler from under a rock. His head had been clean shaven. His sleeveless sweatshirt exposed heavily tattooed arms and hands. Abby's stomach churned. They outnumbered her, and he outweighed her.

"Get her out of my sight," Premalatha hissed.

Dak grabbed Abby by the wrist and shirt and shoved her so hard, she stumbled. He yanked her upright to face him. Abby jumped squarely in front of him, as though to intimidate a new judo partner. She grabbed either side of his sleeveless sweatshirt and pulled him sideways over her extended leg. He fell hard but grabbed her foot. Struggling to wrench it free, she elbowed him in the face and broke free. Running, she felt him lunge at her back. She broke her fall with a roll, but he caught her, slammed his fist into her left shoulder. She cried out in pain and curled up as a protective defense. He levied another blow, striking her high on the right cheek, missing her eye socket. The split-open cheek burned searing hot. She choked back a scream. Dak yanked her upright. He hiked up the back side of her shirt. After twisting the fabric into a wad between her shoulder blades, he dragged her down the incline toward the gate.

A few feet past the garden fencing, Abby saw Jack and Tom leap up and then scramble toward her.

"What the . . ." Tom yelled.

Jack shouted over Tom, "Good God, man! Let go of her." Jack rushed toward Dak like a football lineman.

Dak, the ex-con, pushed back. "You, too, buddy," he shouted. "Outta here."

"Civilized men do not hit women," Jack yelled.

Abby flailed against Dak as he shuttled her to the gate area. Her defiance was putting her and Jack at risk. "Forget it, Jack," she yelled.

"Let her go!" Jack shouted. He threw a jab at Dak. The bodyguard lost his grip. Abby broke free. She stumbled and fell. But now Dak had turned his rage on Jack. As they pounded each other, Tom and the goateed guy, who'd come back on the scene, tried to break up the brawl.

"Run, Abby. Run!" Jack yelled, dodging a punch. "I got this." He followed a quick jab with a cross and a hook. Dak hit the ground and began writhing and moaning.

Abby took off running. A shot rang out. She stopped. Spun around. *Oh, my God . . . Jack.*

A group of men had gathered, with guns pointed at Jack, but he didn't appear to have been shot. The goateed man and Tom had wedged themselves between Jack and Dak. Tom was trying to push Jack toward Abby. She raced back, clutched onto Jack, and held him as he stumbled alongside her to the Jeep. After yanking open the passenger door, she pushed Jack into the car, then ran around to the other side and slid in behind the steering wheel.

"You okay to drive?" Jack asked.

"Silly question," said Abby.

She glanced over. He had his shirt balled up under his nose to stem the tide of blood trickling down. Abby shifted the gear into reverse, wheeled the car around, and pushed the gas pedal to the floor. She drove through the woods in a tense silence, constantly checking the rearview mirror for unwanted company. Only on transitioning from the graveled lane to the main road did she dare look over at Jack. He had leaned forward to wipe his sweaty, bloody face on his T-shirt. There were fresh red spots on his hemp-colored shorts.

"Might be a drop or two on the floor," he said with a distinct nasal twang.

"Well, they could have shot you. Is that what you mean by beating a guy into a brisket and pounding his cabbage?"

Jack chuckled. "Aye. And I fear I am a wee bit out of practice. Still warming up, I was, when his fist hit my nose. Put me off my game."

"Oh, is that what happened?"

Abby rubbed her temples, waiting for an approaching truck to pass. It carried old furniture pieces, tied down with bright yellow rope. After the truck had passed, she pulled out onto the asphalt roadway. Glancing into the rearview mirror again, she felt relief at the sight of dust swirling up behind the Jeep; no other vehicles were following them. The mirror reflected, however, the bluish-purple shiner around her eye and the snail trail of drying blood on her lacerated cheek. The churning she felt earlier in her stomach had evolved into full-fledged queasiness. She swallowed against the bilious taste in her mouth. If she felt terrible, she was pretty sure Jack felt awful, too. He kept shaking his punching hand, as if he couldn't feel his fingers.

"Might throw up, Jack," she said, leaning more toward

her open window. "I think I could do with a cracker or some soda water."

"I should have punched that brute's lights out for man-handling you," he said, apparently reliving the incident in his mind.

"It's over, Jack."

"Yeah . . . yeah. So, crackers . . . I've got some at the cottage. And there's beer, but no soda water. We're not far, are we?"

"No," said Abby. "But what about your rental car? You left it in town."

"Well, I suppose if you could fetch me for the funeral tomorrow, I could pick it up after the burial."

Abby had all but forgotten about burying Fiona. "Yes, of course I'll come get you."

He ran his hand over his head twice, roughing up his light brown hair and not bothering to smooth it back into place. "What a pair we are, huh?"

"Tweedledee and Tweedledum." Abby tried to grin, but it hurt. "I'm sorry I got us into that mess. I should have backed down sooner."

"And I'm going to remember that about you," Jack teased. "I'll wager that if anything gets Tom to leave that place, it'll be to escape the clutches of that Baxter woman. I'd be worried, too, if she had designs on me. Tom told me that their leader, Hayden Marks, arranges and performs marriages, often splitting up spouses and marrying them off to others. Tom said if Marks forces him to marry that woman, there is going to be hell to pay."

"Good Lord. That sounds like a fate worse than death," Abby said.

Jack nodded and grew quiet.

With their drama over and the tension finally leaving her body, Abby considered female rivalry as a motive for

Fiona's murder. When she realized Fiona wasn't going to divorce Tom, Premalatha could have envisioned a more permanent solution to secure the man she wanted to marry. If that was the motive, did she also have the means and the opportunity? Kat had mentioned a phone call that Premalatha had made to Fiona at the time of her death. If she'd called her from the commune, that suggested that Premalatha could not have been with Fiona. What about Dak?

On the console, her phone rang, jangling her nerves and jarring her from her thoughts. Clay's image showed up on the screen. Abby slid her finger across the screen and tapped the green speaker icon.

"Is everything okay?" she asked.

"Why wouldn't it be?" Clay replied. "When are you coming home, woman?"

"Why? Is something wrong?" Abby exchanged glances with Jack, who now sported a bemused expression. Contrary to his usual politeness, he seemed all too ready to listen to her conversation with Clay. Abby could have removed the call from the speaker, but then she'd have to pull off the road. It was mid-afternoon, time marched on, and she still hadn't gotten through her to-do list.

"You've got to see how far along I got in the master bath today. I just had to pop out a small section to accommodate the jetted tub measurements. The framing is done, and I've got most of the copper piping done. Tomorrow I'll be ready to feed the electrical cabling through the studs. Shoot, at this rate, you could be soaking in your new tub by the weekend."

"Oh, that's lovely!" Abby exclaimed. "So . . . nothing wrong on the farmette?"

"No. Although, I can't hear a thing with that nail-gun compressor going. Or when I'm drilling, for that matter.

But while I was eating a sandwich, I noticed your red-colored chicken limping around."

"Ruby? Did she pick up a piece of glass or a thorn during her dirt scratching?"

"I wouldn't know. Oh, and you might want to know that a bunch of your bees left their hive and are circling a limb of that huge peppertree out back."

"A low limb, I hope," said Abby.

"Not hardly. More like twenty feet up."

Abby groaned. "Dang it . . . Those limbs are rigid. And I'm going to need a spring action to shake the bees loose, so they fall into a hive box." She let a sigh escape through her teeth. "And how am I gonna get up there?"

"You'll be glad to know that I put a tall ladder on my purchase order for the materials delivered today. If you get home before dark, you can use it. I'll help. Otherwise, bee rescue will have to wait until tomorrow. I don't mess with bees after dark."

"So, I'm on my way. I haven't gotten your extra nails yet, but the DIY place stays open until nine o'clock. Be there as soon as I can."

Jack sneezed.

Out of habit, Abby said, "Bless you."

"You got somebody with you?" asked Clay.

Abby caught her breath. She looked in horror at Jack, whose eyes expressed a wicked amusement.

"Wuh . . . I told you about my friend Fiona, who passed away." Abby tried to sound matter-of-fact to reassure him. "I'm driving her relative home."

"Just so long as it's not a hot hunk." Clay cleared his throat. "You've got one of those renovating your house, and tonight could be your lucky night."

Abby's cheeks grew hot. Was Clay trying to embarrass

her? She wanted to hang up. If he felt uneasy over the possibility that she was with another man, just wait until he saw her shiner. How was she going to explain that? "Listen . . . let me call you back in a few. Okay?"

Silence ensued for a moment.

Clay's voice came through. "Whatever." His tone sounded like someone had just punctured his party balloon. Abby suspected that when she finally did get home, he would be in a mood and would be displaying that passive-aggressive behavior she hated.

"Later," Abby said, feigning cheerfulness. She tapped the phone to end the call.

Her heart galloped as she struggled against familiar hurt and lingering uncertainties about her relationship with Clay. She stole a look at Jack and wondered what kind of explanation she could give. To her surprise, no explanation was necessary. He had rested his head against the seat back and closed his eyes. Abby sighed in relief that he wasn't going to question her. But then again, why would he? Clay had made things pretty clear.

Abby drove to the turnoff at the big red barn and then navigated the Jeep up the bumpy driveway to Fiona's cottage. Once the car was parked and turned off, she sat gripping the steering wheel, in no hurry to move.

"Your hand still hurt?" she finally asked Jack, locking eyes with him.

He nodded. "Uh-huh. Your cheek?"

"Yes."

"Not life-threatening injuries," Jack said in good cheer. "And comforting to know that a doctor lives next door."

"Most likely blitzed out. In a stupor." Abby knew her words were unnecessarily negative, and that wasn't like her. Clay had put her in a dark mood. She inhaled deeply, let the breath go, and looked around. "But you know what . . . ? I don't see the doc's car. Oh . . . that's a scary thought."

Jack looked at her. "Just means we're alone up here on his ten acres. Why does that scare you? You think I'm going to take advantage of you?"

Abby laughed nervously. "Well . . . one can always hope," she said in a jesting tone. "No, it's just that Dr. Danbury shouldn't be drinking and driving." She tried to hide the fact that it did worry her to be alone on the mountain with Jack, because she could no longer deny her attraction, and it was getting harder not to show it. But Abby would not let herself go there, because doing so would just muddy up everything. They needed clear heads to solve this case.

The stifling heat inside the cottage took her breath away. "Sheesh, you could fry an egg on the floor in here."

"I should have left the windows open," Jack said. "But last night it was darn cold up here, and that wind off the Pacific comes through with a piercing howl. Keeps you awake at night." He began to open the windows one by one.

Abby hurried to the kitchen and filled two resealable sandwich bags with ice from the refrigerator's freezer. Then she pulled out a chair, sat down, and used her elbow on the tabletop to support her hand as she held one of the ice packs in place over her eye and cheek. She pointed out the other ice pack to Jack as he walked through the kitchen on his way to the bathroom. When he returned, she noticed he had cleaned up the dried blood on his face and had brought a damp washcloth and a tube of antibiotic ointment.

"Good on you, Abby, for insisting I not toss this tube during our purging of the place." He laid the ointment on the table. "Now, let me see that cut." After pulling up a chair to face her, he sank onto it and leaned forward to scrutinize her wound. "I'll have you right as ready in the blink of a crone's eye." He placed his hand around the back of her head. At his touch, Abby inhaled an abrupt breath and winced, not so much from pain as from the anticipation of it. With the damp cloth, Jack traced the edges of the laceration. His stroke was sure and steady. He paused to give Abby an arresting look.

Feeling a rush of adrenaline racing through her body, she closed her eyes, hoping she hadn't telegraphed anything.

"Now . . . just relax. I've got you. Tilt your head back a little more against my hand. That's my lass." The ointment smeared light as a butterfly wing fluttering along the length of the cut. The touch of the fingers soothed her. Then . . . there was no touch. No movement.

Abby opened her eyes to find Jack's eyes smoldering with intensity as he gazed at her, his lips so close they would have touched her if she'd nodded forward. He said nothing. She said nothing, but her cheeks flushed with warmth.

"You know, Abby," he said, his voice a husky whisper, "you smell awfully sweet for someone who's just been in a fight."

Abby's lips curved into a smile. "And here I thought I needed a shower."

He leaned back, pulled the neck of his T-shirt up to his nose, and sniffed. "No, if anyone needs a shower, it would be me." He rose and moved his chair back to its original position at the table.

Abby's thoughts raced back to when they first met. Having been interrupted during his shower, he'd answered the door annoyed. But then later on, when she had helped him sort through Fiona's things, he'd greeted her in an unbuttoned shirt, revealing a lean muscular torso. A shiver ran through her. *Oh, Lord. Don't think about that now.* Clearing her throat, she said, "Let me see your hands. You were shaking one of them pretty hard in the car."

"Aye. Jabbing that bollock brain was like a bare-fisted punch at a dicot angiosperm."

She looked at him, bemused. "Come again?"

"Hardwood tree."

"Yeah, well, your lightning jab broke his hold on me." Abby noted the impish grin that lit up his face, and turned her attention to his hands. "Bruising and swelling, but no cuts. Use that ice pack on them. Got any painkillers?"

"Oh, yes." He opened the fridge and took out two bottles of Guinness, popped off the caps, and handed her a bottle. "The liquid variety."

"I can see that," said Abby, suppressing a smile. She tapped her bottle against his.

Jack took a swig. "I'll just change my shirt," he said, then set the bottle on the table and hustled off to the bedroom.

When she could no longer tolerate the ice against her eye, Abby tossed the ice pack in the sink. She sipped from the beer and moseyed to the screen door at the back of the house, where an audible breeze rustled through the pines and redwoods. Looking out at the edge of the clearing between the house and the trees, Abby spotted the doc's cat stalking a bushtit. The bird flitted between a patch of sweet broom and a thicket, as if teasing the cat.

"Mind the hole," Jack called out from the bedroom doorway behind her.

Abby stopped short. She glanced down at the rug partially covering the hole. How could Fiona have allowed the hole to go unrepaired? With her landlord right next door, it could have so easily been fixed. As Abby thought about it, a realization began to emerge. *Hole! Oh, sweet*

Jesus. She leaned down and pulled the rug back. "Jack, bring a flashlight, will you? And a cap or something for my hair."

"What? What's going on?" Jack asked.

"Just trust me."

A moment later, he handed her a blue plastic flashlight and an Andean-style woolen cap with earflaps, a braid down each side, and one garnishing the top.

"Seriously?" Abby handed him her bottle of beer, took the flashlight, and plucked the cap from his fingers.

He winked at her. "In case you haven't noticed, I've got a big head. It's not easy to find caps that fit."

"And it's only going to feel like a hundred degrees with all my hair under that hat, but never mind." She pulled on the hat, flicked on the flashlight, and looked at him with an expression of childish delight. "Spell *hole* backward."

Shaking his head, he stared at her like she'd lost her mind. "Okay. I can do that. . . . E-l-o-h."

"Precisely. Your sister's secret code. High time we found out what's in that hole."

Abby knelt and then lay flat on the floor, her face over the hole. She shined the light in. "Um . . . don't see anything. Maybe if I can squeeze my arm farther in and get my head down in there for a better look. Hang on." She moved into position. "Okay, let's see. Okay, okay. There it is."

"What? What do you see?" Jack asked.

Abby wiggled, willing her arm to reach farther, but soon realized her effort was futile. "Shoot. Can't reach it. And if I can't reach it, how in the heck did Fiona get it there?"

"What? How did she get what there?" Jack's tone sounded impatient.

Abby felt his body stretching out on the floor beside her. She wiggled and stretched some more.

"Pull your head out of that hole," he demanded. "Let me try."

"Would if I could," Abby called from under the floor. "How about a little help?"

Jack shifted his position. Abby figured he was up on his knees. She felt his hands around her hips, pulling her back until her head was out of the hole.

"There's a light-colored fire safe down there, and it's got a combination lock. I'm betting there are four numbers in the combination."

"The year Fiona was born." His eyes were shining when Jack took the flashlight from her. He wasted no time investigating the hole. "I see it."

Abby said, "Think you can reach it?"

"Doubt it." He tried. No success. "We need something with a hook. Let me think." He sat upright, with his back to the wall. "But what? We threw almost everything out."

Abby pulled on the side braids of the woolen cap. "There's a poker in the living room. And a three-prong trowel out by the garden fence. I remember seeing it when you showed me Fiona's garden. If you cut these hat braids off, we've got yarn to tie the trowel to the poker."

Jack uttered a long, low "Ohhh." After a moment, he said, "Genius. Going to the garden. Back in a minute."

Abby's phone buzzed with a text as she was pulling the poker from the tool stand next to the fireplace. Certain that it was Clay again, she figured it could wait. But curiosity got the better of her. She removed the phone from her pocket and glanced at the screen.

Just FYI, girlfriend. Health Dept. just closed down the smoothie shop.—Kat.

Abby texted back. **Holy chicken feathers. I want all the details, but busy right now. Will call you later.**

Sitting next to the hole, she looked out the back door at Jack hurrying toward her. She had the pole for the hole, and Jack had the hook. *Time to go fishing.*

Tips for Making Scented Dusting Powder

Scented oil derived from chamomile, lavender, lemon balm, patchouli, peppermint, rosemary, or other herbs can be used to create your own signature dusting powder. To make six tablespoons (two ounces) of scented dusting powder, thoroughly mix four to five drops of scented herbal oil with one tablespoon of corn-starch. Next, mix in five tablespoons of unscented talcum powder. To retain the fresh scent, the dusting powder is best stored in a jar with a screw-top lid. Use a powder puff, a cotton ball, or a brush to apply it.

Chapter 14

A male hummingbird does not penetrate the
female to mate—he presses his cloaca against
hers in a cloacal kiss that lasts three to five
seconds.

—*Henny Penny Farmette Almanac*

Abby lay stretched out on the floor, watching Jack maneuver the hooking tool they'd made by using the yarn from his cap braid to bind the fireplace poker to the garden trowel. After numerous unsuccessful attempts, he finally connected the trowel end of the tool to the handle of the fire safe beneath the floor. Concentration furrowed his brow as he inched the safe with precision toward the hole in the floor.

He stopped with a sudden gasp and drilled her with a blue-eyed stare. "I do believe it's within my reach. Take the tool," he said, handing her the makeshift rake. "Mind the yarn. I want you to rebraid it and stitch it back on my cap, where you cut it off."

"Seriously?" she asked.

"Oh, quite," he said with a straight face. He put his arm into the hole until his upper shoulder nearly disappeared.

What a picture this is. Abby thought about capturing it

with her smartphone camera app but abandoned the idea when Jack, grunting, pulled the fire safe upward. He set it on the floor with a thud.

She reached up and removed his knitted cap from her head. Her reddish-gold locks tumbled in a loose mass over her shoulders. "Here you go," she said, tossing the hat to him. "You should have put it on before you put your head down there." She leaned over and plucked a cobweb from his hair. "Hope the spider wasn't still in it."

"Indeed," he said. "I should have thought of that. You know, it might be my favorite piece of clothing, that cap."

"You're kidding, right?"

"You've got to have your head covered if you are braving the cold wind in the high Andes."

"And when are you going there again?"

"Maybe never. But you never know."

"So . . . let me get right to work on that braid, then," Abby said in jest.

He smiled broadly, with amusement lighting his eyes. "You know I'm pulling your leg, right?"

Abby pursed her lips to keep from saying what she was thinking. *Oh, believe me, I know when you're pulling my leg.* She felt a little giddy.

Jack turned the safe upright and took a look at the numeric pins of the combination. "I'll punch in Fiona's birth date, but I'm going to need that key in your pocket," he said.

He spun through the numbers of the combination. Then he slid the key Abby handed him into the lock. It clicked and released. Jack let go a high-pitched squeal.

Abby jumped. "You scared me. What was that?"

"That, my girl, was the sound of happiness, the kind of joy that screams for a wee bit of bubbly."

"Shouldn't we see what's inside the safe first?"

"Right, you are. Come to think of it, I don't have anything with bubbly. Beer either. Rain check that idea," he said.

"Let's take the safe to the living room," Abby suggested. "We can examine the contents there without worrying about anything flying down that floor hole."

"Good on you, Abby. Always one step ahead."

After pulling Abby to her feet, Jack reached for the metal fire safe and carried it to the couch. He parked himself with the safe on his lap, then patted the couch seat beside him. "Come sit here."

Abby positioned herself right next to him. When he flipped open the safe's lid, she took note of a few papers, a framed picture, and a small ledger. The white envelope marked with the word WILL caught her eye. "You should open that," she said. To her surprise, he handed it to her.

"It saddens me to see it. I can't imagine she had much to leave anybody. And I would so much rather have her than a token of her life."

Abby lifted the flap of the unsealed envelope, pulled out the document, and read it. "I don't know if you'll welcome this news or not, but she left you the botanical shop. It says here that you can keep it or sell it to pay off the five-year loan she secured to start the business."

"Running a shop? I don't think I'm cut out for that sort of thing."

"Tom gets her jewelry," said Abby. "Well, I guess there's no surprise there. He already has it . . . or had it. I guess Lidia Vittorio at Village Rings & Things has it now."

Abby felt Jack push against her to look at the will. The warmth of his body was a tad unsettling, but she continued to read and share Fiona's bequests and instructions with Jack. "Says here there's a life insurance policy for fifty thousand, with Tom as the beneficiary. . . . Oh, but there's a proviso." Abby pointed to a line near the bottom of the page. "Tom gets the money only if he leaves the commune." Abby cocked her head to look at Jack. "Fiona seemed intent on Tom making a clean break with that cult. Perhaps she grasped better than anyone else what an isolated life he lived up there, with Hayden Marks and Premalatha Baxter dictating when and where he could go and taking his hard-earned wages."

Jack asked her in rapid-fire succession, "So how could the commune loan Fiona money? Do you think the leader wanted it paid back right away and knew about that policy? Do you think they could seize Fiona's insurance money from Tom to settle the debt?"

Abby looked astounded at Jack's insightful perceptions and chose her words carefully. "I think it's not only possible but also probable. And to answer your question about how Fiona could get a loan from the commune leader and his minions in the first place, I'd say they've got lots of money, unlike before. Fiona told me that before the previous leader returned to India, the community scraped to get by. Now the commune organization finances legitimate businesses, like Smooth Your Groove and Ancient Wisdom Botanicals. As a nonprofit, they seek and get donations. Let's not forget the residents who work and contribute their wages, and their families who lend support."

Jack nodded. A muscle quivered in his jaw. He reached into the safe and took out a silver filigree frame that held a photograph of Fiona, bedecked in a red scarf and hat and throwing a snowball. Tom, bundled in a pea jacket, jeans, and muck boots, apparently had been hit by a snowball and stood sideways, with his hands in a defensive position. "Check out Red Riding Hood and her wolf having fun in the snow." He peered closely at the image. "Looks like the picture was taken up here, behind this house. See all those Christmas trees? A whole section of them."

Abby pulled the frame toward her to inspect the photo's background more closely. "You're right. I wonder who took this picture. Dr. Danbury?"

"But surely, it doesn't snow here in the mountains, with the ocean just over those ridges, about thirty minutes away?"

Abby released her grip on the picture frame. "Sometimes it does."

Jack thumbed through the ledger. When a folded sheet of paper fell out, he handed it to Abby and continued to examine the ledger entries. "These entries make no sense. Just numbers and notations, with no documentation key for deciphering anything," he said.

Abby unfolded the sheet of paper and quickly read it. "Well, this explains a lot. That ledger belongs to Laurent. Probably, it was what he was looking for when he burgled her shop."

Jack's brows shot up. "So that's why she went to all the trouble to hide it in the safe under the house."

Abby nodded. "I'm speculating about this, but perhaps Fiona wrote out this letter as a means of self-protection. If anything untoward were to happen to her, somebody at some point would discover this and learn the truth. She's telling us from the grave what she feared could happen. The letter explains that she knew what Laurent was doing and accuses him of stealing from her and selling illegal drugs. He packaged them in tins, otherwise used for mixtures of blended herbs and cut tobacco marinated in molasses, which are smoked in hookah pipes."

Jack laid the ledger in the safe and leaned over to scrutinize the paper with Fiona's handwriting that Abby held. "But how did he have access?"

"He worked there for a while. Could have made a key." Abby scooted to create a little space between herself and Jack and then twisted slightly so she could look directly at the handsome Irishman. "Don't you remember the HELP WANTED sign in the botanical shop's front window? Fiona was looking to hire a store clerk, but while she went through the interviewing process, she likely paid Laurent to help her." Abby gazed into his blue eyes. "Come to think of it," she said, "Fiona could not keep those smoking herbs in stock during his tenure, or at least that's what she told me."

She stared again at the note in Fiona's handwriting, with its explanation of the notations in the ledger. "Each type of drug had a code name, and the amount sold, the date, and the customer's name. Premalatha's name shows up a lot."

"I suppose she would have met Laurent at Ancient Wisdom Botanicals. Otherwise, how would their paths have crossed?"

Abby chuckled. "Las Flores is a small town with a small-town consciousness. People know who the residents are and who the outsiders are. Whom to trust, and whom not to trust. It wouldn't surprise me if the briefcase Laurent carried from Fiona's shop contained his drug stash. Probably already had another place lined up. Just so he could keep doing business as usual. Fiona trusted him, but he was just using her."

"My sister trusted everybody," Jack said with an exasperated sigh. "That was her undoing." He crooked an arm around the back of his head and stared out the bank of windows that looked out over the distant mountain ridges.

"The police will want to see this," said Abby. She carefully refolded the paper and placed it back inside the red ledger. As she did, a small object protruded from the bottom of the ledger—a necklace bearing a number eight charm. A cold shiver shot through Abby's body. After pushing the necklace back into the ledger, Abby closed the safe's lid and spun the tumblers. So . . . Fiona would have had insider knowledge about the significance of those necklaces. There was no need to burden Jack with an explanation about that now, she decided. That discussion could be put off awhile.

Abby considered the slow and methodical way the commune had evolved under the tutelage of Hayden Marks. He used isolation tactics. Moreover, he wielded a renegade authority to dominate the community, performing sham marriages and forcing wedges between legitimate husbands and wives. Wasn't that how many cult leaders gained control? Through dividing and conquering and also through isolating members from their families? Brainwashing certainly appeared to be the root of Tom's plight. He had seemed too scared to leave. Abby sighed heavily.

When she stirred to get up, Jack clamped his hand gently on her knee. "I know you need to go, but I don't want you to. I like your company."

Abby arched a brow and grinned. "And I like yours, too, but . . ."

"Well, there you go again with those buts."

"But, Jack, much as I'd love to hang out here, I've still got errands to run and dinner to cook and chores to do."

"Okay, then. Take me with you into town. I'll get my rental car tonight, so you won't have to deal with that tomorrow, before the funeral. But I'm going to ask for one more teensy favor. It's important to me, and not just because it means a little more time with you."

"And what would that be?"

"Fiona's body is at the church. I wonder, do you think you could spare the time to accompany me there?"

"Uh . . . um . . . I . . . uh—"

"Somebody ought to say the rosary for her. . . ."

How could they go into a church, the pair of them, looking like they'd just gotten the worst end of a street brawl? How could she possibly conceal her black eye and her cut face? In spite of those reservations, Abby couldn't bring herself to say no. Her intention to help Jack through the awful process of dealing with everything while his heart was raw meant doing this, too, barring incapacitation. She wasn't incapacitated. And Fiona wasn't just a victim; she was a good friend. But now, with stops at the police station and the church, how would she explain to Clay why she'd gotten home so late?

"I can't go to church looking like this. I don't suppose you have a shirt I could borrow? My blouse looks like I've been wallowing with a pig."

His expression brightened. "I've got shirts in the dirty, the dirty-dirty, and the dirty-dirty-dirty basket. From which basket do you want me to pull it?"

Abby laughed out loud. "Oh, good Lord. Seriously, Jack? You don't have a clean shirt?"

"To do laundry, I have to be in the mood," he replied with a boyish smile. "I've not been in the mood," he said, laughing.

"Oh, never mind." She brushed her hands over her blouse, as if by some miracle, the soil from her wrestling with Dak could be rubbed out. "Let's just go, but we have to drop that off at the police station first." She pointed at the fire safe. "And let me answer any questions, if they arise, about why we look the way we do. Let's just stick together. We don't want conflicting stories out there, and for all we know, Premalatha and Dak could come here complaining that we assaulted them."

He rose and helped her to her feet. Then, without warning, he pulled her into a tight embrace. "Yes, on all accounts, especially about sticking together."

Abby's legs felt like jelly. Her heart hammered. She closed her eyes for a brief moment and melted into the warmth spreading through her body in the embrace of his strong arms. *What am I doing?* She eased out of his arms and said, "What if the church is being used this evening? Sometimes the church allows a couple of other priests to hold charismatic Masses."

"Never been to one of those," said Jack.

"It's Mass, but more like those held during the first centuries of the Roman Catholic Church, with lots of music, praying in tongues, and anointing of the sick with holy oil."

"Well, we can't know until we get there," said Jack.

"You're right about that. The church secretary will have gone home for the day, and I don't think they put the dates for those special Masses in the church's regular recorded messages."

After explaining to the officer at the Las Flores Police Department how they came by the safe and how it was relevant to the open murder case, Abby drove Jack to Holy Names. The funeral home had delivered Fiona's casket, which rested on a stand in a private area to the side of the cavernous interior. Only two other parishioners, whom Abby didn't recognize, occupied the place. Jack and Abby lit candles and quietly said the prayers of the rosary. Afterward, Abby dropped Jack off where his car was parked near Tilly's Café, made a quick stop for the nails that Clay wanted at the DIY center, and headed out of town to her farmette. Hoping to make it before dark, she arrived just after sunset.

Sugar rushed toward Abby, and Clay called Abby's name, as she headed toward the side gate to the backyard with her daypack and the box of nails. She frantically brain-stormed simple explanations for why she looked as though she'd been in a brawl, without admitting she had.

"Abby, the bees—" He stepped forward, looked her up and down. "My God, woman, what happened to you?"

"Obviously, I ran into something. I can be a klutz at times . . . but do you mind waiting until breakfast for the highlights? I know I'm late, and I'm sorry."

"Fine. Are you sure you're okay?"

"Perfectly." As much as she wanted to take a hot shower and to climb in bed, Abby knew Clay expected her to cook something. After all, he'd been working on her farmette all day. She'd have to praise him for whatever work he'd done in the master bathroom.

"I know what it is to be drop-dead tired," Clay said. He opened the gate, took the nail box from her, and set it on the ground. After drawing her into the yard and latching the gate, he embraced her tenderly, ignoring Sugar's incessant whining for attention. Abby pulled away long enough to kneel and hug Sugar.

"Good girl. I missed you, too. Settle down, now. Quiet."

Clay pulled her close again. "How about I tell you," he whispered in her ear, "that I've already eaten and so have Sugar and the hens? I refilled the chicken feeder with crumbles, checked the water level in the dispenser, and brought in the eggs. And the bed's already turned down."

"Music to my ears," Abby whispered back. Her eyelids felt heavy, but she dared not close them out of fear of falling asleep right then and there, on her feet, in his arms.

"Let's go inside," he murmured.

"Mmm . . . yes. If we don't, the mosquitoes will have us for dinner."

* * *

Abby awoke from sleep as a breeze gusted through the harmonic chimes beyond the bedroom window. Lying on her back, with her head resting on the cool cotton pillow, she breathed in the scent of night-blooming jasmine and tuberose mingled with Clay's citrusy aftershave. She could hear Sugar snoring like a big dog at the foot of the bed.

Turning her head slightly, she opened her eyes to narrow slits. Clay rested next to her in a semi-upright position against a pillow, scrolling through images on his laptop screen. Her eyelids fluttered closed, and she lay listening to his pattern of clicking and stopping before clicking again. It was kind of nice having his company, although it no longer felt as special as it once had. Still, he loved her and wanted to give her his life, or so he'd said. She would give their relationship a chance. *Scroll . . . stop . . . linger.* When Abby opened her eyes to see if he was shopping for building materials, her breath caught in her throat. He wasn't shopping for building materials; he was shopping for a woman. Abby's heart scudded against her chest wall. *Oh, no . . . no, no, no, Clay.*

Apparently unaware Abby was watching, Clay spent a minute more gazing at the woman with long raven-colored hair, who wore tight jeans and cowboy boots. The name Randi was printed in big sparkly letters on the paper fan she held, as if her very presence could turn up the heat. Clay clicked off Randi, only to pause again to view a woman with toffee-colored hair who wore red lipstick and a frilly knit shirt with an image of the state of Texas outlined on it. When he reached for his smartphone, Abby felt her anger rise like a simmering pot on the verge of a boilover. *The Lone Star State . . . Oh, really? His next port of call? A new location, a new woman?* She could hear him entering the woman's information, or at least she assumed that was what he was doing. Abby closed her eyes, feeling too tired and too angry to confront him. She lay still as a corpse, listening to her heart gallop like a stallion fleeing a wildfire.

As if mirroring her discord, the chimes clanged from a sudden wind gust. She rolled away from him to face the window, slowed her breath, and tried to center herself. Her mind struggled to process her discovery. What possible explanation could there be, except that he was surfing dating sites? *Why are you so surprised? Despite what he said when he showed up here, he just needs a place to land between jobs. He must have figured he could rekindle your feelings for him faster than a rooster could hop a hen.* Abby pulled the sheet over her eyes to blot her tears.

She lay there for a long time, so long it seemed like several hours had passed since Clay had turned off his laptop and fallen asleep. Even after she'd reasoned through her feelings of betrayal, she couldn't stop obsessing about exactly when he might leave her. He would have the electrical work on the master bath completed sometime tomorrow. The next day, most likely, he'd get the windows and insulation in place. Then the backer board would have to be installed before he could move in the jetted tub and the showerhead. He would need another day or so to hang Sheetrock. Hopefully, he'd stay long enough to tape and plaster the walls. That would leave her with sanding, tiling, painting, wiring the lights, and laying the floor— jobs he knew she could handle. It would just take some time. Oh, how perfectly he had played his hand. She wanted to punch him.

After some deep breathing to calm down, Abby remembered that Clay had mentioned his truck would arrive on Saturday. By her rough calculations, he'd likely be free to leave on Tuesday or Wednesday. Clay must have had a pretty good idea of his exit date from the moment he waltzed into her house. Abby wished he could have just been straight about it, could have told her the truth. Why had he felt it necessary to give her the "I can't live without you" speech? And she'd bought his act, which lessened her guilt about spending so much time on Fiona's murder case and with Jack. Fuming inside, Abby decided to let the future unravel. Why confront Clay when she wasn't thrilled to be in this relationship, anyway? Maybe the wisest thing would be to remain civil and keep up appearances until he left. She hated dramatic scenes and honestly just didn't have the energy to "go there."

The next day, before sunup, Abby checked on Ruby after feeding and watering the chickens. The Rhode Island Red hen had no problem running to the feeder or following Abby around in the run. Perhaps Clay had misread Ruby's walk or imagined a problem when there wasn't one. However, the bee swarm was another story. Abby thought about not bothering to ask him to help her and trying to retrieve it herself. But it was too high. She needed a pair of helping hands. Luckily, he was nearby and eager to assist. Perhaps he felt guilty about surfing the Internet for a new paramour, she thought.

Abby donned her beekeeper's suit and positioned the empty hive box under the swarm. Without a second suit for Clay, she relegated him to remaining on the ground while she climbed the ladder and, on her cue, to pulling hard on the rope to dislodge the bees. Worried that the bees might also just fly off, Abby devised a means to try to capture the greatest number of them and, hopefully, the queen for her hive. In the garden shed, she located a five-gallon plastic bucket and cut away the bottom. Using duct tape, she attached a black plastic contractor's bag to the bottom opening, and using wire and a couple of screws, she connected an extendable painter's pole to the bucket's top rim.

Pulling her elbow-length goatskin gloves over her bee suit sleeves, she told Clay what he needed to do. "Stand to one side, and when I give you the signal to pull, give the rope a hard yank." Abby hustled up the ladder and positioned the plastic bucket on the pole directly beneath the swarm after extending the pole to reach the swarm. She made a motion like pulling on a bell and readied the makeshift swarm catcher.

Clay jerked so hard, he snapped off the end of the limb. Luckily, most of the swarm dropped into the bucket and right on down into the contractor's bag, just as Abby had envisioned. She descended the ladder, struggling not to drop the bag of bees, while Clay took off running. Thousands of bees, still sensing the queen's pheromones, which were telling them to swarm, encircled Abby.

"Get farther back," she called to Clay. She could see angry scout bees buzzing past him as he watched the spectacle.

Abby turned the makeshift swarm catcher upside down and shook the bees into the empty hive box. She adjusted the box's position so its opening faced the tree that had just held the swarm. That would make it easier for the bees still circling to find their way into their new home. After laying aside her makeshift swarm catcher, Abby walked over to the patio and retrieved ten wax frames, drained of honey and previously cleaned by the bees. These she inserted into the hive box. Slowly, she slid the lid along the box top, leaving a two-inch gap for any bee laggers to make their way in.

With the bees dealt with, Abby unzipped her suit and stepped out of it. She folded it and placed it in the large basket that held the smoker, pellet fuel, the powdered sugar medicine, the hive clamp, and the wax scraper. She took the basket of materials and the swarm catcher back to the apiary. Before returning to the patio, she dropped to her knees by a raised bed and picked some fresh strawberries for breakfast.

"So what's your plan today?" Clay asked after they'd dined on yogurt, fresh berries, and toast spread with homemade apricot jam. "I feel bad that we've hardly spent any time together." He handed Abby his empty yogurt bowl. She set it on hers, strolled to the sink, and placed the bowls alongside the mugs of coffee and glasses of juice they'd drained.

"'Fraid I'll be gone most of the day, dealing with things in town again," she said in a quiet tone. She avoided looking at him, hoping not to slide into the anger simmering under her calm exterior. "I've got to take care of some farmette business and attend Fiona's funeral." She changed the subject. "There are sandwich fixings and potato soup in the fridge . . . and don't go claiming that you can't cook, as it's something we used to do a lot together."

"I remember," he said, pinning her at the sink and slipping his arms around her. "When will you be home?"

Abby shrugged. "I'm not sure. Why?"

"Well, I thought that if I knocked off early, we could share a glass of wine and cook dinner together. After that, we could see what kind of trouble we could get into."

Perfectly understanding his intention, she nudged him back, reached for the tea towel, and began to wipe her hands. "I'll let you know if I'm going to be later than seven o'clock." She hung the towel over the oven door handle and leaned down to pat Sugar on the head.

"I hope you don't think I'm pushing you, Abby," said

Clay. "I can't change what I did before, but I'm trying to make it up to you now." His tone became animated. "You just wait. Your master bath is going to be so dramatic, it'll stop traffic on Farm Hill Road."

"It's a little early for such hyperbole, isn't it?" She forced a smile. "But you must know that I appreciate your efforts, Clay. I am truly grateful."

Abby opened the patio slider and pulled back the screen door. Sugar bounded out, and Abby followed, then closed the door behind her, hoping Clay wouldn't follow. Walking the farmette with Sugar had become one of the most relaxing things she did. Today, more than ever, she wanted to stroll solo through the orchard, past the raised beds of strawberries, over to the herb garden and the vegetable patch, and then back to check on the chickens and bees. Luckily, Clay didn't follow, which, as she walked quietly with Sugar, soon brought Abby a measure of peace. She stopped to listen to a mockingbird sing its bright song—*thweeet-thweeet-thweet, right-here, right-here, worky-worky-worky*. A few minutes later, the nail-gun compressor started up, drowning out the bird's song.

Potato Soup with Fresh Herbs

Ingredients:
4 tablespoons unsalted butter
1½ pounds russet potatoes, peeled and cut into 1-inch dice
1¼ cups chopped yellow onions
1 teaspoon salt
Freshly cracked black pepper, to taste
3½ cups chicken stock

1 tablespoon finely minced fresh herbs (equal parts parsley, English thyme, lemon balm, chives, and marjoram),
plus a pinch for garnishing
½ cup half-and-half

Directions:

Melt the butter in a large heavy saucepan over
medium-low heat. Add the potatoes, onions, salt, and
pepper and gently stir to coat the potatoes with the butter. Cover and cook for 10 minutes.

Add the chicken stock and the herbs to the potatoes,
cover, and cook over medium heat until the potatoes
are soft, about 15 minutes.

Pour the potato mixture into a food processor or a
blender and puree. Return the soup to the saucepan
and stir in the half-and-half. Adjust the seasoning.

Pour the soup into a tureen or soup bowls, garnish
with the remaining herbs, and serve at once.

Serves 4

Chapter 15

When the old honeybee queen dies, the first
new queen to emerge from her cell will sting
the other queens to death; only one queen
rules the hive.

—*Henny Penny Farmette Almanac*

Abby stood in the apiary, with her hands clutching the
metal lid of the new hive box. Her psychic and emotional equilibrium had been knocked out of balance. Irra-
tional as she knew it to be, she had somehow managed to
turn the anger she felt toward Clay inward, blaming herself. Why had she let him convince her they could pick up
the pieces and move forward? Why had she believed him,
instead of trusting her own intuition? Why, when her heart
had finally healed, had she set herself up for disappointment? She didn't need Clay, she didn't need any man, and
the years he was gone had taught her that. Besides, there
were other men around, like Jack or Lucas.

The sound of the bees, their vibration, and the smell of
their honey comforted her so much, she'd lost track of
how long she had remained near the hives. More than anything else, she wanted to avoid Clay. She would not liter-
ally or telegraphically communicate her disappointment.

She refused to give him the satisfaction of knowing that he still had the ability to wound her.

Leaving the comforting presence of the hive, Abby returned to the house and gathered her clothes for the funeral. She carried them into the small bathroom. After showering and drying off, she slipped into a belted, knee-length black dress with cap sleeves and a wide cowl collar, and French heels with ankle straps. She twisted her reddish-gold mane into a French twist, anchoring it with pins and a hair clip embellished with roses worked in marcasite. She decided to keep her makeup understated. She applied an ivory foundation over her face and chose a lipstick and blush in a tangerine hue to complement the color of her blue-green eyes. A pair of silver and onyx drop earrings and dark sunglasses completed the solemn, respectful look she sought.

Driving the Jeep along the silent black ribbon of asphalt to Las Flores, Abby thought about Tom and Fiona. Their love might have seemed true and strong to Fiona, but if it were, indeed, so strong, why wouldn't Tom break his ties to the commune? Why had he sought a divorce instead? Abby could only imagine what their relationship might have been like as best friends, lovers, spouses . . . and now he was left to bury her. Tom probably felt guilty, as if his leaving had led to her death. *How do you go on after something as horrible as that?* She thought about two lines in a poem by Henry Scott Holland, long since dead himself: *There is unbroken continuity. Why should I be out of mind because I am out of sight?*

Abby hit the scan button on the radio until she found some agreeable music to keep her company on the way into town. After arriving at her destination, she dashed up the steps of the Church of the Holy Names and hurried into the narthex. Girding herself against the guilt she felt for lapsing in the religion dutifully instilled in her, she dipped her finger in the basin of holy water and made the sign of the cross. Her French heels clicked against the patterned marble floor as she approached the glass doors to enter the nave of the church. She strolled into the interior, now bathed with light streaming through old-world-style stained-glass windows depicting the Stations of the Cross. The doors creaked shut behind her.

Father Joseph had already led the procession of the flower-draped coffin and the congregation down the aisle and was sprinkling the holy water. The church smelled of lemon-scented wood polish, candle wax, camphor, and the scent of flowers—gardenias, lilies, lavender, and sweet peas. As she approached the altar, Abby spotted Jack, paused to make a slight bow before the altar, and then sidled over to the pew. She genuflected and trod softly over to where Jack sat with his hands in his lap.

"Hi," she whispered, scooting into the seat.

Attired in a white button-down dress shirt, a black suit, and a black-and-gray-striped tie, Jack looked up and acknowledged her with a smile. Despite the somber occasion, he exuded masculine vitality. Squeezing her hand, he whispered back, "Thanks for coming," and then, "Your cheek looks puffy. . . . How's the eye?"

Abby lifted her sunglasses so he could see the black and deep red circle surrounding it. She watched Jack's lips tighten into a thin line. He hung his head, as if he blamed himself for the whole affair. After the opening song, for which they stood, and the prayer that followed, Abby stole a glance at those gathered behind them. Tom sat two rows back, flanked by Premalatha Baxter and Dak Harmon. They stared at the coffin. Tom's puffy red eyes and grim expression seemed to reflect a man lacking a rudder and floating adrift in dangerous waters. He looked over at

Abby. Apparently sensing her concern for him, he touched his heart with his hand and nodded.

A few townspeople and Main Street shop owners had come to pay their respects, but it still wasn't much of a crowd. Abby spotted Kat, dressed in a tailored suit, at the back of the nave and a man Abby didn't recognize but suspected was an undercover cop, across the aisle from Kat. Abby took comfort in the knowledge that cops often showed up at wakes, the funerals of homicide victims, and celebrations of life gatherings. They would come not only to observe the friends and family of the deceased, but also to notice if one or more of the individuals in attendance were suspects or persons of interest. No place was sacred if cops had sufficient reason to arrest someone.

The church secretary stepped before the podium situated on the right side of the church, in front of the baptismal font. Pushing back her short, gray hair to tuck the tips of her wire-rimmed glasses behind her smallish ears, she began her reading. The woman's monotone set Abby's thoughts adrift . . . back to happier times when she and Clay were both on the same page about their feelings for each other. But, like a meteor in the night sky, that love— if it truly ever was that for him—had flamed out. At least this time, Abby knew the way forward. This time, she would be the one to sever the fragile thread that held them together. She forced her thoughts back to the funeral.

After listening to the readings from the Old and New Testaments, Abby heard the double glass doors at the back of the nave creak open, and she turned to see Laurent Duplessis slide into a pew. Later, during Father Joseph's short homily about the gift of life and the inevitability of death, she heard the doors open again. Someone had either come in or gone out, but since the priest was looking right at her, Abby didn't turn around.

By the time the Mass had ended and they'd caravanned to the graveside at the Church of the Pines—roughly a mile from town and up a mile or so in the mountains—for the final Rite of Committal, Abby noticed Laurent Duplessis had not come to the site. Then Father Joseph spoke. "The earth is the Lord's and all it holds, the world and those who live there. . . . Who can stand in his holy place? The clean of hand and the pure of heart . . ." At one point, Tom cried out in aching agony, his lament sounding sorrowful enough to summon Fiona's spirit. Abby trembled and fought against the tears stinging the backs of her eyes. Despite her eyes brimming with tears, she saw Premalatha reach out for Tom's arm to steady him. He jerked from her touch.

After the recitation of a psalm, there were other prayers. Then a parishioner played a haunting rendition of "Amazing Grace" on the uilleann pipes. Six men lowered the casket into the ground. And then . . . it was over.

After the commune people had left and the few townsfolk had departed, Jack thanked Father Joseph and left the grave diggers to do their work. As he'd ridden with Abby and Kat to the cemetery, Jack remained only long enough to say a private good-bye and then rejoined the two women at the Jeep.

"So what now?" Jack asked. He rubbed the right jaw of his cleanly shaven face as his question was met with Abby's silence and Kat's blank stare. He sighed and said, "In our family's ancestral village generations upon generations ago, according to my grandparents, we'd lay out our deceased family member in nice clothes for the final viewing. The menfolk would arrive, their pockets bulging with bottles of spirits. The women would make food enough to feed half the county, and then we'd open a window for the spirit to depart. Of course, if the wind was wailing and the rain sheeting, we would crack that window a wee bit, but only for as long as we thought the spirit might be around. We'd eat and drink ... mostly drink ... and tell stories about the times we'd spent enjoying that person's company."

Jack paused to chuckle. "Mind you, sometimes this would take all night. Come morning, with our heads pounding from hangovers, we'd drag ourselves to the church for Mass and then follow the casket, the poor deceased's body bumping along the country road to the cemetery. We'd face that freshly dug hole and lay our loved one in it." He paused again, this time looking wistfully toward the sky. "Then we'd drink some more. At least, that's the way it used to be."

"Sounds like we should have a drink," Abby said.

"Couldn't hurt," Kat agreed.

"And what about your associate, Kat?" Abby asked.

"He's busy back at the church," Kat replied.

"Busy? Doing what?" Jack asked.

"Inviting Laurent Duplessis down to our police station for a little chat," said Kat. "Otto is probably having a go at Duplessis now."

"To discuss the robbery or the murder?" Abby asked.

"That too." Kat massaged the corner of her eye with her middle finger. "We had plenty of questions about that botanical shop burglary. Then Fiona's note that you brought to the station last night, thank you very much, raise more than a few questions, so we wanted to see what Duplessis had to say." Kat flicked a speck of an undetermined origin from the shoulder of her dark suit jacket. "My shift ended a half hour ago, so what about that drink ... ? Black Witch okay?"

Abby shot a questioning look at Jack.

"Sure," he said.

Kat leaned closer to Abby and whispered. "The place has a new, superhot part-time bartender, who just might be working tonight."

Abby's brow shot up. "Yeah? I thought you and Lucas Crawford . . ."

"Yeah, well, let's not go there."

"Let's do," Abby protested.

"Can it wait until you and I are alone?"

"Sure," said Abby, all the more intrigued by Kat's reticence.

Twenty minutes later, Abby parked the Jeep on Main and led Kat and Jack into the Black Witch. She threaded her way through the crowded bar and climbed onto a tall wooden stool near the dartboard and the back bathrooms. Kat took the other stool, while Jack dragged over a third, wiping peanut shells from its seat.

Kat surveyed the room. "I can't believe this place is so packed. Happy hour is still forty-five minutes from now."

A bleach-blond waitress—one of the old-time workers at the bar—appeared. "What's your poison?"

Kat followed Abby's lead in ordering a glass of merlot.

"Make mine a Celtic Barrel Burner," Jack said.

Abby and Kat both snickered.

"What's so funny?" he asked.

"Sounds as dangerous as a Kamikaze," said Kat.

"Or a Revolver. We make those, too," the waitress said. Her wrinkled lips parted into a tired smile. She spun around and wove her way back to the bar with the drink orders.

Jack removed his tie, unbuttoned his shirt collar, shrugged off his jacket, and laid them on the stool. Rolling up his white shirtsleeves and exposing muscular arms covered in light hair, he leaned in and said, "If you ladies will excuse me, I'll make a quick trip to the men's room."

When he'd gone, Abby nudged Kat with her shoulder. "Okay, it's just the two of us. Now spill."

"What?" Kat's blond brow furrowed, as if she'd totally forgotten.

"You know what." Abby eyed her intently. "You and Lucas Crawford . . . details, please."

"Well, I'll be happy to provide the nonexistent details after you've told me the truth about that black eye."

Abby touched the tender cheekbone just under the edge of the afflicted eye. "I thought you knew. I explained last night at the police station. Dak Harmon and I had a misunderstanding while I was visiting the commune, and we got into a tussle."

"I just heard about the evidence you turned in, not the tussle."

"The long and short of it is that Harmon got into a tizzy when I didn't jump at his order to get off the commune property. We got into a little shoving match, my eye got hit by an elbow, and I left with Jack shortly afterward. End of story."

"No, not the end of story. I expect you to tell me what happened up there."

"Honestly, Kat, nothing worth mentioning happened, and you are stalling. Jack can verify my story when he returns from the bathroom."

Kat arched a brow and remained defiantly silent.

"I'm waiting," Abby said.

Kat let go an exasperated sigh. "Lucas and I never even got out of the starting gate. Turns out we're ill suited."

"But you liked him, set your sights on him."

"Oh, yeah, well . . . ," Kat said. She slipped off the dark gray suit jacket and laid it on her lap. She spent a few seconds fiddling with the Victorian floral pin at the throat of her crisp, buttoned-up white blouse. "It takes two, now doesn't it?" Her eyes swept the room and then went back to Abby. "You know me better than anyone else, so I'll use an analogy you'll instantly grasp. In Jane Austen's *Pride and Prejudice*, which guy would you fall for? Mr. Darcy, who has that quiet, smoldering intensity? Or the charming, seductive bad boy, Mr. Wickham?"

"Oh, you know who I'd choose. What's your point?" asked Abby.

"I don't have enough patience for a Darcy type—the handsome, secretive fellow who can't be pushed, the one who takes his own sweet time about everything."

"So your fling is over?"

"What fling? I would not describe what happened—or, more correctly, did not happen—as a fling. I don't think anyone has a fling with Lucas Crawford." After folding her napkin into what looked like a piece of bad origami, Kat fixed her attention on the waitress, who was approaching with their drinks.

The waitress slapped three more napkins down on the table and set the drinks on them. "Anything else?" she asked, taking the bills Abby had placed on the table and counting out the change.

Kat hesitated and then asked, "Will Santiago be tending bar tonight?"

The waitress shook her head. "Dunno. I just got here myself. I can check for you." She sauntered away.

As if preparing for an affirmative answer, Kat slid her hands over her new Roaring Twenties haircut. "Oh well."

Jack returned, swung a long leg over the bar stool, and slid onto it.

Kat lifted her glass. "Here's to the past remaining in the past. I, for one, am always ready for a new beginning."

Catching a glint of interest in Kat's eyes as she tapped her glass against Jack's, Abby lifted her glass and said,

"New beginnings." Then she did something that surprised even her. She reached for Jack's hand and gave it a gentle squeeze.

The Celtic Barrel Burner

Ingredients:
½ shot Baileys Irish Cream
½ shot Jameson Irish Whiskey
¾ pint Guinness Stout

Directions:
Pour the Baileys Irish Cream into a shot glass. Next, pour the Jameson Irish Whiskey over the Baileys. Pour the Guinness Stout into a chilled pint-size beer mug or beer glass and let it settle. Add the contents of the shot glass to the stout. Drink at once, as the beverage tends to curdle and becomes less appetizing if it sits.

Serves 1

Chapter 16

Watch out if your rooster lowers his head and struts around you—take it as a sign of fowl aggression.

—*Henny Penny Farmette Almanac*

Tires crunching against gravel alerted Abby that someone had rolled into her driveway. She had been sorting snap peas on the patio but got up to greet her visitor as Sugar bounded across the yard with a *yip*. When the dog's tail began waving, Abby knew it was a friend, not a foe, who'd come calling at her farmette. Still, Houdini, who could never be accused of shirking his duty as a rooster, hustled the hens—whom Abby had let free range in the yard—closer to the chicken coop.

"Hey, girlfriend," Kat called.

"Hey, yourself . . . What brings you all the way out here?" Abby picked up another pea, ran her nail along the ridge to open it, dropped the four peas into a bowl, and discarded the shell in a basket on the ground.

"I had to take care of some business out this way, and now I am on my way back to town. But I thought since I was so near, I'd quench my thirst and see that master bathroom Clay's been working on. Where is he, anyway?" Kat sank into a patio chair.

Abby arched a brow. "Why? Is there a problem?"

"No. Just curious," Kat said, stretching out her long legs.

"I suppose he's somewhere in Las Flores."

"How did he get there? Your Jeep is parked out front."

"His truck. Five minutes after the transporter arrived this morning and unloaded his pickup, Clay hopped into his truck and told me he was going to buy four recessed-light kits and a bathroom exhaust fan. And he suggested that when I'm done sorting the peas," she said, laying aside the basket of shells and the bowl of peas, "I could go ahead and finish hanging the drywall."

"How nice of him to give you something to do . . . because everyone knows you have way too much time on your hands," said Kat.

"Yeah, well, it was just the smaller pieces of drywall. It's done. He's gone. And, frankly, I hope he stays gone for a while. I could use some thinking time. Sweet tea?"

Kat smiled. "Oh, I thought you'd never ask. I'm wilting in this heat."

Abby traipsed into the kitchen. She took out a couple of tall glasses, filled them with tea from the fridge, and plopped in sprigs of mint from the plant in the garden window. After stepping back out through the open slider and screen door, she handed a glass of tea to Kat.

"You said you were around here on business. What kind of business?" asked Abby, sitting back down and touching the cool glass to her warm cheek.

Kat took a swig of sweet tea before answering. "A garbage truck nearly sideswiped a cow on Farm Hill Road."

"Sheesh, that could have been disastrous," said Abby

before taking a sip. Using her forefinger, she pushed the mint sprig deeper into her glass.

"Turns out that heifer belongs to your handsome neighbor, Lucas Crawford. When I told him one of his cows had escaped from its pasture and a garbage truck had narrowly avoided hitting her, he showed more animation than when we shared ice cream in town. I watched him swing upon that horse of his faster than a felon on a jailbreak."

Abby smiled at Kat's analogy. "Oh yeah? Horse, huh?"

Kat looked off philosophically. "Damn fine man, that Lucas. Too bad we couldn't get a little something going."

"Yeah, too bad," Abby said in sympathy, feeling secretly delighted, but not wanting to telegraph it to Kat. She took another sip of tea and turned her gaze toward the hill and Lucas Crawford's old gray barn.

The chatter coming through Kat's radio drew Abby's attention back. The dispatcher was asking for Kat's location.

"Uh-oh," Abby said with a frown. "Our illustrious police chief checking up on you?"

Kat nodded while pushing the button on her two-way. She gave her location as Farm Hill Road, between the Henny Penny Farmette and the Crawford Ranch.

Abby listened intently. The dispatcher requested that all available officers respond to a ten seventy-one near Ridge Top Road. Shock registered in Abby's body. Her pulse raced. That road intersected the main traffic artery near Dr. Danbury's cottage. Knowing that a ten seventy-one was Las Flores Police code for a shooting, Abby fought against mounting concern for Jack and the doc. She took a deep breath and reminded herself not to make assumptions or jump to conclusions.

"I've gotta go," Kat said. She chugged down the rest of her tea before setting the empty glass on the table, said,

"Thanks," and sprinted back to her cruiser. Abby and Sugar followed.

"Kat," Abby called out, "that's near Dr. Danbury's place."

"Know it."

Abby called out again as Kat climbed into the cruiser. "Text me. I'll be worried sick until you do."

"Affirmative," Kat called out. She started the engine and flipped on the lights and the siren. The cruiser's tires spun against loose gravel as the car tore out of the driveway and sped off.

Covering her nose and mouth with her hand against the cloud of white dust and listening to the siren's wail grow fainter, Abby stood rooted on the spot and fretted. A drive-by shooting was an all-too-familiar occurrence in nearby Silicon Valley, but in the mountain foothills of Las Flores, it was unheard of. Abby's thoughts turned to her recent altercation with the commune people. She texted Jack, but with no reply, she stood rooted in her driveway, in the hot sun, with a cold chill descending upon her like a vapor.

By nightfall, Abby still had not heard from Kat. Jack hadn't replied to her text, either. To keep from obsessing about the shooting, she busied herself by working on organizing receipts and stapling them to sheets of paper marked HONEY/BEE EXPENSES, CHICKEN SUPPLIES, GARDEN EXPENDITURES, and RENOVATION/BUILDING MATERIALS. Around eight o'clock, Clay strolled into the house with a pepperoni pizza, a bottle of a red blend wine, and an apology for being gone so long. Sugar still barked at him as if he were a stranger, but eventually settled down next to Abby on the couch.

"I've got the light and fan kits in the truck. Put out the pizza with some napkins, and I'll be right back," Clay said, with a devilish grin.

Somebody's in a good mood. Abby tucked the pages of receipts inside four manila file folders and carried them back to the small credenza in her makeshift office at the end of the hallway.

"I don't feel much like eating," she said when Clay had finished lugging in the boxes from the supply store.

"Why's that?" he asked, putting the boxes on the floor next to the wall and proceeding to whip out his pocketknife to cut the foil from the wine bottle. He thrust the corkscrew into the bottle, twisted it a few times, and eased out the cork. After finding two wineglasses in the cupboard, he took them down and poured a splash of red into each.

"I guess you forgot that I'm not a fan of pizza," Abby said, sliding into a chair next to his at the dining table and taking from him the glass of jewel-colored wine. She hesitated in telling him what was really on her mind—that she was worried about the shooting, Jack's safety, and the reason why Kat hadn't yet texted or called.

He shot a peculiar look at her and then reached for a large gooey slice of pizza. "Suit yourself," he said and wolfed down the slice.

It had been four hours since Kat had been dispatched to the scene. Abby would never intrude when Kat was out on a call, but the waiting and not hearing from either Kat or Jack was crazy making. Now, after swallowing a small bite of pizza and telling Clay not to buy pizza again, because she could make a more wholesome version using garden herbs, homegrown veggies, and slices of fresh mozzarella and goat cheese, Abby felt the phone in her pocket vibrate. She dropped the pizza onto her plate, wiped her hands on the napkin, and plucked her phone from the appliquéd pocket of her yellow print sundress. Finally, the update she had been expecting had come as a text. But as she glanced at the screen, Abby saw it wasn't Kat's message, but rather Jack's. **Tom critically wounded. Meet me at Las Flores Community Hospital.**

Abby looked up at Clay, who seemed wholly occupied with pigging out on pizza and wine. He reached for the bottle and began to refill his glass. She put her hand over her glass, scooted her chair back from the table, and said, "None for me, Clay. Sorry, but I've got to go."

Training his dark brown eyes on hers, Clay frowned and opened his palms in a gesture that suggested he was waiting for her explanation.

"Fiona, the friend we buried yesterday . . . Well, now her husband has just been shot," Abby said. "He could die."

Clay's brow shot up, and then his expression turned into a scowl. "Let me get this straight. Just why do you have to go?"

"Because Fiona's family has asked for me. Look, I'm sorry. But these things happen."

"Only to you, Abby. Only to you. You don't work for the police department anymore, and you're not a victims' advocate. I can't see any good reason why you have to go, unless it's to avoid being with me."

"Good grief, Clay. This is not about you. And now isn't the time to cop an attitude. Save it for later." Abby dumped her slice of pizza in the garbage and set her dish in the sink. She dashed to the bedroom for a summer sweater and her purse. Sugar, apparently picking up on Abby's anxiety, began to whine.

"You want me to drive?" Clay called out from the kitchen.

"No," Abby replied, kneeling to hug Sugar. She returned to the kitchen with the sweater, her purse, and the car keys. "Do you mind if I leave Sugar here? I don't think hospital security will let me take her inside, and I don't want to leave the poor baby in the Jeep for hours." Abby hurried back to the dining table to grab one of the six water bottles that she always kept in the bar area opposite the table. She resisted her natural inclination to tell him more about her plans; he hadn't exactly been forthcoming as to where he'd been all day.

Clay bit into another slice of pizza, took a moment to chew and swallow, and another few seconds to wash the bite down with wine. "You're planning to be gone for hours?"

Abby heaved an exasperated sigh. "I don't know. It could be a while."

Clay stared at his pizza. "Fine. Leave me. Leave your dog. We're getting used to your absences."

"That remark is so unnecessary, Clay. I'll be back as soon as I can. In any event, I'll text you."

"Whatever."

Clay's irritation riled her, propelling Abby out the door and to the Jeep. Inside it, she started the engine and reminded herself to breathe through her tension and to let it go. Clay had apparently forgotten that he was a guest in *her* house. Yes, she'd been away a lot, helping Jack clean out the cottage, attending Fiona's funeral, and now keeping a possible vigil at the hospital. Friends helped friends. And if Clay wanted to fault her for that, so be it. He was the darling boy child in his family, the bearer of the family's hopes and dreams, always getting his way. Abby reminded herself how self-focused he could be. *Well, the world doesn't spin around you, Clay. And I'm not thinking about you anymore . . . tonight.*

At the first traffic light in town, Abby braked for the long red light and glanced down at the message from Kat on her phone screen. **Vic is Tom Dodge. Transported. Finished working the scene. Need to interview him.**

The light changed to green, and Abby pushed hard on the gas pedal. The Jeep responded with a squeal of its tires. The hospital was still a half mile away. Abby wanted to get there as quickly as possible, but in one piece. Tom just had to pull through—the police would need to hear his version of the shooting. If he died, it would mean the already overtaxed LFPD would have two murders to investigate at the same time and Jack would have lost two family members. So occupied were her thoughts in making a linkage between Fiona's murder and the attempt on Tom's life that Abby nearly missed the turn into the hospital parking lot.

Not finding Jack in the waiting area of the emergency room, Abby approached the triage nurse, a perky young woman in green scrubs, and asked where she might find the patient with the gunshot wound who had been transported in earlier by paramedics.

The nurse trained her green eyes on Abby and asked, "Are you family?"

"I'm a friend meeting his family, who is already here," Abby told her.

"They took him to the OR, second floor. There's a waiting room up there near the surgical suites, but if you hit the surgical ICU or ward, you've gone too far." The nurse pointed to the gray door marked STAIRWELL. She then reached for a clipboard with paperwork for her next patient.

Abby hurried to the door, pushed it open, and entered the dank, cool stairwell, where she sprinted up the concrete steps. Pushing open the second-floor door and stepping out into a hallway, she saw a sign with an arrow indicating the direction to the waiting area. She spotted Jack pacing toward her. She dashed into his embrace.

He exhaled a long sigh. "Thank you for coming, my girl," he said, stroking her hair. "Can you believe this?"

"Thank God it wasn't you," Abby said, easing out of his embrace to glance toward the operating-room doors. The area smelled of air freshener, used to cover up the other disagreeable scents that permeated the environment, but Abby could still smell them—antiseptic mouthwash, hand sanitizer, iodine, alcohol, and stale coffee.

Jack led her to a dimly lit alcove with six identical chairs next to a small table, with a slew of magazines strewn about. He fixed his pale eyes on hers, as if anticipating a barrage of questions.

"What exactly happened?" Abby asked.

"The police say it was a drive-by. Tom was alone in his truck and, apparently, the target," Jack said. "An eyewitness in a Ford Escort had followed Tom for some distance when a motorcyclist cut in between the Escort and the truck. When the road straightened out of the switchbacks, the biker pulled even with Tom's truck and fired two shots into the cab."

"Oh, my gosh," Abby said. "Then what happened?"

Jack took a deep breath and exhaled. "The truck went into a skid. Tom—despite being seriously wounded—apparently fought for control of his pickup. You know, Abby, there are places up there where there are no guardrails. That was one of them."

Abby nodded. "So he got the truck stopped."

Jack nodded. "In the nick of time and inches from a slide-area drop-off."

After a moment of silence, she asked, "So . . . how serious are his injuries?"

"The bullet wound caused massive blood loss. The police told me that the medics decided to transport him right away, instead of stabilizing him on scene. I think he has a collapsed lung, too. They said he needed a chest tube."

"Oh, Lord. Poor Tom," said Abby. "Have you spoken with his doctors yet?"

"Yes. They're encouraging. Told me he's lucky to be alive. Barring complications in surgery, he should pull through."

Abby's mind raced. "But why was Tom the target? His whole world seemed to be that commune."

"My opinion . . . Dak Harmon may have done this," Jack said.

"Hmm," Abby said, wondering why Jack had formed that opinion, except that he'd seen firsthand Dak Harmon's violent streak. Her stomach churned as she recalled how Dak had hit her.

After a few minutes of sitting quietly, waiting for news from the doctor, Abby looked over at the elevator doors that had just opened. Kat strolled out of the elevator, walked toward them, and sank into a chair.

"We're so glad to see you, Kat. Piece this together for us, will you?" Abby said.

Kat began talking even as she removed the flip-over notebook from her shirt pocket. "Well, we're still working it ourselves. As Abby knows, we tend to be guarded about giving out a lot of information until we have a clear picture of the case ourselves, but we do try to keep the victim's family updated." Kat looked over at Jack. "There was an eyewitness driving from Boulder Bluff, on his way home. He witnessed the shooting of Tom by a tall, thin man on a motorcycle, wearing a touring helmet—full face hidden by the helmet mask—black jeans and shirt." Kat peered at the pages of her notebook, flipping through them one by one. "The witness also said he thought there was some kind of scarf sticking out of the shirt collar. He called the emergency number and stayed on scene until the medics and law enforcement arrived."

Abby stopped Kat for a second. "Wait a minute. Did you say that the eyewitness described the shooter as tall and thin?"

Kat nodded.

Abby looked at Jack. "That can't be Dak Harmon. He's stocky and heavyset. So if it wasn't Dak—and why would he want to kill Tom, anyway?—who else could it have been, and what was the motive?"

"We're looking into it," said Kat. "We believe the shooter used a forty-five-caliber automatic pistol. We found a casing on the road. We've got ballistics over at the crime lab, working on it. In the meantime, we just have to wait for input on the size caliber and also the type of firearm. A lot depends on scrutinizing the firing-pin indentations, as you know."

"When you saw Tom, was he still conscious?" Abby asked.

"No," said Kat. "He'd been hit by flying glass to the face and upper body. The gunshot pierced the left side of his upper chest, and he suffered a loss of blood and consciousness. His lips and nail beds were that cyanotic blue hue you get when you're not being properly oxygenated."

"So have you come to check on him?" asked Jack.

"I'm here to interrogate him as soon as he wakes up." Kat chewed her lip. "I'll be brief, but there are facts we need to get."

Abby nodded and put a reassuring hand on Jack's shoulder.

Kat looked at Abby. "With our resources stretched so thin, it could be a while until we get to the bottom of this. What I wouldn't give for a forensic expert all our own to help us to determine bullet distance, angle, trajectory, sequence, and a thousand other little details."

"Maybe the homicide guys helping Otto on Fiona's murder investigation," Abby said, "could look at this, too."

Her optimism was met with a shake of Kat's head. "Not likely."

"Listen, Kat, my gut tells me there's a link between Fiona's murder and the attempt on Tom's life."

"Yeah, I think so, too," Kat said. "But you know we also have to set aside our personal opinions and let the evidence lead us to the right conclusion. The DA can't prosecute a case based on a gut feeling."

"You think Tom knows who tried to kill him?" Jack asked.

"Possibly." Kat returned her notebook to her pocket and folded her hands in her lap. "I certainly think the shooting was no accident."

Jack chewed the corner of his lower lip.

Kat leaned toward him. "You met with Tom recently, didn't you?"

"Yes," he replied. "Abby and I both did."

"Well, technically, *you* met with Tom," said Abby. "I looked around the commune grounds and got this shiner to show for it," she said, pointing to her eye.

"What did you and Tom talk about?" Kat asked.

Jack sniffed and furrowed his brow, as though trying to remember. "I asked him if he had anything to do with my sister's death or if he knew who did."

"And what did he say?" asked Kat.

"He adamantly denied he had anything to do with her death."

"Do you believe him?" Kat asked, pressing on.

"Of course. Tom is no killer."

"Did he know anyone with a reason to hurt Fiona?" Kat asked.

Jack glanced at Abby. "Maybe, but he didn't name anybody," said Jack. Looking at Kat, Jack said, "My brother-in-law said that the commune was changing and that Fiona had been outspoken about it. I guess the new leaders have a life of ease, even luxury, with all the residents working at the commune or in the commune's various businesses. Premalatha, in particular, had a bad history with Fiona, according to Tom."

"Bad history? What are we talking about here?" Kat asked.

Jack straightened and leaned back into his chair. "Fiona told me that once the old leader returned to India, Hayden Marks and Premalatha Baxter were to share equally the old guy's spiritual power. They said he'd passed it on to them. Those two began implementing the changes. Hayden Marks became the 'official leader,' and Premalatha Baxter assumed the role of commune manager and banker. She recently bought a new BMW Alpina for her and Hayden Marks to share. One assumes she used the money collected from the commune folks to make the purchase. I don't even own a car, but I know this much—that particular model costs over a hundred grand."

Kat made a soft whistling sound. "That's a lot of moola."

Jack rubbed his hand across his cheek. "I don't know if this is relevant, but during our conversation that day, Tom told me about a promise he made to Fiona."

"What promise?" Abby and Kat asked in unison.

"My sister told Tom that he had to promise he would leave the commune if anything ever happened to her. And not only that, but she made him swear to go to the police with everything he knew about the place, its dealings, and Hayden Marks and Premalatha Baxter."

"So, did Tom go to the police, like Fiona had asked?" Abby searched Jack's eyes.

Jack looked at her briefly and then turned his attention back to Kat. "No. I think he was scared. Tom said there could be severe reprisals against people who reveal what goes on inside the commune world."

"It appears that's exactly what happened to him after he talked with you," said Kat. "Did Tom reveal anything about Baxter or Marks to warrant involvement by law enforcement?"

Jack arched a brow. "Tom told me Hayden Marks hired outside help for special situations. He told me that two other people who threatened Marks ended up leaving the commune. Tom said no one knew how, when, or why they left. They just disappeared."

Kat leaned forward, with forearms on her knees, palms clasped together. "That sounds ominous. Did he mention any names?"

Jack shook his head. "No. Do you really think Tom's chat with me was the reason he got shot?"

Before Kat could answer, a call came over her two-way. She pressed her fingers to her lips, signaling the need for silence.

"Interviewing Tom Dodge can wait," Chief Bob Allen said to Kat. His voice sounded loud and clear. "We've got an address for the registered owner of the motorcycle used in the drive-by. I need you and Otto to do a knock and talk."

"On it, Chief," Kat said. She rose to leave. Turning back, she told Abby, "Text me when Tom is awake. . . . I need to ask him some questions."

Abby nodded, but before she could ask Kat to inquire of the chief the bike owner's name, Kat disappeared behind the closing elevator doors.

Tips to Ensure Success in the Making of Mead
(Honey Wine)

Mead may have been the first fermented beverage enjoyed by the ancients, brewed before wine, beer, and other alcoholic spirits were created and became popular. The ingredients list for mead is simple enough: honey, spring water, and yeast. Today other ingredients, such as rose petals, orange slices, raisins, cloves, vanilla, and chocolate, are sometimes added to impart unique flavors to the mead. There are many mead recipes on the Internet and in beverage books; however, in all the recipes, honey remains the most important flavor ingredient. When making mead, be sure to do the following:

- Always follow sanitary procedures to avoid introducing bacteria into the brew.

- Always use an organic, unadulterated honey for best results.

- Ensure that there are no bubbles in the mead and that it is clear before bottling it.

- Permit the mead to age several months to temper its sweetness.

Chapter 17

The drones' sole purpose in life is to mate with
the queen, and then they die. Those that don't
mate are useless and are kicked out at summer's
end to conserve the colony's resources.

—Henny Penny Farmette Almanac

Slumped in the hospital waiting room chair, Abby jerked
upright to reorient herself. The elevator doors banged
open, and a man and a woman stepped out, carrying a
cooler, and conversed as they hurried past her. Rubbing
the sleep from her eyes, she looked over at Jack, who apparently had been observing her every movement.

"Sorry . . . uh . . . I . . . How long was I out for?" she
stammered.

Jack glanced at his watch. "Forty-five minutes." As if
something else was occupying his thoughts, his brow furrowed. "What do you think was in that cooler those two
people were carrying into the OR?"

Abby yawned. "Dunno. Maybe a donated organ. They
have to keep it on ice."

"Oh, yeah. That makes sense." He shifted his position
in the chair and crossed his long legs. "You know, you're

kind of cute when you're sleeping." A broad grin creased his cheeks.

"That, I doubt," said Abby. She pulled the band from her hair and vigorously shook her reddish-gold mane before twisting it all back into a messy bun on top of her head. "Did you sleep?"

"No," he replied. "Couldn't. Too much going on in my noggin."

Abby plucked up the remaining errant tendrils and pushed them into the bun. "Boy, do I need a shower," she groaned and then stifled another yawn. "And my teeth feel fuzzy." Remembering that she usually kept a travel toothbrush in her daypack, she picked up the pack and unzipped the side pocket. "Has anyone from surgery come out to give you an update on Tom?"

"Once. The doctor didn't say much, except that Tom made it off the table and is recovering in the ICU," said Jack. He uncrossed his legs and shifted his position again. "A nurse showed me where it is and told me we can have five-minute visits every hour. She told me not to be surprised by all the lines they've got in him. Apparently, he's on IVs, a heart monitor, and a respirator, but they're going to take him off that as soon as he wakes up."

"That's good news," Abby said, rezipping her pack. "I'm sorry to have snoozed through all that."

"Sun's not up yet. You were tired. It's quiet here."

She rifled through her pack's inner pockets. "I guess I don't have that darn toothbrush, after all. Suppose I could get one in the gift shop, but it doesn't open until nine. So . . . what about some coffee?"

Jack nodded. "Sounds good. I smell it, but for the life of me, I can't locate the pot."

"I suppose that's by design," said Abby. She stood and

touched her toes, holding the stretch for a few seconds. "They'll have a pot in the cafeteria on the first floor. Why don't we meet there in five or ten minutes?"

Jack, suddenly enthusiastic, said, "Let's go now."

"If you don't mind, I'd rather have a few minutes to wash my face," she said, reaching for her daypack. "I never look my best crawling out of bed in the morning, so I doubt my appearance is any better after sitting up all night." She only hoped she hadn't snored. With a smile and a squeeze of Jack's hand, Abby left for the ladies' room in the down-stairs ER lobby.

After she'd washed up, brushed through her hair, and applied a swipe of lip gloss, she sent a text to Clay, ex-plaining why she hadn't returned home during the night. To her surprise, her cell phone rang, with Clay calling back. Despite his mood seeming sullen, Abby did her best to sound upbeat as she shared the good news about Tom making it through the night. But from Clay's silences and one-word answers to her questions about whether he had slept well and whether Sugar had been on her best behav-ior, Abby knew he was mad and was not interested in hearing her excuses, no matter how good and true they might be.

In a parting shot, Clay said, "I told you long ago if we ever reached a point where we couldn't make things work, we should just keep on walking. I want you to think about that, Abby."

Abby blew air between her lips. "Look, I guess we can talk about this when I get home. I should be there by lunchtime."

"Whatever," Clay replied. He ended the call.

From the ladies' room, Abby headed to the cafeteria and bought a cup of coffee. Not seeing Jack, she paid the cashier and then located a seat nearest the cafeteria door so Jack would see her when he walked in. After a few sips of coffee, Abby dialed Kat's number.

Kat answered with a sleepy "Yeah?"

"Did I wake you?"

"Yeah. What's up?"

"Sorry. I'll be brief. Thought you'd want to know that Tom is out of surgery and is recovering in the ICU. We haven't seen him yet."

"Huh."

"And . . . I was wondering if you know any more about that motorcycle rider who shot Tom, or about the bike's registered owner."

"Do we have to have this conversation now, Abby?"

"No, of course not." Abby winced. "I'm being thoughtless. I should've known you were sleeping. Call me later, okay?"

"Wait." Kat exhaled a long sigh. "Are you obsessing about something?"

"Only about a dozen somethings. You know me too well. So, let me just ask about one thing that's really bothering me. Tom's shooter was on a motorcycle. Have you and Otto spoken with the owner of that bike yet?"

"Yes," Kat said sleepily. "The cycle belongs to Gus Morales, the mechanic who owns the mountain garage. He keeps a couple of vehicles in his shop as loaners for customers whose cars are in for servicing. One of his loaner vehicles is that older-model Harley motorcycle."

"What's his connection to Tom?"

"None we could find. He doesn't know Tom. Never done work on Tom's truck. But he's got a nephew named Billy, a marketing whiz, to hear him tell it. Billy has generated some business between the commune residents—

those who still have vehicles—and his uncle, who services them."

Abby's thoughts raced ahead. "I get it. So the nephew is responsible for those flyers, too?"

"What flyers?" Kat asked sleepily.

"The ones we were given at the commune when Jack and I went to see Tom the day Dak Harmon and I had our tussle."

"Ohhh." Kat yawned.

"So no one from the LFPD has interrogated the nephew?"

"Not yet."

"But you say that older-model Harley is a loaner? So if that loaner was used by Tom's shooter, whose bike is in the shop, being repaired?"

"One of the commune members who paid for the servicing up front in cash brought in a motorcycle for Morales to fix. That fellow took the loaner bike back to the commune."

"Ah, so . . . it's likely that a resident of the commune owns the bike being fixed in the mountain garage . . . and any commune resident could have access to the loaner. Okay, Kat. Thanks. Go back to sleep, and we'll talk later."

"Huh."

Abby clicked off the call and looked up. Jack stood in the cafeteria doorway, motioning for her to join him. "Hurry. They say we can see Tom now."

The ICU sounded like a brooder room of peeping chicks, with sounds seemingly chirping from every machine. Fully awake but looking exhausted from his ordeal, Tom rested against pillows in white cases, his hand shaking as he tried to scratch an area on one side of his whiskered cheek, beneath the green oxygen mask.

Abby assumed his skin must itch where the tape had anchored the intubation tube in his mouth to the respirator hose.

Jack said cheerfully, "Glad to see you decided to stick around, bro."

Tom managed a feeble grin.

Abby thought he looked like an elf, with his pointed ears and toffee-colored, curly hair. "Did you get a good look at who shot you?" Abby asked pointedly.

Tom shook his head.

She pressed on. "So you don't know if it was a man or a woman on that motorcycle?"

Tom stared at her. "No," he said huskily. His eyelids floated down and then sharply jerked up again. He seemed to struggle to stay awake. He licked his pale, dry lips.

Jack picked up a glass of water with a straw in it and shot a look at Abby, as if to say, "Save the interrogation for later." He helped Tom lift the oxygen mask and pinched the straw closer to Tom's lips. "You know, the landlord offered me a month-to-month lease on the cottage. You'll need a safe place to mend, and I could use help liquidating the store merchandise." His voice had the reassuring tone of an older brother counseling his young sibling. "Unless you would rather be a shopkeeper."

Tom finished his sip of water and adjusted the mask. "Fiona would've liked that," he said, his voice cracking.

The poignancy of Jack's offer suggested to Abby that he had a tender regard for this man who had married his sister. If Tom stayed around to run Ancient Wisdom Botanicals, it would be the new life Fiona had envisioned for him. But it remained to be seen which choice Tom would make. His entrenchment in the commune's cultish life suggested he'd been brainwashed. Perhaps Fiona had understood that better than anyone and had been pressuring Tom more prior to her death. Her confession of love for Tom in her journals and her desire to have a child with him had to make her untimely passing all the more difficult for Tom to bear. But maybe now Tom's life would radically change.

Suddenly, as if someone had stroked her bare arm with a feather, Abby snapped out of her reverie. Her grandmother Rose might have reminded her that unseen presences had a way of making themselves known. Abby looked at Tom, who stared across the room, as if seeing what couldn't be seen. Just then, a nurse popped in.

"How's the pain?" she asked.

"Hurts . . . bad," said Tom. Small beads of sweat had emerged across his forehead.

"The doctor has ordered something to help with that. I'll be right back."

Abby placed her hand over Tom's. "You deserve a rich and full life. Fiona wanted that for you. Not this. Get well soon, so you can get on with it."

"My sentiments exactly," said Jack, setting the glass back on the bedside table. "There's a couch in the cottage with your name on it. I'm heading back there now, and I'll let the landlord know that we're thinking about signing that month-to-month lease. What do you say?"

Tom nodded.

Abby followed Jack into the hallway. "It's a start," she said.

"Yes, it is." Jack gazed into her eyes. "I can't thank you enough for coming. When will I see you again?"

She smiled and, with a toss of her head, said, "Soon, I hope." His expression dimmed, compelling Abby to reach out for his hand. "I hope you know I mean that, Jack."

He brightened and nodded.

*   *   *

Abby stopped by the post office to retrieve her business mail from the box and dropped by the feed store for a bag of scratch grains before returning to the farmette at a little past noon. She felt fully prepared for a face-off with Clay, but his truck wasn't in the driveway. Her heart's heaviness lifted with the realization that she would have some time to enjoy her sanctuary before the showdown with him.

Kneeling to hug Sugar in the backyard, she said, "I've missed you, sweetie. Did you miss me?" The dog backed up and whined, as if directly addressing Abby's question with an affirmative reply.

Abby checked on the chickens and then the bees. Inside the house, the weariness of the past twenty-four hours settled heavily on her, like a hefty woolen quilt. She longed to dive into the bed for a nap but decided to check out the master bath first. The two large windows were locked in. The tub had been set in place, along with the faucet and showerhead. The lights and switch worked, as did the fan. An old-world vanity, with its single sink set into a marble top and storage for linens behind the large doors at the bottom, lent an air of elegance to the room. But when Abby gazed out the double windows above the spa tub, her breath caught in her throat.

"Oh . . . my. I can sit in this tub with a glass of wine and feel the spa jets massaging my aching muscles . . . all the while gazing up at the ranch owned by that fine-looking Lucas Crawford. What irony. If this isn't the mother of all gifts, I don't know what is."

Around four o'clock Abby awoke from a cat nap, oddly craving chocolate mousse, but all she could do was think about it; she surely didn't have the energy to make it.

Truth be told, she didn't have much energy for anything. She had to push herself to get up, do a basket of laundry, water the plants, eat a small meal, and lock the chickens in for the night. Clay still hadn't called or texted. Maybe he was nursing a wounded ego or just wanted time away from the farmette. Whatever the reason for his absence, Abby vowed to rave about the fine job he'd done with the bathroom when he returned. Around midnight, she decided to call it a day. She showered, slipped into a pair of silk pajamas, and crawled between the cool sheets. She reached out to feel Sugar's soft, warm body next to her. Sleep soon overtook them both.

A gunshot rang out. Beside her bed, the glass window shattered. Startled into wakefulness, Abby dove to the floor. Her senses went on high alert. Her pulse throbbed. Sugar yipped at a deafening pitch. Trying to gather her wits about her, Abby reached up for the knob on the bedside table drawer. Pulled the drawer open. Her fingers stretched to touch the Ruger LCP 380 semiautomatic pistol. She removed the gun and cartridge. Even in the dark, she knew how to load it.

"Shhh, sweetie. Shhh. Quiet." Abby stroked the quivering, whimpering dog. She strained to make out the sounds outside, determine the direction of the shot. "It's okay," she whispered to the dog. "All okay, sweetie. No worries."

But Abby knew it wasn't okay; she was worried. To call for help, she needed her phone. Abby's heart pounded like that of a thoroughbred entering the final stretch in a horse race. Her situation was dire. She had no backup and no partner. First rule of survival: stay calm, clearheaded, and focused. The daypack was on the bed, but she didn't know which direction the shot had come from. Could the shooter see her? Detect movement? Had she locked the house? A shiver shot up her spine. In a split second, she needed to lock the back door, find her phone, and call for help.

"Come, Sugar." She prayed the dog would follow her. "Let's go, sweetie." Cautiously, she inched over the shards and reached the hallway without cutting herself. And then . . . the kitchen. The dog sat on her haunches at the end of the hall, quiet and still. "Stay," Abby commanded as she crawled into the kitchen.

Easing up to a squat, Abby then rose and flattened her body against the wall. Like a silent shadow, she moved past the refrigerator, washer, and dryer until she reached the slider. She realized she had only partially closed the vertical blinds. Too late now. She searched for movement in the blackness beyond the door. Back by the henhouse, she saw a flash of light, like a match to a cigarette . . . and then it was gone.

Feeling for the door latch, she located the metal tab and plunged it down into the locked position. Inhaling and slowly letting the breath go, she crept along the wall to the safety of the hallway where Sugar was waiting. "Good girl."

Now to get the phone. Abby crept into the bedroom. Keeping her body below the bed frame, she stroked her hand along the top of the mattress, feeling for the daypack. When her fingers touched the rough canvas of the pack, she pinched it and pulled the pack toward her. With the pack on the floor, she remained quiet for a millisecond, listening. The stillness of the night drilled on in her ears like a high-pitched whine from electrical wires. Had the shooter finished his smoke?

Crawling back into the hallway, Abby pulled the zipper across its slide and opened the pack. She pulled out the phone. Pushed the button on the side. The green screen lit up with the time, 3:30 a.m. Abby tapped the icon for contacts and then the entry for police dispatch.

"What's your emergency?" the female dispatcher asked when the call connected.

"Attempted one-eighty-seven," Abby whispered as loud as she dared. "Two shots. Fired at me through my bedroom window."

"Is the shooter still there?"

"Think so. Yes."

"Your address?"

"Henny Penny Farmette on Farm Hill Road."

"Your name?"

"Abigail Mackenzie."

"Stay on the line with me."

Abby assumed that the dispatcher was sending the message out to all cruisers and emergency vehicles in the area.

"Are you in a safe place?" the dispatcher asked.

"Not really. The hallway."

"Can you safely get to a room with a locking door?"

"Will try."

"Police are on their way. Don't hang up."

Abby moistened her lips. "Okay. I know the drill."

With her gun in one hand and the phone in the other, Abby crawled on all fours down the hallway, with Sugar padding alongside. At the master bathroom, Abby abruptly stopped . . . listened. The patio slider lock jiggled. Her heart raced. In her head, alarm bells sounded. She had only a minute or two to hide somewhere. *But where?* She felt for the handles on the vanity double doors . . . then stopped. *Even if I fit, Sugar won't. Not an option.*

The assailant's heavy footsteps clomped beyond the exterior of the broken bedroom window. Paused.

Easy way in. Minutes . . . maybe seconds . . . all I've got, if that. Abby crawled from the master bath to the hallway's small office area. *Maybe we can hide under the desk.* She inched forward. Found the desk but was blocked by a large cardboard box. Then it dawned on her. The bathtub box. If it held the tub . . . Abby felt for the lid. Lifted it. Laid the phone inside. She hoisted up Sugar, set her inside, and then crawled in.

A loud thud at the front of the house told Abby the intruder had walked on past the broken window to check the front door. He had knocked over a metal chair on the porch. But why hadn't he used the broken window? Maybe worried about getting cut, leaving blood at the scene. Maybe this wasn't some amateur shooter?

Abby hugged Sugar in a one-arm hold. She reached up and closed the box lid. Pointing the gun straight up, she waited, ready. If the killer lifted that lid, she would shoot. Period. Sugar stopped panting long enough to lick Abby's bare forearm.

Anxiety. We're both feeling it. Abby heard the lock and the knob on the front door being twisted. Nausea swept through her. The lump in her throat couldn't be swallowed. Her pulse pounded. Holding Sugar snug, Abby hoped she could muffle any bark against her bodice. All was quiet for a moment. Then . . . glass crashed again on the bedroom floor as pieces were kicked out from the window. *So here he comes.* Panic ran riot inside her. Abby's sweaty palm quivered against the gun handle; her trigger finger trembled.

The sound of a heavy foot landing on the floor . . . then the other foot made Sugar's lean body tense. Glass crunched like ice shards crushed under a heavy roller. Sugar jerked her head at the sound.

"No . . . no barking," Abby whispered. She trained her

focus on hearing the footsteps as they walked into the master bath. She heard something else.

A faint siren sounded in the distance. Grew louder. The heavy footsteps returned to the bedroom. Crunched more glass. A man's voice cursed as he banged the wall to scramble out the window. The siren screamed, as if only yards away. Gravel crunched under tire wheels. Rubber screeched to a halt. Abby lifted the box lid. A brilliant light flashed on outside. So the cops had turned on their searchlights. Abby exhaled through pursed lips. Let the weight of the gun relax against her chest.

"Police are here," she told the dispatcher before laying aside the phone.

More sirens screamed as another emergency vehicle arrived, and pandemonium ensued. She heard multiple voices shouting. "Drop the gun. Drop the gun. Hands up. On the ground. Spread 'em."

Abby helped Sugar out of the box and then climbed out herself. She put her gun back into the drawer. Slipped a robe over her pajamas and hurried to the front entrance of her farmhouse. Abby took Sugar's panting as a level of high anxiety, but what could she do to assuage the dog while chaos was still going on? She flipped on the indoor and outside lights and saw the suspect being placed in the backseat of the cruiser at the front of her property.

"You okay?" an officer called out to Abby through the screen door she'd opened.

"I am now," she said, stepping into the pink flip-flops she kept on the front porch. "Heck of a quick response. Where were you? On a stakeout at the pancake house at the end of Farm Hill Road?" she teased.

The cop grinned. "Something like that."

"I want to see him . . . the idiot who shot out my window."

The officer led her to the cruiser and opened the door. Dak Harmon, hands cuffed behind his back, glared at her.

"Know him?" asked the officer.

Abby's stomach churned. She had the urge to throw up. She swallowed. "Yes. That's Dak Harmon. Did you find the gun he used?"

"Sure did. Did he assault you, ma'am?" The officer added, "Physically, I mean."

"Uh, no."

"That is bruising around your eye, isn't it?"

"Oh, this," Abby said, touching her eye. "Yes, well, he did do this, but not tonight. That's a whole other story."

Diverting their attention, a young rookie cop walked through Abby's side gate from the backyard to the front driveway. "Sarge, there's an older-model Harley parked on the other side of the property, behind the chicken coop. The motorcycle engine is still warm," he said. "And there is a blood trail, indicating the suspect was heading away from her house in that direction."

Abby locked eyes with Dak, who glowered back at her. "So," Abby said, "the commune kicks out the smart people and keeps the Neanderthals." Addressing the senior officer, she said, "Take him away."

The officer slammed the cruiser door, tapped the hood, and the cruiser pulled away.

Abby walked back to the front door and waited until the sergeant had finished speaking to his rookie. Then she escorted the senior officer into the bedroom to show him the window damage. Pointing to the blood on the sill, she said, "He couldn't shoot me, so I guess he thought he'd come through the window and finish me off. Stupid lout would leave his DNA all over the place."

"We'll need your statement," said the police officer.

"And I'm ready to give it," said Abby, "but what's the chance that you might share with me the license plate of the motorcycle he was riding?"

Chocolate Mint Mousse

Ingredients:
½ cup bittersweet chocolate chips
3 tablespoons strong coffee
1 tablespoon kirsch, Kahlúa, or brandy
4 large eggs, at room temperature, separated (preferably organic eggs from free-range chickens*)
⅔ cup granulated sugar
¾ cup heavy cream
½ teaspoon finely minced fresh chocolate mint, plus 4 sprigs, for garnish

Directions:
Combine the chocolate chips, coffee, and kirsch in a double boiler or a medium saucepan and cook over low heat, stirring continuously, until the chocolate has melted and the texture is smooth and even. Remove from the heat.

Separate the eggs, placing the yolks in a small bowl and the whites in a medium bowl.

Whisk together the egg yolks, sugar, and the minced mint and then fold the yolks into the melted chocolate mixture. Whip the cream until firm peaks are formed. Spoon the whipped cream into the chocolate and then gently fold in using a rubber spatula.

*Pasteurized eggs may be substituted for the organic eggs if there is a concern about the risk of bacteria in raw eggs.

Beat the egg whites until stiff peaks form. Gently fold the beaten egg whites into the chocolate mixture. Spoon the mousse into dessert cups or ramekins and chill, covered, in the refrigerator for 4 hours or overnight until the mousse sets. Garnish each cup with a sprig of mint, fresh raspberries, or shavings of white chocolate and serve.

Serves 4

Chapter 18

A pawful of honey could mean the wrathful
sting of a thousand bees.

—*Henny Penny Farmette Almanac*

By the time the police had collected all the evidence, had removed the crime-scene tape, and had given Abby permission to clean up the broken glass littering her bedroom floor, the sun had left the eastern-facing windows. Breakfast and lunch had come and gone. The cops had pried a bullet from the wall and had bagged and tagged the shell casings. They had arrested Dak Harmon and carted him off to jail. With the gun seized as evidence and the motorcycle impounded, the case against the bodyguard strengthened.

Abby rested in her grandmother's rocker on the patio, sipping from a mug of iced coffee, glad the ordeal was over. She listened to the songbirds' cacophony and watched Sugar's tail wag where it stuck out of the lavender thicket.

"I'll bet you slept better than I did," Clay called out to her as he rounded the house to reach the patio. He looked like he had come from an all-night party and needed only a shave and a comb-through to restore his sexy good looks.

"Why do you say that?" asked Abby.

"Just that it's always so peaceful here."

Resisting the urge to detail her harrowing night, she asked a pressing question. "And where did you sleep last night?"

"In my truck at the downtown park."

"Well, that's just weird. Why did you do that?"

"Lost track of time playing darts at the Black Witch with some of the guys." He groaned. "We drank way too much whiskey. Somebody—I don't recall his name—gave me a lift back to my truck. I couldn't drive. I figured it was safer to stay put."

"Why didn't you just park in front of the bar on Main Street?"

"The downtown was packed. No space on Main, and all the action seemed to originate in that downtown park. Leastways, that's where the drinking started . . . at the booths set up to get people interested in going over to the fair. Guess the fair has almost wrapped up its run. Anyway, one of the booths promoted local wine and cheese. They hook you on the samples and urge you to go to the fair, pay the entrance fee, and buy quantities of the wine and cheese you liked."

"Uh-huh. So you had cheese and a drop of wine, and they convinced you to buy the wineglass etched with the chamber of commerce logo before you could sample more. Am I right?"

"Somethin' like that." He rubbed a sandpaper cheek and changed the subject. "Any coffee left?" he asked, then darted into the kitchen before she could even answer.

Abby had expected him to be bruising for an argument, but he seemed to be in a cheery mood. *How nice.* She sank deeper into the chair and rocked. He hadn't bothered to inquire about how she'd slept. *Oh, that's right. It's always all about you, isn't it, Clay? And you probably haven't got a clue how tired I am of dealing with your crap.*

Her gaze swept across the lawn, past the citrus trees, all the way out to where the white climbing rose scampered up the six-foot chain-link fence and spilled over with thick sprays of blooms. The perfusion of rose blooms partially blocked the view into the wooded acre behind her property. Where the rose ended, the chicken run stretched to the henhouse. It, too, obscured a section of the back fence. Past the chickens' house and run, the fence began again with a metal gate that opened between the two properties. There had never been a need to lock that gate. As she stared at it, Abby figured Dak Harmon must have checked it out and known he could easily slip onto her property from the rear. And showing up at three thirty in the morning could have been a calculation against being seen.

Her attention shifted back to Clay, who had strolled onto the patio and had taken a seat to sip his mug of coffee. "Nice to finally have some time together," he said. "What do you think of your master bath?"

"I love it." *That's what you want to hear, isn't it? When you do something for someone else, it's never out of the goodness of your heart, but for the adulation you receive. I get that now.*

"Don't worry about ever paying me back. I'll think of something. It's ready to use," Clay said, grinning. "I've been thinking about getting a piece of teak to wrap around the top edge of the tub. I can cut a track and install a glass enclosure so water spray won't hit the floor."

"Sounds lovely," Abby said, thinking that although teak and glass would add a level of elegance, it seemed so unnecessary for such a small bathroom. She knew if she said anything about his idea, he'd take offense, see it as an affront to his creativity, so she said nothing else about it.

"Teak and glass will have to wait." Clay's expression darkened. He turned to look at the rose on the back fence.

"Why?" Abby asked, wondering what had caused his whole demeanor to shift. Maybe she hadn't waxed effusive enough with her compliments.

A corner of his mouth drew up slightly, the way it always did when he found something difficult to say. "You know I'd never knowingly hurt you, Abby, right?"

She drilled him with a questioning look. "Suppose so. Why? What's going on?"

"When I came here, I thought things were going to be just like the old times. We were always good together. But you've changed. Most days, you're gone."

"But I tell you when I'm going and where. And when I come back, I tell you what I've been doing. My friend Fiona was murdered. When a victim's family is grieving and needs help, I'm not the type of person to turn my back to them."

"Yeah." He took a sip of his coffee. "I guess I was fooling myself, thinking it would be like before between us. It's true what they say. You really can't go back. It's never the same."

"Oh, come on, Clay. You know as well as I do, relationships take time and effort . . . by both parties."

"And that's my point exactly." His expression hardened. "So why do I feel like I am a party of one? You're not the way you used to be."

"Why do you say that?" Abby asked, her fingers tightening around the coffee mug.

"You really want to know?" He eyed her suspiciously. "It used to be that you were always here, working next to me on the house or in the gardens. Now you are never here. Don't make time for me. I've even had to hire a day laborer just to help get that master bath to where it is."

"I didn't ask you to build me a master bath."

"No, you didn't. I was doing it out of the kindness of my heart."

Abby tensed, swallowed her retort. *Yeah, right.*

"I thought it would be nice if we built something new together, and not just that bathroom."

Abby stared at him. If he was trying to sound hurt, it had come across like sarcasm. *How dare you pick a fight so it seems like your imminent departure is my fault?* Unable to hold her frustration inside, Abby said, "You better take a picture of the tub before you go, because I am moving it out to repair the wiring. I heard arcing in the wall when I turned on the jets. If I didn't know better, I'd swear you were trying to electrocute me."

"Oh, come on. Are you accusing me of trying to kill you?"

"The alternative is to think that in your haste to get recognition, you aren't careful. Think back, Clay, to when I first bought the place and all the neighbors came round to marvel at your work in the kitchen. Then one morning I went to make coffee and barely missed being buried under the light soffit when it fell from the kitchen ceiling. Apparently, after all the compliments, you'd forgotten to finish screwing it in place. The soffit and the tub are like our relationship—both presentations that serve some obscure purpose of yours but are never meant to be permanent. Well, Clay, hear this. In my world, I need things to function correctly. The soffit didn't. The tub isn't. And we're not."

He glared at her and set his mug down harder than necessary on the glass patio table. "Forget it. I guess we're beyond talking things through." He exhaled heavily.

Pushing a wayward strand of hair from her face and tucking it behind her ear, Abby mustered her last bit of strength to return his stare. "You know what . . . ? Just go. I don't need this."

His expression seemed grim. "Fine."

Abby looked away; she reminded herself that two couldn't argue if one left. After standing up and stilling the rocker, she started for the kitchen.

Clay reached out and clamped his hand on her forearm. "You never loved me."

"And you never loved me. Honestly, Clay, I'm tired of playing nice, of tap-dancing around your moods all the time, hoping I haven't said something that's going to set you off. I don't want to live my life that way." She looked at him coolly. "So go, already. Texas this time . . . right?"

His dark eyes registered surprise. "What makes you say that?"

"You shouldn't surf the Net, looking for your next conquest, Clay, when you've just convinced the person lying beside you that she's the one that rocks your world. She's the one you love."

His lips thinned into a tight line. . . . Eyes imparted hurt and hostility. He released his grip on her arm.

Abby summoned all the strength within her. "Just go. We're done here." She marched back to the kitchen to put her mug in the sink. Holding on to the counter with a white-knuckled grip, she struggled to remain resolute.

Through the open slider, he called out, "Fine. I can make it to Los Angeles in eight hours, two more to Phoenix. I'd like a shower before taking off . . . if that's okay with you."

"Be my guest. Clean towels are on top of the washer." Abby busied herself with rinsing the mug and then placing it on the top shelf of the dishwasher.

Clay grabbed a towel. "Why are you so mad?"

"I'm not," Abby shot back. "I'm worn out by what

happened here last night, when you were doing whatever you were doing in town."

"What happened?"

"Someone tried to kill me. Did you not notice that the bedroom window has been shot out?" She turned to look at him. His expression registered shock.

After a pause, he shot back, "And yet you keep involving yourself with criminal investigations, like you are still a cop." He slammed the bathroom door.

Abby exhaled heavily. *Yeah, that's right. Make it my fault. Easier to look into the mirror then, isn't it?*

Fifteen minutes later, he reappeared in the living room, where Abby sat curled on the couch, sorting packets of seed she'd saved over the winter in labeled envelopes. He had towel dried his hair, shaved, and dressed in khakis, a narrow leather belt with a sleek silver buckle, brown lace-up oxfords, and a tomato-colored polo shirt with a Ralph Lauren label. After stashing his dirty clothes in a white plastic bag, he hoisted it under his arm and carried it, along with his suitcase and laptop bag, out the front door to his truck.

With both anger and sadness surging inside, Abby watched him leave the house. He still had the power to hurt her. And even if they couldn't be a couple, the bonds they'd formed long ago were proving stronger than she had realized. She placed the seed packets in the small cardboard box, rose, and strolled out to the front porch, with Sugar by her side. Her eyes burned, threatening tears, but she fought against them.

In the gravel driveway, Clay slammed his truck door and walked back toward her. His dark eyes locked onto hers; the scent of his soft cologne permeated the air. He stood in front of her, his expression dark and pouty. "Guess this is it." His tone sounded husky and slightly hostile.

Her chest tightened; her stomach twisted into knots. "Yes," she said. After a pause, she added, "Whatever it is you are seeking, I hope you find it. I think we know it was never me or the farmette."

He stared at the tassels on his brown oxfords. When he lifted his gaze to look at her again, his eyes shimmered. "Take care of yourself, Miss Abby Mac." He swung himself up into his truck and started the engine. A moment later, he drove away . . . out of her life.

When Kat called in mid-afternoon to see if Abby might want to come into town and meet her for coffee, Abby declined. She hadn't moved for hours after watching the dust settle in her driveway. She had not expected the deluge of tears after Clay had gone nor the conflicting feelings that had emerged after her tears dried. Feeling vulnerable and exposed, she had no desire beyond sheltering herself in solitude and the company of her chickens and bees and Sugar's unconditional love.

"Not today," Abby said.

"It's because of what happened last night, isn't it? Word of the shooting at your place is all over town. I wanted to make sure you're okay."

"I am . . . or, at least, I will be," Abby said, eyes misting up again. She sniffed.

"I heard you were there alone when Dak Harmon tried to kill you." Kat took a big breath and let it go. "Why wasn't Clay there? Of all nights, where was he?"

"He didn't want to get a DUI. He told me that he spent the night in his truck in the downtown park."

"And that would be a lie. Sorry to be so blunt."

"I know," Abby said. "He should have come up with something a little more creative. Everybody knows about that fence going up around that park when the town hosts the fair. The irony is that if he'd waited one more night, the fair would have been over, the booths in the park dismantled, and the fence taken down." Abby cleared her throat. "He probably met someone. Oh, well. It's a moot point now."

"How so?"

"He has gone. This time to Texas."

"You sad?"

"A little. But my heart gets lighter when I see that new master bath he built. Honestly, Kat, it tops any bathroom you might see in a fancy magazine."

"And I still haven't seen it. Don't know when I can get there again, though. The heat has turned up on Fiona's case now that Harmon is in the slammer. We've got ballistics going over the gun and casings."

"Anything from the motorcycle in the mountain garage that Gus Morales is repairing? I've been thinking how tidy it could be for the case if that tire tread matched the partial tire print at the scene of Fiona's burning car."

"Uh-oh," said Kat. "Hold on, Abby. The chief is calling me. I swear that man has eyes *and* ears in the back of his head."

Abby waited while Kat took the other call. When she again picked up the thread of their conversation, Kat's tone sounded urgent. "I have got to go. Chief wants me to bring Premalatha Baxter in for another interview. Get this. The gun Dak Harmon used to shoot out your window is registered to her."

"No kidding?" Abby twisted a clump of her hair around a finger as she thought about that development. "Well, you know . . . Premalatha wore a tunic when Jack and I last saw her, and it was hot enough to fry an egg on the hood of my car. Make her push those sleeves up when you get her into that interview room."

"You think that nicotine patch belonged to her, right? They probably both smoke. Dak had a pack on him when he used you for target practice. And thanks to his stupidity, we've got his DNA on the discarded butt he dropped at your back fence."

"Saliva sample," said Abby.

"Premalatha denied being a smoker, but we'll ask her again. Now, Abby, forget about Clay. Get some rest. Sleep, chocolate, and a new man will fix what ails you."

After hanging up from the call, Abby spent the next half hour stapling screen wire to the exterior of the house, over the hole where the large window used to be. And as an extra measure against any mosquitoes and other insects entering the house, Abby also stapled sheets to the interior wall as temporary curtains. She hadn't finished pushing in the last staple before her cell phone rang. A neighbor wanted to order three jars each of Abby's apricot jam and backyard honey—the result of word getting around that both had been judged blue-ribbon winners at the county fair. And the calls didn't end with that one.

A family who lived a mile north of Dr. Danbury's place wanted fifty sample jars of farmette honey to give away as favors at their daughter's upcoming wedding. The cash deal carried a proviso—Abby would be required to deliver the sample jars directly to the home of the bride's mother. Abby's excitement mounted as she mentally tallied the income that the wedding order would generate and the potential windfall that might follow if the wedding guests became regular paying customers. But even as the thought of an improved cash flow invigorated her, a sobering thought intruded. Was there honey enough to fill the orders? Abby quickly checked the shelves above the washer and dryer. Eight small jars. Not enough. Next, she removed the lid from the white five-gallon honey bucket on the kitchen counter, but it had been drained until nearly dry.

Abby racked her brain. Who might have extra jars that she could buy back until she could open the hives to see if she might take another frame or two? Abby thought of Smooth Your Groove and Fiona's botanical shop. The former had been forcibly closed and locked by the health department. That left only Fiona's stash. And as she recalled, Fiona kept a few jars in her shop and held back the others in the storage shed near her cottage.

"By any chance are you in the cottage?" she asked after Jack answered her call.

"That I am. For the last quarter hour, I've been chatting up Paws, the landlord's long-haired, six-toed kitty. The big boy just invited himself in. Popped up the hole, he did. I've put out a tin of fish for him and a bowl of crackers for me. So, what can I do for you?"

"I'm short honey for orders I have to fill. Fiona bought two cases from me. She told me she was going to put out a few jars for sale and stash the rest in her storage shed near the cottage. Could I—"

"Buy it back? No. Come up and get it. That would be spot-on lovely."

"Could I come now?"

"I'll put out more crackers," he said with a chuckle.

"Okay if I bring Sugar?"

"Only if you promise that she doesn't remember how I previously threw the two of you out."

Abby laughed. "Don't know about that. Can't speak for Sugar."

After clicking off the call, Abby searched the laundry basket. She pulled out a folded pair of jeans and a pale green T-shirt that still held the scent of fabric softener, slipped out of her work clothes, and put the jeans and T-shirt on. From the guest bath, where she stood in front of the wall mirror, vigorously brushing her hair, she heard her cell phone alerting her to an incoming text. It was from the police chief, saying his wife wanted honey for her church—eight-ounce jars, fifteen total. Abby texted back, **I'm on it. If I have enough on hand, I'll deliver tomorrow.**

After nuking a clean, moistened washcloth in the microwave for a few seconds, Abby shook it out, tested the heat, and then draped it over her face. She dried her face with a towel and applied a light foundation, some blusher, a dab of mascara, and a couple of strokes of plum lip gloss. After grabbing a yellow paisley-patterned scarf and a heavily embroidered jeans jacket, she stuffed the pockets with treats for Sugar. She looked approvingly at herself in the armoire mirror before locking the kitchen slider and exiting the house through the front door.

The drive into the mountains before sunset had always seemed romantic to Abby, especially in late spring. She likened it to an arty Italian film with evocative cinematography—you could almost smell the earth, warm and fragrant with hedge roses, ripe grapes, and wild thyme. You could almost see a light sifting of dust floating over the patchwork hills and the medieval stone houses in villages where bell towers rang out the canonical hours. The mountains soon worked their magic on Abby. So peaceful and absorbed in thought was she that she nearly missed the big red barn turnoff, hitting the brakes just in the nick of time.

Only too eager to stretch her legs and sniff the environment, Sugar leaped from the Jeep as soon as Abby had opened the door. Jack jogged down to the mailbox and greeted her with a bear hug. Sugar yipped until Jack held out his hands, palms down, for her to smell. Her tail began to wag.

"Have I passed her sniff test, Abby? Or should I be afraid she'll take my ankle off when I stand up?"

"Oh, *please*. She weighs thirty-five pounds. How could she possibly hurt a big guy like you?"

"Yeah, well, I can think of some ways. It's the ones at the knees you have to watch out for . . . never know which spot they'll go for." He grinned and tried stroking Sugar's head, but she wouldn't back away from him.

"She'll settle down," said Abby. "Do you see that shed over there? You've got the key to it, I hope," said Abby as she advanced on the path past the mailbox.

Jack abruptly stood from where he'd squatted to pet Sugar. He reached into his long, straight-leg jeans and fished out a silver ring with several keys. "Let's find out." They walked over to the shed, with Sugar leading the way, nose to the ground.

"Gosh, why does it smell like a garbage dump?" Abby asked.

Jack wrinkled his nose. "That would be because it is. The landlord stacks his refuse bags next to that black barrel. There he incinerates them." Jack tried a key in the padlock. It released. After removing the lock and unlatching the door, he pulled the door open and waved Abby inside.

"Why let the bags just pile up like that so near the cottage?" said Abby. "You'd think there would be—"

"Rats?" Jack asked.

Sugar's shrill, high-pitched *yip-yip-yip* interrupted.

"Yes, rats," Abby replied, hurrying over to quiet Sugar. "*No*. Get outta there. Now."

Sugar pawed at the mound of plastic and paper bags of

refuse. Abby tried grabbing her, but Sugar leaped from her reach, dashed to the other side of the bags.

"If she comes this way," Jack said, "I'll try to snatch her."

"It could be a rat or a mouse that's got her so excited," said Abby. "She's definitely more interested in the garbage than the treats in my pocket. If I gave her a treat now, it would just reinforce the barking behavior."

"Oh," Jack said, tapping his temple. "Now you're going all dog whisperer on me. Brilliant. So what's your strategy?"

"Beats me," said Abby. While she considered her options, Sugar plowed through the pile, knocking over bags, causing their contents to spill out. She leaped up and raced after a field mouse zigzagging toward the mailbox, up the path, and under the cottage.

"Over soon," said Abby. After a few minutes of frantic barking, Sugar abandoned the mouse to sniff around the bushes at the entrance, where the cats had undoubtedly marked their territory. "Oh, my gosh, Jack," Abby said, looking at the strewn contents of a bag near his feet. "Don't move."

Jack frowned, as if he feared the escaped mouse had a companion that was about to disappear up his pants leg. "What? That broken teacup?" He reached down.

"No. Don't . . . don't touch it," Abby demanded. "That teacup is one of Fiona's. I recognize it because it belongs to that set of china I helped you pack up."

"So it is. Good eye."

"I've got a hunch the detectives will want to check out the items in that bag—the cup, those wadded paper towels, and that disposable cup with the Smooth Your Groove logo."

"Clues?" he asked.

"I don't know. It's probably a long shot. Just the same, I'm calling it in."

* * *

Twenty minutes later, Abby and Jack stood near Dr. Danbury. Still in a stupor, the doc had stumbled outside to watch the police retrieve the plastic bag and its contents. He wore a wrinkled short-sleeve cotton shirt under farmers' overalls. His oiled silver hair lay flat; he seemed to need his cane to stand upright. By the time the two cruisers pulled away, the sun had dropped low behind the blue-green mountain ridges. Fog like fingers of smoke inched through the dark valleys below. Dr. Danbury asked Abby if she and Jack would like to come over and help him finish a bottle of a local vintner's pinot noir.

"I'll have to pass," Abby said. "Thanks anyway. But, Doc, do you mind if I ask a question?"

"Be my guest," he said, using a ropy-veined hand to smack an insect that had alighted on his hairy arm.

"Do you remember seeing Fiona on the morning she died?"

"Nope. Couldn't have," the doctor replied.

"Why is that?" Abby asked.

"I stayed overnight in Las Flores. My son's got himself a nice condo. It's right downtown. His fiancée and I took him to the country club to celebrate."

"Yeah? If I may ask, what were you celebrating?"

"His birthday. I spent the night on his couch." He cleared his throat. "Don't much like driving in the dark."

"And that's your Volvo there?" she said, pointing to his wagon. "What about that ATV in your garage? Does anyone ever take it out for a spin?"

"Nope. Got it for my boy four or five years ago. He used to tear all over the mountain. Not now. His girlfriend never went in for that sort of thing." He paused. "You interested in buying it?"

Abby smiled. "Nah. Just curious. So, to be clear, you

weren't here during that twenty-four-hour period when Fiona died?"

"Nope."

"And none of your neighbors have reported seeing anyone messing around on your property?"

"Nope. That neither." He thrust his hands into his pockets. "S'pect the wine's breathed plenty long enough now," Dr. Danbury said. "You joining me or not?"

Abby shook her head. Jack had walked a few paces away to gaze at the rising full moon as the curved sliver steadily ascended to become a luminous golden disk. "Dr. Danbury wants to know if you'd like to have a drink with him, Jack."

"Oh, no. Thanks, Doc." Jack turned to face them. "Abby and I are going honey hunting."

Apparently, Jack's remark made no sense to the doctor, who spun around and walked with his cane back to his door.

When the doctor had left them, Abby said, "I kind of like the honey-hunting idea. It sounds like we're primitives going out to find hives in the wild."

"It might interest you to know that in Nepal, there is an ancient tradition of gathering honey from the hives of wild bees. Honey gatherers have two tools—rope ladders and long sticks . . . well, three, if you count smoke—to raid the hives on towering cliffs. It's risky."

"Luckily, we won't need ropes, smoke, or sticks. And we don't have to go far, just to that shed over there," Abby said with a grin. She took hold of his arm and steered him toward the shed.

"Did you know the largest honeybee in the world is the *Apis laboriosa*, and it's found in Nepal?" Jack asked.

"I did not," Abby replied as they approached the doorway of the shed. The shed's exterior was illuminated by moonlight, but the interior was as dark as a covered well. "Did you know it's next to impossible to find the honey in the dark?" She was about to add, "I'll just get my flashlight from my pack," when he pulled her into an embrace.

"Who says I can't find honey in the dark?" He tilted her face upward. His fingers trailed along her cheek.

Abby felt giddy. Her heart pounded like a thundering river. As he leaned in, Abby anticipated his kiss, but instead, he nuzzled his face against her neck, reached out into the darkness, and flipped on the light switch. Directly in her sight line, on a metal-framed utility shelf, rested the case of honey and six jars bearing her farmette label.

"Oh, you're good," she said, at once relieved at what had not happened and at the same time wishing something had. "If you'll carry the case, I'll grab these jars."

After they had loaded the honey into the Jeep, an awkward moment passed between them until the lightbulb in the shed sputtered off. They both turned to look at it. It flickered back on and then off again. A loud *pop* sounded, and the light went out.

"Jesus, Mary, and Joseph. I'd better turn off the juice. Don't want to burn down the shed," Jack said.

Abby chuckled. "No, that would never do." She reached down to stroke Sugar, who was pawing at her legs. "We'd better go," said Abby, lifting Sugar's warm, round body into the Jeep. "I've got my pooch to feed, my chickens to check on, and honey jars to fill with what little honey I have in the house."

"Well, if you must," Jack said. "I could help, if you like."

"Really? When did you last fill a honey jar?"

"Well, actually, never. But I'm a quick study. Besides,

after we fill them, we can drive around delivering honey to all your customers, and I can amuse you with stories. So, what do you say?"

Abby thought about his proposition. *A sexy guy who tells the truth, is willing to help, and takes direction. What's not to like?*

"I'm game. Do you think you can find your way to Farm Hill Road? Turn right and look for the mailbox with the chicken on it. Actually, it's a rooster with tall tail feathers, but it marks my driveway. If you can get there by eight o'clock in the morning, I'll have coffee ready and some killer apricot honey bread in the oven."

Apricot-Craisin Honey Bread

Ingredients:
Vegetable oil spray, for greasing the loaf pans
1 cup diced dried apricots
½ cup Craisins
½ cup organic honey
¼ cup canola oil
⅔ cup boiling water
2 cups whole-wheat flour
2 teaspoons baking powder
¼ teaspoon baking soda
1 cup chopped unsalted pecans
½ cup evaporated milk
1 large egg

Directions:
Preheat the oven to 350°F. Lightly spray three 6-x-3-inch loaf pans with the vegetable oil spray. Place the apricots and the Craisins in a medium

bowl and add the honey, oil, and boiling water. Set aside and let cool.

Meanwhile, sift together the flour, baking powder, and baking soda in a large bowl. Add the pecans.

In a small bowl, whisk together the milk and the egg. Pour the egg mixture into the reserved apricots and Craisins and mix well.

Add the apricot-Craisin mixture to the pecan-flour mixture and stir until all the ingredients are well combined.

Pour an equal amount of batter into each of the prepared loaf pans. Allow the batter to settle. Bake for 30 to 35 minutes. Test for doneness by inserting a toothpick into the loaves. It should have no batter on it when extracted.

Cool the mini loaves and then invert them onto a clean surface. Wrap them in foil. Let the honey bread rest overnight for the best flavor.

Makes 3 loaves

Chapter 19

For a flock of appreciative clucking followers,
sprinkle dried mealworms over a dish of greens.

—*Henny Penny Farmette Almanac*

At first light, Abby ran the water in the tub of her new master bath, but the water from the spigot remained as cloudy and slightly greasy as the previous time she'd cracked it on. It dawned on her that the water had to run awhile to get rid of the flux from the new copper pipes. It was normal with new piping. Still, she wasn't about to turn on the jets. But as she thought about it, maybe a bath wasn't such a good idea. Jack might arrive early, before she had prepped everything. After turning off the water and dashing to the guest bathroom, she showered and did a quick blow-dry of her hair.

Choosing a lightweight turquoise summer knit dress with hidden pockets, a scooped neck, and a flared skirt, Abby pulled it over her head and stepped into a pair of black flats. She gathered her reddish-gold locks and anchored them with a black elastic band at the base of her neck. Finally, she put on her favorite turquoise, amethyst, and seed pearl earrings and then admired her image in the mirror. She hoped the look would please Jack.

After tying on a clean white pinafore apron, she began to load the dishwasher with jars and screw-top lids, rather than the ring lids she used for jam. Abby set the dishwasher running through its hottest cycle, but then she heard a ruckus from the chicken house. Dashing out the patio door and across the lawn, she saw a small fox pawing at the structure's window.

"Oh, no, you don't," she yelled, plucking two apricots from the tree and lobbing them at the fox. The fox leaped from the henhouse and scampered up the chain-link fence.

Abby stood in the chicken run until the hens had settled down. The black-and-white wyandottes resumed their alto-toned, gravelly *g-rack*, *g-rack*, *g-rack*. The white leghorns clucked in a higher pitch. Blondie, the Buff Orpington—who could be a broodzilla when she was in her broody cycle—began scratching a hole for her dirt bath. And Houdini, the rooster, let go a shrill, yet manly *cock-a-doo-dle-doo*. Abby knew they wanted out of the run to free-range forage, but that wasn't going to happen while there was a predator in the area. Where there was one fox, more were likely, perhaps a den of them. She could still see the fox sitting on its haunches on a hill at the rear of the wooded acre. No way was she letting her feathered friends out today. Abby checked the feeder hanging from its chain and the water dispenser. Both were half full, so Abby left the run and returned to the farmhouse.

Back inside the kitchen, she turned on the oven and set about making a batch of apricot honey bread. With the three loaf pans in the oven for the next thirty minutes, Abby carried a chair over to the washer and dryer area. From the top shelf, she took down two cardboard boxes, each holding a dozen jars of apricot jam. She set the boxes on the dining-room table.

After putting the chair back from the washer and dryer area and tucking it under the dining table, Abby then returned to the kitchen. She poured a cup of nuggets into the dog food bowl and fresh water into the canister of the water dispenser. Next, she made a pot of coffee. When it was ready, she poured herself a cup and leaned over the counter with a pencil and paper to write out the sequence of her honey and jam deliveries, starting with the chief's at the police department.

Jack arrived punctually at eight o'clock that morning, dressed in a T-shirt featuring a blue morning glory and, beneath the image, its identification, *Ipomoea tricolor*. He wore tan cargo shorts and sand-colored lace-up espadrilles. His hair lay in loose curls across his forehead, making him more boyish-looking than usual. Sugar behaved as if Jack had become her best friend; her tail wagged wildly when he strolled into the yard through the side gate. Abby didn't try to conceal her delight at seeing him, too. She gave Jack a quick hug and offered him a tour of her farmette, with Sugar bounding happily around them.

His face beamed a smile as his gaze swept over her property. "Oh, yes, Abby. Show me this place you've created out of an old field," he said happily.

At the Black Tartarian trees, he picked a bright red cherry with a hole in its side. "Oh, well, what's a small peck out of the side of an otherwise perfectly good cherry? I don't mind sharing with the birds," he said, then popped the cherry in his mouth and promptly spit out the seed.

At the row of early bearing peaches, he gently squeezed three golden fruits until he was satisfied he'd found the ripest specimen. He offered it to Abby. When she shook her head, he peeled off the skin, ate the peach with relish, and tossed the pit to the ground. They walked a short distance farther and reached the apple trees.

He gave her a sexy look. "I feel like I'm in the Garden of Eden," he said. "But the temptress hasn't offered me the apple."

Abby laughed. "You'll have to wait."

"Oh, isn't that always the way? Eve didn't hesitate to offer one to Adam."

"She would have if they were standing by this tree."

Jack's expressive eyes danced as he regarded her quizzically.

"Well, just look at them," said Abby. "They're the size of acorns. These apples won't be ripe until autumn."

"Autumn, you say? What a pity. I might be gone by then." His eyes regarded her, as if he was gauging her response.

Abby dropped her gaze.

"Or I might just stick around."

"Would that be such a bad thing?" Abby teased.

His eyes locked onto hers with seemingly seductive intention. "No, not at all. By autumn, your apples might not be the only sweet thing I taste in your garden."

"Oh, my," said Abby, pretending to fan away her fluster with the skirt of her apron. "I think we've dallied long enough. Better have our breakfast and hit the road, or I'll be late with my deliveries."

Inside the lobby of the Las Flores Police Station, with the honey order for Chief Bob Allen's wife, Abby overheard two female dispatchers arguing. Apparently, they were both dating the same man.

"Yeah, well, he is serially monogamous," the older of the two women asserted.

"You think I don't know what that means?" said the younger dispatcher, running her fingers through her edgy bicolored black-and-platinum hairdo. She flipped her hand dismissively toward the other woman. "He dumps his current girlfriend to pursue a new one. I'm the new one."

"Don't get your hopes up, love. He hasn't dumped me yet, and I don't intend to let him." The beads braided into her mocha-colored hair gave the older woman an exotic look. "You forget, I'm from Colombia, and there we fight for our men. I'm telling you it's not over until I say it is."

The tone of the argument quickly escalated. Abby frantically pushed the buzzer on the wall, waited, and pushed it again. Nettie appeared on the other side of the glass window, her forehead creased in a frown. Alarmed and shaking her head, apparently at the argument, she told Abby through the speaker, "Be right with you."

Abby pointed to the counter and motioned for Jack to put the case down next to the jars she'd already placed there. They waited as Nettie disappeared and returned with Chief Bob Allen. He went over to the dispatchers and called out the warring women.

"Who were they arguing over?" Abby asked Nettie as the chief took each woman aside for a talk.

Nettie rolled her eyes. "Bernie in the evidence room."

Abby burst out laughing. "You're kidding, right?"

Nettie shook her head. "Mr. I'm here for a good time, not a long time."

Abby shook her head and feigned a serious look as the chief looked over at her. The room became as quiet as a hot jar of jam before the seal popped.

"This way," the chief said after he opened the security door for her and Jack to enter. "My office is down here at the end of the hall. Officer Petrovsky and I have been interviewing a suspect in your sister's death, and I'd like to fill you in, Mr. Sullivan."

"A suspect? Any chance it's Premalatha Baxter?" asked Abby.

He nodded, leading them to the institutional chairs opposite his massive desk. "She denies any knowledge of the murder." The chief motioned for them to set the case and the jars on the desk and take a seat.

"You have proof to the contrary?" asked Jack.

"Yes, Mr. Sullivan, we do. Her fingerprint was on the broken teacup that Mackenzie's dog uncovered. We were able to match the one on the teacup with prints in the state's system because of a background check on Ms. Baxter when she applied for work in a casino. We can also tie her to the burning car crime scene through that nicotine patch that Mackenzie found in the nearby weed patch. Claims she is a closet smoker, mostly herbs through a water pipe but also tobacco. She conceals her habit and also the patch she wears to quit."

Abby felt pleased but maintained a solemn expression. "But, Chief, Fiona knew Premalatha smoked. She had to know, because Premalatha and Dak stopped by Ancient Wisdom Botanicals, asking for an herb blend for smoking, the day before Fiona died. I was there and saw the exchange. Fiona told Premalatha that the blend was out of stock."

"Yes. I read your statement. We're convinced that we've got your sister's killer, Mr. Sullivan, but we know she had to have help moving the body. We're still piecing that part of the case together."

"But you have Dak Harmon in custody," said Abby. "He's got to know what went down."

"He's not saying. We read him his rights, and he lawyered up."

"Isn't it true that the two of them were providing alibis for each other? They were at the commune that morning. They had lunch there together with the leader and everyone else."

"True," said Chief Bob Allen. "Premalatha told us that around ten thirty on the morning Fiona died, she tried to phone Fiona to apologize for their public argument at the smoothie shop. Her cell phone records indicate that she made that call."

Abby had a sudden thought. "How long was their conversation?"

"Less than two minutes."

"Okay, I'm going to suggest something," Abby said. She then phrased her theory with flattery for the chief. "You've probably already thought of this, but here goes. What if Premalatha went to the cottage and gave Fiona poison in a cup of tea or in a smoothie she prepared in a Smooth Your Groove cup? I've been reading up on this, and Jack knows about it, too. This poisonous plant called monkshood has pretty flowers, but all parts of the plant, including the roots, are poisonous. Let's say that Premalatha makes a tincture from the plant, which they grow up on the commune land, and puts the drops in the tea or the smoothie. Then she convinces Fiona to taste a smoothie recipe she'd like Fiona to approve for the smoothie shop. Seeking Fiona's approval might have gotten the result she intended. That is, for Fiona to taste the smoothie. Maybe Fiona already had a cup of tea, and Premalatha doctored it, too, or perhaps Premalatha made her a cup of tea if Fiona complained of not feeling well after tasting the smoothie." Abby took a deep breath and exhaled.

"Go on," said the chief. His elbows rested on his desk, and his thumbs and forefingers pressed against each other.

"To create an alibi for herself, Premalatha uses her cell phone to call Fiona. Getting a message, she listens and maybe leaves one for Fiona. All the while, she's standing right there in the cottage as Fiona is dying. Then Premalatha cleans up, putting everything in that trash bag to toss onto the refuse pile where Dr. Danbury stores his trash to be incinerated. And since Dr. Danbury spent the night in Las Flores, celebrating his son's birthday, there was no one else at the estate the morning Fiona died."

"That's right," said Jack. "Tom told me he'd asked permission from Premalatha to go to Fiona's cottage that night to discuss their divorce. Also, he said he had that winery renovation job to go to early the next morning . . . the morning Fiona died."

"For your sister," Abby said, glancing over at Jack, "it was just a stroke of bad luck that no one was on the property that morning. Premalatha had already decided it would be the last time Tom would spend the night with Fiona." Abby exhaled deeply and looked back at Chief Bob Allen.

"I'm still listening." The chief leaned back in his chair and quietly tapped a finger against his desk.

"I think that Premalatha and her accomplice loaded Fiona's body in her car. They took two vehicles to Kilbride Lake. There they placed Fiona into the driver's seat but forgot to adjust the seat forward so Fiona's feet could reach the gas pedal. Premalatha is roughly five feet, nine inches. Fiona was about five-three."

"Uh-huh," said the chief. "And so . . ."

"So, Premalatha and her accomplice set the car on fire to get rid of the body and any trace evidence," Abby said. She looked over at a stone-faced Jack before continuing. "They ride back to the commune, leave their vehicle, probably a motorcycle, in the woods near the commune. That way, they can part company and slip onto the grounds unnoticed from different directions, as if they'd been present at the commune all morning."

Chief Bob Allen had been staring intently at Abby as she spoke. He sniffed deeply. "Initially, we thought Dak Harmon might have helped move the body. That partial tire print at Kilbride Lake has some similarities to the tread on the tires of the mountain garage loaner motorcycle—the one he uses when his is in the shop and the same one he rode to your house, Abby."

Abby sat a little straighter. *Thought it might.*

The chief leaned back and put his hands behind his head. "But you know as well as I do that because tires are so generic and are sold so widely, it would be difficult to tie a suspect to any one vehicle in that location. And that is true even if the print happened to be a good, usable impression. It's a little too circumstantial. Others could have easy access to that bike."

Abby nodded. "True, but who would also have motive and means and access to that bike? You said the impression appeared similar to the tread on that bike's tire."

"Wish it were a full print, but it's not. Fingerprints can get us a conviction, but a DNA match would tie up the evidence with a sweet little bow. We have it with the nicotine patch linking Premalatha to the burned car and her print on the teacup. But we all know she had help."

The chief hadn't lobbed any cheap shots at her yet, and Abby wondered if he would. Maybe since she'd brought all that honey, he was making nice, treating her like a colleague rather than a cadet. "Somebody drove the body to the lake in Fiona's car, while the accomplice followed on or in some type of vehicle. Let's say it was a motorcycle. They would have staged Fiona's body behind the steering wheel and torched the car. Was an accelerant used?"

"Yes," said the chief.

"So, where's the container? If the killer and an accomplice made their getaway on a motorcycle, they probably used lighter fluid. Easier to take the container with them than a gas can. If Dak Harmon didn't help with disposing of the body, then who did? Who else had the motive to take Fiona's life and also had access to that bike?"

Chief Bob Allen rubbed a bushy brow with four fingers of one hand while he stared at Abby, as though staring could elicit from her the answer he didn't have.

Abby thought for a moment. "Hayden Marks has a motive. Fiona threatened his hold over everyone."

The chief leaned forward. "Well, we're not ready to hold the press conference yet, but there was a second print, a thumbprint, recovered from the trash. The bag that held the broken teacup contained a print that belongs to Marks. He's an ex-felon who served time for grand theft of firearms."

"Wonder if he knows how to ride a Harley," Jack mused.

The chief nodded. "Oh, he does. Marks had a previous affiliation with a gang of outlaw bikers."

Abby smiled. "So that's it. Hayden Marks puts Fiona's body in the car. He drives it to the lake. They set the car on fire, and then Marks gives Premalatha a ride back to the commune on that motorcycle."

"There's another piece of linkage in all this," said the chief. "As part of the state's mandate to reduce prison populations, Hayden Marks was released early. He was sent to the same conservation camp, or 'fire camp,' as Dak Harmon and a few other prisoners to help fight California wildfires."

"So with Baxter and Harmon in jail, why haven't you arrested Marks?" Jack asked.

"Well, there's a problem. He's taken off," the chief said.

"We've alerted the local airports, bus terminals, and train stations. And we've put out a BOLO on him and that new car."

Abby chimed in. "Driving a hot new BMW Alpina B-seven isn't too stealthy. It won't be difficult to spot it."

"He probably didn't have a choice with his bike in the mountain shop, being repaired," said the chief, rising to lift the case of honey from his desk and to set it on the floor by the window. "Two residents saw Marks drive away from the commune. But we'll find him. And now with a plausible scenario and incriminating evidence to support it against those three, we'll soon have them all behind bars. Premeditated murder, with poison as an aggravated factor, is a capital murder charge. That means the death penalty is on the table."

Jack stood and extended his hand, his eyes shining with gratitude. "Thanks for the update, Chief. Finally closure."

"Good work, Chief," Abby said, rising from her chair.

"How much do I owe you for the honey, Mackenzie? My missus is going to—" His words stopped with the knock at the door.

Nettie popped in. "Chief, we've got a hit on the BOLO. A sheriff in Santa Cruz County is calling. Someone thought they saw the car. Do you want to take it here? Line two."

The chief pursed his lips. He nodded.

Against a desire to dally long enough to find out more about the BOLO, Abby said to the chief, "We'll settle up later with the money. Give you some privacy to take that call. Fingers crossed." She and Nettie walked back to the lobby, with Jack following.

A few minutes later, Abby pulled out of the police parking lot and steered the Jeep on a course into the mountains.

"Getting those killers behind bars is one thing. . . . Do you think the police will have enough evidence for the court trial?" Jack asked, unpeeling the wrapper from a piece of gum. He offered the gum to her.

She waved off the gum and said, "You can be sure that Chief Bob Allen and his team will do everything they can to bring a solid case to the district attorney."

"Good." Jack slipped the gum package back into the pocket of his T-shirt and settled back into his seat. He stretched out his bare, muscular legs. "There was a gorgeous moon and a clear sky last night. What's up with all this fog today?"

"Microclimates. The mountains are different from the valley." Abby tapped a button on the radio and turned to her favorite soft jazz station. As she entered the first big turn on the slick asphalt road, she gripped the steering wheel a little tighter. "Here in the Bay Area, we can have sun in the valley and fog and drizzle in the mountains. The outside temperature can change thirty degrees from one microclimate to another, like in the summer, driving from San Jose to San Francisco."

"Oh." Jack leaned back and closed his eyes, apparently enjoying the ride. "I like your taste in music," he said. "How far do we have to go now?"

"A few miles," said Abby. Her tension lessened as they drove toward the summit for the delivery to the wedding customer. A late-season storm was expected to blow through. If they were lucky enough to get any rain in the valley, it would be spotty, but the winds buffeted her Jeep now and already the mountain mist had become heavy, so rain could hit at any moment.

"Where is this Kilbride Lake?" asked Jack.

"It's not too far from where you're staying in the cottage. I could take you to see it before we make the delivery, if you like. It's a really pretty area, although today the lake water is probably choppy and reflecting the gray sky."

He spoke in a voice tinged with sadness. "It's where the killers took her and tried to burn . . . I want to see that spot."

"You got it," said Abby. She negotiated the curvy road for another half mile, cringing on the approach into the two most dangerous curves. She'd not soon forget that Timothy Kramer in his silver pickup had once forced her off the road, had taken a shot at her, and later had set that wilderness cabin on fire. For an instant, her thoughts turned to that harrowing experience. But then the Santa Cruz County Sheriff's Department had found him and arrested him. It was unlikely that local law enforcement would return to those wooded forty acres. Oh, but Hayden Marks could have.

"Oh, my gosh!" exclaimed Abby at the sudden realization. "Mind if we take a brief detour, Jack? I have a sudden urge to check that land behind Doc Danbury's estate. I think it's possible that Hayden Marks knows about that area. He could be hiding back there. And that could be why law enforcement hasn't found him."

With the two curves behind her, the road again climbed. Abby remained vigilant on the road since the cliff side had no guardrail. The rocky, tree-studded cliffs plunged eighty feet below. On the mountain side, blind curves presented another hazard to drivers. On a clear day, Abby enjoyed the drive, but when there was fog and the road was wet, like today, she hit the brakes a lot . . . and now she needed to use the wipers.

The fog concealed the drop-offs from view but did little to lessen Abby's anxiety. Despite her defensive driving, the Jeep hydroplaned after reaching the red barn. *How ironic*, Abby thought. *Hydroplaning in an area where the fog bank has thinned and visibility has improved.* Still, she navigated the series of curves before the road straightened out again.

Then she spotted the NO TRESPASSING sign in white paint on the big board nailed to a tree that indicated the turnoff to the cabin in the woods. She followed the rutted road to the high hill and the stand of oaks, remembering the shot Kramer had fired at her. Shaking off the memory, she peered down toward the clearing where the cabin once stood.

"I can't make out much of anything," said Jack, leaning in to wipe the inside of the windshield with his hand.

"I was hoping the fog would be evaporating here, like it was at the barn," said Abby. She stared at the wispy sheets wafting by in front of the Jeep's headlamps.

"Ah, Abby, 'tis like we're ghosts in a netherworld," said Jack, slipping into his Irish brogue. "No one here to see. No one to bother us. It gives me ideas, it does."

Abby smiled and drilled him with a playful gaze. "Yeah? What kind of ideas?"

Jack unfastened his seat belt. His eyes conveyed desire. "This, for one," he said, leaning in.

Abby anticipated his kiss, but it never came. Instead, Jack's attention was diverted as he turned abruptly to face the source of the lights that had flicked on in the clearing. Abby stared, too. The lights appeared to be the high beams of a vehicle. Whatever kind of vehicle it was, the darn thing was headed straight for them. Abby didn't have time to debate whether or not to make a U-turn. The champagne-colored Alpina streaked past, swerving at the last minute.

"It's him . . . Hayden Marks. He almost killed us," Abby cried out.

"I see him. Go . . . go. Go after him, Abby. He's getting away."

"Too dangerous, Jack. The fog . . . can't see—"

"He's got to be stopped. Think of Fiona."

Flipping into a U-turn, Abby hit the gas. "You're right.

For Fiona . . ." *And my brother.* "Call it in, Jack. The phone is on the console. We need backup."

Abby drove as fast as she dared in the deadly fog, following the Alpina's taillights. Jack alerted dispatch. At the NO TRESPASSING sign, the Alpina turned onto the asphalt road and picked up speed. Abby followed. Nearing the red barn, she saw the fog had receded over the edge of the mountain.

"Thank God. I can see." Abby breathed. "There. There he is," she said, pushing hard on the gas pedal.

"We're closing in, Abby. Closing in."

Abby hardly heard Jack. Her thoughts raced ahead to the two most dangerous curves on the mountain. The Alpina had entered one of them. Then, in a millisecond, Abby heard the crash as the Alpina hit the granite wall. She watched the car flip into the air. Fly off the edge. Plunge down the cliff.

Abby's heart caught in her throat. Her fingers tightened into a death grip on the steering wheel. She tapped her brakes, knowing if she hit them hard, the Jeep would fishtail on the wet asphalt. She would lose control. End up just like Marks. When she got the car to a nearly full stop, she guided the Jeep into a slow roll onto the narrow turnout.

Jack jumped out. She followed. They raced to the cliff's edge to peer over. Flames from the Alpina leaped high into the air. Loud popping sounds followed, shattering the mountain's silence. Abby trembled, and Jack reached out to pull her close. He stroked her hair as they stood staring at the spectacle below.

"No one could have survived that," said Abby. She sucked in a mouthful of air and blew it out between pursed lips. "How ironic. What he tried to do to Fiona's body, he ends up doing to his own."

"It's divine justice," Jack said, drawing her closer.

Within minutes, sirens screamed in tandem on approach. The arrival of the first emergency vehicle, with its lights and siren on, shattered the quiet peace of the mountains. Cal Fire followed closely behind the deputy sheriff's cruiser. Abby slipped out of Jack's embrace when the deputy pulled in behind her Jeep. He got out and approached them. Abby recognized him from police work back in the day.

"You all right?" asked the deputy.

"Uh-huh," Abby said. "The driver is the murder suspect Hayden Marks. My friend here is Jack Sullivan. We saw Marks lose control of the Beemer, hit, flip, and fly over." She let go a sigh. "Guess Chief Bob Allen can cancel that BOLO he put out on Marks."

The deputy nodded. "We'll need your statements," he said, raising his voice to be heard over more sirens approaching.

"No problem," said Abby.

"Seeing as how it's you, Mackenzie, I don't see why we have to detain you."

"Nor do I," said Abby. "The chief knows how to reach me. So we'll let you get on with your work preserving the scene."

The deputy nodded and walked over to the fire truck.

Abby's trembling subsided once she and Jack had returned to the Jeep and she was driving back to town. Hitting the brakes to let a cruiser pass, she made a mental note to call her wedding party customer to set up another delivery date.

"Listen, Jack, I'll keep my promise to show you Kilbride Lake, but it'll have to wait for another day. The mountain's going to be shut down to through traffic. I can't make my honey delivery, and you can't go home. So, lunch at my place?"

His eyes brightened, lighting his handsome face. "You'll

not have to be twisting my arm for that," he said, feigning the Irish accent.

"Lovely." Abby turned the volume up on the soft jazz and was soon bobbing to the beat of the music. "So, what about egg salad sandwiches, sweet tea, sheet cake, and lemon ice cream with fresh berries? The sun should be out down on the farmette, so we'll dine on the patio, under the umbrella, and watch the birds and the bees."

"Ohhh, Jesus, Mary, and Joseph! The birds and the bees, you say? Now you've got my attention." He turned in his seat and played with a tendril of hair behind her ear. "Oh, Abby," he said in a breathy voice. "I'd love to share with you what I know about that."

Abby smiled wickedly. "I thought you might."

Lemon Ice Cream with Strawberries

Ingredients:
1 cup superfine sugar
¼ cup fresh lemon juice
1 tablespoon lemon zest
1 cup heavy cream
1 cup whole milk
⅛ teaspoon salt
1 cup fresh sliced strawberries

Directions:
Combine the sugar, lemon juice, and lemon zest in a large bowl.

Slowly pour the cream, milk, and salt into the lemon-sugar mixture and stir constantly until the sugar is completely dissolved, about 2 minutes.

Pour the lemon-cream mixture into freezable individual molds or bowls or into an ice cube tray, and then cover with foil and freeze until the ice cream is completely firm, about 3 to 5 hours, depending on the type of mold used.

Unmold the ice cream, garnish each serving with the sliced strawberries, and serve at once.

Serves 4

Acknowledgments

My heartfelt gratitude goes to Aaron Pomeroy for your encyclopedic mind and insight into law enforcement. Whenever I have a cop question, you've got the cop answer. Please know I deeply appreciate your help, and if, inadvertently, I have made any mistakes, they are all mine.

Thanks also to Heather Pomeroy for the ongoing support and enthusiasm for my Henny Penny Farmette cozy mysteries. Your paramedic background and also your experience as an evidence technician in a small-town police department have proven invaluable to me.

I also want to thank Madison and Savannah for all their questions, feedback, and ideas. There's always something new to learn from you two.

Books and magazines about beekeeping line my bookshelves, but for fast answers to my questions about bees, I know I can rely on Botros (Peter) Kemel and Wajiha (Jill) Nasrallah. You have taught me most of what I know about keeping bees and harvesting honey. Together, you have a wealth of knowledge and generously share it. Thanks to you both.

For her unwavering support of the Henny Penny Farmette, I offer my thanks to Jeanne Lederer. The element of setting in a story can serve many purposes: it can be a place of sanctuary and safety or of fear and uncertainty. Your mid-century stone house in the woods serves as a scary counterpart to the sheltered farmette of my protagonist, permitting me to generate fictional threads of rising tension from that wooded acre.

To my architect husband, Carlos J. Carvajal, who teaches me what I don't know about renovation and has patiently answered all my remodeling questions in connection with this story, I offer my heartfelt appreciation. My son Josh deserves my thanks for untold hours helping me build and maintain my Web sites. Also, Josh and Carlos, you both have earned huge hugs of appreciation for a willingness to be first-level taste testers for all my recipe creations and modifications.

For her continuing belief in me, I offer thanks, along with a huge hug and a kiss, to my agent, Paula Munier. I've been honored to have you as a lifelong friend and fellow author. Your dazzling mind and astonishing talent never cease to amaze me.

I offer my deepest appreciation to my brilliant editor Michaela Hamilton, whose insights are spot on and whose guidance is always so welcome.

Finally, I want to thank all the folks at Kensington Publishing for their knowledge, expertise, and support of my Henny Penny Farmette mysteries.